THE KIND ONE

TOM EPPERSON

FIVE STAR

An imprint of Thomson Gale, a part of The Thomson Corporation

THOMSON
★
GALE ™

Detroit • New York • San Francisco • New Haven, Conn. • Waterville, Maine • London

LIBRARY OF CONGRESS CATALOGING-IN-PUBLICATION DATA

Epperson, Tom.
  The kind one / by Tom Epperson. — 1st ed.
    p. cm.
  ISBN-13: 978-1-59414-617-6 (hardcover : alk. paper)
  ISBN-10: 1-59414-617-9 (hardcover : alk. paper) 1. Amnesiacs—Fiction.
2. Gangsters—Fiction. 3. Nineteen thirties—Fiction. 4. Los Angeles (Calif.)—
Fiction. I. Title.
PS3605.P59K56 2008
813'.6—dc22   2007041312

First Edition. First Printing: January 2008.
Published in 2008 in conjunction with Tekno Books and Ed Gorman.
Printed in the United States of America on permanent paper
10 9 8 7 6 5 4 3 2 1

To Stefani

"No man goes as far as he who knows
not whither he goes."

—Oliver Cromwell

★ ★ ★ ★ ★

1

★ ★ ★ ★ ★

1

"Say," said Darla, "where'd you get that cupcake?"

"They're on that table," I said. "Over there."

"I love cupcakes."

"Want me to get you one?"

"No, honey, I'll get it. Oops!" Somebody bumped up against her, and she sloshed some of her drink on the sleeve of my coat. She brushed at my sleeve with her hand. "Sorry, Danny."

"That's okay."

She was pretty plastered. She was wearing a slinky gold lamé gown with gold high heels. She had soft wavy gold hair. She was a singer that didn't sing anymore. "His eyes?" she said, whispery, like it was a secret.

"Whose eyes?"

"You know. *His.*"

"What about them?"

"Last night I had a dream about them."

"What did you dream?"

"That I put them out. With sewing scissors. Because I couldn't stand them anymore. I couldn't stand the way they looked at me."

"Why would you have a dream like that?"

"Geez. I can't imagine."

I had a thought, and I started to say something, but then the thought started to slip away, it was like a helium balloon a kid was holding by a string and then he let the string go, and I watched it float away into the blue.

Darla drifted off into the crowd. The way her gown was, her back was naked nearly all the way down to her butt, and I watched her shoulder blades and her backbone moving under her skin.

We were at a party at Bud Seitz's house. The place was packed to the gills. It was a chilly night in mid April, but the house was hot. It smelled like sweat, smoke, booze, and perfume. Everybody was talking and laughing like it was a contest to see who could talk and laugh the loudest. On the phonograph was a song that I'd never heard before:

Something strange happened to me,
Lost my heart so suddenly,
Suddenly I found myself in a dream . . .

The new mayor's brother, Joe Shaw, was there. Several cops, including Jack Otay, head of the Gangster Squad. The head of the Police Commission, a short fat bald guy named Nuffer. John Hobbs, a newspaper reporter. Arnold Dublinski, Bud's lawyer—Blinky people called him. Plenty of girls—starlets, dancers, extras, waitresses, manicurists, shopgirls, cigarette girls, hatcheck girls, switchboard girls, and half a dozen out and out whores. And some of Bud's guys, the guys that were in the coziest with him: Teddy Bump. Tommy and Goodlooking Tommy. Nucky Williams. Nello Marlini. Dick Prettie. And me.

I finished eating my cupcake, licked some frosting off my fingers. Doc Travis moved past me, walking on his knuckles. He grinned at me and smacked his lips.

I made my way over to the bar. The bartender was a tall blond Russian named Anatoly, who was also Bud's butler.

"Another scotch, please, Anatoly."

"Of course."

Anatoly was wearing a white shirt and pants and a red velvet vest. He had two fingers missing from his right hand. I'd heard he'd been this rich count in Russia and got his fingers shot off when he was fighting in the Revolution against the Communists.

"Were you really a count?"

He shrugged. "Past is past. In America, no one cares about past. I am trying to be good American now, Danny."

"I care about the past." I took a solemn sip of my scotch, as though toasting the past, then somebody slapped me on the back.

It was Police Commissioner Nuffer.

"What's the good word, Danny?"

"I can't think of one."

Nuffer laughed like I'd made a hell of a joke and slapped me on the back again.

His double-breasted suit was like a sausage casing that could barely contain its contents. Anatoly gave him another drink. He took a gulp of it. His face was red and sweaty, and he looked like a man with a fever.

Bud had told me last week I wasn't acting friendly enough to his friends, so I made an effort with Nuffer.

"So how are you doing these days, Mr. Nuffer?"

"Hanging in there, my boy, hanging in there, as the condemned man said on his way to the gallows." Nuffer's eyes narrowed as he looked around the room. "Quite a shindig tonight. Your boss knows how to throw 'em. What do you think the odds are of my getting laid? Mm, look at that tasty-looking young lady on Lieutenant Otay's arm. Jack! Jack! Join us!"

Jack Otay came over with a big-busted redhead in an orange dress. Nuffer was about eye-level with her chest, which seemed to suit him just fine. "Please introduce us, Jack."

"Well, this here's Clover, I believe," said Otay. "Or was it Daisy?"

"*Violet*," said the girl. "Violet Gilbertson. Pleased to meet ya."

"Pleased to meet *you*, Miss Gilbertson. I'm Wendell Nuffer."

"No kidding. My daddy's name is Wendell."

"And I'll bet you're a daddy's girl, Miss Gilbertson."

Violet smiled down at Nuffer; it looked like she'd used about half a tube of lipstick on her mouth. "Definitely. And you can call me Violet."

"I hope I have a chance to call you Violet many, many more times tonight."

"Well you never know," she said coyly, swaying a couple inches closer to Nuffer's flushed face, and then she looked me over. "You got a name?"

"You mean you don't know who you're talking to?" said Otay. A cigarette dangled out of his smirking mouth. He had a big square-jawed head that was handsome in an ugly way, or maybe vice versa. I'd heard that he was an expert in the third degree— that he had a special pair of pigskin gloves that he put on whenever he was about to work somebody over.

"This here's Danny Landon," continued Otay. "Two Gun Danny Landon."

"He's practically famous," said Nuffer. He and Otay exchanged a look. "In certain circles."

"Famous! Gosh, Danny," said Violet, nearly smacking Nuffer in the face with her breasts as she swung them around toward me, "I'm sorry I didn't know who you were. See, I ain't lived here very long, so I don't know who everyone is yet."

"Where did you come here from?" asked Nuffer.

"Iowa. I was Miss Iowa Pork Queen of 1933."

"You don't say."

"Yeah, when I won that I thought, Violet, your luck is finally changing, and I decided it was a good time to leave Iowa."

"It's probably always a good time to leave Iowa," Otay said, and then we all heard a lot of screaming and crashing around and commotion in the next room. Everybody went rushing out to see what was up.

I saw Darla stumbling up the stairs; she was crying and her arm was bleeding and she had blood all over her gold gown. Bud Seitz and Dick Prettie were hurrying up the stairs to help her.

Nello Marlini was standing next to me and I asked him what happened. "Darla was eating a cupcake and Doc Travis tried getting it but she wouldn't let him have it. Then he bit her on the arm and then Goodlooking Tommy started kicking the hell outa Doc and Doc ran off screaming his fucking head off."

Bud had seen *Tarzan the Ape Man* and decided he wanted a chimp like Cheeta and that's who Doc Travis was. He called him Doc Travis because supposedly he looked like this old bootlegger friend of his who had that name. The human Doc Travis had a cabin in the woods on Lake Arrowhead, and he disappeared completely in 1929 except for his head which was found floating in the lake.

I had spent a lot of time with Doc (the chimp). We'd sit in the sun together out by Bud's swimming pool. He liked to comb through my hair with his fingers, I don't know what he was looking for, fleas or lice or dandruff, and sometimes he'd find something and put it in his mouth. He seemed fascinated by my dent. I have a dent on the right side of my head. He'd gently touch it with his big black fingers, trace its route about an inch and a half up my forehead and then into my hairline where it goes under my hair about three inches and all the time he'd be making these soft cooing noises. I'd always found Doc to be affectionate, humorous, and good-natured, and never known him to bite anybody.

A tit poked me in the arm and I looked over and there was

Violet. Except I got mixed up about her name and said: "Hello, Clover."

"My name ain't Clover damn it. So what are you famous for? How come they call you Two Gun Danny?"

But before I could answer Dick Prettie came walking back down the stairs and came over to me. "Gotta talk to you, kid," he said, pulling me away from Violet.

"Bud wants us to take care of Doc."

"What do you mean take care of him?"

"You know what I mean." He saw the look on my face. "Lookit, I like the monkey too. But orders is orders."

We started walking through the house looking for Doc. Bud had declared the party over so everybody was leaving; out front I could hear car doors slamming and engines starting up. "How's Darla?" I said to Dick.

"They're sending for the doctor. But she's all right."

"You know how strong Doc Travis is. If he'd really wanted to hurt her, he could've ripped her arm right outa the socket."

Dick sighed, like he was bone-tired. "Yeah, I know." He was wearing a brown suit and a tie with yellow flowers on it. The suit looked too big on him. Suits usually looked too big on him, since he was the skinniest guy I've ever seen that wasn't dying of something. Even his moustache was just this skinny little brown line.

"I wonder why he bit Darla," I said. "He likes Darla."

"I heard Tommy and Goodlooking Tommy got him drunk."

"Drunk?"

"Yeah. They was giving him bottles of beer all night. Beers and monkeys don't mix, I guess."

We found him in the billiard room. It had red carpet and gold walls and paintings of half-naked French women. Doc was sitting up on the pool table rolling balls around, making them bump against each other. He looked up as we walked in then went back to rolling around the balls. He acted like we weren't even there. I think he knew he was in trouble.

We stood by the table staring at him.

"What are we supposed to do?" I said. "Take him out in the desert?" Because if we were supposed to take him out in the desert we could just let him loose or give him to somebody and Bud would never be the wiser.

"Nah. We gotta take him out in the back. Bud wants to watch."

The seven went rolling into the twelve which bumped against the three.

"We don't have to do this," I said.

"What do you mean?"

"You and me and Doc—we could just walk outa here, get in my car, and start driving."

"Yeah? And which way we gonna drive?"

"Well, we go west we hit the ocean. So I figure we head east."

"Danny, even if I was nuts enough to risk my life for a fucking monkey, how far do you think we'd get? You don't just drive away from Bud Seitz and that's the end of it. And another thing. Where's your sense of fucking gratitude? Bud's took real good care of you ever since you got hit in the head. You'd be selling apples on a street corner if it wasn't for him. And you know I ain't saying that to hurt your feelings."

"Yeah. Yeah, I know."

I stood there a minute and thought about things; then I started walking toward the door.

"Danny, where you going?" Dick sounded worried.

"I'm coming back."

I went in the party room, went over to the table where the cupcakes were. I took one and wrapped it in a napkin and put it in the side pocket of my coat.

I went back in the billiard room. Doc was still playing around with the balls.

"You were bad, Doc," I said. "Real bad."

Doc looked over at me. He whimpered and twisted his lips around on his teeth. I held my hand out and then he leapt into my arms.

"Let's go for a little walk, Doc."

I walked out of the house carrying Doc, with Dick walking behind us. I said softly into Doc's ear: "Did Goodlooking Tommy kick you? One of these day's I'm gonna kick Goodlooking Tommy." Doc had this strong musky smell I liked; I always liked the way animals smelled even when it was kind of bad like a dirty dog that had been rained on but I didn't always like the way people smelled.

When we got outside I put Doc down. Bud had a big two-story Spanish house with tall palm trees all around it. It was set on a lot of property; there was a swimming pool and a pool house and a tennis court and then a garden with all sorts of plants and flowers and thick green grass and everything was surrounded by a tall stone wall that had barbed wire spiraling along the top of it.

I held Doc's hand and we walked out into the night. It was cold enough that our breath was making clouds. I could hear Dick behind us coughing every now and then; he coughed a lot because he smoked one cigarette after another. The swimming pool had lights under the water and was blue and still and frozen-looking. Bud had had sand hauled in to make a beach around the pool. The beach had its own seagull, tethered to a big rock by a ten-foot length of cord tied to its leg. The seagull seemed asleep.

We walked on past the tennis court and then out on the grass and among the flowers.

"Let's stop here," said Dick.

I looked back at the house. On a second-floor balcony,

silhouetted against the light from his bedroom, Bud Seitz was standing. He was like a shape cut out of a sheet of black paper. I could see the burning tip of his cigar.

"I'll do it," Dick said.

A breeze was blowing in the tops of the palm trees and they were making rustling sounds and moving against the clear, brightly starred sky. Doc was looking up at me, waiting patiently, on his best behavior now, wondering what I was up to.

I squatted down beside him and said: "Look what I got for *you.*" He watched me as I took the cupcake out of my pocket and unwrapped it from the napkin then he took it from me eagerly and started to eat it. He was making little happy grunts. He had a real sweet tooth.

I looked up at Dick, standing a step or two behind Doc. He looked like he was about to be sick. He took out his .32 revolver from under his coat. I stood up and took a step back. Dick leaned over and put the barrel of the gun a few inches from the back of Doc's head. Then the gun spurted orange light and Doc pitched forward facedown onto the grass.

He wasn't quite dead yet. I saw his hands pulling at the grass. And then Dick leaned down and finished him off.

"Quit blubbering," said Dick. "If the guys seen you carrying on like this . . ." He shook his head darkly.

We were in Dick's car. He was taking me to my hotel. After we'd buried Doc, we went back in the house and I grabbed a bottle of Johnny Black and guzzled about half of it. Then I went kind of nuts and started stumbling around and yelling that we shouldn't have done it and it was pure murder and Dick had hustled me out of there and into his car. We went down La Brea then left on Hollywood Boulevard.

It was the middle of the night, and Hollywood seemed un-populated, except for a few shivering whores and some bums sleeping under Hoover blankets. Pretty soon we pulled up in front of the Rutherford Hotel.

The lobby was empty. The elevator boy was some old geezer that looked about ninety. "What floor?" he said.

He was wearing a too-small blue uniform, and he had a huge red and yellow boil on his forehead that looked like it was about ready to pop. I couldn't take my eyes off it. He knew what I was looking at, and he started getting mad. "*What floor?*" he nearly yelled.

"Eight," I said. "I live on the eighth floor."

He scowled at me and spat some tobacco juice into a spattered Chase & Sanborn coffee can then took us up.

We went in room 807 and I went in the bathroom and pissed and puked then came back and flopped on the bed. Dick was standing with his hands in his pockets looking bleakly out the window.

"This is a crummy hotel," he said. "In a crummy town. On a crummy night."

"I'm moving as soon as I can find something. Bud gave me a raise."

"Yeah? Great. *You* get a raise. That's rich."

He walked over to the bed and untied my shoes and took them off. They made clunking noises as he dropped them on the floor.

"I'm leaving now, kid. Sleep it off. I'll see you tomorrow."

"Don't leave yet. Tell me something."

"Like what?"

"Tell me about why they call me Two Gun Danny."

Dick sighed. "Ah, Danny . . . it's three o'clock in the fucking morning."

"Come on, Dick. Please."

Dick shook his head but at the same time he lit up a cigarette so I knew he wasn't going.

"You, me, and a couple other of the boys—one night we drove down to Long Beach. We took a water taxi out to the *Monfalcone*. It was one of them gambling boats. It was out past the three-mile limit, so it was all strictly legit."

"But what we were gonna do—that wasn't legit."

"That's right. We was on a heist job. We was gonna heist the dealers and the customers and we heard there was a safe with a hundred fifty G's in it and we was gonna heist that too. But that wasn't all."

"We were gonna sink it. Sink the *Monfalcone*."

"You wanna tell the fucking story? Yeah, that's right. We was gonna set it on fire and sink it 'cause Bud had a beef with the owner. And we didn't care if everybody on it drowned like rats.

"The main gambling room was the greatest place in the world. It had green carpet and chandeliers, and roulette wheels and dice tables and slot machines, and all the customers was dressed up like a million bucks. And the dames was all gorgeous, all of 'em looked like Ginger Rogers. Dozens and dozens of Ginger Rogers."

"Too bad we had to burn it up," I mumbled. "Too bad we had to sink it."

"Yeah, too bad. But orders is orders. So we was taking a little look-see at things when you got recognized by some muscle that worked for the boat and he started to take his piece out. But you slugged him in the jaw and knocked him colder than a mackerel and grabbed his piece and pulled out your own piece and jumped up on a blackjack table and yelled: 'Ladies and gentlemen, this here's a heist!' "

I was lying flat on my back, with my eyes closed. The room was spinning around me like a roulette wheel. Dick's voice seemed to be coming from further and further away.

"Then all these guys come running in the room, some of 'em had sawed-offs and some of 'em had pistols and you was screaming that they was dirty sons of bitches and blazing away at 'em with a gun in each hand."

Two Gun Danny. Then I couldn't hear Dick anymore. I was in endless night, floating on a raft on an infinite sea. And the water was filled with floundering Ginger Rogerses in golden gowns. And they were in danger of drowning, but I welcomed them on my raft, one and all.

2

I drove through Hollywood in my yellow '33 Packard Club
sedan on a sunny Monday morning. I passed a church with a
sign in front that said: "The eyes of the Lord are everywhere." I
had to slow down when a baseball bounced out on the street in
front of me; a kid ran out after it and as he bent down to pick it
up he looked up at me and I felt this sort of shiver like I'd lived
through this before, except the kid with the tousled hair chasing
the brownish battered ball was me, and the guy behind the
wheel of the Packard was . . . *who?* Then the kid ran off and I
felt like me again and drove on.

I turned down La Vista Lane. It was a little street of modest
pale houses and skinny palm trees south of Melrose and east of
Vine. I parked in front of the Orange Blossom Bungalow Court.
A sprinkler was going and made a rainbow over the sloping
lawn. I climbed seven steps to a sidewalk that ran straight back
from the street between identical tan tiny stucco houses, four
on each side, facing each other across a courtyard. The
courtyard had a couple of dwarf orange trees loaded with green
half-grown oranges.

I knocked on the door of the first bungalow on the left. Edna
Dean opened the door. She was the Orange Blossom Bungalow
Court manager. She had a long face with a sharp chin and she
wore glasses with wire frames. She smiled and showed a set of
teeth that were way too bright and perfect to be real.

"Oh hi, Danny. I got the place all ready for you. Let me get the key."

A sour smell wafted out the door. I assumed Mr. Dean was in there somewhere. When I was here before, he never said a word, but just sat in a chair with a filthy blanket over his lap. A fly was buzzing around the room, and Mr. Dean followed it with his watery blue eyes. He needed a shave, and he smelled like he hadn't had a bath in weeks. Mrs. Dean explained that he'd been laid up for the last few years after an accident at a mackerel cannery in San Pedro. He looked baffled as he watched the fly, like he couldn't figure out how his life had come to such a pass that he didn't have anything better to do than watch a fly buzzing around.

Mrs. Dean came back out. She was wearing a drab dress that hung on her like a gunnysack and she had booze on her breath. "Nice day, isn't it? I hope you like it here. It's a pretty nice group of people, I guess, but they come and they go. You've come. You'll go. Just don't have any wild parties or play your radio too loud and we'll get along just fine."

We headed up the sidewalk.

"Did you hear about Dillinger?" she said. "It was just on the radio. They had him and his gang cornered in Wisconsin, but they all escaped in a blaze of gunfire. They killed one federal agent and an innocent bystander. I'm just scared to death of gangsters. Nobody's safe these days."

A little girl, maybe ten or eleven, was squatting on the sidewalk, drawing hopscotch squares with a piece of chalk.

"Hi, Sophie," said Mrs. Dean. "Meet your new neighbor, Mr. Landon. Danny, this is Sophie Gubler."

The girl winced. "You *said* it."

"Said what?"

"My *last name*. You know I hate it."

"Oh Sophie, there's not a thing wrong with your last name.

Gubler's a perfectly fine name."

The girl winced again.

"What would you like your last name to be?" I asked.

She liked that question. "Well in school we studied this French queen, she told her people to eat cake so they cut off her head. Her name was Marie Antoinette."

"You'd like to be Sophie Antoinette?"

She shrugged. Her knees were poking up from under her cheap print dress and were scraped up pretty good and blotched red with Mercurochrome. I said: "What happened to your knees?"

"I was skating down the street and this dope opened his car door right in front of me. What happened to your leg?"

"My leg?"

"Yeah. I saw you limping on your leg. You hurt it or something?"

"Sophie," frowned Mrs. Dean, "that's a personal question."

"My *knees* are personal. He asked me about my *knees.*"

"I got hit in the head. With a lead pipe. See?"

I took my hat off and inclined my head. Sophie stood up to get a better look at my dent. "Gosh. And you got hit in the leg too?"

"Nah. But it mashed my brain, and it made it so's my left leg and my left arm don't work so hot anymore. But they're getting better."

Sophie nodded, looking me over, not feeling sorry for me, just interested. But Mrs. Dean looked embarrassed. "Let's go, Danny," she said quietly.

We walked on toward my bungalow, the last one on the right. In front of the third on the right a guy was kneeling and weeding in front of a carefully tended flowerbed. He was wearing brown trousers, a loose white shirt, a big sombrero, and gardening gloves. A black and white cat was keeping him company. He

25

gave us a friendly, gap-toothed grin over his shoulder as we walked by.

"That's Mr. Dulwich," said Mrs. Dean as she nodded at him genteelly. "An Englishman. A real gentleman, too. I've had nary a lick of trouble from Mr. Dulwich."

Mrs. Dean unlocked the door of my bungalow and we went in. She looked around the living room with a pleased expression. "I had a nigger named Matilda spend the whole day cleaning in here. You could eat off the floor if you wanted to. Because nobody cleans like Matilda." Then she gave me the key. "Well this is yours now. If you need anything you know where to find me. Do you play checkers by any chance?"

"Checkers?"

"My husband loves checkers with a passion. If you ever feel like a game, just come on over. And I'll pour you a cup of jackass brandy to boot."

"Okay, Mrs. Dean. Thanks."

She left. The key was cool in my hand. I was all alone in my little bungalow. I thought it not bad for forty bucks a month.

One reason I took it was, it was furnished, with some battered mismatched odds and ends. I sat down on a tattered black davenport. I took my hat off and placed it down beside me, then sat there with my hands on my knees trying to remember if I knew how to play checkers. Red and black squares. Take your jump. Crown me. Yes. I knew how to play checkers.

My head hurt. I always kept a little tin of Bayer aspirin in my pocket. I got up and went in the kitchen. No glasses. I'd have to buy some. I'd have to buy a lot of things. I didn't really own anything, except a toothbrush, a shaving kit, a couple suitcases of clothes. And the car. It used to be Bud's car. He gave it to me. After I got hit in the head.

I put two aspirin in my mouth, turned on the tap, put my cupped hand under the water, and washed the aspirin down.

Then I went in the bedroom.

A bare mattress lay on a rickety frame. I needed sheets, and pillows. On the mattress was a tea-colored stain almost exactly the shape of the state of Texas.

I lay down on the bed, avoiding Texas. The box springs creaked. I put my hands behind my head. I planned to stay here till my headache went away.

I heard something, and looked toward the window. Sunlight was pouring in. A fly was buzzing and butting its head against the glass. The fly was green, bright as a jewel.

3

I pulled into the parking lot of the Peacock Club. It was on the north side of the Sunset Strip, just down the street from the Clover Club.

It was early afternoon, and the club wasn't open yet. Inside Bud Seitz sat in his usual U-shaped booth, just to the right of the stage.

Every table had its own little wooden peacock, and the walls and ceiling were covered with painted peacocks, and there were a thousand or a million or who knows how many eyes of the tails of the peacocks looking at you. The club was called Cicero's before Bud bought it. He changed the name and the look because when he was a kid growing up in New York he went to the Central Park Zoo and fell in love with the peacocks. On opening night he had three dozen live peacocks brought in. They were supposed to just walk around looking proud and pretty but almost immediately it got out of hand. People got drunk and started chasing the peacocks around trying to pull out their tail feathers and the peacocks were screaming and crapping all over everything and then one of them flew up on a table where there were candles burning and its tail caught on fire. The burning peacock flapped around the room and everybody just went nuts, guys in tuxes and girls covered in jewels were yelling *fire, fire* and running toward the exits, movie stars were cursing and swinging their elbows and knocking people down and the funny thing was, the newspapers the next day didn't print a thing about it. Sure, they had stories about the gala opening of the Peacock Club and pictures too, but everything went swimmingly and everybody had a grand time according to the reporters who were all on Bud's payroll.

One of those reporters, John Hobbs of the *Los Angeles Times*, was sitting with Bud in his booth. Nucky Williams, Nello Marlini, and Arnold Dublinski were there too. There was so much smoke rising out of the booth it was like it was on fire with Nucky and Nello and Blinky smoking cigarettes, Hobbs a pipe, and Seitz a cigar. I didn't smoke. It gave me a headache.

I sat down with them. Eddie, the waiter, brought me a cup of coffee. Everybody was drinking coffee. Bud had a firm rule that nobody could have a drink before sunset. Sitting over at the bar, Tommy and Dick Prettie were also drinking coffee. Tommy in particular was a real booze hound, and I could see him in the mirror staring at all those shiny bottles of liquor behind the bar like sundown couldn't come fast enough.

Bud was forty-two but looked older. He had a narrow face with deep grooves in it, slightly buck teeth, bushy eyebrows, and small brown eyes that could scare you to death when they looked at you in a certain way. He was starting to lose his hair. He was maybe five-ten and a hundred sixty pounds.

He was always dressed to the nines. Today he was wearing a gray suit, a gray shirt, and a white tie, with a white carnation in his buttonhole.

There was no way you could describe Bud as handsome, but girls were always all over him. Maybe it was just a matter of him having a lot of dough and being a big important guy. Or maybe some girls actually liked him.

It wasn't like Bud was getting laid by a different girl every day though. He was very careful about girls, because he was scared of catching something from them. Before he slept with somebody she had to go to his doctor to get a clean bill of health. He had a thing about germs, about cleanliness. He showered three times a day. He didn't like to shake hands with people. He always had to have a box of Kleenex tissues near him and every five or ten minutes he'd wipe his hands.

He also had a thing about order. Let's say that on his desk were a fountain pen, a cigar box, and a letter opener, then they had to be lined up a certain way, and if anybody moved them even half an inch when he wasn't around he'd blow his top. And he couldn't stand to have anything pointing at him. Once this little bookie named Louie Vachaboski put his cigarette down in an ashtray with the lit tip pointed right at Bud. Bud picked up the cigarette and dived over the table and grabbed Louie by the throat with one hand and with the other hand mashed out the cigarette in Louie's left eyeball. Louie cut loose with these high-pitched, girlish screams, which got him nicknamed "Fay Wray" after the screaming blonde in *King Kong.* When Bud was done with Louie, he had to wash his hands about fifty times to get rid of his germs.

"She's a milestone around my neck," Bud was saying. He was talking about his wife, Bernice. They'd been married ten or twelve years but the last two years they'd been living in separate houses, Bud in Hollywood and Bernice in Beverly Hills.

"She spends my dough like there ain't no tomorrow. And she's always calling me up and pestering me about dumb shit. Like she calls me last week, she likes sunbathing naked by her swimming pool and she says these two kids that live next door are always climbing up in a tree to get a gander at her. She says she opens her eyes up and sees them two kids staring down at her and jacking off and she wants me to take care of 'em. What am I supposed to do, send some of you guys over to bump 'em off? Shit, the truth is I feel sorry for them kids if they're so desperate they gotta jack off by looking at Bernice's fat ass."

Everybody laughed. John Hobbs puffed on his pipe and said:

"She still won't give you a divorce?"

"Nah, she's a Catholic. She thinks the Pope'll send us both to hell if we get a divorce. And she says she still loves me too much to let me go to hell. I tell her the Pope's gonna try and send me to hell anyway 'cause I'm a Jew. But she won't listen to me."

"We need to get something on her," Blinky said. "So she'll cooperate."

"Yeah," said Bud. "Like she's fucking a nigger. Something like that."

Hobbs wrote something down in a notebook. He was wearing a tweed coat and a red bowtie, and he had a lazy eye that gave him a slightly loony look. He said: "Maybe I can look into it."

"It oughta be a famous nigger," said Nucky. "Not just some regular nigger."

"There's no such thing as a famous nigger," said Nello.

"What the fuck's Jack Johnson then?" said Nucky. "Danny? You ever hear of Jack Johnson?"

"Sure. He's a boxer."

"See? Even Danny knows who Jack Johnson is."

"But he's all washed up now," said Nello. "He ain't had a fight in years."

"That don't matter. He's still famous."

"He *used* to be famous. He ain't now."

"Why don't both you guys shut up?" said Bud. "You're giving me a fucking headache."

Stan Tinney brought a girl over to the booth. Stan used to run some big club in New York till Bud had brought him in to manage the Peacock. He was an older guy, with white hair and heavy, black-framed glasses. Stan could hire anybody he wanted as long as it wasn't a girl. Bud had to approve any girls.

Stan introduced Armilda Lee Keddy to him. Said she was up

31

for the job as the new cigarette girl.

"What happened to Betty?" said Bud.

"She quit, Bud. She took a job over at the Pom Pom Club."

"You telling me she's going to work for those cocksuckers?" Bud looked incredulous. Stan shrugged.

"I even offered her a raise."

"Even offered her a raise," repeated Bud, shaking his head; then he turned his attention to Armilda Lee. "Where you from?"

"Ada, Oklahoma."

She had brown hair, dimples, and a hayseed accent; her jaws were working hard on a piece of gum.

"Another dumb hick from Oklahoma," said Bud pleasantly. "Just what this town needs."

Armilda Lee giggled, her dimples deepening.

"Spit it out."

"Huh?"

"The gum. Get rid of it."

Armilda Lee quickly spit the gum out in her hand, then put both hands behind her back.

"People chewing gum. It makes me sick."

She looked scared and said: "I'm sorry, Mr. Seitz."

"Lemme see your legs."

She hiked up her skirt a foot or two. We all inspected her legs. Armilda Lee Keddy had killer legs.

"Armilda Lee, if I hire you, do you promise never to go to work at the Pom Pom Club?"

Armilda Lee's face lit up. "Oh yes sir, I swear to God, I'd never do nothing like that. And my daddy's a preacher, so I don't take swearing to the good Lord lightly."

Bud bared his buck teeth in a smile. "Well hallelujah, sister. Welcome to the Peacock."

Stan led the ecstatic Armilda Lee away. "I need to talk to Danny," said Bud. "So everybody kindly clear out."

Everybody did. Bud plucked out a tissue from the box and wiped off his hands, then added it to a white puffy pile of used tissues. He chewed on his cigar, looked at me through the smoke.

"How you been doing, Danny?"

"Fine."

Eddie came over, warmed up our coffee, took away the Kleenex.

"You ain't seemed yourself lately. I'm thinking maybe you're sore at me."

"Why would I be sore?"

"Maybe you're wondering why I made you take care of Doc, since you liked him so much."

"Yeah, I guess I was wondering that."

"You've forgot a lot, and so now I'm trying to teach some of it back to you. Sometimes it becomes necessary in life to do stuff we don't wanna do. It ain't easy, I know. I've done a lot of stuff I didn't wanna do. But, like I said—sometimes it's necessary."

Since I couldn't think of anything to say, I was glad Darla picked this moment to walk in.

I watched her slide into the booth, kiss Bud on the cheek, smile across the table at me. "I'm not interrupting anything, am I? Eddie?" she called out to the waiter. "How's about some orange juice?" She took Bud's cigar right out of his mouth and lit a cigarette with it. If anybody else had touched Bud or something belonging to him without his okay he'd have probably broken their arm, but he was just watching her with this goofy grin on his face, like he was some yokel in a carnival tent in Tennessee and she was a shimmying hoochie koochie dancer.

"Whatta you been doing?" he said.

"Nothing. I do nothing all the time now. It's what I do for a living."

"It's good you come by. There's something I wanted to talk

to you about. You and Danny."

She looked at me curiously. I shrugged.

"It's like this," said Bud. "It's getting around town that you're my girl."

She blew a stream of smoke in his general direction. "Is that what I am? Your girl?"

"Sure. Sure you are."

"I thought I was your mistress."

"I don't like the sound of that, 'mistress.' 'Girl''s nicer."

"Okay. So?"

"So I got a lot of enemies. I ain't the easiest guy to get to, but they might try to hurt me by hurting you."

Eddie came back with the orange juice. Darla took a long drink like she was really thirsty. Then she looked back at Bud.

"Hurt me how?"

"Use your imagination. So I don't want you going nowhere alone no more. Danny'll go with you."

Darla looked at me. "He'll be my bodyguard, you mean?"

Bud nodded. My heart started beating a little faster.

"I don't need a bodyguard."

"I guess you got wax in your ears, baby. I just said you do."

Darla drank the rest of her juice, then set the glass down so hard on the table she was lucky it didn't break. "I *don't* need a fucking *body*guard!" She slid out of the booth and began to flounce her way toward the exit.

"DARLA!"

She stopped in her tracks and looked back at Bud. Everybody else in the place was looking too, Eddie and Dick and Tommy and Nello and Nucky and Blinky and John Hobbs and Stan Tinney and Armilda Lee and the peacocks and this little Chinese guy that was sweeping up with a broom. When Bud spoke again, it was so quietly you could hardly hear him.

"Where you going?"

"To the beauty parlor." It was like her voice had shrunk several sizes.

"Danny'll drive you. Wait outside for him. He'll be there in a minute."

She just stood there, with everybody looking at her like she'd been hit in the face with a rotten tomato. Then she turned and walked out.

Bud's cigar had gone out. He put a match to it and puffed a few times, then gave me a crooked grin.

"Broads, huh?"

"Yeah."

"I'm giving you a lot of responsibility, Danny. But I think you're ready for it."

I nodded.

"Lookit, you and me both know you can't never trust a broad. They're just born troublemakers. But don't ever let her make any trouble between you and me. You know what I'm saying?"

"I think so."

"Don't ever let her tempt you. Just imagine she's got a big sign hanging in front of her snatch. Private Club. Members Only. No Trespassing."

"Okay."

"That's it then."

I got up, walked away a couple of steps—then turned back toward the booth.

"Bud?"

"Yeah?"

"I won't ever let anybody hurt Darla. I promise."

Bud looked at me. Nodded a little.

I walked out to where she was waiting.

4

Darla was always reading magazines about houses, like *House Beautiful* and *American Home.* Today, as we drove away from the club, she was looking through *House and Home,* and acting like I was invisible.

"Darla, don't be mad. This wasn't my idea."

She discovered a hangnail, scratched at it with her thumbnail, put it to her teeth and tried to bite it off.

She was wearing a soft yellow sweater, a gray skirt, silk stockings, and gray, low-heeled shoes. She was hardly wearing any makeup because she hardly needed any makeup. I remember the night I first saw her sing and I thought she wasn't the best or the worst singer in the world but she probably was the prettiest girl in the world.

She'd started singing at the Peacock Club about five months ago. Within a couple of weeks, Bud had sent her to his doctor for a check-up. A couple weeks more and she showed up wearing a ring with a ruby the size of a marble, then six or seven weeks ago Bud had made her stop singing because he didn't like other guys looking at her.

She opened her purse and took out a little silver flask. She unscrewed the cap and took a drink, then gave me a smirk. "Vodka. He can't smell it on me. And what he can't smell can't hurt him." She offered the flask to me, but I shook my head. "Oh, come on. I know you're dying for it. I can see it in your face."

"No thanks."

She shrugged and returned the flask to her purse. I noticed a charm bracelet on her wrist—a silver chain a-dangle with a star, a crescent moon, a heart, a man's hat, a Scottish terrier, a mermaid, an owl, and a lightning bolt.

"I like your bracelet."

"Yeah?" She raised her arm up and looked at it herself; sunlight was angling in on her side of the car, and the charms trembled and glittered in it. "Bud got it for me. To make up for what you guys did to Doc."

We were rolling down the big hill on La Cienega. I turned left on Fountain. She said: "It's okay, Danny. I don't blame you for it."

I realized my fingers were squeezing the wheel so hard they were turning white, so I loosened my grip.

"I guess it was all my fault," said Darla. "I should've just given him the cupcake."

"So you didn't know about it. About what Bud was gonna have us do."

"Course not. I loved Doc."

Darla was spending most of her time at Bud's house these days, but she still kept her apartment, in a building on Fountain near Fairfax. She wanted me to stop off there so she could check her mail and pick up some things.

I parked the car out front but when I started to open the door she put her hand on my arm.

"No, Danny. You stay here."

"But—but Bud said—"

"I know what Bud said, but let's get something straight. We're both stuck with this situation for now, but that doesn't mean I want you following me around everywhere like you're my little poodle. I'll be back in five minutes."

Fifteen minutes later I was getting worried. I started thinking I'd been on the job less than a half hour and Darla was maybe kidnapped already, she was trying to scream out my name but she had a gag in her mouth and two muscle-bound goons were throwing her in their car and I got out and headed toward the apartment house.

It was a five-story yellow-brick building. One of those swank kind of places, with a green awning. The door to the lobby swung open and the doorman held it for Darla, who had an armful of clothes. She saw me and said: "Gimme a hand."

As I was taking the clothes a young, tall guy in a sharp suit came out of the lobby and walked past us. He gave Darla a grin and a rakish wink.

I watched him walk toward the street, resetting his snap-brim hat on his head; he had a happy-as-a-clam look about him.

"Who's that?" I said.

"I got no idea."

"He winked at you."

"Danny, if I had a nickel for every time a guy winked at me I'd be richer than Rockefeller."

I put the clothes in the car and we drove off. Darla lit up a Lucky Strike and tossed the match out the window; then she leaned back against the door and blew smoke at me and gave me a long look.

"I get it now."

"Get what?"

"You're not my bodyguard. You're a spy."

"A spy?"

"Bud thinks I'm sneaking around behind his back seeing other guys. So what did you think, Danny? That I'd been up in my apartment balling that guy that winked at me?"

"I didn't think anything."

★ ★ ★ ★ ★

Evelyn's Klip n' Kurl was on Beverly Boulevard. I started to go in with Darla, but she blocked the doorway. "Sorry, Danny. No boys allowed." She opened her purse and pulled out a bill. "Here's ten bucks. Go buy yourself a nice steak. Or a not-nice girl. Or whatever you want."

I stiffened a little and stared at the money.

"No thanks."

Darla sighed, and returned the ten to her purse. "All men are morons. You included. Just get lost for a couple of hours, okay?"

She shut the door in my face.

I walked off slowly down the street. It was warm and sunny, and I took my coat off and slung it over my shoulder, and loosened my tie.

An old Apperson rattled past, its tailpipe billowing smoke. A slack-jawed woman was driving, leaning forward with an anguished look on her face, clearly desperate to either get somewhere or get away from somewhere.

Two teenage girls were looking at me kind of wide-eyed and giggly as they walked by. I'd forgotten about my gun in my shoulder holster, and I put my coat back on.

An ice cream cone minus the ice cream lay smashed on the sidewalk. A pair of sparrows pecked at the brittle bits of cone.

Step on a crack. Break your mother's back.

There was a filling station on the corner. A sign above a red Coca Cola cooler said: NO LOAFING. I opened the lid, reached down into the icy water, pulled out a dripping bottle of Coca Cola, paid for it, and immediately went on my way.

I walked down the street trying to remember just one thing about my mother. Name? Age? Height? Weight? Color of eyes? Color of hair? For just a moment I thought I glimpsed some glimmering something, some look in her eyes as she looked at me as I stood in some ghostly, long-lost doorway, but it was gone before I could nail it down.

A guy with no legs was sitting on the sidewalk in front of a hardware store. He was selling combs and brushes out of a suitcase. A sign said: WAR VETEREN—I LOST MY LEGS FOR YOU.

"How much?" I said.

He scrutinized me from under his battered hat.

"Brush is two bits. Comb's a dime."

"I'll take a brush and a comb."

"Okey doke. Pick 'em out."

I picked out a black comb and a pink brush; then I dug in my pants pocket for some change.

"I was watching you coming up," he said. "I thought you was a war veteran too the way you was walking. But now I see you close up I see you ain't nearly old enough."

I handed him a quarter and a dime.

"Nope. Not old enough."

I started to walk away, but then he said: "Hey mister, I'm awful dry. How's about lending me that sody pop?"

I gave it to him. He looked up at me and gave a harsh, nasty laugh, as though he'd just put something over on me.

I went back to my car, which was parked just down the street from the beauty parlor. I slid behind the wheel, slumped down, tugged down the brim of my hat.

I went to sleep fast, and started dreaming. I dreamed about a girl, but it wasn't Darla, she was dark where Darla was fair but she was nearly as pretty but I didn't know her name, and then I dreamed about a train and the clackety clack of its hard wheels, clackety clack, clackety clack . . .

I woke up. I looked at my watch. I'd gotten myself lost for the requested period of time.

I went in the beauty parlor.

Darla was sitting in a chair leafing through a *Ladies' Home*

Journal. A hatchet-faced woman dressed like a nurse was standing beside her. Darla's hair had disappeared into fifteen or so gleaming metallic curlers, which were attached to a tangle of black electrical cords which snaked down from a sinister-looking black apparatus a couple of feet above her head.

I couldn't help but laugh. Darla looked up at me and said: "Stop it." Then she said: "Hey! Stop it!"

Then she threw the magazine at me, but she too was laughing.

5

We came out of the Klip n' Kurl. "I'm hungry," Darla said.

"What are you hungry for?"

"Fried chicken. Lots and lots of hot and greasy fried chicken."

"You know the Hottentot Hut?"

"Sure. Let's go."

People were getting off work, and there was a lot of traffic. I was glad I didn't have a regular job and my job was driving Darla around. She went in her purse for the vodka and finished it off, then had me stop at a liquor store to buy some more. She tried to get me to join her again, and I said no again.

" 'Cause it's not sundown yet? He's not God, Danny. He can't see what we're doing."

"He might have somebody watching us," and I checked the rearview mirror. "Somebody might be tailing us."

"You mean a spy that's spying on the spy?"

"I'm not a spy."

"It's no fun drinking alone. You're a goddamn party pooper."

Somebody like Darla was practically always going to get what she wanted from somebody like me. I'd never had vodka before, and I hated it. I thought it tasted like rubbing alcohol. But pretty soon as the bottle passed back and forth I felt like busting out in a song.

I couldn't remember ever being as happy as I was driving north across Hollywood toward the Hottentot Hut with Darla. I felt like we were escaping something, like school, or prison, or like the car had plunged off a bridge into a river and sunk to the bottom but we had gotten out and now we were holding hands as we floated upwards in a swirl of silvery bubbles, any moment now we would break the surface and look at each other and laugh because we were Danny and Darla and we were still alive.

We drove up Highland Avenue then across the Cahuenga Pass and onto Ventura Boulevard. The parking lot of the Hottentot Hut only had two or three other cars in it. As we walked inside, Hawaiian music was playing. A ceiling fan made of dried palm fronds swished over our heads.

We took a table, and ate ourselves silly. Washed down the chicken with cold beer. Darla's hands and lips shined with grease. She wiped off her mouth with a paper napkin then reached across the table and wiped my mouth off. "You're a funny fella," she said.

"Yeah?"

"All that Two Gun Danny stuff. Just doesn't seem to fit you."

"I guess I must've been different before I got hit in the head." I was quiet for a minute, chewing, thinking. "I was Bud's favorite, so they say. Before—you know. Now I think I disappoint him all the time."

"Maybe it's a good thing you disappoint him."

In a little while she said: "I need to make the river run." She got up and went to the ladies' room.

A guy at the next table leaned toward me. "Hey, bub. What did you do to deserve it?"

"Deserve what?"

"That goddamn gorgeous girl."

I just smiled and shrugged. He laughed. I didn't mind him thinking what he was thinking.

When she came back to the table she was dancing along with the music like a hula hula girl, hips slowly swaying, arms moving in a wavelike way. She sat down and gave me a dreamy smile. "Aloha, Danny."

"We better get going. Bud's probably wondering what happened to us."

"Fuck Bud."

I paid up and we left. The sun was gone and the stars were out. We drove back over the Cahuenga Pass. Darla was curled up in a corner of the seat, arms crossed, eyes closed. She sighed, and murmured something.

"What?" I said.

"Mutual Movies Make Time Fly."

I'd heard that before—it was the motto of a movie company. She kept talking but didn't bother to open her eyes. "You like my hair, Danny?"

"Sure."

"You should've told me, then. When a girl gets her hair done, that's what she wants to hear."

"I like your hair."

She wiggled around a bit to get more comfortable. The headlights of oncoming cars lit her up, and left her dark, and lit her up, and left her dark.

I dropped her off at the Peacock Club, then drove home. Except I figured out I wasn't ready to go home, so I stopped off at Healy's Bar. It was on Vine near Melrose.

As I walked up to the entrance, an old stewbum stumbled out, looked at me with amazement, and said: "Brian!"

"You got the wrong guy," I said. I tried to walk past him, but he grabbed my arm. He had a black stocking cap pulled down over his forehead, and his breath smelled like his insides were rotting out.

"You ain't Brian Dunnigan?"

"Nope." I pulled my arm away and went in.

It wasn't a place for fancy people. It was long and narrow and dark, like a tunnel to nowhere, and had that vomity dead-end smell joints like that always have. A smoke-dimmed picture of Custer's Last Stand was hanging on the wall. Kid McCoy was sitting at the bar with his drinking pals George and Sonny. They all greeted me by name, they were happy to see me because they knew I would buy them all a drink. I got a vodka for myself.

"How can you drink that belly-wash?" said Kid McCoy. "Only queers and Communists drink that shit."

"I know a girl that drinks it. She got me started."

"A girl, huh?" He shook his head and stared broodingly into space like I'd just explained everything.

McCoy had been the middleweight champ of the world back in the 1890's. The phrase "the real McCoy," meaning the genuine article, came from him. He'd got in a fight in a saloon with a guy who'd refused to believe he was Kid McCoy. When the guy woke up ten minutes later, he rubbed his jaw and said: "Geez, I guess that *was* the real McCoy."

McCoy got really rich then spent every dime on women and booze and the high life. He was married nine times. Then he met somebody he wanted to make wife number ten. But she started getting nervous that he wanted to marry her for her money, because she was getting divorced from this wealthy guy and was about to make a big pile of dough on it. She started talking about maybe moving to New York after the divorce instead of marrying McCoy, so one night he got drunk and shot her in the head with a .32 revolver. And then he left her apartment and ran amok and shot and wounded three other people before the cops finally stopped him. Both the judge and the jury went easy on him because he used to be famous, and all he got was an eight-year bit in Quentin.

He'd been out a couple of years now. He'd gotten married

again. He had a head like a potato with some messed-up hair on top.

"Nothing weakens a man like pussy," said the Kid.

"How true," said George. "One curly little pussy hair is stronger than the strongest rope or steel cable."

"Depends on whose pussy it's from," said Sonny philosophically. "Some old ugly bitch—one of her pussy hairs wouldn't be all that strong."

"Eye of the beholder," said George. "Believe it or not, there's probably a woman somewhere on the planet who would even find *you* sexually attractive."

"Hardy har har," said Sonny.

"I can hardly get a hard-on anymore, thank god." George included us all in a fond smile. "It's much more pleasant sitting here with my friends sharing a drink in a convivial setting than chasing around town after some treacherous little chippie whose *only* goal is to break my heart."

George wasn't shy about letting people know he was a college graduate and he used to have a top job at an oil company till he lost it due to drink. He wore shabby but once-fine suits. His spectacles and pipe gave him an English-professor air.

Sonny was from West Virginia. He had thin reddish hair and his skin was so white he approached albino status. He said he used to have a good job at the Chrysler plant in Maywood till he had to bust the boss's jaw because he wouldn't get off his back then got thrown in the clink for assault for a year.

Kid McCoy reached into a big jar of boiled eggs sitting on the bar, two for a nickel. The eggs were floating in a piss-colored liquid, and I watched his gnarly-knuckled dirty-fingernailed hand fishing around until he snagged a couple. He bit one in two and held the other out to me.

"Hungry?"

"No thanks. I just ate."

"*I'm* hungry," said Sonny.

McCoy tossed him the egg. "You're always hungry, you scrawny hillbilly sack of shit."

"Them eggs ain't free," said Henry, the bartender. "The owner comes in and counts ever one of them eggs. If everything don't add up, my pay gets docked."

McCoy started to reach in his pocket, but George stayed his hand. "It's on me, Kid." He threw a nickel down on the bar, it rolled and wobbled around like it was drunk then toppled over.

"That's one for the history books," said Sonny. "George paying for something."

"You mock me as you eat the very egg I paid for."

Sonny finished the egg then picked up a yellow egg crumb off the bar and ate that too then licked his fingers. "You know what the problem is? The problem is, we got some people eating five times a day, and other people going five days without eating."

"You sound like a socialist," said George.

"Well if a socialist is somebody that wants to string ever rich guy up by his heels and gut him like a hog, I guess I'm a socialist."

"You're probably going to vote for that fool Sinclair."

"Who?" McCoy said.

"Upton Sinclair. He's a writer running for governor. Don't you read the papers?"

"I only read the papers if they got a story about me. I love reading about me. But I ain't been in the papers for years."

"Why do you say he's a fool?" I said.

"Because he believes in the improvability of the human heart. And he thinks he can actually beat the powers that be. I personally prefer to keep our corrupt status quo. Why? Because you can always trust a dishonest man. Now I realize that sounds like a paradox. What I mean is, you can trust our present leaders to act in a predictable fashion, which is to do everything they can to line their own pockets and the pockets of their cronies. But an idealist might do anything. Society would be disrupted. Chaos might ensue!"

"Five days without eating," mumbled Sonny, who seemed faint with hunger himself, or maybe just drunk.

George said: "What are your political persuasions, Danny?"

I tried to remember but came up dry. "I don't guess I have any."

"I believe we've found a free thinker. A man with a mind of his own! That calls for another round, Henry."

So I bought another round, and another, then started feeling as wobbly as the nickel and knew it was time to go.

There were these two guys at the other end of the bar I should have paid more attention to. I hadn't seen them in Healy's before. They must have watched me pulling out a fat roll from my pants pocket to pay for the drinks. They must have seen how drunk I was as I headed for the door and how I was limping on my left leg. They probably pegged me as any easy mark. Not knowing, of course, that I was Two Gun Danny Landon.

My car was parked about a hundred feet from the bar. The traffic light at the next corner was changing colors but it could have saved itself the trouble since there wasn't a car on the street. The only living thing I saw was a skinny yellow alley cat that looked me over, then trotted away briskly like it suddenly remembered it was late for a previous engagement.

I heard their shoes on the sidewalk behind me. When I looked over my shoulder, they started running at me. I tried to land a Sunday punch on the nearest guy but missed completely, and took a fist in the face and one in the gut then hit the sidewalk.

They were about my age. They were dressed maybe just a little bit better than tramps. They didn't say a word as they proceeded to kick the living shit out of me. A foot connected with the back of my head and it was like I'd taken a direct hit from a lightning bolt as light exploded inside my skull. Then I felt them going through my pockets. I heard one of them say: "Come on, hurry, hurry!" He sounded scared. Maybe they'd never done anything like this before. Maybe they hadn't eaten in five days and they were desperate.

Then I could hear their footsteps moving off. I pushed myself up off the concrete. Saw them walking quickly, and excitedly counting my money. It was mainly ones, so they'd probably be disappointed.

I was on my knees now. I reached in my coat and took out my gun. I pointed it at them.

One of the guys happened to look over his shoulder and saw me and got kind of a *yikes!* look on his face and yelled something at his buddy and they started to run. I kept the gun pointed at their bouncing backs, shifting the aim slightly from one back to the other.

They reached the corner where the traffic light was, headed down a side street, and disappeared.

6

Luckily, the Orange Blossom Bungalow Court was just a few blocks from the bar, so I managed to drive home okay. But I couldn't make it all the way up the seven steps that led up from the street. I sat down on the fifth step, and put my elbows on my knees and my head in my hands.

I felt like I'd spent the last few hours rolling around inside a cement mixer then had climbed out and been trampled on by a runaway horse. My head was killing me. Blood was dripping out of a cut on my cheek.

I became aware of the presence in my stomach of the chicken dinner from the Hottentot Hut, it was like an animal that wanted out and I stretched out my neck and spewed puke down the steps. A few seconds passed, and I did it again. Then I heard myself groan, and I sat there with my eyes closed and my nostrils filled with the stink of the mess I'd made.

"Danny?"

I looked up. Somebody was standing over me, lit faintly from behind by a street light.

"Who's that?"

"Lionel Dulwich. Your neighbor."

"Oh."

"I don't mean to intrude, but—you seem to be a bit under the weather."

"I'm okay."

I put my head back in my hands and closed my eyes.

"Are you sure?"

I nodded; then I felt his hand on my shoulder.

"Come on, old man, you're being silly, you're *not* okay and I'm taking you inside."

I didn't argue with him. He helped me up, then we headed up the sidewalk that ran between the eight bungalows. I was feeling dizzy, and the sidewalk seemed to move beneath me like I was walking across a trampoline.

"How'd you know my name?" I said.

"The day you moved in, I overheard you talking to Mrs. Dean and Sophie. Sorry. Didn't mean to eavesdrop."

I remembered the grin from under the Mexican hat. He guided me toward his bungalow. "I keep a medical kit in preparation for every sort of emergency: earthquake, fire, flood, famine, pestilence, war—and young neighbors coming home late from an adventurous night on the town. There's Tink coming to greet us. Hello, Tink!"

The black and white cat was looking out the screen door at us. We went inside. Dulwich had me sit down in an armchair, then went in the kitchen to get me a glass of water.

His bungalow was exactly like mine and not at all like mine. Mine was shabby and depressing, but Dulwich's looked like a home. The furnishings were classy and comfy and some of them seemed like they might have cost a pretty penny. A floor lamp with a lampshade covered with long-tailed monkeys and many-colored parrots sent a soft warm light spilling across the room. On the wall was a painting of a beautiful girl with long blonde hair; she was dressed like a princess from the days of King Arthur and was standing on a rocky gray cliff and gazing out at a stormy sea. A cabinet radio was playing an elegant sunny song, like something Fred Astaire and Ginger Rogers might dance to. And Tink sharpened her claws on a Persian rug then walked over and sniffed at my shoes.

They were spattered with vomit, as were my pants legs. The cat opened its mouth and wrinkled its nose and generally acted like it had never encountered anything so disgusting before as me. Dulwich walked back in with the water.

"Getting better acquainted, are we? Tink is short for Tinker, which is short for Tinker Bell. And Tinker Bell rules the house."

I drank half the glass, then took the aspirin tin out of my pocket.

"Head hurt?" said Dulwich.

"Yeah."

I drank down the aspirin, then gave the empty glass back to Dulwich. "Thanks."

"Let me take your hat and coat."

I handed him my hat, then winced a little getting out of my coat. He looked at my dent, looked at my gun; then he went away again.

On top of the cabinet radio was a photograph in a silver frame. It showed a young man in a soldier's uniform. He had light-colored hair parted in the middle and a strong chin with a cleft in it. He was as handsome as a motion picture star. He was looking right in the camera, and smiling a little.

"Aubrey Joyce," said Dulwich. He'd come back in the room with his first-aid stuff. He looked at the picture smiling a little like Aubrey Joyce. "The look on his face is so characteristic of him. That sly, mischievous, I-know-something-but-I-shan't-tell-*you* expression."

"Who is he?"

"He was my best friend. We were in school together. We were twenty-one when the war started, and we both rushed to enlist. Or rather, he rushed to enlist, and I rushed to keep up with him. He was mad for glory, mad for medals, and he won more than a few. But of course his mood darkened as the war progressed. He was seriously wounded on three separate occasions. He could have gotten out of the war if he wished, but he always insisted on returning. Not because he still believed in the war, but because he thought his men needed him. His 'lads,' he called them. 'My lads are helpless without me,' he would say. 'Who else is going to wipe their silly little noses for them, and make sure they eat their vegetables and say their bedtime prayers?' He survived the war, rather miraculously I thought, but then died six weeks after the Armistice. On Christmas Day. Of the Spanish flu." Now Dulwich smiled ruefully at me. "Sorry. Didn't mean to get into all of *that*. Now let's take a look at you."

With a wet washcloth, he wiped the blood off my face. His touch was gentle, nearly tender. He had sandy hair that fell over his forehead, hazel eyes, a large round nose, a wide mouth with big lips, and ears that stuck out from his head. He was over six feet, and very thin. He was wearing soft tasseled slippers, and an exotic-looking silk jacket with a sash; the jacket seemed to have a hundred shimmering colors in it.

He peered at the cut on my cheek. "Don't believe we need stitches. But this will sting a bit."

He soaked a piece of cotton with some rubbing alcohol and dabbed at the cut. "What happened?"

"I was coming out of a bar, and two guys jumped me. And stole my dough."

His eyes drifted to my gun.

"Smith & Wesson? .38?"

"Yeah. I couldn't get it out in time. Otherwise . . ."

Dulwich thoughtfully said: "Mm," and put a band-aid on my cheek.

"Vision all right? Not blurred?"

"It's fine."

He began putting away his first-aid stuff.

"I'm terribly curious about what you do. Would it be impolite to ask?"

"I work for the Los Angeles Projects Corporation." That wasn't untrue. Bud had a company, and that's what it was called. "I'm sort of a . . . a guard."

"I see."

"Well, thanks for the help. I should go."

"You're quite sure you're all right?"

"Yeah, I just need to go to bed. I had a lot to drink."

He grinned at me; the space in the middle of his front teeth was big enough to slip a kitchen match through. "A bit sozzled, are we?"

"Yeah. If sozzled means drunk."

He got my hat and coat for me and walked me to the door. His cat followed us, and he scooped her up in his arms.

"Well, thanks again, Mr. Dulwich."

"What are neighbors for, hm, Tinker?" he said, scratching her head. "And by the way, please just call me Dulwich. *Mr.* Dulwich brings my father to mind, and the less he is brought to anyone's mind the better. And only my mother and my lovers call me Lionel."

"You can call me Danny."

"Good night, Danny."

"Good night, Dulwich."

I limped away across the lawn. Looked back once—and saw Dulwich and his cat still in the door, watching me go.

7

"No wonder they call you the Kind One," said Max Schnitter. Bud had just been telling him what happened to this guy named Sal Tagnoli. Bud used to own this little speakeasy just south of downtown on Flower, and he had a nickel slot machine in it. And every night Tagnoli would come in, and he'd make out like a bandit on that nickel slot. So Bud got the idea that Tagnoli was cheating the machine somehow. But when he confronted him, Tagnoli denied it. He said how do you cheat a fucking slot machine, and Bud said maybe with magnets or some kind of tool and Tagnoli said search me and Bud had him searched but they didn't find anything. Tagnoli said: "See? I'm just lucky."

But Bud wasn't convinced. He had the boys take him into the back room and work him over, but Tagnoli continued to insist he was just lucky. "I'm gonna cheat Bud Seitz for a buncha fucking nickels?" he said. "You think I'm crazy?" Then Bud turned him over to Nucky Williams. Nucky slipped on his brass knuckles, which was Nucky's thing and how he got his name. He made Tagnoli's face look like a ripe tomato splitting open but he still just kept screaming that he was lucky. Then Teddy Bump took some wire pliers and started working on his nose and nipples and nuts and toes, but that didn't do the trick either.

So Bud was really exasperated now. He had the guys tie Tagnoli up and throw him in Bud's car along with the slot machine. They drove to San Pedro and got in a boat and went out about halfway to Catalina. Then Bud had Tagnoli tied up to the slot machine, and he told him: "This is your last chance, Sal. Tell me how you was beating my machine."

Tagnoli started yelling: "Bud, you gotta believe me, I'm just lucky! I been lucky ever since I was a little kid! I'm just one of them lucky guys!"

Bud just sighed and said: "Sal, you're tied up to a slot machine and you're about to be dropped in the fucking ocean. How lucky can you be?"

Then Sal started screaming his head off in Italian and they threw him over the side, and Max Schnitter laughed and said: "No wonder they call you the Kind One."

We were at the Surf Club in Redondo Beach. We were in a private room where there were some card and dice tables and a row of slot machines. Sitting in a booth besides myself and Bud and Schnitter were Teddy Bump and Vic Lester, a pug-nosed little guy with Schnitter.

Schnitter was about sixty, and maybe an inch or two north of five feet tall. He was bald and had pointy ears that gave him a slightly inhuman look, like an evil elf. I'd heard he was from Germany, and he'd got a job on a ship as a cabin boy when he was twelve. Then he jumped ship in Panama and walked all the way to America and now he was one of the most powerful guys in Los Angeles.

Guys like him and Bud had made most of their money from bootlegging. Repeal had happened just six months ago, which had basically jerked the rug out from under them. Now they were scrambling around trying to get into new things.

"We put too many of our eggs into one single basket," said Schnitter, who still had a slight German accent.

"That's it exactly, Max," said Bud. "You need a lot of different baskets, so in case you got some D.A. with a bug up his ass about this thing or that thing you won't be totally fucked."

"And the secret of success is simple," Schnitter said. "You must give the people what they want. The government did not have the right to deny a hard-working citizen a drink on Saturday night. Neither should it have the right to tell a man he cannot wager a portion of his wages on the roll of a die; that he cannot enjoy the sexual favors of a beautiful young lady in exchange for a few of his hard-earned dollars; that he shouldn't forget the burdens of existence for an hour or two by smoking opium or snuffing cocaine."

Bud wiped his hands on a tissue. "Danny, you oughta be taking notes when this guy talks. He's a fucking genius."

Schnitter smiled at me. He had sharp eye teeth, like Dracula. He was holding a snifter of brandy in his palm. He sloshed it around gently.

Teddy Bump had a laugh like a dying hyena and he let it loose now. "What's so funny?" said Bud.

"That dame over there. The fucking ash from her cigarette fell down the crack between her tits and she's going nuts."

The pug-nosed guy looked over and started laughing too; his laugh was a lot like Teddy's.

I excused myself to go to the can. There was crushed ice in the pisser. It steamed and crackled and melted as I hosed it down. I had an image of a little boy peeing in the snow, the little boy seemed to be me and then he vanished.

I washed my hands, and looked at myself in a mirror over the sink.

"Danny Landon," I said softly.

There was a guy standing next to me combing his hair. "What's that, Mac?"

"Nothing." I dried my hands and went out.

But I didn't go back to the private room. I went in the bar.

It was crowded. A chubby Negro in a white suit was playing the piano and singing "Stardust":

"You wander down the lane and far away,
Leaving me a song that will not die—
Love is now the stardust of yesterday . . ."

It was a sad kind of a song, but he was smiling as he sang, and seemed like the happiest guy in the room.

Tommy and Goodlooking Tommy were sitting at the bar arguing about something. They were both very drunk. "Shanghai Sally!" said Goodlooking Tommy, and Tommy said: "You're full of shit!" Spit was flying out of their mouths they were getting so mad.

The bar was so full of smoke I wanted to call the fire department. I went outside to get some fresh air.

Dick Prettie was standing there, one hand in his pants pocket, the other holding a cigarette. "Who's Shanghai Sally?" I said.

Dick laughed. "Them two dumbbells still going at it?"

"Yeah."

"There's this broad that works as a bouncer in this joint in Pedro."

"A broad?"

"Yeah. She weighs about two fifty and she's got tattoos of dragons and shit all over her arms. Goodlooking Tommy says her name's Shanghai Sally. Tommy says her name's Cairo Mary."

"You know which one it is?"

"Sure. But I'm staying out of it. Both them Tommys is fucking nuts."

The sea breeze was blowing in on us and it was cold and I shivered a little. Out in the distance in the dark I could see white lines of foam where the waves were coming in. "Let's go walk on the beach," I said.

"What for?"

"The hell of it."

"I'll get fucking sand in my shoes."

"Ah, come on."

So we left the lights and the smoke and the noise of the club behind us and went out on the beach. There was half a moon and plenty of stars. And miles out on the ocean I saw the lights of a ship. I wondered if it was a gambling ship, like the one I'd helped to heist and sink.

Dick stumbled and started cursing. "It's happening already, I'm getting sand in my shoes! I can't stand the way it feels in between my fucking toes!"

I wondered what Darla was doing. Seitz had banished her from his presence for a few days, because it was that time of the month for her and he couldn't stand to be around her when that was going on.

"So how's it going with Shitter?" said Dick.

"Okay, I guess." I saw some seaweed washed up on the shore that looked like a tangled clump of snakes. "He called Bud 'the Kind One.' "

"Yeah?"

"Seems like I remember somebody else calling him that once."

"Sure, it's a nickname. It's kinda like a joke, see? 'Cause kind ain't the first thing you'd think of calling Bud Seitz."

"Who started calling him that?"

He stopped to light up a new Old Gold. He cupped the flame of the lighter against the wind. His gaunt face was lit up, and the angles were filled with shadow. "It was this Mexican girl. Emperatriz.

"She was his girl for a while. He met her in Tia Juana, at Agua Caliente. She was there with this rich Mexican asshole old enough to be her grandpa. Bud told her what horses to bet in a couple of races, and she cleaned up. Then she dumped grandpa and came back up here with us.

"She was a gorgeous broad, but she was also nice. She was nice to people that most people don't give a shit about.

"There was this kid, Flumentino. He worked in the kitchen at the Peacock, sweeping up, taking out the garbage, that kinda shit. He had a long neck and big ears and he was always smiling at everybody. Everybody thought he was a dummy, but maybe that's just 'cause he didn't speak no English to speak of.

"Anyway, Emperatriz was nice to Flumentino, and maybe he got the wrong idea. One night, him and one of the cooks, they'd been nipping at a bottle all night, and I guess he musta got pretty plastered, 'cause when Emperatriz walked by he grabbed her by the ass. And Bud happened to walk in right at that moment and he seen it.

"Jesus Christ, Danny, what they did to that poor kid. They cleared the kitchen out and tied him up and put him up on this counter where the cooks do their chopping. When they got done with him, they had to put him in four different gunnysacks to get him outa the kitchen. And then I got stuck with the job of going out in the desert to bury the sacks."

"What was Emperatriz doing during all this?"

"Begging. Pleading. Screaming. But it didn't do no good. And after that she started calling Bud *el Benévolo*. The Kind One."

"What ever happened to her?"

Dick took a drag on his cigarette—took his time blowing the smoke back out. "I don't know. She just kinda disappeared. Went back to Mexico, I guess."

We started walking again. The sand sucked at my shoes. The waves slid up the beach then slipped away.

"Was I there?" I said.

"Was you where?"

"In the kitchen. That night."

Dick was quiet a minute. "I think you was outa town. On business."

I wondered what business I was on. We heard some laughing

and screaming—a happy kind of screaming—then we saw a guy and a girl playing around in the water. Dick said: "Shit. They're naked."

They looked young, maybe seventeen or eighteen. They were chasing each other around and grabbing each other and kissing and then they'd laugh when a wave hit them and by the light of the half of the moon I could make out the nipples on the girl and the hair down between her legs and my heart felt like it was about to bust I wanted so bad to be out there in the waves chasing around a girl, not her, not Darla even, but the girl I dreamed about sometimes, the girl with the dark hair and the olive skin.

"Looks like they're having fun," Dick said wistfully.

"Yeah."

"You know the last time I screwed a broad that wasn't a whore?"

"No."

"Me neither. Probably when Babe Ruth was still a pitcher."

We walked a little further, then Dick said: "Hey, lookit!"

We'd found their clothes on the sand. A "his" pile and a "her" pile.

"I know what," said Dick. "Let's bury 'em!"

"Their clothes? What for?"

" 'Cause it'll be funny as hell."

I thought about it a minute. "Nah. Let's just leave 'em alone."

"Well, no way I ain't gonna get a fucking souvenir."

He rummaged through the "her" pile then pulled out her underpants. He held them up dangling in front of his eyes and grinned then stuffed them in his pocket.

We headed back up the beach. When we got close to the Surf Club we saw a couple of guys duking it out on the sand. We got a little closer and saw it was Tommy and Goodlooking Tommy.

It looked like Goodlooking Tommy was getting the worst of

it. By the way, it wasn't like Goodlooking Tommy was really that goodlooking. Nello Marlini was twice as goodlooking as Goodlooking Tommy, girls were telling him all the time he was a dead ringer for Rudolph Valentino. But it got confusing having two guys named Tommy around, so since one of them was goodlooking in comparison to the other, who was very ugly, he got hung with the name Goodlooking Tommy. The alternative would have been for Goodlooking Tommy just to be Tommy and for Tommy to be Ugly Tommy.

We ran toward them, as well as you can run in the sand, yelling at them to stop it.

But they ignored us. Goodlooking Tommy tried to kick Tommy in the balls but Tommy dodged it and grabbed hold of his leg and started twisting it till he fell down. Then Tommy jumped on his back and started pounding on his head with his fists and yelling: "SAY IT! SAY IT! SAY IT!" and Goodlooking Tommy said: "FUCK YOU!"

Tommy suddenly whipped out his revolver and put it to Goodlooking Tommy's head and pulled back the hammer.

"Say 'Cairo Mary,' damn it, or I'm putting a bullet in your fucking head!"

Dick and I jumped on Tommy and dragged him off. His gun went off with a heartstopping pop and a bullet flew out over the ocean. Dick was beside himself.

"Jesus Christ, Tommy, are you crazy? Bud's gonna cut all our fucking balls off!" Because Bud couldn't stand for us to get out of control in public. Unless, of course, he'd given us the say-so.

"Dick," said Tommy, "you know what her fucking name is. Tell him. Tell the prick."

"I'm staying outa this."

Goodlooking Tommy stood up, brushing sand off his suit. He shot his cuffs, straightened the knot in his tie. "Everybody but this shitstick knows her name is Shanghai Sally."

"Shut up," said Dick. "You guys are like a couple of fucking kids. I don't wanna hear nothing more about it."

We all started walking back toward the Surf Club. By the time we got there the Tommys were laughing and joking around about something. I'd noticed they had memories like dogs or cats, not usually seeming to go back more than a minute or two into the past.

I went back in the private room. Everybody was standing up and getting ready to go. "That musta been the longest piss in history," said Bud when he saw me.

"Sorry, Bud. I went for a walk."

Max Schnitter was smiling at me with a slightly puzzled expression, as though he couldn't quite figure out what to make of me. "It was good to see you again, Danny," he said, holding his hand out.

I shook his hand and said: "Good to see *you* again, Mr. Shitter." Bud glared at me, but Schnitter didn't act as if he'd noticed.

"So, Max," said Bud, "lemme talk to Blinky about a couple of things and then I'll call you."

"I'll be looking forward to it," said Schnitter. He didn't stick his hand out to Bud because he knew how he felt about shaking hands.

We all headed toward the door. Teddy Bump was walking in front of us with Vic, Schnitter's guy. They were talking and swapping their hyena laughs with one another like they'd suddenly become best buddies.

A fat-assed woman wearing a fox stole that had the sad head and bushy tail of a fox hanging off it squealed as a clatter of quarters came out of a slot machine. A long-legged cigarette girl snarled at some drunk: "Hey, keep your stinking mitts offa me!" White dice tumbled across a green table as the shooter yelled: "Fever in the fuck house!"

I noticed people looking at us respectfully as we passed, like we were all big important guys, like we had the world by the tail, by its bushy tail.

We stopped off at a table near the door where some guys were playing cards. "Hey, Floyd," said Bud, "let's see what kinda balls you got. Let's cut the cards for 10,000 bucks."

Floyd, who had three or four chins spilling out over his collar, looked around at the other guys at the table, who were grinning at him expectantly; then he set down the deck in front of Bud.

"Okay, Bud. Let's go."

"Go ahead, Danny," said Bud.

"Huh?"

"Cut the cards."

"Aw, no, Bud, not me—"

"Go ahead, kid. I got a feeling."

People at other tables were watching now. The cigarette girl paused in her tour of the room, and waited high atop her legs. I felt my heart speeding up as I reached for the deck.

Three of hearts.

The guys at the table started to laugh—Floyd too, his chins shaking. The cigarette girl smirked at me. But Bud didn't bat an eye.

"Hey, it ain't over yet. Floyd?"

Floyd shook his head and sighed like this was all a tiresome formality and reached over and cut the cards.

Deuce of spades.

The guys at the table were howling now. I heard some cheers and applause coming from some of the other tables. The cigarette girl gave me a nice smile, showing rosy gums and even white teeth. And Floyd's face and all his chins were turning as red as a brick. "You know, Bud, I don't actually have that kind of money on me right at this moment—"

"Don't sweat it, Floyd. I know you're good for it. Just bring it around tomorrow."

Then Bud slapped me on the back as we went out. "See, kid? You're a winner."

Bud and I were in the back seat of his bulletproof black Lincoln sedan as it sped northward on Sepulveda toward Hollywood. Teddy Bump was driving. Dick and the two Tommys were behind us in another car.

Bud was smoking a cigar and sipping some whiskey on the rocks; he was in a good mood.

"I figured something out tonight. It's like silent pictures and pictures with people talking. Most of them old movie stars couldn't make the switch. It turned out the guys had voices like fairies and the broads sounded like cats that was getting their tails stepped on. Same thing since they made booze legal. A lotta guys are gonna fall along the wayside. But not me. I'm gonna be smart about all this."

I nodded. Bud rattled around the ice in his glass. "What do you think of Schnitter?"

"He's okay."

"What's the matter with him?"

"I didn't say anything was the matter with him."

"Come on, Danny, I know you. Spit it out."

"Well . . . if you were to eat a bunch of bad oysters and you're puking your guts out all night, and then you finally fall asleep, but you're still sick, and you're having these horrible dreams, they're like the worst nightmares of your life, and you're thrashing around in bed and moaning . . . well, Schnitter's the kind of guy you might be dreaming about."

Bud puffed on his cigar and looked at me.

"That sounds nuts, I guess."

"No, Danny, I understand your meaning. I've noticed you're

usually very sharp about people. I always take what you say very serious."

We rolled on through the dark awhile, and then: "Bud? Can I ask you a question?"

"Sure."

"How old am I?"

He seemed taken aback. "How old are you?"

"Yeah."

He looked away from me and out the window. There wasn't much to look at.

"Twenty-five, kid. You're twenty-five."

8

"Smell me," said Darla.

She offered me her wrist. I could see green and blue and purple veins under the skin which seemed as thin and white as tissue paper.

It made me dizzy she smelled so good. Like sticking my head in a bucket of flowers. "Nice," I said.

"It's Mitsuoko. Jean Harlow's favorite. I bought twenty bottles."

We were driving away from Bullock's Department Store on Wilshire. On the radio the announcer said Clyde Barrow and Bonnie Parker had been killed by lawmen in Louisiana.

"So they finally got them," said Darla.

I'd been guarding her body for three and a half weeks. I was obviously an intimidating force, since there hadn't been a single attempt to attack or kidnap her.

I'd taken her, in puffy pants and high black boots, to her weekly horseback-riding lesson at the DuBrock Riding Academy. I'd driven her, pale and sweaty and gritting her teeth, to see a Dr. Siegel in Beverly Hills for some kind of "female" complaint. I'd eaten triple-decker ice cream sundaes with her at Eskimo Ice Cream, which was a building shaped like an igloo, and had platefuls of steaming, gleaming, tender pork ribs at the Pick-a-Rib Barbecue Pit on Melrose. I'd gone with her to a bar in Malibu because she said they served great silver fizzes there, that's a drink made with egg whites; I couldn't have choked one down on a bet but she drank three then we drove on up the Coast Highway to Point Dume. It's a finger of land sticking out in the ocean where Santa Monica Bay ends. We got out of the car and walked around. It was windy and the water was blue and there weren't any clouds. A couple of hundred feet from shore a sea lion was sunning itself on a big rock. You could look up the coast and see the rest of California disappearing into the distance, and you could imagine disappearing into that distance too, not looking back, just traveling forever.

Point Dume was where Darla told me all about Darla.

She grew up in a speck-like town on the prairie called Nebraska City, Nebraska. Her father was the postmaster. One winter when she was twelve there was a terrible blizzard and no one could get out of the house for days. Her father just sat there drinking moonshine out of a mason jar and getting more and more worried because he couldn't get the mail out to people and he felt like he was letting everybody down. Darla said she and her father were sitting at the kitchen table and her mother was standing at the stove cooking breakfast and her mother told her father to quit feeling sorry for himself. Her father didn't say a word, just got up and started walking toward her mother and then Darla saw a gun in his hand and he shot her mother in the back of the head. Then he turned and looked at Darla.

The wind was howling outside and snow was blowing past the windows and she could see in her father's eyes that he was about to kill her. She jumped up and ran in the bathroom and locked the door. He started beating on the door then throwing his weight up against it, and she tried to get the window open but it was jammed shut then he burst into the room.

She got in the bathtub like it was some kind of protection and tried to squeeze herself up into a little ball as he walked over and looked down at her. "No, Daddy, don't!" she said, and he smiled at her and said: "Aw, honey, I wouldn't never hurt you, I'm your daddy," and then he shot himself in the side of the head.

She was sent to live with her uncle Gideon. He lived on a farm out in the middle of nothing. He and his wife didn't have any children. She was an invalid and seldom left their bedroom.

Darla had to do all the cooking and cleaning like the stepchild in a fairy tale. She had to bring in water from the well and feed the chickens and once she even had to help Uncle Gideon slaughter a hog; she held on tight to the hog's hind legs so it wouldn't run off while Gideon beat it in the head with a sledge hammer.

One day Darla was sitting in the outhouse when she became aware that Gideon was spying on her through a crack in the door.

As the weeks went on it seemed like every time she looked around she'd find her uncle's eyes on her. She was only twelve but she'd developed early and she looked sixteen, and she knew enough about the facts of life to know what was on Gideon's mind.

She was out in the barn gathering eggs on a day in early spring when Gideon came in. He came up behind her and put his hand on her bottom and started rubbing and squeezing it. She told him to stop and he said: "I'm just giving you what you been wanting, you little whoremongering bitch."

She tried to get away but he chased her around the barn, giggling all the while like they were two kids playing tag. She started taking eggs out of her basket and throwing them at him, and he dodged and giggled till one hit him in the forehead. Then his face turned dark with anger as he wiped off the dripping mess, and she made a break for the ladder that led up to the hay loft. She nearly made it all the way up but then he grabbed her by the ankle and pulled her down, then, still holding on to the one ankle, he dragged her over to a pile of hay. He yanked her dress up and her drawers down and climbed on top of her. She said the sounds he made while he raped her reminded her of how the hog sounded when it was being killed.

When Gideon finished he became enraged and slapped her face again and again. He said it was her fault he'd fallen into sin and it was her fault his brother had killed himself; he was sure Darla had tried to tempt his brother into doing what Gideon had just done and he had to kill himself to keep from doing it. As he got up and buttoned his britches he told her not to tell anybody what had happened or else he'd throw her down the well then say she'd killed herself because she couldn't live with all the lies she'd been telling.

She ran away, but Gideon called the sheriff on her and he caught her and she was back on Gideon's farm in less than a day.

Gideon told her if she was going to act like some kind of sorry no-account dog that wouldn't stay in the yard unless it was tied up then that was how he was going to have to treat her. He chained her to the stove. He brought her food and water twice a day, and the only time he let her loose was to go to the outhouse. He'd go with her and stand in the door to make sure she didn't run off.

Darla said that after about a week she wrapped the chain around her neck and tried to strangle herself, but it hurt too bad so she gave up.

Finally one night her aunt Bess crept out of the bedroom, wearing a flowing white nightgown that made her look like a ghost. She had a key. Darla could hear Gideon snoring as Bess unlocked the padlock. She whispered: "Now you just run, honey, you run away fast as you can. I'd go with you if I could." So Darla snuck out of the house and ran down the road and the sheriff didn't catch her this time.

She walked for two days, hiding whenever a car went past, till she happened upon a hobo jungle near a railroad yard. Three hoboes were cooking some stew and Darla was starving and they fed her. She stayed with them a few days and they were really nice to her. Darla said it was kind of like a Shirley Temple movie, three loveable tramps adopting a cute little runaway girl; one of the tramps even looked and talked like Wallace Beery, but then they all got liquored up one night and tore off her clothes and took turns with her.

So she ran off again. She hitchhiked. She tried to accept rides only with older husband-and-wife-looking couples who seemed unlikely to attack her. When asked what her story was, it never occurred to her to tell the truth; she would just say she was on her way home after visiting relatives. Her rides would often feed her and sometimes give her a buck or two.

Darla drifted eastward across the country; her only goal was to put as much distance as possible between herself and Nebraska. That summer she got caught in a thunderstorm out on a road in Indiana. She'd always been terrified of lightning and so she jumped in the first car that stopped.

It was a Model A Ford driven by a young Army lieutenant. Within ten minutes his hand was on her knee and headed north. She sunk her teeth in his arm and he yelled and she opened the door and flung herself out.

She bounced and tumbled in the rain till she came to a stop with her left arm sticking out at a crazy angle. The lieutenant's car slowed down a minute then sped away.

Darla found herself just outside the city limits of Elwood, Indiana. She walked into town, her broken arm hanging. Lightning struck a tree in front of her and a big limb fell down on the ground. She saw a sign in front of a house that said: Woodrow Ames, M.D.

Dr. Ames turned out to be a tall silver-haired old man who set her arm with gentleness and skill. He complimented Darla for not crying or crying out. He was nearly finished when she started getting bad stomach pains then blood came pouring out from between her legs. He called to his wife to come and help, and the Ameses and Darla were all astonished when a tiny half-formed baby plopped on the floor like a dead fish.

Darla hadn't known that her uncle Gideon or one of the tramps had gotten her pregnant. She began to cry and she told them everything. She begged them not to send her back to Uncle Gideon, and Dr. Ames said don't worry, the only things that man deserved were a vigorous horsewhipping and a long prison term.

Dr. Ames and his wife had a daughter but she had grown up and had her own children and moved away, and now they were very lonely. They looked on Darla as a gift from God. They moved her into their daughter's old bedroom. They felt bad about what had been done to her and they couldn't do enough for her. They bought her new clothes and shoes and ribbons for her yellow hair and whatever kind of bright gewgaw a girl twelve going on thirteen might desire. They told everyone in Elwood Darla was the daughter of a distant relative who had died. They said they would like to adopt her legally if it was all right with her and she said yes.

On Sundays, they took her to church. She had a fine singing voice and joined the youth choir.

In September, she enrolled in school. She was in the eighth grade. She felt much older than her classmates and didn't make any real friends. But she found herself popular because she was so pretty and everyone was eager to sign the cast on her nearly mended arm, and she liked school and studied hard and made good grades.

In December, there was a lynching.

An old white woman named Bathsheba Butler had been found in her house robbed, raped, and stabbed and hacked to death with a pair of gardening shears. Earlier that same day, a colored man named Beau Jack had done some yard work at her house, and he'd been seen trimming some bushes with those very same shears.

Beau Jack was arrested and put in the local jail. That evening a mob formed and took him from the jail and out to the edge of town. They stood him in the back of a pick-up truck under an oak tree with a big horizontal limb; Darla found out it wasn't the first lynching that had happened there.

It seemed like the whole town turned out, and people were acting excited and happy, like it was the Fourth of July and they were waiting for the fireworks. Near the outskirts of the crowd Darla saw the mayor talking to the police chief; they were both laughing and smoking cigarettes. Some kids were playing Pop the Whip.

Crisp brown leaves covered the ground. It was very cold, and it was sleeting, and the sleet made a frying sound on the dead leaves.

The scene was lit up by the headlights of several cars. Beau Jack had his hands tied behind his back. He looked to be about thirty. He was tall, broad-shouldered, and well-muscled. He was naked. He was bleeding from many places. He'd been whipped and beaten, and his right ear and his private parts had been cut off.

He was shaking all over, whether from the cold or fear or the shock of his wounds Darla couldn't say, but his face as he looked out over the crowd was completely blank. Somebody said: "Dumb nigger don't even know what's happening to him," but Darla understood the blankness.

They put the rope over his neck, and somebody started up the truck. But there had been a lot of rain lately, and the truck only moved a foot or two before it got stuck in the soft ground. Beau Jack stumbled a little but regained his balance. Good-natured jeers came from the crowd as they struggled to get the truck moving. The tires spun in the mud. A big fat guy named Donnie Collins unwisely got right behind one of the tires and was splattered head to toe with mud, which caused a lot of laughter. Finally the truck got traction and lurched away, and Beau Jack swung and jerked at the end of the rope for several minutes till he was still. Then people got out their cameras and posed in front of the dangling corpse.

Darla was there with Dr. and Mrs. Ames. Bathsheba Butler had been his patient and the life-long friend of both of them. Mrs. Ames couldn't bear to watch, she hid her face in her husband's chest, while Dr. Ames looked grim but he never turned away.

Darla told me she didn't care what that poor coon had done, he didn't deserve what had been done to *him,* at the very least he should have got a fair trial. And the whole town had just stood there and watched and nobody had said a thing, including her beloved Dr. Ames. And the people had brought out their own children to see the torture and killing of Beau Jack, and it was evil, purely evil, out there on the edge of town, evil in the leaves and evil in the sleet and evil in the headlights and the stark shadows and evil even in Darla, she had stood there with the rest and hadn't said a word, it didn't matter she was only thirteen she should have said *something.*

At church that Sunday, she looked around at everybody, and she'd seen many of them at the lynching and if they'd been a bunch of naked wailing witches leaping around a fire at midnight she would've had more respect for them, it just made her sick them singing hymns about going to heaven and acting like they were so godly and so good.

She started having bad dreams about her and Beau Jack, although sometimes her eyes were open so they couldn't be dreams: Beau Jack would be crouching in the bathtub as her father stood over him with a gun, Darla would be standing naked on the truck with the rope around her neck and the tires churning the mud and throwing it up into the headlights, she would be holding on to Beau Jack's legs as Uncle Gideon beat him in the head with a hammer, and she and Beau Jack would be fleeing the hobo jungle, running away together into an eternal night.

Elwood, Indiana had seemed like a haven to her at first, but now it seemed a dark place, full of ghosts and sorrow. It seemed like Nebraska all over again, a place she needed to leave.

It was the Ameses' habit every Sunday after church to go to the Totempole Grill for a fried chicken and waffles dinner. A few weeks after the lynching they were there when Darla overheard the waitress talking to a man at the next table; he said he was a traveling salesman for Morrill Meat and was just passing through. When he got up to leave, she excused herself, saying she needed to go to the restroom, but she followed the man outside. She asked him if he could give her a ride to the next town, and he looked her up and down and grinned and said you bet, hop in, and Darla never saw Elwood or the Ameses again.

For the next several years she wandered around the middle part of the country, making it a rule never to return to a place once she'd left. By the time she was fourteen she looked twenty; she lived her life as an adult, and thought of herself as one too. She had little trouble getting a job as a waitress at one greasy spoon or another. Sometimes when she left a job she'd clean out the cash register on her way out; she said she'd steal a hot stove in those days. She got caught by the law once, but she slept with the sheriff and he let her go.

She turned eighteen in Aurora, Illinois. One day she was at a picture show, watching *Hills of Peril,* a Buck Jones western. She was nearly the only person there. After the movie was over she started talking with the owner; the place was named the Dream Theater, and she asked him why it was called that. He told her it was because he thought "dream" was the most beautiful word in the English language.

Darla started going to the theater at least once a week, and she found herself looking forward as much to seeing the owner as the picture. His name was Goldsborough Bruff. He was forty-eight. He got around on crutches, because one of his legs was missing just below the hip. He had dark wavy hair with gray streaks in it.

One night he told her his ticket girl had just quit and did she want the job? And so Darla gave up waitressing and began working in the Dream Theater.

It was an old drafty building that leaked in the rain and there never seemed to be very many customers but she loved it there. She sold tickets and candy and soda pops and popcorn and helped Mr. Bruff change the titles on the bright marquee and put his messy office in order. She would come in even on her days off to help him out.

Bruff didn't have a wife or any close relatives. He told her he had grown up in a wealthy family but his father had lost everything in the Panic of '93. When the Spanish-American War started he joined the Army, and was very disappointed that the fighting was over before he could get into it. But eventually his outfit got shipped to the Philippines to fight the rebels there. One day a donkey wandered into their camp. He and some other soldiers went over to take a look at it. The donkey was carrying some packs on its back, and Bruff saw smoke curling up out of one of the packs an instant before the donkey exploded. Several soldiers were killed, and a dozen or so were wounded; Bruff woke up without a leg.

Darla told him a little of what had happened to her, and she saw tears welling up in his eyes as he listened, and she thought she had never known anyone so kind.

She'd been working there about three months and she was up in the projection booth with Bruff helping him get the picture ready for the Saturday matinee, when she sensed that he wanted to kiss her. She said it's okay, Mr. Bruff, go ahead, and he did so. He said he was in love with her and wanted to take care of her forever and for her to be his wife but there was something she needed to know: his war wounds had left him unable to father children. She said the last thing she wanted was to have a bunch of bratty kids and as far as what went along with having children she'd already had more than enough of that and could live without it just fine and she loved him too and the answer was yes.

Darla said they were very happy for a while as they planned their wedding and honeymoon, but then he started acting sad and glum. He said she was a beautiful young girl with her whole life ahead of her, and it was selfish of him to allow her to join up her life with that of an aging cripple running some falling-apart picture show that barely made a dime. She said she was old enough to know her own mind and they loved each other and that's what counted and she didn't want to hear anything more about it.

One day she came in for work and didn't find Bruff in his office, then went up to the projection booth and that was empty too. But then she looked down and saw Bruff sitting in one of the seats, right square in the middle of the big empty theater, facing the curtained screen.

She went downstairs. Bruff's crutches were propped up on the seat beside him. His eyes were closed and his chin was on his chest. She thought he was asleep, but then touched his shoulder and knew he was dead.

The doctor said it must have been a heart attack, but Darla wasn't so sure. She said that Bruff was still often in terrible pain because of his war injuries, and he'd take such great quantities of morphine he'd be so woozy he could barely keep his eyes open. She thought that maybe he'd accidentally taken too much.

Darla discovered that Bruff before he died had changed his will and left her everything—which basically meant his little house and the Dream Theater. She knew she couldn't stay in Aurora with him gone, so she sold the theater and the house, and after the bank loans were paid off, she was left with a little over 3500 dollars.

Around that time she happened to read an article about Los Angeles in a magazine. The article's name was "The Newest City in the World." That sounded good to her, and so she booked a seat on the Santa Fe Chief.

"How old are you, Danny?" asked Darla.

We were still in the Mitsuoko-smelling car, heading north on La Brea.

"Twenty-five," I was pleased to be able to say.

"Me too. Think you'll live to be thirty?"

"I don't know. I never thought about it." I thought about it. "I guess so."

"I think I'll be real lucky if I live to be thirty. I don't think the odds are in my favor at all."

"That's just plain dumb. Why would you say that?"

Darla shrugged. La Brea crossed Franklin then ran up a little hill and ended right in front of Bud's house. I stopped the car. Usually someone was around to open the gate, but I didn't see anybody.

I tooted the horn, and someone came running.

9

"So you don't remember a thing," said Dulwich.

"Not before about ten months ago," I said. "They told me a bunch of guys jumped me in Ocean Park, and one of them hit me in the head with a lead pipe. But all I remember is waking up in a hospital and seeing a nurse putting some flowers in a vase. And I said: 'Those are beautiful flowers,' and she gave me this big smile and said: 'Weeellll . . . welcome back, honey!' "

"Do you know why you were beaten?"

"No. Nobody knows who the guys were. My wallet was missing. Maybe they just wanted to rob me. Or maybe they knew me. Maybe they wanted to get even with me for something."

"Who took care of you afterwards? Do you have family members here?"

"The guys I work with. They took care of me."

"The guys at the . . . what was the name . . . the Los Angeles Projects Corporation."

I nodded. I sipped my tea. It was in a delicate cup that had a red and blue oriental dragon twisting around it.

We were in Dulwich's living room. Aubrey Joyce smiled musingly at us from his perch atop the cabinet radio. There were some tasty little sugary cookies on a saucer on the coffee table. Next to the saucer was a book, lying open and facedown: *Is China Mad?* by Baron Auxion de Ruffe.

"You ever hear of Bud Seitz?" I said.

"The hoodlum?"

"I guess so. That's who I work for."

"Really."

"Yeah."

Dulwich looked at me with interest as he nibbled on a cookie.

"I sunk a ship once."

Dulwich looked surprised. "An entire ship?"

"Yeah."

"Just you?"

"No, me and some of the boys. It was a gambling ship. The *Monfalcone.*"

"Oh, I remember that. It was about four years ago, wasn't it? It went down near Long Beach."

"Right."

"But I remember it being an accident. An inebriated cook, a fire in the galley, something of that sort."

"It was no accident. It was a heist job and a sink job. 'Cause Bud had a beef with the owner."

"Is it tea time, old chap?"

We looked toward the door. Sophie Gubler was standing there, peering in through the screen, her hands cupped around her eyes to block out the sunshine.

"It is indeed," said Dulwich. "Would you like to join us?"

Sophie came in and eyed the coffee table. "I'll join you in cookies," she said, and took one.

"Why aren't you in school?" said Dulwich.

"It's summer, dummy. School's over." She took another cookie while still chewing on the first one. "Well, is it?"

"Is what what?"

"Is China mad?"

"The whole world's mad."

"You shouldn't put a book down like that. It's terrible for it. It'll break its back."

"You're quite right." Dulwich picked the book up, turned

down the corner of a page, and closed it.

"You shouldn't bend a page like that—"

"Oh, that's enough. Be quiet."

Sophie looked at me for the first time.

"Hi, Danny."

"Hi, Sophie. How are you today?"

"Fine." She plucked at her dress. She suddenly seemed a little shy. She turned back to Dulwich. "Where's Tinker Bell?"

"The last confirmed Tinker Bell sighting was on the foot of my bed, where she was observed to be taking one of her not infrequent catnaps."

"Can I go see her?"

"Of course."

Dulwich waited till Sophie disappeared into his bedroom, then said softly: "Poor girl. She loves animals, but that beastly mother of hers won't let her have a pet."

I'd seen her mother a few times in the courtyard, usually hearing her first, clicking quickly down the sidewalk on her very high high heels. She wasn't much older than me. She was pretty in a trampy way, with wiggling hips and platinum blonde hair obviously out of a bottle. Her name was Lois.

"I don't know why Mrs. Dean puts up with her behavior," Dulwich sighed.

"What kind of behavior?"

"Well, she's had a succession of male 'houseguests,' each more unsavory than the last. She introduces them as 'my cousin Joe' or 'my uncle Roy' or 'Mr. Ritter, an old family friend.' And then in the middle of the night one hears an ungodly yowling and yodeling emanating from her bedroom as she and Mr. Ritter talk over old times. I consider myself the least prudish of men, but really! It's hardly a proper environment in which to raise a child."

Sophie walked back in, looked at us suspiciously. "Were you

talking about me?"

"Not at all," said Dulwich. "How was Tinker?"

"Still asleep. Her whiskers were twitching. She's probably dreaming about catching birds." Sophie turned to me. "Mrs. Dean hates her. She feeds the birds, and Tinker hides in the bushes then runs out and tries to catch them."

"*Does* catch them, sometimes. I like our feathered friends as much as Mrs. Dean does; however, she obviously hasn't read Darwin, and understands nothing about the survival of the fittest and the balance of nature and so forth. She actually suggested once that I give Tinker away. I replied: 'Mrs. Dean, with all due respect, I suggest that you go climb a tree.' "

Sophie giggled. "Think about it. Think about Mrs. Dean climbing a tree."

"I've had a sudden inspiration," Dulwich said.

"What?" said Sophie.

"There's a new Clark Gable picture playing. Who would like to go?"

"Oh, I would, I would!" said Sophie, bouncing up and down.

"Danny?"

"Sure."

"Can we go in your car?" asked Sophie.

"Fine by me."

"Have you seen Danny's car?" she said to Dulwich. "It's a doozie!"

"Oh really? I thought it was a Packard."

She rolled her eyes. "That's dumb."

"But Sophie," said Dulwich, "you should go ask your mother for permission."

"She's at work. But she wouldn't care. She likes it when I'm not around."

Dulwich rose from his chair. "Then let us heed the words of the Persian sage: 'Up! Up! Only a little life is left, the road before you is long, and you are immersed in illusion!' "

The movie theater was on Wilshire and Western. Fortified with popcorn, candy, and icy cups of soda, we walked across crackling peanut shells to our seats.

Claudette Colbert played this rich girl engaged to marry this rich guy, but he was a jerk, and so she ran away. She was in Miami, and she took the night train to New York. And it became this big national story for some reason, and Clark Gable was a newspaper reporter, and she left the train and got on a bus and Clark Gable was there except he didn't tell her he was a reporter. And then they started to fall in love, and then everybody on the bus started singing "The Daring Young Man on the Flying Trapeze," and it was funny: at night I'd lie awake for hours dying to go to sleep but I couldn't, but during the day I'd find myself falling asleep when I didn't want to, and I fell asleep now.

I dreamed about Doc Travis and Doc Travis. The monkey and the man. We were driving in my car, on a road that ran through the desert. Nobody said anything, but everybody was happy. Then Sophie elbowed me in the ribs.

"Hey, wake up, you big boob, you're snoring!"

"Sorry."

I don't know what happened while I was asleep, but Claudette Colbert was in New York now and was about to marry the jerk again, but then Clark Gable showed up, and there'd been some kind of misunderstanding between them, but her rich father, who you didn't like too much before but now started to like, saw that Clark Gable was a fine fellow and a perfect husband for his daughter, and so Clark and Claudette ended up together, not that you'd ever really doubted that they would.

It was a good movie, what I saw of it. We walked down Western afterwards, and we started singing that trapeze song.

Like I said, I was really happy when I was driving with Darla to the Hottentot Hut, but I was drunk then, and I was sober now, and I was just about as happy.

We went in a drugstore and sat down at the soda fountain. The skinny young sodajerk's face was covered with jerkblossoms. He made us three chocolate sodas. They were fifteen cents apiece. Dulwich tried to pay, but I wouldn't let him.

"But it's not fair, Danny, you've been paying for everything."

I shrugged as I peeled a twenty off my roll. I was aware of Sophie looking at all the dough with big eyes. "You can get it next time," I said.

Truth was, I was flush these days. The day after we went to Redondo Beach Bud summoned me over to his booth at the Peacock Club. He handed me an envelope and said: "Your cut for your cut."

"Huh?"

"Twenty-five percent. For cutting the cards."

There were twenty-five hundred-dollar bills in the envelope. He was watching my face and smiling.

"Gee, Bud," I said, "you didn't need to do this."

"You deserve it. The sky's the limit, kid."

The sky's the limit. For some limping guy who couldn't sleep except when he shouldn't and usually had a headache and couldn't tell you his middle name. I basically just didn't get it. Didn't get Bud Seitz, didn't get myself, didn't get how I could ever have sunk a ship.

"Here's your change," said the sodajerk. I left fifty-five cents on the counter. His red infected face lifted in a grateful grin. "Oh, thank you very much, sir."

"Want your cherry?" said Sophie to me. I shook my head. She plucked the cherry off the whipped cream and popped it in her mouth, then turned to Dulwich. "Want your cherry?"

"Yes, darling, but I believe you want it more."

"Thank you so much, dah-ling."

Sophie was a plain little girl, but there was something about her that made you think she might someday be a pretty woman. She had brown eyes, a small snub nose, a longish face. Her mouth was wide and kind of drooped down at the corners like she was used to frowning but when she smiled it was a great smile. Her hair was short, brown, and straight, and fell over her forehead to nearly her eyebrows. There were eleven freckles scattered across her nose and cheeks. She was wearing a yellow-and-white-striped dress that wasn't very new or clean and hung down loosely over her bony, angular body. But her shoes did look new: shiny black mary janes worn over sagging white socks.

She mumbled through a full mouth: "I'm catching the night train to New York. Who wants to come with me?"

"I've lived in New York," said Dulwich, "and have no wish to return."

"What did you do in New York?" I said.

"Oh, I did a bit of scribbling. Mainly for a silly little publication named *Top Hat.*"

"You're a writer?"

"A scribbler. And then I came here to scribble for the movies."

"You write for the *movies?*" said Sophie skeptically, as though he'd claimed he flew back and forth to the moon every day.

"Oh, that's all in the past. It's not as easy as it looks. Although one of my scenarios was actually produced. *The Doctor of Devil's Island,* it was called. It was hysterically funny, but unfortunately it was a drama. I wrote it under the *nom de plume* 'John Ross.' Secrecy was necessary, since my mother would never have approved of my writing for the moving pictures." He spooned some ice cream into his mouth, and groaned. "I believe I need to have my stomach pumped."

It was late in the day as we drove back home in my shining

yellow Packard. Sophie sat between Dulwich and me. "Watch me wave like a queen," she said. She put on a kind but remote smile, and waved her hand in a slow arc of three or four inches at the pedestrians on Western Avenue.

We walked up the seven steps and between the dwarf orange trees whose ripening fruit glowed in the deepening dusk. Music and light were coming out of Sophie's bungalow, the third one on the left.

"Mother's home," she said in a flat voice, then turned to Dulwich and me. "Thanks for taking me to the movies. I had a nice time."

"It was our pleasure, Sophie," said Dulwich.

We watched her walk inside. We could hear Lois Gubler laughing like a jackass at something, then some guy laughing back, then the music got louder.

Dulwich invited me in for some whiskey.

I settled down on the sofa. Dulwich turned on the radio to a live classical music broadcast from the Hollywood Bowl.

After several sips I closed my eyes, and felt my brain pleasantly baking in the warm dry heat of the whiskey.

"*Plenum opus Dei,*" said Dulwich.

I opened my eyes and looked at him. "The full work of God," he said.

I continued to observe him blankly.

"Everything comes from God, or nothing comes from God. Everything is random, or nothing is random."

"Are you sozzled?"

He laughed. He was sitting in his easy chair. He'd put on his many-colored silk jacket and his slippers with the golden tassels on them. His cat was in his lap, and he was stroking her, and smoking a pipe.

My eyes wandered over to the painting. "She looks like Darla," I said of the girl on the cliff.

"Who's Darla?"

"Bud Seitz's girlfriend. I'm her bodyguard."

He looked at me awhile through the drifting smoke.

"Are you in love with her?"

"I guess so."

"Is that a good idea?"

"I don't know. Maybe not."

"Oh well. I've been known to fall in love with inappropriate people myself." He looked at the painting. "Aubrey painted that, you know."

"Yeah?"

"Yes, he was quite talented. And the girl there is his fiancée. Edith Wick. It was his last gift to her. He was barking mad in love with Edith. I thought her a rather routine sort of girl, but you know how love transfigures its object. At any rate, after he died, she couldn't stand to have it around so she gave it to me. And then she couldn't marry another fellow fast enough."

We lapsed back into silence. My brain baked, the cat purred, the smoke floated. His pipe kept going out, and he kept relighting it. Finally I said: "Your smoke smells funny."

"That's probably because of the nature of what I'm smoking."

"What is it? Marijuana?"

"Opium. Like a puff?"

"No thanks."

"It's one of the bad habits I acquired in Mesopotamia, during the war. I spent a good part of it as a prisoner of Johnny Turk, and it wasn't terribly fun. But I befriended one of the guards, a very sweet and gentle boy named Harutiun. I called him Harry. He actually wasn't a Turk, but an Armenian. Since the Turks were massacring the Armenians at the time, life was a bit awkward for him. His captain was not a bad sort, and was protecting him, but I shudder when I think of the fate that may have finally befallen him.

"Ah, the Turks, Danny. Quite a people they are. Once I saw them punish a young Arab boy for stealing a horse. They nailed horseshoes to the soles of his feet. Then they tied a rope around his neck, and made him walk around and around a stake in the ground for days, till they tired of their sport and shot him.

"As I said, Harry and I became friends, and he shared his opium with me. He was well educated, and spoke English. He had a mystic bent. We used to argue about whether men had souls, and if so, did they exist before birth, or did God just create them as needed, like a cook popping a new batch of cookies in the oven? And what about donkeys? And if God knew the future, how could we possibly have free will?"

Dulwich gave me a wry smile, and said: "Confessions of an English opium smoker." He was silent awhile, contentedly petting his cat and puffing on his pipe. And then he closed his eyes, and quoted some poem from memory:

Pierce thy heart to find the key;
With thee take
Only what none else would keep:
Learn to dream when thou dost wake,
Learn to wake when thou dost sleep . . .

10

Dick Prettie and I rolled east on Route 66 past rabbit ranches and poultry farms, and through vast orange and lemon and avocado orchards, the trees whipping by in ruler-straight lines that made you dizzy to look at. Dick was reading the paper while I drove.

"Fucking Yankees won again," said Dick.

"How long have I been here?"

"Huh?"

"In Los Angeles. How long have I lived here?"

He turned the page of the paper without looking up. "Beats me."

"Well, how long have you known me then?"

Dick shrugged. "I don't know. Three years maybe?"

"Somebody told me the *Monfalcone* sank four years ago. So you must've known me at least that long."

Dick put down the newspaper, lit up a cigarette. "I'll take your word for it. I'm no good with dates. I can't hardly remember when my own fucking birthday is."

"What was I like then?"

"What do you mean?"

"I mean was I the same kind of guy as I am now?"

Dick sat silently and smoked.

"Dick?"

"I'm thinking. I'm trying to remember."

"Where did I live? Did I have a girlfriend? What did I do

when I wasn't working?"

Dick looked uncomfortable. "Ah, I don't know, kid. You kinda stayed to yourself. You were . . . mysterious, I guess you could call it. Nobody knew nothing much about you."

"I think maybe I'm from New York. I mean originally."

"Yeah? Why's that?"

" 'Cause when I see New York in the movies, it kind of reminds me of stuff I dream about."

Dick didn't say anything. He returned to his paper. I had to swerve to avoid a run-over dog.

"Jesus," said Dick.

I looked over at him. He was looking at the paper.

"Listen to this. 'CIGARETTE GIRL FOUND DEAD IN DESERT.' 'The body of a 26-year-old woman was found dead in the desert near Lancaster Tuesday, the Sheriff's Department reports. Betty McWilliams—' "

"Betty?" I said.

"Yeah, fucking Betty. '. . . had been missing for about three weeks, according to co-workers at the popular Pom Pom Club on Sunset Boulevard, where she worked as a cigarette girl. The Sheriff's Department said her body was in a state of de . . . de . . . com . . . pi . . .' "

"Decomposition?"

" '. . . which made it difficult to determine the cause of death. Foul play, however, is suspected.' " Dick looked at me. On the best of days, his face was pretty pasty, but now he looked like a ghost. "Jesus, Danny."

Betty had been this big happy friendly girl from Minnesota. I remembered how when she worked at the Peacock Club Dick had always been watching her and mooning over her but had hardly ever said a word to her because he was shy around girls. He'd been in love with her, for all I knew.

"Poor Betty," I said. "I wonder who killed her."

"Yeah, I fucking wonder," said Dick bitterly.

"What do you mean?"

"Skip it. Shut up. Drive."

I drove through Monrovia, Duarte, Glendora, La Verne. Just outside Upland, an old truck was on fire by the side of the road. Black smoke twisted up. A ragged family was standing around staring bleakly at the truck. A kid in overalls and no shirt was holding a birdcage with an agitated blue jay in it. The cage looked way too small for the bird.

Mountains in front of us got bigger and bigger. In San Bernardino we left Route 66 and took the Rim of the World Highway, and pretty soon we were up in the mountains and looking down at where we'd been. We'd been driving inland nearly three hours, but still we could see at the limits of our vision the dreamy glitter of the Pacific.

We were on our way to Lake Arrowhead, because a bunch of high muckypoos were meeting there: Bud Seitz and Max Schnitter and Loy Hanley, an old bootlegging partner of Bud's, and Joe Shaw, the mayor's bagman brother, and Lieutenant Otay of the L.A.P.D., and Police Commissioner Nuffer. Word was they were supposed to cook up some grand plan together for running the rackets in Los Angeles.

The road wound up and up through thicker and thicker stands of pine, and right on top of a mountain we found the jewel-like lake. On its shores were hotels, cabins, tourist camps, and lodges, and a little village with places to eat and shop and dance and drink.

A motorboat was cutting across the lake, throwing up white wings over the blue water, and a guy and a girl on water skis skimmed along in its wake. Even at a distance you could tell the skiers were young, tan, goodlooking. Rich, probably, too. Perfect people on a perfect lake.

We saw a sign that said Birkenhead Manor, with an arrow

that pointed up a road that ran through the pine forest. A blonde was bouncing along the road on the back of a horse, and she smiled at us as we cruised by. Dick was positive it was Ginger Rogers, but I had my doubts.

After a quarter mile or so, the road ended at Birkenhead Manor. It was three stories, wood and stone, and like something you might see on a picture postcard from Switzerland. Two cheerful college-boy types met us as we pulled up; one drove my car away ("Quite a snazzy car, sir!") and the other took care of our bags.

Under the name of the hotel, a stone lion was standing on its hind legs on top of a column; its front legs were holding on to another column, and it looked like it was trying to hump it. Then when we walked in the lobby there was a stuffed grizzly bear rearing up on its hind legs about ten feet in the air, teeth bared and long claws sticking out of its paws.

"I hate fucking animals," said Dick. "I wanna see animals I'll go to the fucking zoo."

"But you liked Doc."

He grimaced. "Doc was different. Doc was like a person. What did you have to bring him up for?"

A girl was standing at the front desk with her back to us chatting with the desk clerk. She was wearing gray slacks and a red blouse and a red beret-like hat with a black fluffy ball on top. She had dark hair under the hat and her bare arms were a creamy olive color. When she turned her head a little in our direction, my heart picked up its pace and even on my limping leg I seemed to skim over the polished wood floor like the golden skiers across the lake. I touched her shoulder, and said: "Gwynnie?"

Then she turned and looked at me. Nice brown eyes, but not *her* brown eyes.

"Sorry. I thought you were someone else."

She kind of looked me over and said: "Maybe I'm sorry too."

"You gentlemen checking in?" said the desk clerk to Dick and me.

"Yeah," I said, then someone touched *me* on the shoulder.

I turned around, and nearly bumped into a pair of big tits.

"Hi ya, Two Gun Danny," said the redhead standing there.

It took me a moment to place her.

"Clover," I said.

"*Violet.* Violet Gilbertson."

"The Pork Queen."

"It's all coming back to you."

"What are you doing here?"

"I'm here with Wendell. You know, Mr. Nuffer?"

"Yeah? Where *is* Wendell? Mr. Nuffer."

"Up in his room, changing into his bathing suit. *I* got a new bathing suit. Wait'll you see it."

"I'd rather see *you* in a bathing suit than Nuffer," said Dick. "That's for fucking sure."

Violet tittered. I looked around. Dick was signing the guest register. The girl that looked like Gwynnie was gone.

Bud and the rest of the guys hadn't arrived yet. I got my key and went up to my room. It was a great room, on the third floor, with a wide window looking out on the lake.

Above the bed was a painting of an Indian village on the banks of a river. An Indian boy was standing knee-deep in the water. He'd just speared a fish, and was holding it up, and it was shining in the sun. Two pretty Indian girls were standing at the edge of the river and looking at the kid like he was their hero. And an old man was sitting back in some green shade watching the youngsters and smoking a pipe.

Beneath the painting the bed looked broad and inviting. I took two aspirin, and lay down, and pondered the question: Who the hell is Gwynnie?, till I fell asleep.

11

Everybody had dinner that night in the Big Boulder Dining Room, called that because at one end of the room was a little waterfall trickling down over a tall pile of big boulders with a pool that had live trout in it. I was sitting at a table with Nucky and Nello. Dick was standing over by the waterfall, smoking a cigarette and looking at the boulders. Then he got all excited and started pointing at something.

"Hey, lookit, lookit, lookit! Get over here! Look at this!"

So we went over and looked. Guests of the hotel who were famous were asked to write their names on the boulders, and I'd already seen the autographs of Cary Grant, Buster Keaton, Myrna Loy, and a lot of others. Now Dick was pointing at one of the names. "What's that say?"

" 'Ginger Rogers,' " read Nello.

"See? I told you Danny and me seen her today on a fucking horse!"

"That don't prove nothing," said Nucky. "That don't prove a goddamn thing."

"Nucky's right," said Nello, who came over from Italy when he was a kid and still had a little bit of an accent. "She coulda wrote that years ago."

"Like hell she could have. She ain't been famous for years."

"Ever place we go you say you see Ginger Rogers here or Ginger Rogers there," said Nello. "But nobody else ever sees her."

"Danny seen her."

"Well, maybe it was her," I said. "But maybe it wasn't."

"Oh fuck you, guys, I know she's here someplace," and he started looking around the room like he expected to see her sitting at one of the tables stuffing her angelic face with mashed potatoes.

I looked at one of the other names and said: "Who's Laura La Plante?" But nobody answered me. Dick threw his cigarette in the water, and they all headed back to our table.

A trout glided over and took a look at the cigarette butt. Decided it wasn't food, and finned away.

I looked over at the table where Bud was sitting with the other big cheeses, along with Violet and Darla. Darla was watching me, and now she smiled. Bud saw the smile, and looked at me, and smiled too.

I smiled back. Everybody was smiling.

There was a fancy little club on the other side of the hotel called the Moonlight Room. At the entrance was a poster showing a blonde in a red glittering gown, standing there with her hands spread out and her mouth open; she was Sally Layne, "THE GIRL YOU WONT FORGET."

She was onstage in a spotlight singing as we walked in. She appeared to be wearing the same gown as on the poster, it seemed to be made of a billion beads, each one catching the light. It all felt a little eerie, because she was singing that same song that I'd heard at Bud's party:

> "Suddenly I found myself in a dream,
> One sweet kiss did it to me,
> I got dizzy instantly . . ."

We took a table, and ordered drinks. At another table we saw the two Tommys, yakking it up with a couple of touristy-looking girls.

Dick was drunk, and he was getting drunker. He didn't say a word for a while, just glared at Nucky and Nello. I thought he was still sore about Ginger Rogers, but that turned out not to be it.

"So which one of you monkeys did it?" he said.

"Did what?" said Nello.

"I'm talking about Betty. The cigarette girl."

Nello and Nucky exchanged a look. Dick turned to me. "Nucky told me once how he strangled to death this broad in Jersey with his fucking tie. I'm thinking maybe that's what he done to Betty."

"But why would he want to kill Betty?" I said.

"That's a good fucking question," said Nucky. He was a plug-ugly little guy, with a mashed-in face and eyes with no more expression than a chicken's. He leaned a little closer to Dick. "You got a problem with me, you skinny prick, maybe you oughta talk to Bud about it."

Dick stared into the lightless eyes of Nucky, then muttered: "Fuck yourself," and got up and headed for the exit.

Nello called after him: "If you run into Ginger, tell her I said hello!"

Nucky and Nello laughed. Now a girl came over, all giggly and blushing, and asked Nello to dance. Wherever we went, girls flocked around Nello, like they were pigeons and he was birdseed. He got up with a shrug and took her out on the dance floor.

"Fucking Nello," said Nucky. "He needs two dicks he gets so much pussy," and then he said: "I'm getting a whore tonight, kid. Want me to get you one while I'm at it?"

"No thanks."

"You know, I never see you with a broad. You ain't queer or nothing?"

"Nah."

"Saving it for your wedding night? At Niagara fucking Falls?"

I pretended to laugh. "Yeah, maybe something like that."

"Or maybe you're saving it for Darla? Or maybe you *ain't* saving it for Darla. If you know what I'm saying." And he laughed.

It was smoky as hell in the Moonlight Room, so I decided to get some fresh air. I went through French doors out onto a wide terrace and into actual moonlight.

A well-dressed elderly couple was strolling along arm in arm. Their hair was so white it seemed luminous. They nodded at me in a familiar fashion as if this was a regular walk they took and they were used to encountering me at this point on *my* regular walk.

A guy and a girl were sitting on a bench feverishly necking. The girl's eyes opened for a moment and saw me in an unseeing way then her face disappeared behind his shoulder like she was a swimmer and he an overwhelming wave.

I walked across the flat stones of the terrace to the stone balustrade. I faced the forest. Sipped my whiskey. Looked up at the shaggy silhouettes of the pine trees against the moon-drenched sky.

I heard someone walking up behind me.

I turned and saw an uncertain smile and a glass of champagne, then one of the girl's high heels caught in one of the stones and she tripped and pitched forward. I grabbed her arms and she splashed champagne on me.

"Dear Lord," she laughed, "what an entrance! I'm always spilling things on people."

"And I'm always getting spilled on."

"That could make us a swell team. So do I still look like her?

In moonlight?"

It was the girl that looked like Gwynnie, and: "Yes," I said.

"My name's Janet Van der Eb," and she held her hand out and I shook it. "I'm also known as the Girl You Won't Forget, though *my* won't has an apostrophe in it, unlike *that* little ninnie's," and she jerked her thumb back toward the Moonlight Room, where through the French doors I could see Sally Layne still singing. "I think the illiteracy rampant in America these days is simply shocking, don't you?"

"I'm Danny Landon."

"Yes, I know. I asked around. You're one of *them.*"

"Who?"

"The gangsters."

"The gangsters?"

"Oh, don't play innocent. Everyone's talking about it. It's extremely exciting. The rumor is that Lucky Luciano is here, or was here, or will be here soon. Is that true?"

"Not that I know of."

"How disappointing. As you can probably tell, I like gangsters. I respect them. In the United States of Hypocrisy, they are our only genuine citizens. I predict that at the end point of capitalism, we shall *all* be gangsters. *All* be carrying submachine guns in violin cases, and taking people we don't like on one-way rides. Oh dear. I am blabbering a bit, aren't I? It's the champagne. Mother told me to stop, but I just wouldn't listen."

I asked her where she was from.

"Philadelphia. You've heard of Philadelphia cream cheese, haven't you? Well, the Van der Ebs practically invented it. I don't say that in a boastful way. I think cream cheese is a ghastly stuff, don't you? The Van der Ebs have unleashed a horror upon the earth, and we must certainly pay for it, if not here then in the Hereafter. Amen."

"You're here with your mother?"

"*And* father. They're inside, listening to the Girl You Wont Forget. You know, Sally what's-her-name." She finished off the last few drops of champagne, then set the glass down on the balustrade. It immediately tipped over, and I caught it, as she reached in her purse and pulled out a silver cigarette case. I was sorry I didn't have matches because I would haved liked to have lit her cigarette because however drunk and sort of loony she was she was disturbingly beautiful.

"This is my graduation present, you see," she said as smoke drifted out of her lightly lipsticked mouth. "This here trip. To Sunny California. I'm a Rumson girl, I was voted 'Best All-Around Woman' in the Class of '34, but now I have to decide what to do with the rest of my life. I'm considering writing an obscure and unpublishable book. Applying Freudian methods of analysis to the masterpieces of American literature. *Moby-Dick* speaks for itself naturally, but what of that sunny innocent boys' book *The Adventures of Tom Sawyer*? It's not what it seems. Think, for instance, about Tom getting lost with Becky Thatcher in the cave. The entrance to the cave is the vagina. The cave itself represents the dark, unplumbed mysteries of sex. Injun Joe, of course, is Tom Sawyer's id. The episode is about repression. Injun Joe must die so that Becky Thatcher may remain a virgin."

She blew smoke past my ear.

"How many men have you killed?"

"I don't know."

"I'm getting goosebumps. Why do you limp? Were you shot in the leg?"

"No."

"I didn't mean to offend you. I think a limp in a man is awfully attractive. I have an uncle who came home limping from the Great War, and I adore him dreadfully. A limp means, I have been through something difficult, but I am still walking. I am indomitable.

"You keep looking at my lips. What does that mean?"

Wondering if I was taking advantage of a crazy person, I leaned down and kissed her.

She tasted like champagne and cigarettes. She had a lively tongue, and her hands went under my coat and rubbed my chest, and tugged at my tie, and then she whispered: "Officially I'm still a virgin, but that doesn't mean I'm not quite a creative girl." I was mulling over what she might mean when with the deftness and speed of a pickpocket she snatched my gun out of my shoulder holster and then holding it in both hands pointed it at me as she crouched down and backed away giggling uncontrollably.

"Janet!" I said. "Be careful with that!"

"It's so heavy! It's like a brick!"

The necking couple was staring at Janet in alarm. The guy said: "That's not a real gun, is it?"

There was a flash and a bang, and I heard the bullet whistle past my ear. The necking girl screamed. Janet dropped the gun and it clattered on the terrace. She stared down at it in shock; then she clapped her hand over her mouth and cried: "Oh my god!"

I quickly moved to pick up the gun and reholster it. The neckers hurried off hand in hand in a huff. A smell of gunpowder hung in the air. Janet's hand stayed over her mouth, trying to stifle hysterical laughter.

The French doors opened and Darla came out. She eyed Janet and me like a mother who's just come in a room where two kids have obviously just committed some rowdy act but she can't figure out what.

"What's so funny?"

"You didn't hear it?" I said.

"Hear what?"

"Nothing."

"Nucky told me you were out here."

"Nucky!" snorted Janet.

Darla looked at Janet with puzzlement and distaste. "Who are you?"

Janet sighed, and wiped away a tear just under her eye. " 'She wiped away a tear of laughter.' I'm sorry. I plead guilty to conduct unbecoming a Rumson girl. I'm Janet." She looked at me. "My parents and I are leaving in the morning, Danny. For Lake Tahoe. We specialize in lakes. So I guess this is good-bye."

She approached and then as she leaned in I put my hand on my gun in case she was planning to go for it again but all she did was whisper in my ear: "Room 225. I'll leave the door unlocked, my darling." She brushed my earlobe with her lips, then Darla and I watched her walk back inside.

"What was that all about?"

"She reminds me of somebody I think I used to know."

"Oh, Danny, you're starting to remember?"

"I think so. A little."

"That's great."

"Where's Bud and everybody?"

"Discussing 'important business.' They told Violet and me to get lost. The crummy bastards."

The sounds of Sally Layne and her band floated out onto the terrace. We looked back into the Moonlight Room, could see Sally Layne dramatically lit up in the dark, covered in the cold fire of her gown.

"That should be me," Darla said softly.

"You miss singing?"

She nodded. She looked at me. "Wanna go down to the lake?"

We were the only ones on the little road. The pines crowded in close as the lights of Birkenhead Manor disappeared behind us. All we could hear was the wind in the tops of the trees and our shoes on the pavement.

" 'Member that bear in the lobby?" said Darla.

"Yeah."

"Think there's any more like him out here?"

"I doubt it. I think the pioneers killed all the bears and the Indians and so on."

"It's still pretty scary though."

"Wanna go back?"

"No." And then her hand found mine.

"Danny?"

"Yeah?"

"I hear the guys talking about you sometimes. I hate to say it, but—it's like they're making fun of you. It's like they don't respect you."

"What do they say?"

"They make jokes about you being stupid. 'Cause you can't remember stuff. Which shows you how stupid *they* are. And they got this name for you."

She hesitated.

"What?"

"Limpy. Two Gun Limpy Landon."

"Dick? He calls me that?"

"No, not Dick. I think he really cares about you."

"And Bud? What does he say about me?"

"It's funny with Bud. I can tell he really likes you. But he never wants to talk about you. Except to make sure you haven't been getting fresh with me."

"How come you're telling me this?"

"I just think you should know who your friends are. That's all."

It seemed like there were about ten times as many stars up here in the mountains as down in the city, and they shined above us between the pines like a parallel heavenly road. I started thinking as we kept walking and didn't find the lake that maybe we'd taken the wrong road and we were lost like Tom and Becky and I would have to save her from Injun Joe; then we came out on the lake.

We could see the lights of hotels and cabins on the dark shores, and from the south, where the little village was, we could hear faintly voices, music, laughter. The wind moved on the lake and turned the reflected moon into wiggling quicksilver. The wind was chilly, and Darla shivered; I took my coat off and draped it over her shoulders.

We walked a bit. We saw the lights of a boat out on the lake, then heard the low growl of its engine. I wondered if we were anywhere near where they found Doc Travis's head.

"Does it ever seem strange to you?" said Darla. "Just being alive? Why is there anything here anyway? The lake. The stars. You and me. The world would make a lot more sense if it just didn't exist."

"I love you," I said.

"Oh Danny. No you don't."

"Yes I do."

Silence from Darla.

"Don't you like me a little? Sometimes I think you do."

"Sure I do. I like you a lot. That's why I don't want you to get hurt."

"I'm not gonna get hurt."

She stopped walking and we faced each other.

"Listen, Danny. Take my word for it. You don't wanna be with somebody like me."

"Why not?"

"You just don't. That's all."

Darla was looking up at me, and I saw the glistening of her

eyes in the moonlight; then it was like my heart stopped and the moment seemed to stretch on forever, her eyes in the moonlight on the shore of the lake atop the mountain. But when I moved a little closer to her, she immediately turned away and said firmly: "Time to go back."

We were walking back toward the road when we heard groaning. My first thought was somebody was hurt or sick; then we saw Teddy Bump.

He was leaning up against a tree with his eyes closed and his mouth ajar. A guy was kneeling in front of him and his head was moving back and forth. They were into the woods twenty feet or so, but if they'd been looking to conceal themselves they'd picked a bad place since a shaft of moonlight hit them like a spotlight.

Darla giggled. Teddy heard her and opened his eyes. He stared at us in horror, then the guy on his knees looked over his shoulder; he had a pug-nosed face, and I saw it was Schnitter's guy Vic Lester.

"We'll leave you two lovebirds alone!" called Darla, then, both laughing, we walked away quickly.

We were back on the road that led up to the hotel when we heard shoe leather cracking along at a great pace behind us. It was Teddy. He was walking so fast, arms pumping and hips rolling, that he looked like a contestant in a walking race. As he went by us he snarled: "Don't either of yuz say a fucking thing!"

"Or what?" said Darla.

"Or else!" yelled Teddy.

"Don't threaten us, you bastard!" said Darla, then she grabbed my shoulder for balance and snatched off one of her shoes and flung it at Teddy. It sailed over his head and landed in the woods.

Teddy, arms swinging savagely, disappeared around a bend in

the road. Darla limped like me in her one shoe as we went over to look for the other one. It took us about five minutes to find it.

12

I returned to my room, and fell asleep under the painting of the peaceful Indian village. Dreamt all night of massacres, and bugling, and scalping, and bodies floating down the river.

At one point I woke up with a rockhard hard-on and the conviction that Janet Van der Eb was in the room. My heart was racing and I looked around wildly, then seemed to see her in silhouette, standing at the foot of the bed, gazing down silently at me. The silence should have been a clue it was all an illusion, and after a few seconds she melted back into the general darkness and I fell asleep again.

When I woke up for good it was nearly nine. I felt exhausted, as though I'd spent the whole night doing calisthenics and running laps around the hotel.

I shaved and brushed my teeth then went downstairs.

Darla was in the lobby, sitting around a coffee table with Violet and Wendell Nuffer. Darla was writing a message on a picture postcard, Nuffer was reading the sports pages, and Violet was leafing through a *Photoplay* with Clark Gable on the cover sporting a roguish grin. They were all drinking coffee; Violet was also chewing gum and smoking a cigarette.

"Good morning, my boy, how did you sleep?" said Nuffer heartily. He was wearing white trousers, white shoes, and a shimmering silk shirt with an orange and green and yellow tropical fruit design. "I slept like a top myself. The mountain air, the mountain air!"

"Anyone hungry?" I said.

"I'm sorry, Danny, we all just finished breakfast. And what a breakfast it was!" He patted his huge stomach. "What did I have? Five trout and ten eggs? Or was it the reverse?"

"I don't know, Daddy," said Violet, "but it was sure good."

Darla glanced up from her postcard. " 'Daddy'?"

Nuffer squeezed Violet's knee. "She likes to call me that."

"I'll bet because you got the same name as her father," I said. "Wendell."

"You have an excellent memory. I don't know if you're aware of it, Darla, but Danny was there at the very moment when Violet and I met. At that momentous moment, I might say. I know we've known each other only these few short weeks, but in the deepest depths of myself I feel as though I've known Violet forever. Her sense of humor, the joy she takes in the little things, not to mention of course her green eyes, her red hair, her fair form . . . it's hard to imagine their absence from my life. It must have been a very impoverished life. But it all seems so long ago, I can hardly remember."

Violet beamed at Nuffer, smacking her gum rapidly. "I just love the way Daddy talks. Don't you?"

Loy Hanley came walking up. He was six-four, with a hard lean body, weathered reddish-brown skin, and high cheekbones over hollow cheeks and a thin straight line of a mouth. He was wearing a gray suit, black cowboy boots, and a string bowtie. He hailed, I'd heard, from Texas.

"Me and some of the fellers is fixing to go fishing," he said. "Any of y'all wanna join us?"

Nuffer patted his stomach again. "No thank you, Loy. I'm too busy digesting fish to catch them."

"Danny?"

"I don't think so. I don't even think I know how to fish."

"Oh, there ain't nothing to it. You just bait your hook and

throw it out in the water."

"What are you gonna use for bait?" said Violet.

"Minners."

"What's a minner?"

"Little bitty fish. 'Bout as long as your finger."

Violet took a drag on her cigarette and looked Loy over; the butt of the cigarette was stained red with her lipstick. "You gonna go dressed like that?"

"Naw, I'm gonna change into my fishing britches. Where you from anyway, Violet? You don't talk like you're from California."

"Iowa."

"Iowa, huh? I used to do a little bi'ness up in Waterloo."

"I was Miss Iowa Pork Queen of 1933."

Hanley stared pointedly at Violet's breasts. "Miss *Pork* Queen! I woulda thunk they'da made you Miss *Cow* Queen!"

Violet giggled while Hanley guffawed and Nuffer chuckled uneasily and turned red.

"Well, see y'all later," said Hanley, and then his long black-booted legs carried him off across the lobby.

"Don't you think Mr. Hanley looks *just like* Gary Cooper?" said Violet.

"More like Boris Karloff," grumbled Nuffer. He made a show of returning to the sports pages, folding them noisily and then holding them up so they hid half his face.

"Daddy?" said Violet.

"Hm. Jigger Statz went three for four. He's been on quite a tear lately."

"Daddy?"

He continued to ignore her. She put her hand on his arm and made him lower the paper; then she pinched his fat pink cheek.

"Smile, Daddy."

But he just gazed back tragically at her. She tickled him under the chin with her finger like he was a baby.

"Smile, Daddy! Smile!"

And suddenly he burst out in a great laugh and grabbed her and kissed her and then looked at us utterly happy like he'd just won the grand prize.

"Isn't she amazing?"

Pretty soon after that they walked off to the elevator, holding hands.

"I felt bad for Mr. Nuffer," I said.

"I feel bad for his wife and kids."

Darla licked a stamp and put it on the postcard. It had a picture of Birkenhead Manor on it, with the caption: "The Mile-High Paradise In The Pines." I asked her who she was sending it to.

"Dr. Ames and Mrs. Ames."

I was surprised. "You're still in touch with them?"

"I don't know. I've always felt guilty about how I just walked away without a word, so a couple of times a year I've been sending them a postcard. Just to let them know I'm okay. I don't put a return address, so there's no way for them to write me back. I don't even know if they're still alive anymore. They'd be in their eighties now."

"I'll bet they're alive. And they'll be real happy to get this, and see you're staying in such a beautiful place."

Darla gave me a sad smile. "You're so sweet."

I went in by myself to the Big Boulder Dining Room, and had what Daddy had, the trout and scrambled eggs, called "world-famous" on the menu. On my way out I was walking through the hallway that led to the lobby when I saw Nucky and Goodlooking Tommy sitting at the shoeshine stand. The shoeshine boy was this old colored man named Timothy; he was the only Negro I'd seen at Lake Arrowhead.

Goodlooking Tommy was reading *The Racing Form* while he

waited for Timothy to finish up Nucky's shoes. He saw me and motioned me over.

"So what's the word?"

"What's the word on what?"

"On how it's looking from Bud's corner."

"What do you mean?"

"I hear Max and Loy ain't getting along. And Bud's been like a referee in a prize fight."

"You've heard more than me then."

"I thought you was always in the know with Bud."

"He hasn't said ten words to me since we been up here."

Goodlooking Tommy looked at me skeptically.

"Yeah?"

"Yeah."

Now Nucky was inspecting Timothy's handiwork. "Looks real good, boy. A hell of a shine."

"Thank you, suh," said Timothy. He had white curly hair like a lamb, and skin the color of milky coffee.

Nucky dug in his pocket, and pulled out a silver dollar.

"Here's a nice shiny silver dollar. I think you deserve it. Don't you?"

Timothy smiled, revealing three or four snaggly teeth. "If you think so, suh."

"Well, I think so."

Nucky held out the silver dollar, and Timothy put out his palm; then Nucky gave Goodlooking Tommy and me a quick wink and moved his hand half a foot and dropped the coin. It clanged on the rim of a brass spittoon then vanished inside.

Goodlooking Tommy laughed, then said low in my ear: "Nucky hates niggers."

"Yeah, I can see."

Timothy was staring at the spittoon; dripping brown spittle glistened around the rim.

"Well ain't you gonna get your dollar, boy?" said Nucky. "You don't wanna hurt my feelings, do you?"

Timothy looked into Nucky's chicken eyes, then: "No suh," he said slowly. He reached in the spittoon. His hand was just small enough to get in there. He fished around a minute, then pulled out the dollar.

It, and his hand, were covered with a slime made of spit and tobacco juice and cigar and cigarette ashes. I watched Timothy reach for one of his red shoeshine rags to clean off the slime as Nucky and Goodlooking Tommy laughed. And then I walked away.

13

"I'll bet you think my name's not really Vera Vermillion."

I shrugged. I held no opinion on the subject. She pulled a business card out of her purse and handed it to me.

Vera Vermillion
"One in a Million"
Actress - Singer - Dancer - Et Cetera
The Mel Goldberg Agency
Normandie 3215

It seemed like every girl came with some sort of motto or slogan up here. One in a Million. The Girl You Wont Forget. Best All-Around Woman.

I started to hand the card back but she said: "Keep it. You never know when you might need an et cetera."

It was the middle of the afternoon. I was killing time till tonight when there was going to be a birthday dinner for Max Schnitter. I'd gone in the hotel bar looking for some company, but it'd been empty except for the elderly couple I'd encountered on the terrace last night. They smiled and nodded at me, and I smiled back and took a seat at the bar. I was drinking a beer, and hoping Bud wouldn't catch me at it, when Vera Vermillion came in.

She was a big girl, nearly as tall as me, with a little begirdled waist separating big shoulders and breasts from wide lush hips. She was wearing a clingy reddish-orange dress with matching high heels. An extravagantly colored feather boa was wrapped around her neck, and a little hat with more feathers was perched atop her thick auburn hair.

She flounced across the room looking flustered and exasperated. She plopped herself down on a barstool and ordered something called a blue moon. It looked like a glowing blue martini. She slurped some down, and it seemed to hit the spot as she sighed and relaxed a little; then she noticed me.

"I nearly killed a fucking deer," she said.

"Really? Why?"

"Jesus, it wasn't on purpose. I was driving up here and three deers ran across the road and I nearly hit one of 'em. Jumped right over the hood of my car, I nearly had a heart attack. I hate to drive in the first place. Usually Mel, my agent, he drives me. But we were driving down Melrose yesterday and a bee flew in the window and stung him right in the eyeball. Poor Mel, that kinda shit only happens to him. So he's back in Hollywood in bed with an ice bag over his eye and I gotta drive up here by myself. Up in the goddamn mountains with deers jumping over my car like the cow jumped over the fucking moon. Whew! At least I made it." Then she took another drink, and said: "Hi, I'm Vera Vermillion."

And I told her my name and that's when she gave me her card.

"So what did you come up here for?" I said.

"I'm doing a show tonight."

"What kind of show?"

"Well, it's for this guy's birthday party."

"Max Schnitter?"

"Yeah. You know him?"

"A little."

"You gonna be there?"

"Yeah."

She smiled at me and primped her hair a little. "I guess you'll be seeing more of me then."

"I guess so."

"You must be in the mob, huh?"

She seemed impressed. I shrugged.

"Your name's not really Vera Vermillion, is it?"

She laughed. "Nah. Susie. Susie Pulaski. I'm from Chicago."

"Why'd you come to Los Angeles?"

"Why do you think? To be in the movies, like every other girl. So I'm living downtown near Pershing Square, and I'm taking a trolley car out to the beach, and there's this little guy in a bowtie looking at me. I think he's trying to pick me up, and I'm ignoring him, then he says, Mae West has only got one thing that you don't have. An agent. And I says, are you an agent, and he says yeah. And I says how do you know I don't have an agent, and he says if you had an agent you wouldn't be riding in some dumpy trolley car. And I says *you're* riding in a trolley car, what kinda lousy agent does that make *you*, and he says it makes me a very good agent, 'cause I've just discovered the next Mae West."

I looked again at the business card. "Was that Mel Goldberg?"

"Sure was."

"So how's it going?"

"You know, Danny, it's tough. They say only one in a million make it to the top in Hollywood, but that's why I chose my name. Vera Vermillion, 'One in a Million.' But you wanna hear something interesting?"

"Sure."

"Mel became not only my agent, but also my husband."

She held up her hand to proudly show off a big diamond or something pretending to be a big diamond.

"That's great, Vera. Congratulations."

"That little guy'll do anything for me, it nearly killed him not being able to bring me up here, I nearly had to tie him down to the bed. And the last thing he said to me when I was walking out the door was, Susie, you're the only thing I've ever loved. He's always saying that to me, you're the only thing I've ever loved." She frowned. "And sometimes I treat him like shit too."

Her glass was empty now, so I bought her another blue moon, which she seemed very happy to get.

"Don't get the wrong idea, Danny, I ain't some kinda lush. I don't usually drink like this, but them fucking deers nearly scared me to death. I can't get 'em out of my head. Jumping over my car like that." She sighed. "The things a girl does to get ahead. It's just I hear that clock ticking all the time. I'm not as young as I look, you know."

"No?"

"How old do you think I look?"

"Oh, I don't know."

"Go ahead. Guess."

"Thirty?"

Vera looked disappointed. "I'm twenty-nine."

"Oh."

"I'm scared time's running out on me. I don't wanna wind up some flea-bitten old floozy living downtown in some crummy room."

"That's not gonna happen."

She eyed me over her beautiful blue drink.

"You're nice."

"Thanks. So are you."

"When we get back in town, if you ever wanna call me, that's okay. You got my number."

I looked at the card again. "That's Mel's number."

"Just call it and ask for me. Mel won't mind."

"He won't?"

"We got this understanding. Mel and me, we love each other, but all that bedroom stuff, that ain't part of the deal. See, when he was thirteen, he had the mumps, and it caused his tetiscules to stop growing."

"His what?"

"Tetiscules. You know, his manly parts."

"Oh."

"They're like little peanuts. So he's not much good to a girl, in that department. But I'm not complaining. 'Cause like I said. We got this understanding."

I felt like changing the subject.

"So I don't know anything about agents. How does Mel go about getting you a job?"

"Well in this case, Mr. Seitz called up and asked for me personally. He saw me perform once. I do this thing with peacock feathers." She looked uncomfortable. "Look, Danny, the only reason I'm doing this thing tonight is 'cause it's a hell of a lot of dough for Mel and me. Just remember, I really do act and stuff. Like it says on the card."

"What are you gonna be doing?"

"I'll be wrapped up like a present, then Mr. Schnitter's gonna unwrap me, then I'll sing 'Happy Birthday' to him, and then—well, you get the picture."

"Mm."

"Is he a nice guy? Mr. Schnitter?"

"You know, I don't really know him that well."

Teddy Bump came in, with Tommy. They took a table in the corner. The waitress went over, and they ordered coffee.

Teddy had a funny kind of a face; his eyelashes were unnaturally long, and he had bushy eyebrows that seemed to be growing too far up on his forehead. Right now he was giving me one of those if-looks-could-kill looks. Vera looked over and saw it too.

"What did you ever do to him?"

"Saw him."

"Saw him what?"

"I better not say."

"Ain't you the mysterious one."

14

The hotel shut down the Moonlight Room that night so we could have Schnitter's birthday dinner there. Everybody sat at a long table and ate big pink slabs of prime rib. Bud was hosting the dinner, so he sat at the head. The important guys, Schnitter, Loy Hanley, Joe Shaw, Jack Otay, and Nuffer, were clustered up around him, and then came the rest, us Seitz guys, and some Schnitter guys and Hanley guys. There were about twenty of us all told. No Darla or Violet or any other girl.

We were all in tuxedoes. I'd rented mine in a store downtown on Broadway. The clerk that helped me was this pissed-off little Russian who spent the whole time cursing out Roosevelt as a tool of the Bolsheviks and Jews. I asked him if he happened to know a Russian count named Anatoly who'd got two fingers shot off in the Revolution. He said it didn't ring no bell.

Waiters moved in and out keeping the food and booze coming. It was loud and there was lots of laughing and if there was any tension between anybody I didn't see it.

A guy in a powder-blue tux with curly golden hair and a sissy kind of a face sat at a baby grand playing soft swoony tunes that nobody seemed to be listening to but me.

Doc Travis was being reminisced about.

"You know how ugly Doc was," said Loy Hanley. "But I 'member a time I thought he was the prettiest sight this side of heaven."

"What happened?" said Bud, already beginning to grin.

"Well Doc was living in a tent in the desert out east of Yermo. There was a natural spring the Indians used to use, so he had all the water he needed for his operation. He kept his still hid in a old abandoned copper mine. So I drove out there in this big old Chevrolet truck with a load of sugar. It was more like a trail than a road, and by the time I got out there it was nearly sundown. Doc said he'd just finished up a new batch of turtle juice; that's what he called moon. He said I oughta just stay out there tonight and him and me could sample the new stuff and I could drive back with my load of moon in the morning.

"Well we sat there in his tent that night, drinking by the light of a kerosene lamp—and by god that goddamn turtle juice nearly took the top of my head off. After a hour or two all of a sudden Doc let loose with this big long scream, like he'd just been pushed off the top of a mountain, then he keeled over sideways and his head hit the ground so hard it bounced, and then he started to snore. But I stayed awake and kept drinking that dadgum turtle juice."

Loy knew how to tell a story, already he had everybody laughing; now he leaned in a little and lowered his voice a notch.

"And then I commence to hearing things. First I hear a coyote yipping, then a wind kicks up and starts the tent to flapping and snapping, then I think I hear people whispering to one another, like they's out there in the dark creeping up on us. I get it in my head that the Dry Squad has done found us and they're fixing to lower the boom.

"Doc always kept a loaded thirty-thirty handy, so I took one more swig of turtle juice, then I grab up the rifle and go charging outa the tent. And the wind's blowing sand in my eyes, but I think I can see people, some of 'em kinda hunkered down and others running away, so I go running through the greasewood bushes hollering my head off and shooting off the rifle, then that's the last thing I remember for a while.

"When I come to, I'm laying on the ground. I think it must still be nighttime, 'cause my eyes are open but I ain't seeing nothing. But the funny thing is, it's hotter'n hell. The sand's burning my skin, and I'm thinking there has to be a fire, but how could there be a fire if I can't see it, and then it comes to me: Loy Hanley, you are one dead son of a bitch, and your mama was right, you've done gone to hell. 'Cause I was remembering what I heard the preacher say when I was a kid, that hell's a place of utter darkness, that the fires of hell burn without no light.

"But then I'm thinking, if I'm in hell, how come I'm laying in the sand with the wind blowing over me, and then I figure it all out. I'm still in the desert out east of Yermo, and the sun's come up, but I can't see it 'cause Doc's turtle juice has made me go stone-cold blind!

"Well sir, I'm scareder than shit, I get up and start hollering for Doc: Doc, Doc, where are ya, come get me! But Doc don't answer back. So I'm in the middle of the goddamn desert and I'm blind as a bat. And it's a hunnerd twenty degrees, and I don't have no water, and my tongue's so swole up it's sticking outa my mouth. So I start stumbling around yelling and moaning, and I run into a cactus and get a pussful of needles, and then I take a step and there ain't nothing under my feet and I'm falling and I don't know whether I'm fixing to fall five feet or a hunnerd feet.

"And then I find myself waking up for the second time. Somebody's splashing water on my face and saying Loy, Loy, are you all right? And then I open up my eyes and there's Doc Travis. I ain't blind no more! And I say: Doc, if you wasn't so ugly, I'd kiss you right on your fucking mouth!"

Everybody laughed. Jack Otay said: "You know that old bastard was wanted for the same murder in two different countries?"

"How could that be?" said Joe Shaw.

"He stuck a knife in a guy in Mexicali, Mexico. Then the guy got in his car and drove over the border and died in Calexico, California. So he got charged in both countries."

"What finally happened?" said Nuffer.

"The main witness against him had a bad accident. Drowned to death in a dry river bed."

"Some witnesses just seem to have the shittiest luck," said Bud.

"We all miss Doc," said Schnitter, slicing his knife through a juicy piece of meat. "But we all know there's a reason he's not sitting here with us at the table tonight. He showed a lack of loyalty. An unwillingness to work as part of a team."

This seemed to be directed at Loy Hanley.

"Well, hellfire," said Hanley, "let's drink to teamwork!" and everybody bumped their glasses together and mumbled: "To teamwork."

"This ain't a wake," said Bud to one of the waiters. "Tell Goldilocks to pep it up a little."

The waiter went over to the piano player and said something, and the piano player glanced worriedly at Bud then started playing a rollicking version of "Bill Bailey."

I was sitting next to Nuffer, who was getting drunk as fast as he could. His face was florid with sunburn. He gave me a blurry affectionate smile, and patted my arm. "I like you, Danny. You're a nice fella."

"I think you're a nice fella too, Mr. Nuffer."

"Nice fella. So therefore I think there's something you need to know."

"What?"

He moved his mouth close to my ear. "A rumor has been afloat today. To the effect that you and Darla were observed together last night by the lake."

"Yeah, so?"

"Not to put too fine a point on it—the lady was seen with your dick in her mouth."

I looked down the table at Teddy Bump. Caught him in the middle of one of his dying-hyena laughs, his mouth open and full of food.

"But that's not what happened—"

"Shhh!" said Nuffer so sharply my ear was sprayed with spit. "The truth doesn't matter. Only appearances matter," then he squeezed my knee under the table. "A word to the wise, hm?"

After dinner, the waiters brought around brandy and cigars.

"Want my cigar?" I said to Dick Prettie.

He shrugged, and put it in his pocket, then lit up his own. As usual, his clothes didn't fit; the sleeves of his tuxedo jacket were too short, and his collar was too big for his long skinny neck.

He still seemed to be in a sour mood. He studied the smoke curling up from his cigar.

"You know, when I was growing up, no way I ever coulda imagined smoking a cigar like this in a joint like this. But now I'm here, who gives a fuck?"

Joe Shaw started coughing and clearing his throat like something had gone down the wrong way, then he slowly stood up. Bud tapped on his brandy glass with a spoon and shouted to the loud table: "Hey, pipe down, you fellas! I think Joe's got a few words he'd like to say."

"Thanks, Bud. Well, I got a few words, then my brother's got a few more words." Shaw was burly and pleasant-faced, with little glittery eyes and a dimple like a bullet hole in his chin. "I wanna thank you guys for inviting me up here, and I've had a great time the last two days. And on top of everything else, I got to see the Eighth Wonder of the World: Wendell Nuffer on water skis! Wendell, when you fell off them skis, I was afraid there wasn't gonna be any water left in the lake. But luckily it all ran back in."

Nuffer laughed harder than anybody.

"My brother was sorry he couldn't make it up here himself, but I just finished talking to him on the phone, and filling him in on what we all been talking about. Frank said he can't wait till we all get back in town so we can continue making Los Angeles the Greatest City in the World!"

Loud applause. Joe Shaw took a piece of paper out of his pocket and unfolded it. "Now let's move on to what this night is all about." He looked at Max Schnitter. "Max, Frank wanted me to read this to you.

" 'Dear Max: Heartiest congratulations to you on your birthday! Max, you're what the American Dream is all about. A poor immigrant kid who started from scratch and is now leading a prosperous, productive life and providing employment for a lot of people. I'm proud to call you my friend,' and it's signed: 'Frank Shaw, Mayor of Los Angeles.' "

More applause as Joe Shaw sat down and Schnitter stood up. Everybody was puffing away on their big cigars and the room was becoming as smoky as a battlefield.

"Thank you, Joe. And I'm proud to call the Shaw brothers *my* friends. And to the rest of my friends here: Thank you very much for this birthday dinner in my honor."

Somebody sneezed so loud it was like a window falling shut and then they blew their nose.

"Life is a forward motion, we are always marching into tomorrow. But an occasion like this sends us the other way, back into the labyrinth of memory."

He smiled a little, baring his eye teeth as he gazed off into the smoke.

"My first night in America. I had slipped across the border from Mexico into Arizona. I had no passport, no papers of any kind. I barely knew any English. I was fourteen years old.

"I was hungry and tired, and I walked into a bar. It was full of Mexicans and Indians. Not any whites but me. I put my last few coins on the bar, and ordered a glass of beer and a sardine sandwich.

"There was an Indian boy and an Indian girl also sitting at the bar. I don't know what their relationship was. Husband and wife? Boyfriend and girlfriend? Brother and sister? All I know is the girl was beautiful. Long black braids. Brown eyes that had no bottom to them.

"I smiled at her. And she smiled back at me. And her husband, boyfriend, or brother watched. And that night I learned my first lesson in America: Never get in a knife fight with an Indian."

Schnitter paused and took a sip of his brandy to allow for the laughter.

"When I got out of the hospital, I traveled west. When I arrived in California, I thought I had arrived in paradise. The warmth, the sunshine, the oranges hanging in the trees. But when I tried to pick one of those oranges, I was chased away by a man on horseback. And I learned that even in paradise, a price must be paid for oranges.

"And so I got a job, picking lima beans, and I thought my back would break. Then ten years later I went back to that same tree, or one very much like it, and I picked an orange, and I peeled it, and I ate it, and that day no one tried to chase me away—for I was now the owner of the grove.

"I enjoyed eating that orange as much as I have ever enjoyed anything, before or since. And my birthday message to you, my friends, tonight, is, savor all your victories, great or small, because ultimately there is just one rule in life: Everybody loses everything."

Schnitter sat down, to somewhat befuddled applause. Bud

stood up, and started singing: *"For he's a jolly good fellow,"* and everybody else joined in as the piano player vigorously played along. As they reached the first *which nobody can deny* the blue lights in the Moonlight Room began to fade till all you could see were the fiery tips of everybody's cigars. Then a spotlight hit a curtain on the stage. Then, as the song concluded, the curtain opened to reveal Vera Vermillion.

She was lying on the stage wrapped in cellophane and tied up with red ribbons. She was completely naked. She was very white in the light, except for her auburn hair and her abundant pubic hair and her big pink nipples.

"She's all yours, Max!" said Bud. "Go ahead! Unwrap her!"

Shnitter looked as if he'd just as soon be someplace else, but he managed a smile and walked toward the stage, accompanied by ribald cries of encouragement. He knelt in front of her, and pulled at the ribbons, and it quieted down in the Moonlight Room, and you could hear the crinkling of the cellophane, then you could hear Schnitter mutter: "What the fuck is this?"

Now Schnitter stood up, and turned and faced us in the bright round light. His pointy-eared face was contorted and terrible. He shouted: "What the fuck is THIS?!"

15

She'd suffocated, evidently.

Nucky and Nello had been in charge of her. They'd wrapped her up a little before dinner started. They said the last they saw of her she was fine, except she'd been drinking like a fish all night, so at some point she must have passed out, which must have been why she didn't yell for help or something before she died.

Max Schnitter seemed to think the whole thing was some kind of practical joke on him, and he stormed off with his guys. Hanley, Shaw, and Nuffer bailed out of there pretty fast too.

Bill Flitter, the hotel manager, who looked like his name, and seemed terrified of us, called a doctor and the San Bernardino County sheriff.

Bud sat at the table wiping off his hands with one Kleenex after another. "Some fucking mess," he said glumly.

Jack Otay said: "Don't sweat it. We'll fix it."

Vera Vermillion lay on the stage in the cellophane and ribbons, looking very white, lonely, and pathetic. And still. So still. Finally a waiter flapped out a tablecloth and let it settle down upon her.

The doctor and the sheriff showed up. The doctor was an old, white-haired guy that looked just like the picture I had in my head of Dr. Ames. He examined the body, while Otay and the sheriff went off in a corner together. I'd have expected somebody that was a sheriff to look lanky and tough, like Buck

Jones, the cowboy movie star, or maybe Loy Hanley, but this guy looked more like Oliver Hardy or Wendell Nuffer, wearing bright-red suspenders and a straw hat, and mopping his sweating neck with a handkerchief even though the room wasn't hot.

Turned out the sheriff and Otay were old pals. Every winter they'd go south to El Centro together and shoot ducks. After the doctor finished with Vera, he went over to Otay and the sheriff, and the three of them talked for a while as Bud and myself and the rest of the guys watched. At one point they all busted out laughing, and the sheriff slapped Otay on the back.

"Hey, they're laughing," said Nucky. "That's a good sign."

"You better hope it's a good sign, you fucking moron," said Bud.

Finally the three shook hands all around, and Otay came walking back.

"The doc says it looks like a heart attack. 'A tragedy in one so young,' he said. Nothing nobody coulda done."

Bud sighed with relief.

"Thanks, Jack. I won't be forgetting this."

"Glad to be of help," said Otay with his usual smirk.

Now Bud addressed us generally.

"I don't want some headline-happy reporter getting wind of this. You know, 'Dame Dies At Wild Party Attended By Mayor's Brother.' Talk to the waiters and the busboys and the guy that ran the spotlight and anybody else you can think of. Spread around some dough. Tell 'em to keep a lid on it if they know what's good for 'em."

We heard a thud. The piano player had fainted. He was lying near his piano all crumpled up in his powder-blue tuxedo.

"Poor Goldilocks," said Bud. "I guess the excitement was just too much for him," and everybody laughed.

Two guys dressed in white came in and loaded the body on a stretcher and lugged it off into the night. I went up to my room without trying to bribe or threaten anybody. Took two aspirin and filled up the bathtub with the hottest water I could stand.

I eased myself in and lay there with just my nose and eyes above the surface like a crocodile. It seemed strange and somehow impossible I'd been talking to Vera this afternoon and now she was dead. I thought if I hadn't bought her that second drink maybe she would have stopped drinking and maybe right now she'd be frolicking with Max Schnitter in his room instead of riding in an ambulance down a twisty road with the guys in white.

I was barely awake now, like my nose was barely above the water. And then I either dreamed, or imagined, or imagined I dreamed, or dreamed I imagined that Vera Vermillion was running naked through the woods around Lake Arrowhead, pursued by three angry snorting deers, and then I snorted up the hot water of the tub and sat up coughing and choking then heaved myself out and grabbed a towel.

Above my bed the Indian kid was still holding up his shining triumphant fish. I wandered over to the window. The moon had gone down, and I couldn't see much, just a few dark trees; they looked like a bunch of guys standing around on a corner with their hands in their pockets and their backs to me, talking about stuff they didn't want me to hear.

I sat down in an armchair. The back of my brain felt like it was teeming with bad dreams, and I was reluctant to go to bed, go to sleep, and unleash them.

I don't know whether I'd been sitting there five minutes or two hours when I heard a ruckus out in the hallway: yelling, and cursing, and crashing around, and I jumped up and yanked on my pants and opened my door.

Wendell Nuffer was crawling down the hallway on his hands and knees, wearing nothing but blue-and-white-striped boxer shorts, while Loy Hanley walked behind him, kicking him violently in the butt with his cowboy-booted foot.

Hanley was wearing trousers and an undershirt. His jaws were working on a piece of gum, and there was something remorseless and impersonal in his face, like a grasshopper chewing its way through a leaf.

Nuffer's body was covered with a glowing-pink sunburn, and he wept and bled from the nose as he crawled and cried out: "No! No! Stop! Stop! Please! No!"

There were spectators: Hotel guests in their nightclothes peeked fearfully out of their rooms. The two Tommys leaned against a wall, smoking cigarettes and yukking it up. Violet Gilbertson, wearing a bathrobe, her hair messed up, stood in a doorway and nervously bit on one of her fingers; it took me a moment to realize she was in the doorway of Loy Hanley's room.

Nuffer finally collapsed to the floor. Hanley stood over him, chewing, hands on hips, not even breathing hard. He said: "You had enough, Nuffer?"

"Yes."

"You ever fuck with me again I'll kill you. You hear me?"

"I hear you."

"Loy?" called Violet. "Come on back."

But Hanley wasn't quite ready to let it go. He stood there, looking at Nuffer, then reached down and jerked his boxer shorts down past his buttocks; then he turned and walked back to his room. "Get back in there, you're half nekkid," he told Violet, then the door closed behind them.

Other doors up and down the hallway also closed. Tommy and Goodlooking Tommy walked away, still giggling.

I went over to Nuffer. His eyes were scrunched shut and leaking tears, snot and blood were dripping out of his nose, and he was gasping and wheezing. His butt was starkly white compared to the boiled-looking rest of him; there was something shockingly obscene about it, like he'd been posed for a dirty photograph.

"Come on, Mr. Nuffer," I said, and I took one of his arms and helped him to his feet. I tugged up his shorts, then led him toward his room. He shuffled along, with the blank eyes of a blind man.

He'd left his door wide open. We went in, and I sat him down in a chair, then went in the bathroom and wet a washcloth.

He stank of sweat and liquor. I wiped the blood off his face and chest. "What happened?" I said.

He looked at me like he'd just become aware of my presence. "Oh, Danny."

I asked him again what had happened.

"I was pretty pickled, you see. Oh yes. Extraordinarily pickled. And Violet and I went to bed. Then I woke up, and she wasn't there.

"Oh I knew right away where she was, my boy, I knew right away, because I saw, you saw, we all saw, how she and Hanley were looking at each other. So I went straight to his room. I pounded on the door. I stood bellowing in the hallway like a bull. Then when he opened the door, and I saw her behind him, I struck him in the face."

Nuffer laughed.

"I was something of a sissy when I was a boy, and I suppose I forgot I'm still a sissy."

And he kept laughing, and it was a scary kind of laugh, like he was on the edge of going loony.

"And oh, my boy, how could it have been any worse! Intoxicated, in my underwear, getting kicked in the hiney by a gangster, while the cheap tramp that caused it all looks on and laughs! Soon the whole town will know! I'll be a laughingstock! And I should be! I'm funny, I'm funny, Nuffer is funny!" He was shaking all over with laughter, and his face was turning even redder if that was possible. "But I won't let it get me down, no, not a bit, my boy, not a bit, because Nuffer has that fighting spirit," and then he began to sing in a hoarse boisterous voice:

"Fight on for ol' SC,
Our men fight on to victory,
Our alma mater dear
Looks up to you,
Fight on and win
For ol' SC,
Fight on to victory,
Fight on!"

16

Next morning I came out of the elevator with my suitcase and saw Dick Prettie in the lobby, looking thoughtfully up at the grizzly bear. He was standing so still that he looked stuffed too.

I walked over and looked up at the bear myself.

"Look at them fucking teeth," he said.

"They're big all right."

"Just think about it. Think about being ate to death by that fucking thing. I couldn't never have been a cowboy. Bears trying to eat your ass. Indians trying to scalp the fucking hair right off your head."

Probably to the great relief of the staff and the other guests, we were all leaving Birkenhead Manor. Bud and Darla walked by, trailed by two college-boy bellhops with their luggage. They seemed to be in a hurry. Darla glanced over at us and waved. I waved back.

"Look at him," said Dick. "Trying to get outa here before he runs into Shitter."

"I guess this whole thing was a disaster, huh?"

Dick shrugged and coughed, which seemed to remind him it was time to light up another cigarette. As he flicked his lighter, Timothy, the old colored shoeshine boy, stumbled out of the corridor where his stand was, pursued by Nucky Williams, who was hitting him with a dead fish.

"I know you did it, you lying nigger!" yelled Nucky.

"No suh," said Timothy, "it wasn't me, suh! Lordie! Stop it, suh! Please!"

Timothy had his arms up, trying to fend off the blows. The fish looked like one of the trout from the pool in the Big Boulder Dining Room. Guests and employees were keeping their distance, some looking scared and others amused. I saw the manager come out of his office behind the front desk, take a quick look, then flit back into his office.

"Nucky, what's going on?" I said. I took a step toward Nucky and the old man. I felt Dick's hand on my arm, heard him say: "Stay out of it, Danny."

Nucky looked over his shoulder at me. He was holding the fish by the tail, and its glassy eye seemed to be looking at me too. "Huh?" said Nucky.

"What's going on?"

"Snowflake here put this fucking fish in my bed—"

"No suh, I didn't do no such of a thing—"

With a smooth backhand motion, like he was playing tennis, Nucky slapped the trout into Timothy's face and shouted: "Shut up!" Now he turned back to me. "He was getting back at me 'cause I dropped that dollar in his spit bucket."

"But how do you know it was him?"

"I seen him last night sneaking around outside my room," and then he said: "What's it to you, Danny? You a member of the National Association for the Advancement of Niggers?"

"Suh," said Timothy, "reason I was up there, I was picking up shoes to shine. Folks put their shoes outside of their doors at night, and in the morning when they open their doors up they find their shoes all nice and shiny."

"I TOLD YOU TO SHUT UP, NIGGER!" and Nucky began to ferociously flog Timothy with the fish again.

"Nucky, stop it!" I tried to grab the fish away from him, then he shoved me and I stumbled back then I started to go for him but Dick grabbed me and hissed in my ear: "Danny, are you nuts?"

Nucky's tie had gone crooked and he straightened it as he stared at me in disbelief with his flat chicken eyes. "Yeah, Dick, that's right. You keep your pal away from me."

Timothy had taken this opportunity to scuttle off and vanish. I could see in Nucky's face that he wanted to do a lot more to me than just hit me with a fish. Dick picked up my suitcase and pulled me toward the front entrance. "Come on, let's get outa here."

We got in my Packard and began to drive down the mountain. "You don't wanna get on the wrong side of Nucky Williams," said Dick. "The only reason he didn't kill you is 'cause he's scared of Bud."

"You mean he's not scared of me?"

Dick didn't answer. Pretty soon the mountains were in my rearview mirror and we'd reentered the flat lands. Orange orchards. Hubert's Rabbit Ranch. People in tattered clothes toiling in emerald fields. We stopped for gas. It was thirty-three cents a gallon. We'd made a deal that if I drove my car Dick would buy the gas, and he started complaining to the sullen kid with the swollen jaw that was manning the pumps that this was fucking highway robbery, gas was twelve cents a gallon in Los Angeles. The kid said: "Lay off me, mister. I just work here. And I got a goddamn toothache."

I found myself glad to get back to the city. It felt like we'd been gone weeks instead of a couple of days. I dropped Dick off at his apartment house on Wilcox, then headed for La Vista Lane.

As I pulled up in front of the bungalow court, I saw Sophie flying down the sidewalk on roller skates. I called out to her, but she didn't look back, then I realized it wasn't Sophie at all, but another little girl who didn't even particularly look like Sophie.

I climbed the seven steps. Fifteen or twenty sparrows and three mourning doves were busy at some birdseed Mrs. Dean had put out. They scattered with a whoosh of wings at my approach, the doves making choppy whistling sounds.

I unlocked my bungalow and went in. It seemed musty and stuffy and still and silent.

I thought I'd drop in on Dulwich. Tell him about my adventures. I could picture the gap in his teeth as he laughed at certain things, the kindness and sadness in his eyes as he listened quietly to other things.

His door was closed. Usually it was open. I knocked. Knocked again. He seemed not to be home. I turned to leave, but then heard: "Who's there?"

But it wasn't Dulwich's voice.

"Danny," I said.

"Who?"

"Danny Landon," I said more loudly to the closed door. "I'm Dulwich's neighbor. Is he there?"

Silence. I was getting an eerie feeling. Maybe Dulwich had been murdered, and his murderer was on the other side of the door, just a foot or two away, trying to decide what to do with me.

"Hello?" I said.

I heard the door being unlocked, and now it opened. Standing in front of me, on the other side of the screen door, was . . . Dulwich.

"Dulwich," was all I could think of to say.

"Hello, Danny," he said very softly.

"I didn't recognize your voice."

He didn't respond. I was alarmed by the way he looked. It was like it both was and wasn't him, as if he was wearing some kind of ghastly Dulwich mask. I couldn't remember ever having seen such bleakness, such despair in anybody's face before.

"Dulwich, what's the matter? What's happened?"

"Nothing has happened. It's just that . . . on some days . . . the fog rolls in."

He mustered up the ghost of a smile.

"But I'm all right, Danny. I'll be seeing you soon."

He stepped back, and slowly shut the door.

I went back into my bungalow.

In the bedroom I took off my hat and coat and my shoulder holster and gun, and sat down on the side of the bed and took off my shoes. Mrs. Dean had given me an old radio. It didn't work very well. I twisted the dial and got nothing but static, then somebody yakking away in Spanish, then finally, faintly, a woman singing:

"Life is just a bowl of cherries,
Don't take it serious,
Life's too mysterious . . ."

The voice seemed to be coming from some immeasurable distance, from the other side of space and time, and suddenly I was surprised by a sob that jumped up through my throat and out of my nose, and my eyes stung as tears ran down my cheeks.

It didn't last long. I lay down on the bed. It had bedclothes now that covered the stain that was shaped like Texas.

I laced my fingers behind my back and looked at the ceiling. There were some interesting cracks up there.

In the living room, the phone started to ring. As far as I was concerned, it could ring till kingdom come and not make me get up. Not make me stop looking at the ceiling, as though this was the very thing I'd been put on earth to do.

★ ★ ★ ★ ★

2

★ ★ ★ ★ ★

1

Sophie had a black eye.

"Where'd you get the shiner?" I said.

She shrugged. "I fell down."

She was sitting on the steps in front of the bungalow court, poking at some ants with a stick. I'd just come back from the store, and was carrying two sacks of groceries plus a brand-new broom with a bright-yellow handle. She said: "What's the broom for?"

"Gee, I don't know. What are brooms usually for?"

"Don't get wise, BB eyes. You need some help?"

I gave her one of the sacks, and we moved down the walk. She was wearing dirty dungarees and a shirt with huge purple polkadots on it. A fashion plate she wasn't. Suddenly she startled the heck out of me by clattering her shiny black shoes across the concrete as she belted out in a high-pitched voice:

"Come and meet those dancing feet
On the avenue I'm taking you to,
Forty-second Street!
Hear the beat of dancing feet,
It's the song I love the melody of,
Forty-second Street!"

I'd come to a dead stop as I watched her. Now she looked back at me.

"Say," I said, "that's pretty good."

"Thanks. I plan to run away and be a tap dancer in New York."

"Why not? Maybe you can be the new Shirley Temple."

"I'm much, much older than Shirley Temple. Anyway, I can't stand that kid. I think she's just a big phony."

"So you seem like you're in a pretty good mood for a girl with a black eye."

She gave me her shy look. "Seeing you—that makes me be in a good mood."

Dulwich's door was open, and we could hear the energetic rattle of typewriter keys, the ding of the bell, and the sliding of the carriage.

"Sounds like he's writing something," I said.

"Yeah. Maybe a new movie! Maybe he'll write a part for me!"

We went in my bungalow. Sophie helped me unpack my groceries and put them away. Coffee, milk, baloney, rat cheese, bread, licorice sticks, and so forth.

She looked at a bar of Lifebuoy soap.

"You know what they call me at school?"

"What?"

"Soapy. Soapy Gobbler."

"That's not very nice."

"Yeah. I hate 'em."

I knew she was lying about her black eye, and I felt like doing something for her.

"Wait here a minute."

I went in my bedroom, rummaged through a dresser drawer, then found the pink brush I'd bought from the veteran with no legs. I returned to the kitchen and presented it to Sophie.

"A brush," she said, looking it over.

"Yeah."

"How much you pay for this?"

"A quarter."

"You got robbed. But thanks anyway."

I walked her to the door.

"You wanna go over and pester Mr. Dulwich?" she said.

We walked over and peered in his screen door. Saw him sitting at his typewriter with his back to us, tapping away furiously.

I knocked on the door frame as Sophie said: "Knock knock!"

Dulwich looked over his shoulder, broke into a grin. "Hello there!" he said as he got up to greet us. I was relieved to see he seemed to be back to his old self, though his smile went away when he saw Sophie's face.

"Sophie, what happened?"

"I fell down. When I was playing."

"And those bruises on your arms? That also happened when you fell down?"

I'd missed them somehow—a purplish cluster of bruises, like a bunch of grapes, emerging from under her shirt sleeves on each of her upper arms.

"Yup," said Sophie.

"And Jerry? Did he have anything to do with your falling down?"

Jerry was her mother Lois's latest boyfriend—a stocky fellow with dark curly hair and a toothy too big smile.

"Nope," said Sophie.

Tinker Bell plodded in from the bedroom, stuck out her front paws and stretched. Sophie said: "Hi, Tinker Bell, have you been sleeping?" and went over to pet her.

"Sorry about the other day," said Dulwich to me.

"Why be sorry? I get down in the dumps too, sometimes."

"Are you writing a movie?" asked Sophie, as Tinker purred under her hand.

"I'm writing a so-called 'detective' story, actually. Or at least trying to write one. I always seem to be finding out things aren't as simple as they seem."

There was a pile of magazines on his desk, and he picked up the top one. On the cover were a tough-looking guy and a sultry blonde in a silver convertible, passing a city-limits sign that said:

NOWHERE

POP. 0,000,000

"Now here's a recent issue of *Super Detective Stories*." He leafed through the pages. "All right. Listen to the beginning of 'Names in the Black Book.'

" ' "Three unsolved murders in a week are not so unusual—for River Street," grunted Steve Harrison, shifting his muscular bulk restlessly in his chair.

" 'His companion lighted a cigarette and Harrison observed that her slim hand was none too steady. She was exotically beautiful, a dark, supple figure, with the rich colors of purple Eastern nights and crimson dawns in her dusky hair and red lips. But in her dark eyes Harrison glimpsed the shadow of fear. Only once before had he seen fear in those marvelous eyes, and the memory made him vaguely uneasy.

" ' "It's your business to solve murders," she said.' "

Dulwich bit his lower lip for a moment as he studied the story.

"The writing's a bit uncouth, perhaps, but I think you'll agree there's a certain seductive energy that lures one on. *Why* is there the shadow of fear in the nameless beauty's marvelous eyes? What do the three unsolved murders have to do with her? And Harrison, our hero, he of the grunts and the muscular bulk . . . why is he so restless and uneasy? What terrible event occasioned the previous appearance of fear in the dark eyes of his exotically beautiful companion?"

Dulwich tossed *Super Detective Stories* back on the pile.

"*My* story seems to have all the dynamic forward motion of the figures painted on Keats's Grecian urn. The spying eye in the keyhole never blinks. The drooping ash at the end of the cigarette in the long cigarette holder held by the willowy blonde never actually detaches itself and falls."

"Mister," said Sophie, "I got *no* idea what you're talking about."

Dulwich sighed. "Precisely the problem."

"You seemed to be typing a mile a minute when we walked up," I said. "Like you were really inspired."

"Misleading. A mouse in a cage running frantically in his exercise wheel. But I should persevere, I suppose," and he smiled cheerfully at us. "After all, one can't honestly call oneself a scribbler unless one occasionally makes some wretched attempt at scribbling!"

Tinker rolled on her back and presented her belly to Sophie.

"She likes to have her tummy scratched," said Sophie, then she looked up at Dulwich. "Would you write a part for me in your story?"

"A part for you in my story," Dulwich mused. "How would that work exactly?"

"It's easy. You just write about a cute smart kid named Sophie!"

"Sophie Antoinette?" I suggested.

Sophie laughed. "Yeah. And her faithful cat Tinker. They can solve crimes together. Tinker can climb trees and look in people's windows and report back to Sophie. And Sophie can wear all kinds of disguises! And she can trap the crooks and—"

"I thought I heard your voice, you little devil!"

We all looked toward the door. Jerry was there, in a red plaid sports jacket with a matching tie. He looked exactly like the door-to-door salesman that he was.

"Your ma's been looking everywhere for you," and then he flashed his smile at Dulwich and me. "Hello, Mr. Dulwich! How are you today, Danny?"

Jerry was one of those people that after meeting you for three seconds remembers your name forever and repeats it every chance he gets.

"Fine day today, isn't it? Not like Foggy Old England, huh, Mr. Dulwich! And Danny boy! When are you going to a ballgame with me! I caught a homerun the other day, and you know who hit it? Jigger Statz! He signed the ball for me after the game, Danny, I'll bet it'll be worth a ton of money someday!"

Tinker disdainfully turned her back on Jerry and went back in the bedroom.

"Come on, Sophie. Your ma's got things she wants you to do."

"What sort of things?"

Jerry's smile started looking a little rigid.

"How should I know? Let's go, Sophie. Quit bothering these two gentlemen."

"Oh, she's no bother," said Dulwich. "Quite the opposite."

"Well, isn't that nice of you to say so! Good seeing you, Mr. Dulwich! And you too, Danny boy!"

Sophie got up and listlessly slumped toward the door. "Bye," she said without looking at us.

We went to the door and watched them walk toward Sophie's bungalow. Jerry put his hand on her shoulder, and she flinched it off like a horse would a horsefly, then they disappeared inside.

"So you think Jerry beat her up?" I said.

"I think it likely, yes. Something happened over there on one of the nights you were gone. I could hear all three of them shouting and shrieking like banshees; it calmed down only when Mrs. Dean came out and knocked on the door and threatened to call the police."

"How could anybody hurt a little girl?"

"Unfortunately, I've grown unsurprised at anything human beings do. Not excluding me. I believe Sophie's ideas for my story are better than mine. I'll make us a cup of tea, and you can tell me all about Lake Arrowhead. Hm, Danny boy?"

It was like I was at the bottom of a deep black well, and I listened to a phone for a long time ringing way above my head, till finally I awoke and stumbled into the living room and picked it up.

"Danny? It's Darla."

It was about three in the morning. I tried to get my wits about me.

"Darla? What's the matter?"

"Nothing, really. I woke you up. I'm sorry."

"S'okay. Where are you?"

"At Bud's. Downstairs. He's upstairs. Asleep. I had the most terrible dream."

A yawn tried to pry my mouth open.

"Yeah? About what?"

"Doc. He was out on the balcony. He was trying to get in. He was beating on the window with his fists. The glass was breaking. He was so mad at me, Danny. So mad."

"What happened to Doc wasn't your fault."

"He's buried out there somewhere, isn't he?"

"Yes."

"Do monkeys have ghosts?"

"I don't know. I don't think so."

A long silence.

"Darla?"

"I'm here. Do you really love me?"

"Yes."

"Good night, Danny."
"Good night."

2

It was funny. It was like the clean mountain air Nuffer was talking about really did have some kind of effect on me. I came back from Lake Arrowhead and started having fewer headaches, and my left arm was feeling stronger when I did my morning pushups, and it seemed like I was walking with less of a limp. And the dark veil separating me from my past seemed thinner now, and a little light was passing through. For instance, not only could I see myself as a kid pissing my name in the snow, but I could see the snow was on the rocky bank of a river, and the river was half frozen, and a skinny mutt of a dog was walking on the ice and I was afraid it would break through, and beyond the river rose the tall buildings of a mighty city.

Also, I understood better how I felt about Darla. I loved her, but I didn't love her without reserve. Because there was the other girl, Gwynnie. The lost girl, the ghostly girl. Who was still loved by some lost, ghostly part of me.

I didn't see Darla for about a week after we got back. I was told she was laid up in bed with a cold, though when I'd talked to her on the phone she hadn't sounded sick, and it didn't seem the right season for a cold. But Bud called me one night and told me to come to the Peacock Club and she was there.

"Feeling better?" I said.

"Sure. I'm on Cloud Number Nine."

We were in Bud's booth. I was on the outside, then next to me was Goodlooking Tommy, then came Bud, Darla, and Moe

Davis, and Nello Marlini was sitting across from me at the other end of the U.

Moe was so fat he could hardly fit in the booth. He probably weighed as much as three Dick Pretties put together. He had a basket of bread in front of him, and he was loading up a piece with one pat of butter after another without even bothering to smear them around. Then he took a big bite and said: "Great fucking bread."

Bud looked pleased. "Baked fresh on the premises every day."

"Yeah? Well my compliments to the chef."

He pronounced the ch in "chef" like the ch in "champ." Butter shined on his blubbery lips, and he was chewing with his mouth open. I noticed Darla was watching him too, like she was about to be sick, then our eyes met and she snorted out a laugh.

"What's so funny?" said Bud.

"I was just thinking about a joke."

"Why don't you share it with the rest of the table?"

"Too late. I already forgot the punchline."

Bud had an office called the Security Finance Company on the second floor of a building on Cahuenga. It was the front for a bookie joint and Moe Davis ran it.

"Guess who I seen walking down the street the other day," said Moe. "Louie Vachaboski."

Bud grinned. "So how's Fay Wray doing?"

"He seemed kinda nervous. But he said to give you his best regards."

"How'd his eye look?" said Nello.

"Kinda squinty. Like he was winking at me."

Everybody laughed. But Darla wasn't laughing. She was sucking down a cigarette, and getting tanked on martinis; the waiter came by and she ordered another one. Bud frowned at her.

"How come you drink so much?" he said.

"How come you commit so many crimes?"

"That supposed to be funny? 'Cause I ain't laughing."

"I wouldn't expect somebody to laugh whose idea of funny was putting out somebody's eye with a cigarette."

It got quiet around the table as Darla puffed on her cigarette and tried to pretend she didn't feel Bud's eyes boring into her; then you could see him deciding to let it go. He looked at Moe as he wiped his hands off with a Kleenex.

"You talk to Phegley?"

Pete Phegley was a lieutenant in administrative vice, and a frequent loutish visitor to the Peacock Club.

"Yeah. He still says he needs twenty percent."

Bud shook his head. "Phegley's already gotta be the richest police lieutenant in Los Angeles, if not the fucking world. And yet he still wants more."

"I think we all got in the wrong perfession," said Moe. "We all shoulda been cops. That way all we'd have to do all day is ride around town and eat free and screw whores without paying for 'em."

"And stick our fucking hands out for envelopes filled with dough," said Bud.

"Why do you put up with him?" I said. "If he's such a prick."

"We can't just go around getting rid of cops, Danny," said Bud, like a patient parent explaining life to a five-year-old. "They're necessary evils."

"Yeah, like broads," said Goodlooking Tommy, and he and Nello laughed.

Stan Tinney, the manager, walked over.

"How is everything? Darla, you're looking lovely tonight."

"Thanks. So where's the body?"

"The body?"

"It's like a wake in here. So I figure there must be a body around someplace."

The club *was* pretty empty. A bored-looking orchestra was

playing, and two or three couples were shuffling round on the dance floor like zombies in a nightclub in hell.

"Well, you know," said Stan, "it's Thursday night."

"Stan," said Bud, "is it also Thursday night over at the Pom Pom Club?"

"Of course."

"And you think the Pom Pom Club is this empty?"

"I've got no way of knowing that."

"Maybe I'll drop by later and see for myself."

"All I know is, the Peacock Club is still a popular place. Especially with the right people. Why, just last night, Lionel Barrymore was here."

"And Dick said he thought he seen Ginger Rogers in here last week," said Nello.

"Who wants to dance?" said Darla.

Silence around the table.

"Come on, it won't cost you much. I'm just one of them dime-a-dance dames."

"You know I got two left feet," said Bud.

"Danny?" said Darla. "You got a dime? I'll dance with you for a dime."

Goodlooking Tommy laughed. "Danny dancing. That's a good one."

Darla glared at him. "What do you mean?"

Goodlooking Tommy was losing confidence.

"Well, you know—his leg, and all."

"I'll give it a try, I guess," I said.

We went out on the dance floor. I didn't remember ever having danced before, but I had a feeling I'd be okay at it; and after a minute or two Darla said: "You dance real nice, Danny."

She was wearing a beige beaded dress with no back; two slender straps made an X centered just below her shoulder blades, and just below the X my hand rested on her bare flesh.

It was a slow song, and she snuggled in pretty tight.

"Were you ever really a dime-a-dance girl?"

"No. But I had a friend who was. Bombina. This Italian girl from Boyle Heights. She worked at a club on the Santa Monica Pier. She said one night she was dancing with a handsome stranger, and she looked down and saw he had one goat foot and one chicken foot. Then her skin started burning where he was touching her, and she looked in his eyes and realized she was dancing with the devil. Then she could feel herself fainting.

"Bombina said the next thing she knew, she was waking up on the beach. She was all by herself. The pier was about half a mile away. And she had burn marks on her arms."

"You really believe all that?"

"Well, I saw the marks on her arms. And they did look kind of like fingers."

We drifted along with the dreamy music; then: "I'm proud of you, Danny," Darla said.

"What for?"

"I heard you and Nucky got into it. Because you were sticking up for a shoeshine boy."

"Where'd you hear that?"

"Oh, a pretty little bird told me. But you gotta be careful, Danny. Don't turn your back on Nucky," and then she giggled. "Nucky the knucklehead. I'm drunk." And then, in a singsongy voice:

> "I had a little bird
> And its name was Enza.
> I opened the window
> And influenza!"

"What's that?"

"Something us kids used to say in Nebraska City. During the flu epidemic."

"You know Dulwich? My neighbor? His best friend died of the flu. On Christmas."

"You really like Dulwich, don't you?"

"Yeah."

"Is he married?"

"No."

"Does he have a girlfriend?"

"I don't think so."

"Is he a fairy?"

"No. Of course not."

"Anyway. I'm glad you have a friend. You should have lots of friends."

So Darla and I danced, us and the zombies, beneath the eyes of the painted peacocks. If we could have danced forever like that, it would have been fine by me. I felt the delicate knobs of her backbone under my fingertips. I smelt her Mitsuoko. I could feel the warmth of her body through the sheer chiffon of her dress and on my neck the warmth of her breath and then the song was over.

We went back to the booth. Bud said: "You looked pretty good out there, kid. You been taking lessons from Arthur Murphy?"

I laughed and shook my head.

Darla took the olive out of her latest martini and put it in her mouth and chewed on it slowly and looked at me.

Nello looked morose. "You know what I seen in the mirror today? Three gray hairs. I can't believe my hair's turning fucking gray already."

"You ever try Grey Gone?" said Darla.

"Naw, what's that?"

"A hair dye. Bud uses it. It works great."

Everybody looked at Bud's hair.

"You dye your hair?" said Moe.

Bud looked steamed. "It's none of your fucking business. And you talk too much, baby," he said to Darla.

"First you don't want me to sing, now you don't want me to even fucking talk."

"That's right."

"Why can't I start singing again, Bud? When I was singing, every night this place was packed."

"And you think that was all 'cause of you?"

"I think I had something to do with it, yeah."

Armilda Lee Keddy walked up in a tiny skirt with a tray of cigarettes.

"How are y'all doing tonight? Anybody need some cigarettes?"

"Gimme a pack of Spuds," said Moe, addressing her legs. He gave her a five for the smokes but when she started to make change he said: "Keep it."

"Oh, thank you, Mr. Davis."

"Moe."

"Moe. You know, you're the first Moe I ever met."

"Yeah?"

"I'm from Oklahoma, and I guess Moe ain't a Oklahoma kind of a name."

"You like working here?" asked Darla.

Armilda Lee smiled at Bud. "You bet I do! It's the best job I've ever had."

"That's good. I just hope things work out better for you than the last girl that worked here."

Armilda Lee's smile faltered a little. "What do you mean?"

"Her name was Betty. She's dead now. Somebody killed her."

"Oh. That's terrible."

"Get lost," said Bud to Armilda Lee.

Armilda Lee sashayed away, looking happy to escape.

Bud glowered at Darla. "What was that all about?"

"What was what all about?"

"You seemed to be inferring something. About Betty."

Darla lit up a Lucky Strike.

"I don't know what you're talking about. I just know I'm sick of you. Sick of this place. Sick of these fucking peacocks."

"Get the hell outa here then." He turned to me. "Danny, take this whiney bitch home."

"I'll go home when I'm good and ready."

The waiter put down a fresh basket of bread in front of Moe.

"Don't make a scene," said Bud.

"Why don't you share some of that fucking bread, you greedy pig?" said Goodlooking Tommy.

"Fuck you," said Moe, and: "Fuck yourself," said Darla, as Goodlooking Tommy suddenly leaned across the table, reaching for the bread.

Out of the corner of my eye I saw a gleam of metal, then there came a deafening bang and a flash of light.

The bullet went in one side of Goodlooking Tommy's head and out the other, blowing blood and brains all over Bud and Darla.

Time seemed to slow down. I saw right in front of me a big revolver with a long barrel. It was pointed at Bud. It felt like I had all the time in the world to reach out and slap down the barrel just as the gun fired again. The bullet blew a hole in the table.

I looked up, and saw a little balding big-nosed guy standing over me; he was wearing a red bowtie and had a bandage over his left eye. He was looking at Bud and screaming: "She was the only thing I ever loved!"

I knew right off it was Vera Vermillion's husband. I lunged at him and wrapped both arms around him and we went to the floor as the gun fired again and the bullet lodged in the ceiling. And then I saw Nello twisting the gun out of Mel Goldberg's hand, and he screamed again: "SHE WAS THE ONLY THING

I EVER LOVED!" But he didn't quite finish the last word because Nello shoved the barrel into his wide-open mouth and all the way down to the back of his throat and pulled the trigger. I could feel his body jump like he'd just got a jolt of electricity, then he was still.

The orchestra had stopped playing and I could hear people running and shouting. I pushed myself up off Mel Goldberg and came to my knees. His unbandaged eye was open and staring up at the ceiling at the peacocks painted there, as a pool of blood, a darker red than his bowtie, began rapidly growing behind his head.

I looked back at the booth. Goodlooking Tommy was slumped across the table, one hand still extended toward the bread. Moe Davis's mouth was ajar and filled up with half-chewed bread; he was gazing down at Goodlooking Tommy, but now he looked over at me and slowly started to chew again. Bud was using one Kleenex after another to wipe the splatters of blood and brain off his face and clothes; he was moving really fast, as if the blood would start burning holes in him if he didn't immediately get it off.

But most of the blood seemed to have landed on Darla. The lustre of her blonde hair was dimmed with blood, and the lit cigarette she was holding in her right hand had actually been extinguished by the blood.

She was sitting there still as a statue. Nothing moving at all except her wildly blinking eyes.

3

The Sunset Strip is on county land between Hollywood and Beverly Hills and thus under the jurisdiction of the Sheriff's Department. Two homicide dicks from the Fairfax station drove up to investigate the killings.

They wore loud sports jackets and powerful cologne; I'd seen them before at the Peacock bar. They barely gave the bodies a glance, told everybody still left in the club to stick around, then disappeared into Stan Tinney's office. Bud and Darla were already in there.

A police photographer, a daffy-looking guy in a derby hat and a green tweed suit, showed up and took some pictures of the bodies. I didn't see him for a while and thought he had left, but then flashes started coming out of the bar, and I saw he was in there with Armilda Lee. She was sitting on a barstool with her pretty legs crossed, and making big dimples for the camera.

After about twenty minutes, the homicide dicks returned. They asked me a few polite questions, and I told them what happened. They had notebooks, but didn't write anything down. Then they said I could go.

I walked out of the club fast. I was in the parking lot and nearly to my car when I heard: "Hey! Danny!"

It was Bud.

He'd changed his clothes, and was all spic-and-span again. He walked up, then solemnly held his hand out. I knew a handshake was a big deal for him.

"Thanks, kid. I owe you."

"What for?"

"You kidding me? You saved my life."

I hadn't really thought of it that way until now. What had happened had just been a reflex. But it was true: I'd helped Bud live and Goldberg die.

"How's Darla?" I said.

"Ah, she'll be all right. She's so soused she probably won't remember a goddamn thing in the morning," and then he smiled a little and gave a puzzled shake of his head. "That Goldberg guy, huh? Getting so worked up about some two-bit stripper."

An ambulance from the coroner's department drove up. Two guys took two stretchers out of the back.

"You got some blood on your clothes," said Bud. "Send me the cleaning bill, okay?"

"Okay."

"Get a good night's sleep. We'll talk tomorrow."

I got in my car, and as I pulled away he yelled: "I got big plans for you!"

I looked in my rearview mirror. Saw him take his handkerchief out, and try to wipe away my handshake.

Instead of turning left, towards Hollywood and home, I turned right, towards the ocean.

It was about a twelve or fifteen mile drive. I highballed down Sunset with all the windows open and the cool night air rushing in and cleaning me like water.

You could tell right where the Strip stopped and Beverly Hills began because all the neon nightlife ended and suddenly great mansions were vaguely visible back in the darkness beyond towering palm trees and high stone walls. Past Beverly Hills were more tony communities, Bel Air and then Brentwood and then Sunset got very hilly and twisty for several miles and trees flashed past in the headlights as I pushed the Packard hard on the curves and the tires squealed and then the road straightened out and I was in Pacific Palisades and I smelled the ocean and then I saw it.

I turned south on the Coast Highway, drove a bit, and then pulled over. I got out, and walked toward the water.

I saw four Mexicans sitting around a fire. They were passing around a bottle of wine. They looked pretty down and out. One of them had a guitar, and was strumming it and softly singing, and you didn't have to understand Spanish to know he was singing one of the saddest songs in the world. He fell silent when I appeared, and all four watched me, a guy in a suit with blood on it limping across the sand, but as soon as I passed out of the flickering circle of firelight I could hear the singer start up again.

I walked down to where the waves had polished the beach and made it slick and shiny. I was glad to get out of my clothes. I waded naked out into the water. It was colder than I expected. I plunged headlong into a wave and came up gasping, but it felt good.

The sky was moonless but stupendously starry. There was one particularly bright star, or maybe it was a planet, hanging just above the rim of the ocean. I swam toward it. It looked pure, sad, and beautiful. It looked like the song had sounded.

After a while I realized that I wasn't much of a swimmer, and that I was fortunate the ocean was pretty calm tonight, and that if I didn't stop swimming toward the star soon I'd never make it back to the beach.

When I got back on terra firma, I couldn't find my clothes. I was thinking maybe I'd been dragged by the current and I'd returned to a different part of the beach, when I saw a dark, oval shape on the sand that I recognized as my hat.

I brushed the sand off, put it on my head, and looked around. The fire was still burning, but the Mexicans had vamoosed.

Not only had they gotten my clothes and shoes but also my wallet and my Smith & Wesson revolver along with its holster. I wondered why they had left the hat. Decided it was probably a reflection of a sly sense of humor.

I looked down Santa Monica ways and could see the lights of the pier and the circling jewel-bright Ferris wheel and I thought about Bombina; then I trudged across the sand back to my car.

Luckily I'd left the keys in it. I drove south on the Coast Highway, then took Santa Monica Boulevard back into Hollywood.

It was interesting driving naked. It was like the dreams I had sometimes of being naked in a public place, except the dreams were always filled with anxiety and shame but tonight it felt just fine. In a way it was more like another type of dream I had, my dreams of flying. I felt exempt from the rules of life as I glided steadily east in my gleaming yellow car.

I was stopped at a red light when a motorcycle cop pulled up beside me. He looked me over, but I guess as far as he could tell I was just a somewhat eccentric fellow wearing a fancy fedora but no shirt, and when the light changed he tipped the bill of his cap to me and roared away.

I turned down La Vista Lane and parked in front of the bungalow court. The street was deserted. No one saw me get out of the car and pad barefooted up the seven steps, but as I was walking between the rows of bungalows I heard someone discreetly clear his throat.

It was Dulwich. He was sitting outside his door on the stoop, smoking his pipe.

"Hello, Dulwich," I said.

"Hello, Danny. Nice night, isn't it?"

I nodded. I didn't stop to chat. Dulwich, for his part, was

careful not to let his face register the least bit of surprise as he watched me and my hat pass by.

4

I saw the postman walk by outside, with Sophie skipping along beside him. She was shouting: "I'm a hit, Abner, I'm a hit!"

"Aw, lemme alone, you crazy kid," said the postman. "And my name ain't Abner!"

I was sitting on my tattered davenport in an undershirt with the *Times*. Matilda, the colored woman that worked for Mrs. Dean, was in the kitchen scrubbing the sink. I'd hired her to come in once a week to clean house and do my laundry.

We'd had several days of very hot weather and I'd gone out and bought a box fan, which was cooling me off but wreaking havoc with reading the paper.

The story I was reading was headlined: "MURDER AND SUICIDE ON SUNSET STRIP," with two smaller headlines: "PEACOCK CLUB SCENE OF HORROR," and "SHER-IFF'S DEPARTMENT BELIEVES LOVE TRIANGLE TO BLAME." It was written by John Hobbs.

"A crazed gunman entered a popular nightspot on the Sunset Strip Thursday night, shot to death one of the customers, then, as hundreds of people looked on in horror, turned the gun on himself. The victim was Thomas McPartland, a 32-year-old life insurance salesman, who was having dinner at the Peacock Club with several friends. Witnesses say the club was packed with patrons when, a little after eight, Mel Goldberg entered the premises, walked up to McPartland's table, screamed 'She was the only one I ever loved!' and shot McPartland through the head with a revolver, killing him instantly. Goldberg then put the gun into his mouth and took his own life.

"Goldberg, 53, was reportedly despondent over the recent death of his wife, Susie, who worked as a strip dancer under the name Vera Vermillion. Goldberg was a self-styled 'talent agent,' though the voluptuous and much younger Vera Vermillion was thought to be his only client. Vera, or Susie, had been ill for many years with a heart damaged by a childhood case of rheumatic fever, and passed away last week.

" 'It looks like the oldest story in the world,' said homicide detective Roy Foster of the Sheriff's Department sadly. 'Mr. McPartland evidently met Vera recently when she tried to buy a life insurance policy from him because she was concerned about her health. It appears that she and the handsome young McPartland then struck up a relationship of an amorous nature. Goldberg found out about it. He went crazy because of jealousy and grief, and the unfortunate young McPartland had to pay the piper.' "

It was the bee's fault. If the bee hadn't flown in the car window and stung Mel Goldberg in the eye, he would have gone up to Lake Arrowhead with Vera, and been able to look after her, and she'd probably still be alive. Him, too. And Good-looking Tommy. The bee killed all three of them.

Somebody knocked. I looked up from the newspaper flapping in the fan and saw a guy on the other side of the screen door.

"Sorry to bother you, mister, but you think you can spare something to eat?"

He was holding his hat in a humble way by the brim with both hands, and looked tired and scruffy.

"Matilda?" I called, and she stuck her head out of the kitchen.

"Yes suh?"

"Would you make this fella something to eat, please?"

"Yes suh."

"Thank you kindly," said the hobo.

He put his hat back on and moved away from the door as Matilda got his food. In a minute or two I heard a sharp female voice: "What are you doing there? You get a move-on or I'm going to call the police!"

Now I saw through the window Mrs. Dean's pinched features and her eyeglasses glinting savagely in the sun. The hobo was attempting to stammer out a reply when Matilda came out of the kitchen holding a plate with a sandwich and an apple on it and a glass of milk. "Tell Mrs. Dean it's all right," I said.

Matilda went to the door and said: "Miz Dean, it's all right. Mr. Landon he tell me to fix him some food."

"Well, Matilda, I'm sure Mr. Landon's not aware that when you start feeding one tramp you only encourage others to come around. They have a way to secretly mark houses to let each other know which ones are hospitable to them and which aren't," and now she addressed the hobo. "And I can assure you the Orange Blossom Bungalow Court is *not* hospitable."

"Okay, okay, lady, keep your shirt on, I'm going," said the hobo, and he started to walk away, but Matilda had pushed through the screen door and it banged shut behind her and she said: "You ain't going no place!"

The hobo and Mrs. Dean both stared at Matilda. She was maybe forty or forty-five, with a pretty but worn-out face, bloodshot brown eyes, and a big behind. She always wore a faded dress and falling-apart men's shoes and a white apron and a green scarf over her hair. I'd seldom ever seen her open her mouth except to mumble some version of yes or no and so I could hardly believe it now when I heard her say: "My grandma that raised me she told me never to turn away nobody that come to your door a-wanting food 'cause it might be a angel in disguise or even Jesus hisself, and even if it ain't, even it it's just a old hobo, you still gotta feed 'im 'cause that's what the Good Book tell us to do. And Miz Dean, you can fire me if you want to but I'm still giving him this here sandwich and this glass of milk."

I'd gotten up and gone to the door by now. "And the apple," I said.

"And the apple. And that's about all I got to say."

Mrs. Dean looked shocked, while the hobo and I were both grinning.

"Well, all right, Matilda," said Mrs. Dean finally. "But as soon as he's finished, please tell him to move along."

Matilda immediately reverted to her usual servile self. "Yessum," she said, as she handed the hobo the plate and the glass.

Mrs. Dean fled back across the courtyard to her bungalow, as Matilda went back inside, and the hobo sat down on my little stoop to enjoy his meal.

He took a drink of milk, crunched into the apple, then lifted up the top piece of bread and examined his sandwich.

"My favorite!" he said. "Baloney and cheese!"

5

Sunday morning I was summoned to the Hollywood Y.M.C.A. Bud liked to have meetings in the steamroom there. I took my clothes off in the locker room and wrapped a towel around my middle. Nucky Williams was sitting in a chair outside the steamroom keeping guard and giving his teeth a thorough going-over with a toothpick. "Hello, hero," he said with a nasty grin. I didn't say a word, and went into the steamroom.

Bud was sitting with some guy I didn't recognize. Bud saw me and lifted a finger to indicate he'd be with me in a minute. The guy was balding and practically chinless and had soft flabby breasts. He was talking fast, with passionate gestures, and Bud seemed to be listening intently. Then the guy stood up and stuck out his hand; Bud, though, pretended not to notice it. Now the guy turned and walked past me, dripping with sweat and smiling like things had gone just great.

Bud motioned me over.

"Interesting guy," he said as I sat down beside him.

"Who is he?"

"Harry Seaburg. He's an inventor. He invented a machine that electrocutes hot dogs."

"Why would you want to electrocute a hot dog?"

"It's a cooking method. Cooks hot dogs faster than you can say Jack Robbins, he said. That way you'll never have to keep a customer waiting while you boil up a new pot of dogs. He says a year from now everybody in America'll be eating electrocuted hot dogs and he's giving me a chance to get in on the ground floor. Nice of him, ain't it?"

"Does his machine have a name?"

"The Electrodog. He's bringing it over to the club tomorrow to demonstrate. You oughta come by. I wanna get your opinion about it."

"I'll be there."

I'd never seen Bud without a shirt before. Even when we were sitting around by the pool he always wore a shirt and long pants. I was surprised by how puny he looked: skinny arms and a sunken chest and a soft little belly. He had quite a bit of chest hair, but it could have used some Grey Gone. There was a roundish scar about an inch wide on the lower left part of his stomach.

"So how you feeling?" he said, and he looked at my dent. "How's them headaches?"

"They're better. I'm feeling good."

"You been seeing Dr. Bartlestone?"

"Not lately. But last time I saw him he said he was pleased with my progress."

"Him and me both. You know, I knew it was the right thing, bringing you into the business," and then he added: "*Back* into the business. You can write your own ticket now, Danny. After what you done for me. Whatever you wanna do, I'll help you get set up. Whores. Numbers. You like the fights, don't you? There's a lot of dough to be made in fights. Or what about the hot-bond racket?"

"What's that?"

"It's a new thing I'm doing. We heist government bonds from post offices and banks back east, and sell 'em out here. We got some dicks in the Bunco Squad working with us. It's a nice way to make some jack without getting your hands too dirty."

"Sounds interesting. But I been thinking about it lately. I'm not sure I'm cut out for this."

"For what?"

"You know—the underworld."

Bud laughed, and shook his head.

" 'The underworld.' You been seeing too many of them Edward G. Robertson movies. There ain't an underworld and an upperworld. There's just the world. Legit and illegit's just two sides of the same nickel. We're businessmen, we're judges, we're wheelers, we're dealers, we're killers, we're everything. You think the Chink that runs the Chinese laundry don't cheat his customers ever chance he gets? And you think if the Chink accidentally gives one of his customers too much change, the customer's gonna say: 'Hey, Mr. Chink, you gave me too much change, here's your money back'? But you want me to set you up in the Chinese laundry business? I'll do it. You can run a whole fucking chain of Chinese laundries. Like I said. You name it. It's up to you."

Then Bud gave me such a long, penetrating look it made me start squirming around a little. Like my toe was hooked up to the Electrodog.

"I need someone near me I can trust. Keep this under your hat, but it ain't going so good with Schnitter. Not with Hanley neither. And I think the mayor's mad at me. That little trip up to the lake blew up in my fucking face. And now I think they're all conspiring together to get rid of me. So I got my guys around me, sure. Like Nucky sitting outside the door right now. But think about it. All my guys are packing. Any one of 'em could knock me off. Who's gonna guard me from my guards? It's like that Roman guy, Julius Caesar. It was his best buddy, Brutal, that slipped in the shiv."

I knew I ought to say something like: "You can trust *me*, Bud," but all I did was nod. My eyes drifted down to the scar on his stomach.

"What happened there?"

He took a look at the scar himself, smiling crookedly. "I got shot. That's where the slug come out." He twisted around, pointed out another, smaller scar on his back. "That's where it went in. S.O.B. shot me in the back."

"Who was it?"

"Night watchman at a warehouse down at the Battery. I was trying to heist about twenty cases of canned anchovies. I thought I'd cased the job out real good. The night watchman was this old redheaded mick that'd spend the first half of ever night getting drunk and the second half pounding the pillow. But I didn't know the mick didn't show up that night and they had another guy working. This other guy didn't give me no chance at all. Just plugged me as soon as he seen me walking away with some of them anchovies."

"How old were you?"

"Sixteen. Just a kid. But I'd been on my own—I'd been part of the *underworld*—ever since I was eleven. That's when my mother died."

"What about your father?"

"I never knew who my old man was. My mother never talked about him."

"What was your mother like?"

"Why all the questions?"

I shrugged. "I'm just curious about you, I guess."

He seemed pleased by that. "Yeah? Well, you can ask me any question you wanna. But I ain't gonna guarantee you I ain't gonna lie." He laughed. "You asked me about my mother. She was nice. Pretty. She never laid a hand on me in anger. I didn't have no brothers and sisters, so it was just her and me. But I didn't see her much. She was working all the time. She worked in one of them places they had 500 girls sewing on sewing machines sixteen hours a day. But then she got sick. I took care of her. I seen a lot of her then." He fell silent, and then: "I don't wanna talk no more about my mother, if you don't mind."

"What happened after you got shot?"

"Well, I dropped them anchovies and run on outa the warehouse. Then I was running down the street. Then I guess I musta passed out, and somebody musta found me and drug me off to the hospital, 'cause that's where I woke up.

"Maybe I'da been better off if I got left on the street. That hospital was a crummy joint. Blood and puke all over the floor. People moaning and screaming. The doctors and nurses didn't give a shit about you, they just wanted to get you outa there 'cause you didn't have any dough.

"Some cops come by and wanted to know how I got shot. I didn't tell 'em nothing. Then another cop come by, he used to know my mother. He was nice to her and me when she was sick. He told me this gang of wops was looking for me, they knew it was me that done the warehouse job and they figured I was trying to muscle in on their territory. He said I was hotter than a dime-store pistol and I oughta get outa town as soon as I could.

"Well, I knew these wops, they'd already killed a good friend of mine, so I didn't need no extra encouragement. I told one of them nurses I wanted my clothes, and I just walked outa there. Nobody tried to stop me. They was glad to see me go.

"I had a girlfriend. She was a year younger than me. She was a real smart girl, had a lotta class; tell the truth, I don't know what she was doing with somebody like me.

"She was still going to high school. So I went over to her school and waited around. Blood was coming through my shirt and it was colder than shit and windy and it was starting to snow. Then she come out, and I told her what happened and how I needed to get outa town, and you know how broads are, she started crying and begging me not to leave her. I told her I didn't have no choice and I needed some dough. She only had something like two bits on her, but she said she knew where her old man kept some dough stashed away at home.

"I waited around till she come back with the money. It was about forty bucks. She brung a suitcase too. She was planning on going with me. I told her that wasn't a good idea, but I promised I'd come back for her when the heat was off.

"So I went down to the train station. All the time I was still bleeding and feeling like I was about to pass out. But I was just scared to death of them wops. I wanted to put as much distance as I could between me and them and still be in America, so that's how I wound up here," and he laughed. "All 'cause of them anchovies. And I don't even like fucking anchovies."

"You ever see her again? Your girlfriend?"

"What do you think?"

There were some guys in the other corner of the steamroom and suddenly they started laughing at something. We looked at them, and they were dim in the steam, faded like an old photograph, and suddenly I had this feeling as though it was a hundred years in the future and everybody in the steamroom was long dead, and Darla was dead too, and Dulwich, and Sophie, and everybody else in the world and every dog and cat and horse and cow and fish and bird, so why did anything we said or did or thought or felt really matter?

"I heard some shit," said Bud. "About you and Darla. Up at the lake." I started to say something, but he held up his hands to stop me. "You don't have to splain nothing to me. I know you and her ain't up to any monkeyshines, 'cause you never would do that to me. Plus you're too smart. But you got any idea who mighta started this shit?"

I thought it best to keep my mouth shut. I shrugged.

"Well, I'll find out. Eventually I always find out everything. But understand something. This ain't about you and Darla. It's about politics. Politics ain't just like when you're electing a mayor, it's all the time and everywhere. People see you rising in the organization, so they wanna throw in a banana peel and hope you slip on it. I just thought you oughta know."

"Okay, Bud. Thanks."

"I'm leaving town for a couple days. On business. Maybe you could take Darla out someplace. Show her a good time. She's been hiding out in her room with a bottle ever since Thursday night. That ain't healthy for her. She's turning into a regular boozehound."

"Okay. I'll see what I can do."

6

That night I dreamed I was pissing my name in the snow. Since I wasn't sure what my name was, I was paying close attention, but I couldn't make heads or tails of it, it was like I was able to write my name but not read it.

A dog was barking, but then it stopped. I looked out toward the half-frozen river.

The buildings of the great city across the river rose black and jagged, seeming more like mountains than buildings. The starving dog I had seen on the ice was gone. I realized it must have broken through.

Panic surged through me. I ran out on the ice. It was clear like glass. I looked down and in the dark water I saw Vera Vermillion.

She was naked. She was on her back. She was looking up at me. Her auburn hair was floating around her head in a snaky tangle. The current was carrying her, and her fingernails were clawing at the ice and making white streaks in it. Shouting her name, I ran to keep up. But she was moving along faster and faster, till finally she was borne away. I felt like I was about to burst with grief. I fell facedown on the ice, and began to cry.

After a while I felt a hand on my shoulder. I looked up. It was my mother.

She was young, maybe twenty-five. She had coppery hair and light-blue eyes. She was smiling at me.

I sat up. She was wearing just a thin summer frock that left her arms bare, and I said: "Aren't you cold?"

"No. Are you?"

"No."

"Don't cry about the dog. It's all right."

"It didn't drown?"

She shook her head. Her face was so beautiful, I couldn't get enough of looking at it. I noticed a faint, crescent-shaped scar on her left cheek. "What happened there?" I asked.

But she just smiled a little, and shook her head again, and laid a finger on my lips. An overpowering drowsiness possessed me. I lay back down, and my eyes closed. I was curled up on the hard ice of a wintry river, but I felt as comfortable as if I were inside on a soft rug in front of a blazing fireplace. I was basking in the warmth of *her.*

Darla didn't look like somebody that had been on a five-day bender. She came down the stairs in a curve-hugging white silk gown with a halter neck and patches of black beads over the left breast and left hip. Three plump pearls dangled from each earlobe, and she was wearing a pearl bracelet on her left wrist.

"New dress?" I said.

"Mm hm. Joan Crawford wore a dress just like this in *Letty Lynton.*"

Anatoly, Bud's eight-fingered butler, held the front door open for us. "You are pretty as princess," he said to her. "On snowy night. In St. Petersburg. Long ago."

"Why, thank you, Anatoly," said Darla with a gracious princess-like nod.

Teddy Bump and Tommy were hanging around outside, smoking and passing a pint of Haig & Haig back and forth. Tommy looked pasty-faced and haggard; even though they used to fight all the time, he'd taken the death of Goodlooking Tommy hard. Teddy glared at us from under his crooked eyebrows.

"Now you boys behave yourselves," said Darla as we walked past.

Teddy looked like he was about to bust he wanted so badly to say something, but all he did was throw his cigarette down and grind it out under his shoe.

I opened the door of my Packard for Darla and she hitched

up her gown and got in. We drove down the sloping driveway to the front gate. Willie Cooney was sitting in a chair reading the funnies with a flashlight. Everybody called him Willie the Coon, though not usually to his face, since he heartily hated Negroes. He had a nose that looked like it had been broken about a dozen times and a jutting jaw and shoulders a yard wide. He'd spend all night at the gate, and I knew there was at least one more guy somewhere out there in the dark patrolling the walls; Bud had brought in extra guys to guard the house when he got back from Lake Arrowhead.

Willie gave us a lazy wave and hit a button, and the tall iron gate rattled open.

We drove down the hill and across Franklin and continued south. It was nearly midnight, and there wasn't much traffic. Los Angeles was mostly a town that went to bed early.

"Ever notice something funny about Teddy's eyebrows?" I said.

"Sure. They're pasted on."

"They're fake?"

"Yeah. And he wears a wig and false eyelashes too. Bud told me about it. He's bald as a billiard ball all over his body. He was born that way. Some kinda rare disease."

"No hair on his arms, or legs, or—?"

"Nowhere. Not even down around his you-know-what."

We both had a good laugh about it. Now Darla had me pull into a filling station to buy her some Lucky Strikes. When I returned to the car, my heart jumped as I heard a gunshot. But it was just a backfire from a red Buick moving slowly by on the street.

Darla touched my hand to steady it as I lit a cigarette for her. She didn't seem to have been drinking, which I was glad of. She was in a good mood, because she was going to sing tonight.

The place we were going was on Adams Boulevard, a little

south of downtown. She said it was one of the first joints she sang in after she'd arrived from Aurora. I asked her what it was called but she said it didn't have a name.

We crossed San Pedro. We were in a neighborhood of once-fine houses that had mostly gone to seed. Now Darla told me to pull over.

"That's it," she said, nodding at a gloomy mansion that didn't seem to have a single light on inside.

"I don't think anybody's home," I said. "Or maybe they've already gone to sleep."

Darla laughed. "They're in there. And they're not asleep."

We were lit up from behind as another car parked. A very dressed-up man and woman got out of a long white Marmon and walked toward the mansion. Darla and I followed.

The couple looked a bit odd, since the woman was about a head and a half taller than the man. We all went up the front steps, and the man knocked on a heavy wooden door. A panel was pulled back, and the stern face of a Negro appeared.

"Open sesame," said the man in a booming deep voice as the woman giggled.

"Well, if it ain't Earl and Shirley," said the Negro.

"Hello, Otis," said Darla.

The Negro's face was split by a big grin and two gold teeth gleamed at us.

"Darla," he said, and opened the door.

We stepped inside. It was nearly as dark inside as out. By the light of a lone candle, I saw that Otis looked like a character out of *The Thief of Baghdad.* He was wearing a turban, a loose silk blouse, and baggy silk pants, and had a wide curving sword hanging from his side. He was about six and a half feet tall.

"Little Brother told me you was coming," he said.

"How have you been?" said Darla.

"The same. Everything been zackly the same round here

cepting you ain't been here but now you back here everything zackly the same."

We walked into a cavernous room lit only by a few candles, the ceiling barely visible in the darkness. The floor was covered in colorful Persian rugs, and all the windows were hidden behind heavy purple drapes. There were several low sofas and low tables, and plush pillows were scattered about on the rugs and people sat or reclined on the sofas and among the pillows. The air was thick with the smoke of cigarettes and reefers.

A handsome young colored man, wearing a white dinner jacket, a red shirt, and a black bowtie, sat at a baby grand playing a lazy jazzy tune. He gave Darla a wink and a wave.

We sat down on one of the sofas. Three waiters, all colored and all dressed like Otis, were moving amongst the customers with trays of drinks. Darla ordered a cherry bomb, and I asked for the same, whatever it was.

I looked over the clientele. Several Negro men were cuddled up with white women, one hefty Negro woman was sitting on a portly white man's lap, and two white women were passionately smooching. Darla was enjoying my obvious amazement.

"You ever seen a joint like this before?" she said.

"Nope. Looks like you and me and Earl and Shirley are about the only regular couples here."

"Take a look at Earl and Shirley and tell me what they're doing."

They were sitting on another sofa. Earl was lighting Shirley's cigarette; now he applied the flame to a big cigar sticking out of his mouth.

"Earl's lighting a cigar."

"Unh unh. That's Shirley. Earl's the one in the dress."

I looked again. I could see it now. A guy dressed up like a broad and vice versa. I laughed.

The waiter came back with our cherry bombs, which turned

out to be glasses of champagne with cherries in them. Darla ate her cherry, then asked for mine. As I handed it over, Little Brother, the proprietor of the place, appeared. He was a short, light-skinned colored guy dressed like his waiters and doorman except he wasn't wearing a turban. His head was shaved and he had a gold earring in his right ear. He hugged Darla and kissed her on the cheek then presented me with a very limp hand to shake as Darla introduced us.

"Oh, he's cute, sugar," he said to Darla. "If I was you I'd go out and find a judge and get married right now."

"Marriage just means three things," said Darla. "Diapers, dirty dishes, and dinner."

Little Brother laughed extravagantly, then sort of twirled away, at the same time clapping his hands above his head.

"Ladies? Gentlemen? Look who we got here with us tonight! Darla! Yeah, Darla's back! And if we ask her real nice, she might sing us a song or two! With her sweet, bird-like voice!"

The candle-lit couples applauded softly for Darla. She finished off her cherry bomb and handed me the glass and walked over to the piano. She talked briefly with the piano player, then started singing "One Night of Love"—

> When at the break of dawn
> I find my lover gone
> I'll whisper with a smile
> I've lived a little while—
> I've known one night of love.

She seemed in her white gown to be a perfect creature of the smoke and the flickering light. I looked around the room, and saw people looking lost and dreamy as they listened, as if she was a witch casting a wonderful spell. Earl and Shirley got up and started dancing, with Shirley's face buried in Earl's false bosom. The two white women seemed unaware of everything else as they continued to kiss and caress each other; one of them had a cool, aloof beauty that seemed very familiar.

Little Brother came over and gave me a glass filled with a clear green liquid.

"Try this."

I took a sip. It tasted like liquid licorice.

"Not bad. What is it?"

"Absinthe."

"That woman over there? The one in the brown skirt? Is that Greta Garbo?"

Little Brother took a look. "Maybe. Maybe not. When people come in here, they check their names at the door. I'm glad you like the absinthe. It makes the heart grow fonder."

Darla sang more songs, and I drank more glasses of absinthe. I began to see things I wasn't sure were actually there. A gigantic blue and red and green parrot appeared on the arm of the sofa, squawked "So long!" eleven times, then flapped away and disappeared up a staircase. Greta Garbo gave me a sinister smile, then stuck out her unnaturally long tongue at me. A colored guy in a three-piece chesterfield suit was on a sofa with his hand up the dress of a writhing white girl. A big dark dick began to lift up out of his lap like a cobra out of a basket. Bats crawled across the purple curtains.

A waiter approached with still another glass of absinthe, and I raised my arms like a man who was being beaten. "No! No more."

Little Brother sat down beside me. "How you doing, sugar?"

My tongue felt like a dead slab of meat as I mumbled some stuff that even I didn't understand.

Little Brother laughed and said: "I didn't know you spoke Chinese."

I laughed too, a weak, wheezing, old man's laugh. My head started tipping over, it was like it bore no relationship to my shoulders. I felt spit gathering in the corner of my mouth, getting ready to turn into drool.

Little Brother moved very close to my face; he seemed to have the overlarge predatory eyes of an owl. "That girl over there? Singing by the piano? She's very near and dear to me. You understand what I'm saying?"

My head lolled around loosely at the end of my stalk-like neck as I tried to nod.

"She seems to trust you, for some reason. So you take good care of her. You don't, and Little Brother's gonna come looking for you."

He kept talking, but I couldn't hear him anymore because an enormous roaring filled my ears, and then all went black as though I was swept into a railroad tunnel.

8

Clackety clack.

Next thing I knew I was outside the mansion of Little Brother throwing up lavishly and greenly on the lawn.

"Ha ha!" I heard. "Har har!"

I looked up from my bent-over hands-on-knees position, and saw Darla a few feet away, watching me with concern; near her was the white man who'd had the colored woman on his lap. He was an older guy, with a bushy white walrus moustache. He had his hands on his hips and was laughing at me. He said, with an English accent: "Your friend's giving it a bit of the old heave-ho, what?"

"You gonna be okay, Danny?" asked Darla.

I nodded. I noticed it was dawn. I took my handkerchief out and wiped off my mouth. The guy handed Darla something.

"My card, my dear."

" 'Anthony Goodall,' " read Darla. " 'Motion picture producer.' "

"I am not one of those fly-by-night soi-disant producers, ask anyone in the city about Tony Goodall and I am confident they will tell that I am, as you Americans call it, the real McCoy."

"I know the *real* real McCoy," I said.

Tony Goodall laughed again. "Yes, you poor fellow, I'm sure you do." He turned back to Darla. "By dint of long practice, my eyes have become, for all practical purposes, motion picture cameras, and as I gazed upon you tonight I thought I detected that elusive sidereal quality that we are all in quest of. My next film and the next of Ronald Coleman happen to be one and the same. While fox hunting, the Prince of Wales takes a nasty spill from his horse, suffers a knock on his noggin, and develops amnesia. He wanders off on his own. The entire country's looking for him, of course, but somehow, the script's still a bit weak on this point, he winds up in America. He finds work as a common laborer, and falls in love with a very beautiful girl who works as a maid. Inevitably, one morning he awakes and remembers who he is. His dilemma is this: He knows his responsibility is to return to England to be who he was born to be. But if he does so, he'll have to give up the girl, since obviously a mere maid is unfit to be the wife of the future king. It is an impossible choice between duty and beauty."

"So what does he do?" said Darla.

"Oh, I don't know, love, the writers, such as they are, are still hashing all that out. At any rate, that vile horrible witch Joan Crawford *wants* the role of the girl but over my dead body. Ronnie and I are looking for a fresh face. Perhaps you are she."

"Funny you should mention Joan Crawford," said Darla as she gave her gown a pluck.

"Yes, isn't it? Well, I must toddle. I do hope you call. You have nothing to lose but your chains. Ha ha!" And then to me: "I once knew a man whose liver was rotting out who produced vomitus of precisely that color. I'd go to a doctor if I were you."

Goodall doffed his hat to Darla and walked off toward his car. Darla stuck out her arms and closed her eyes and gave a mewing half yawn as she stretched luxuriously.

"What a night. You ready to go, Danny?"

We got in the Packard and drove away from Little Brother's. The days had been hot, but now it was cool. A bit of morning mist hung in the air. We had Los Angeles largely but not completely to ourselves. Plenty of birds were out. A kid in knickers on a ramshackle bike was expertly flinging newspapers at the front steps of houses. A milkman dressed in white was carrying white bottles of milk away from a white milk truck.

Darla was scrutinizing herself with a frown in her compact mirror. "Well, my face doesn't look very fresh right now. Matter of fact, it looks like hell." She snapped shut the compact and returned it to her purse. Then she looked at Tony Goodall's card, tore it in half, and threw it out the window.

"Why'd you do that?"

"Oh, he just wants to screw me."

"Maybe he was on the level."

"What if he was? I was in a movie once. A guy a lot like Tony Goodall got me the role. I had one line in one scene. This mean little kid let loose a bunch of white mice at a fancy party. I had to jump up on a table and say: 'Take me home at once, Alfred!' Then I fell backwards into a bowl of punch.

"They shot the scene again and again. And all these white mice were supposed to be dropping down the fronts of women's dresses and getting in their hair and crawling up guys' trouser legs, and these stuck-up people were running around and screaming and going nuts and it's supposed to be hilarious. And usually I'm scared of mice, but these mice were just so cute. Little pink ears and eyes and feet and tails. And they were getting stepped on, and thrown against walls, and I saw one dragging itself along the floor leaving a trail of blood, and I found another one drowned in the punchbowl. And the director just kept screaming: 'More mice, more mice!' I was nearly hysterical by the time it was all over.

"I know, they were just mice. But it wasn't right, what happened. Nobody cared about the mice. Somebody should've looked out for them."

"So 'cause you had one bad experience, you don't wanna be in the movies?"

She shrugged, and lit up a cigarette. We drove along in silence awhile. My head was killing me. Since I didn't have any water I just chewed up two aspirin and swallowed them. Which tickled my throat, which made me start coughing, which made me feel sick again.

I pulled the car over and jumped out and ran over to the side of the street and threw up in some brownish, patchy grass. We were in a neighborhood of shabby warehouses and machine shops; I saw chalked on the side of one building: "END POVERTY IN CALIFORNIA. VOTE FOR SINCLAIR."

As I walked back, I saw a car about a block and a half behind us, stopped in the street with the engine running, dark smoke drifting up from the tailpipe. It was a red Buick. Two guys were in the front seat, but they were too far away for me to see what they looked like.

I got in my car and drove on. In the rearview mirror I could see the Buick driving on too. I made a left. In a few moments I saw the Buick making the left behind us.

"Don't turn around," I said. "Just look in the mirror. I think we're being followed."

Darla took a look. "Jesus. Are you sure?"

"Pretty sure."

"You got your gun, right?"

Wrong. The Mexicans had my gun, and I hadn't got around to getting a new one.

"Right."

"Who do you think they are?"

"I don't know."

I turned right at the next block, and the Buick obligingly followed.

"Shouldn't we go fast?" said Darla. "Try and lose 'em?"

"Maybe it's better if we don't let 'em know we know they're there."

"But Danny, what if they're about to kill us, or kidnap us?"

"I think they've been following us since last night. I'm pretty sure I saw the same car when we stopped at the gas station to get cigarettes. So if they wanted to hurt us, they probably would've already done it. I think they're just watching us. They wanna see where we go, what we're up to."

"It's Bud. They're reporting back to Bud."

"Most likely."

"Bastard."

She started puffing away furiously at her cigarette, like the cigarette was Bud and she was trying to smoke him up.

"He's completely nuts. I'd leave today, but I know he'd come after me. Betty, the cigarette girl? He had her killed just 'cause she took another *job*. And there was this other girl, this Mexican girl. She was his girlfriend for a while, but finally she'd had enough, and she took off and went back to Mexico. He sent his creeps after her, and they brought her back. She was on her knees, begging for her life. And he shot her. Right in the Peacock Club."

"Was her name Emperatriz?"

"Yeah. So you know about her."

"I didn't know she was dead."

"I know the same thing would happen to me if I ever tried to leave him." Now she gave a long sigh. "Look, I don't wanna drag you into my mess. It's all my fault, and now I'm paying for it. Forget I said anything."

The Buick continued to hang back at a discreet distance all the way to Bud's house. I stopped in front of the gate and beeped. Willie the Coon peered out, unkempt and unshaven; he was peeling a banana, and, through the bars of the gate, looked like he lived in a zoo.

The gate slid open, and I drove up to the house. Anatoly was out by the swimming pool, at the artificial beach. He was barefoot and wearing an undershirt. He was feeding the seagull. He tossed up scraps of food and the gull, flapping around on its ten-foot tether, snapped up the scraps in mid-air. Anatoly seemed to be talking to the gull, while the gull was making screechy cries. Both man and gull seemed happy.

Darla and I went in the house. I could hear somebody snoring somewhere. I walked with Darla to the stairs.

"Thanks for taking me out, Danny. I had a great time."

"Yeah, me too. But I think next time I'll lay off the absinthe."

She smiled. She pulled her pearl earrings off.

"I can't wait to crawl into bed."

She was standing on the second stair, so her head was a little higher than mine. And now she bent down a little and put her hand on the side of my face and kissed me on the mouth for about three seconds. Then she turned, and I watched her hips in the Joan Crawford gown sway their way up the stairs.

I wandered off in search of the snoring. I found Teddy and Tommy asleep in the room where we'd had the party. Tommy was slumped in an armchair, and Teddy was sprawled on his back on a couch. Teddy was the snorer.

I stood above him and looked down at him. His mouth was wide-open. I ripped off one of his fake eyebrows and dropped it in his mouth and walked swiftly toward the door. I heard choking and gagging noises behind me, and then I was outside where the sun was just coming up over the barbwired wall.

9

"I used to doubt the existence of fairies too," said Dulwich to me and Sophie—this in response to Sophie's declaration that she didn't believe in God, ghosts, Santa Claus, fairies, or anything else. "But a summer I spent in Ireland when I was eleven caused me to doubt my doubt.

"I was staying with my uncle and aunt, who lived a few miles outside the little town of Foxford. There was a girl that worked there as a maid, her name was Kitty. A wide, freckled face, a bit on the podgy side, very warm, always laughing and filled with garrulous stories. She was a firm believer in the fairy folk, and she told me about a phenomenon known as the 'lone sod.' That occurs when a place is particularly precious to the fairies, and they cast a spell on the unwary trespassing traveler which makes him completely befuddled and lost and unable to find his way out of the place, until the fairies choose to let him go. She said the only way to break the spell is to take off your coat and turn it inside out and put it back on, but such a maneuver works less than half the time. There was a field just a short distance down the road that had a huge gnarled thorn tree growing in the middle, and Kitty said it was a fairy tree and that I should avoid the field lest I fall victim to the 'lone sod.'

"Well, of course I just considered Kitty to be an ignorant superstitious Irish girl and thought no more about it. Then a few days later came a day of great heat."

"Like today," said Sophie. We were walking back from a

drugstore on Melrose, with ice cream cones we were hurrying to consume before they dripped onto the baking street.

"Like today. My uncle was a very quiet chap who had lost a leg to an infection caused by a Zulu spear at the Battle of Isandhlwana, and he seemed forever to be brooding on its loss. The only time his spirits seemed to brighten a bit was when he talked about his boyhood, which he obviously saw as some cloudless prelapsarian paradise."

Sophie frowned and said: "Speak English."

"My uncle smiled as he told me about a stream that flowed out of the Ox Mountains, it had a deliciously cool pool embowered by blackthorns where he and his young chums used to bathe on hot summer days such as this.

"It seemed like the proper place to go, so I got directions from my uncle and set out on foot. The road looped around the aforementioned field. I could see the thorn tree standing tall and dark and twisted in its center. The field was surrounded by a fence, and in the fence was a gate, and there was a footpath that led across the field. It seemed silly to walk all the way around the field when I could walk directly across it, so I went through the gate and closed it behind me.

"The path seemed to belie Kitty's claims, since it seemed unlikely that if the local folk were afraid of being kidnapped by the fairies they would have crossed the field often enough to have ever worn a path there. Or so it seemed at least to my logical, eleven-year-old mind. The path passed near the thorn tree, and I looked it over as I walked by. Its branches were moving a little in a breeze, which would have been unremarkable if there had actually been a breeze. But the air hung heavy and still. Yet still the branches moved.

"I quickened my pace, and reached the other side of the field without further incident. A stile was there."

"What's a stile?" I said.

"Steps over a fence. Beyond the fence I saw the road. I climbed up the stile, but as I crossed over onto the other side I felt a strange sensation in the pit of my stomach and a ripple of dizziness. But it all lasted just a moment and then I was fine.

"I was puzzled though to find myself, not back on the road, but in another field. I set off down another path, and then I saw before me another large twisted thorn tree, and then I realized, with some consternation, that I *wasn't* walking across another field but was walking back into the *same* field. I turned around, went back to the stile, crossed over the fence again and—well I'm sure you can guess that the experience repeated itself exactly.

"I decided to give up the whole idea of a short cut and to depart the field at the same place I entered. The day seemed preternaturally still as I crossed the field again. I heard no buzz of bug nor chirp of bird. The thorn still seemed to be vaguely gesticulating to me as I walked by.

"I was relieved to see the gate again, and I opened it and passed through. But again I felt the dizziness and the strange feeling in my stomach, and I was dismayed but not altogether surprised to find myself still on the wrong side of the gate and trapped within the field.

"Then I heard human voices. A rickety cart was approaching on the road, pulled by a decrepit donkey. In the cart were an old man and a young boy. I called out to them, but they didn't seem to hear me. I called out louder, and jumped up and down and waved my arms. The donkey glanced my way, but the man and the boy just continued to talk to each other, and I watched the cart trundle on down the road and out of sight.

"At this point I began to panic. It was, as I said, very hot. I felt thirstier than I'd ever felt in my life. And I feared that I would be a prisoner here forever, a poor damned creature roaming from one side of the field to the other ceaselessly seeking an exit that didn't exist. I turned toward the thorn, which was rising up dark and terrible against the blazing blue sky, and I cupped my hands around my mouth and shouted towards it: 'I'm sorry I didn't believe in you! I believe in you now! Please let me go!' And then I tried the gate again, but unfortunately the result was the same."

A mangy brown and white beagle with an oozing sore on its leg had been limping along behind us; now I gave it the soggy remnants of my cone, which it chomped up ecstatically. "But why didn't you just turn your coat inside out?" asked Sophie. "Like Kitty said."

"I wasn't wearing a coat, but I did do this: I took off every article of clothing I was wearing, turned it inside out, and put it back on."

Sophie giggled. "What happened?"

"It worked like a charm. I passed through the gate, and found myself back out on the road, whereupon I resumed my journey to the stream. Taking the long way around, of course."

"Were you still wearing your clothes inside out?" said Sophie.

"No, of course not. I undressed and then redressed properly."

Sophie gave Dulwich a squinty, sideways look. "Did all that really happen?"

He tousled her hair. "I only lie to myself, Sophie. Never to others."

We walked by some kids who'd erected forts made out of lawn furniture and were throwing firecrackers at each other. Today was the Fourth of July.

"Danny and I have a surprise for you when we get back," said Dulwich.

"Really? What kind of surprise?"

"It's a birthday present," I said.

"But my birthday was two weeks ago."

"Uh oh. Looks like we screwed up, Dulwich."

"Indeed. We've made a dreadful error. What do you think we

should do?"

"Take it back to the store, I guess. Get a refund."

"Yes, I do believe that's the correct course of action."

"You better not," said Sophie grimly.

In Dulwich's bungalow Sophie tore the wrapping paper and ribbons off a box then lifted up the top. She pushed aside some tissue paper and said: "Shoes."

"Tap-dancing shoes," I said.

" 'Split clog' tap-dancing shoes," said Dulwich. "The very best one can get, according to the helpful young lady who sold them to us. Beechwood soles and hollow wooden heels that produce a very special sound."

Sophie looked beside herself with excitement as she took her mary janes off and slipped on the gleaming red tap shoes.

"Where'd you get them?"

"This store called Capezio's," I said. "It's on Hollywood and Vine. The salesgirl said Bojangles Robinson gets all his shoes there."

Tinker Bell jumped into the shoe box, and started clawing at the tissue paper. Sophie began clattering around the room in her shoes.

"We guessed at the size," said Dulwich. "Do they fit all right?"

"Perfect. I can run away to New York and get famous now. Like Ruby Keeler."

"No running away," I said.

"You can come too. And Dulwich. And Tinker. We can all run away together."

"That charming sound you're producing," said Dulwich, "reminds me that I really ought to sit down in front of my typewriter and get to work."

"How's your story going?" I said.

He sighed. "Worse and worse, I'm afraid. The patient barely has a pulse."

" 'Scuse me, Tinker," said Sophie as she evicted the cat from the box then gathered up the wrapping paper and the ribbons and her old shoes.

"It's a wonderful present," she said. "It's the most wonderful present I've ever gotten."

Later I sat on my davenport in the living room as the day ended and the dusk seeped in. I'd bought a new Philco radio with some of my gambling winnings, and *Betty and Bob* was playing on it, but I wasn't really listening. I was trying to remember where I'd left my life like a man tries to remember where he's left his hat.

I heard someone walking down the sidewalk, then Sophie appeared at the door. She squinted in through the screen.

"Danny? You in there?"

"Yeah. Come in."

"How come you're sitting in the dark? Why don't you turn on a light?"

"Why should I?"

"I don't know."

She walked around, looking the room over like she'd never seen it before. Then she came over to the davenport, perched on the edge of it. She fidgeted, sighed, tugged at her hair, knocked her knees together. Finally she said: "Thanks again. For the shoes."

"You're welcome."

"I always have so much fun when I'm with you guys. Everybody's always laughing and joking around. How come everybody can't be like that all the time?"

"Beats me. Things just don't work that way, I guess."

Sophie chewed on her lower lip. Betty and Bob blabbered on.

"Knock knock," said Sophie.

"Who's there?"

"Shelby."

"Shelby who?"

"Shelby coming around the mountain when she comes," sang Sophie.

"That's pretty funny."

"Yeah. Do you know any jokes?"

"I don't think so."

"Danny?"

"Yeah?"

"Would you mind if . . . I sat closer to you?"

I was a little surprised, but said: "No. Of course not."

Then she nestled up against me, and I lifted up my arm and put it around her shoulders, and she put her arm across my chest. I could feel her heart tapping fast against her ribs. There seemed to be nothing to her. When you hold a baby bird in the palm of your hand it seems to have no weight, it's like a handful of feathery air, and it felt kind of that way to hold Sophie.

"You remember that brush you gave me?" she asked.

"The pink one?"

"No, the polkadot one, you dummy. How many brushes have you given me? Yes, the pink one."

"What about it?"

"Every night before I go to bed, I brush my hair with it."

"Yeah?"

"Yeah." And then: "I like you *so much.*"

"Well, I like you too."

"A lot?"

"A whole lot."

She sighed; then her grubby-fingernailed hand began to rub my chest, then it slid down to the front of my pants, and she started feeling around for my you-know-what.

I was shocked. I shoved her hand away. I said: "What the hell are you doing?!"

We both sat bolt upright, and stared at each other, both aghast.

"But—I thought—you wanted me to."

"Are you nuts? You're just a kid!"

"Okay. Quit yelling at me. You bastard."

Eyes aglitter with tears, she jumped up and ran out the door. Mrs. Dean had recently replaced the old slack rusted spring on the screen door with a brand-new shiny tightly coiled spring, and it yanked the door shut with a sound like a pistol shot.

10

I dreamt Kid McCoy and I were at Custer's Last Stand. We could see the Indians attacking the soldiers on a grassy hill a couple of hundred yards away, but the Indians hadn't spotted us yet.

I saw a phone booth. I went in it and tried to call home, but nobody answered. Then I saw some of the Indians leaving the scene of the massacre and riding our way. They were nearly naked and covered in blue paint with yellow, lightning-like zigzags and white spots like hail and they were making terrifying war whoops.

I stepped out of the phone booth. "Run, Kid!" I yelled, and the old champ took off in a scampering, monkey-like fashion as spears and arrows whizzed past and barely missed him. I turned and ran too as the Indians bore down upon me, the grass was up around my knees, it was like running through water, then I woke up. It was ten past ten in the morning.

I sat at the kitchen table in my underwear for a while, brooding over a cup of Folger's; then I called up Wendell Nuffer.

He seemed surprised, but glad, to hear from me. He agreed to meet me at one o'clock for lunch at Jack's Steak House.

It was on Santa Monica Boulevard, on the corner of Formosa. We sat in a red leather booth, and drank ice-cold martinis while we waited for our steaks.

Nuffer had been a wreck the last time I'd seen him, but today he seemed relaxed and happy.

"You're looking good, Mr. Nuffer."

"Why, thank you, kind sir." He patted his stomach. "I've lost some weight, on doctor's orders. I've cut down considerably on my drinking, the present martini notwithstanding. In short, I'm feeling, as they say, 'in the pink,' for the first time in many years."

"Why the change?"

He musingly fingered his martini glass.

"When I came back from Lake Arrowhead, I thought about driving to Pasadena and jumping off Suicide Bridge. But then I decided, to hell with the scandalmongers, Nuffer's number wasn't yet up. Now gradually I've come to realize it was all for the best. I'd set myself upon a dark and shameful path. I was keeping company with known criminals. I have a wonderful wife and four beautiful children, but I was willing to risk everything for an alluring piece of tail. And I have to tell you I find myself missing Miss Gilbertson not a whit. Well—perhaps a whit."

He laughed ruefully, and lifted the martini to his lips.

"I plan to leave city government, Danny, in the very near future, and go into some relatively honest line of work—say, graverobbing or safecracking. Or have you heard of the Running Board Bandit? He's an enterprising fellow who jumps on the running boards of cars with women drivers in them and threatens them with a knife and steals their jewelry and purses. I believe this town is big enough for two Running Board Bandits. And I'm sure my doctor would approve; I'd be working all day in the open air and getting plenty of exercise chasing down cars."

Our steaks arrived, carried by a cute little package named Latona.

"You fellas need anything else?" she said. "Another drink maybe?"

"I'm going to be virtuous, Latona," said Nuffer, "and just have a glass of iced tea."

"Same for me," I said.

"Okey dokey," smiled Latona; now Nuffer watched her wiggle off with a look of deep regret.

"It's hard to be virtuous, Danny. So very hard."

He knifed into his T-bone as I shook some ketchup out on my french fries.

"Thanks for meeting me, Mr. Nuffer. I guess you're wondering why I called."

He forked a juicy pink triangle of meat into his mouth.

"As far as I'm concerned, we're friends, Danny. You don't have to have a reason to call me. But I assumed you had one."

"It's like this. A lot of things don't add up. With me, I mean."

"Like what, for example?"

"Well, like my nickname. Two Gun Danny Landon. I got it because a few years ago myself and some of the other guys robbed this gambling ship—"

"The *Monfalcone*. Yes, I know the story. You jumped up on a table and blazed away at your enemies with a gun in each hand."

"Of course I don't remember any of this. I don't remember anything before I got beat up last year."

Nuffer wiped his mouth with his napkin, and gave me a careful, appraising look.

"So what doesn't add up?"

"I've figured out that I don't like guns, Mr. Nuffer. They're loud, and they're scary, and when I saw what a bullet did to Goodlooking Tommy's head it just about made me sick. I can't imagine standing on a table shooting at people like some kind of maniac, like Jimmy Cagney or somebody."

Coincidentally, at just that moment I saw a movie star slide into a nearby booth—except it wasn't Jimmy Cagney, it was Gene Autry, the singing cowboy.

"What else doesn't add up?" said Nuffer.

"I keep getting this creepy feeling that everybody else knows something that I don't. Like everybody's in on the joke but me. Dick Prettie, for instance. Whenever I ask him something about my past, he always gets kind of uncomfortable, and shifty-eyed, and tries to change the subject."

Latona came back with our iced teas. "Guess who just came in!" she said in a loud excited whisper.

"Gene Autry?" I said.

"And he's sitting at one of *my* tables!" She stole a glance at Autry; he was wearing a western shirt and a polkadot bandanna, and had a soft, friendly face. "Isn't he a dreamboat?"

"Perhaps you'll ride off to old Santa Fe with him," said Nuffer. "As he sings to you. On the back of his golden horse."

"That'd be swell," Latona giggled, then she smoothed her skirt down over her hips and sauntered over to his table.

"Imagine the enormous amount of nookie Gene Autry must be getting," sighed Nuffer. "But excuse me, Danny. Go on."

"I'm just looking for someone to level with me. To tell me the truth about me. At least, as far as they know it."

Nuffer smiled faintly.

"You were kind to me that night, Danny. On the worst night of my life, you were the only one who was kind. Ask me anything you want."

"Is my name really Danny Landon?"

"I have no idea."

"What happened that night on the *Monfalcone*?"

"My understanding is it sank after an accidental fire that started in the kitchen."

"Was it robbed?"

"Not to my knowledge."

"Was I on the ship that night?"

"I highly doubt it."

"So the story about me and the two guns is—?"

"Bullshit."

I felt greatly relieved; it was like I'd actually physically been holding those heavy guns in my hands for month after month, and now I'd tossed them down.

"Who started the story?"

"Our friend Mr. Seitz."

"Why?"

Nuffer hesitated.

"Danny, everything I'm telling you is obviously in the strictest confidence. The consequences would be dire for me if this conversation became known."

"Don't worry, Mr. Nuffer. I won't tell anybody."

"This is what I know, in a nutshell.

"A year or so ago, Bud suddenly left town. He was gone for several weeks. When he came back, he came back with you.

"You were taken straightaway from the train station to the Cedars of Lebanon Hospital. You were in very bad shape. You'd suffered a severe beating. You were drifting in and out of consciousness, and you'd lost your memory."

"So you saw me? In the hospital?"

"No. Nobody except Bud saw you until later. Bud said you were alone in the world, and he'd decided to take care of you. He said he was creating a fictitious identity for you—'making up a new life for him,' is how he put it—Two Gun Danny Landon, a tough customer who'd been part of his gang for years. He was expecting everybody to play along with the story or he'd be very disappointed, he said. And he had his reasons for doing what he was doing and they weren't anybody's business but his.

"That's all I know for certain, Danny. Beyond that is just rumors, speculation. It's believed that Bud brought you here from New York. I've heard that you're the son of an old pal of his who once saved his life and now he's taking you under his wing to pay off the debt. I've also heard you're the son of his sister."

"Bud Seitz's nephew?"

"I wouldn't put much stock in that particular story. I don't see much of a family resemblance myself," then he looked at my face more closely. "I don't know. Perhaps the nose. And around the mouth."

I sat there in silence, trying to get my head around all this.

"Danny? Are you all right?"

I nodded. I noticed numbly that Gene Autry was drinking a glass of milk—evidently as wholesome off-screen as on.

"Since I'm already speaking out of school here," said Nuffer, who all the while had been speedily working his way through his steak, and now was on the home stretch, "there's something else I think you should know."

"What?"

"Have you heard of the Combination?"

I shook my head.

"It's simply the people that wield the real power in the Angel City. Some are elected officials, some are businessmen, some are people like your boss. Some might even consider me to be a modest part of the Combination. So here's the word.

"Imagine rats. Imagine they're on a ship. Imagine the ship is sinking. Now I'm not suggesting you're a rat, Danny, but I am suggesting that the future of Bud Seitz in this town is limited, and the more distance you put between yourself and him, the better for you."

"What are you saying? The Combination's gonna have Bud killed?"

Nuffer shrugged. "They're in the midst of a reorganization, let's put it that way." He eyed my plate. "You're not hungry?"

"No. Want my steak?"

"Well, it would be a shame to let something so delicious go to waste."

He stuck in his fork and plopped the steak on his plate. Juice splashed up on the starchy front of his white shirt.

"Damn it!" He started rubbing at the spots with his napkin. "It's always something, isn't it? Now I'll have to go back to work looking like a slovenly pig. Oh, to hell with virtue. Latona? Latona? Two more martinis please!"

As I drove home from Jack's, a bit of song came into my head, I didn't know how I knew it—

> Mother of Christ,
> Star of the sea,
> Pray for the wanderer,
> Pray for me.

11

Bud killed Tommy at about three-thirty on a Thursday after-noon.

It was two days after my lunch with Nuffer. I was sitting around the Peacock with Bud and Dick and Nello and Willie the Coon. The club didn't open up till six, so we had it to ourselves. Everybody was drinking coffee and smoking and making the usual numbskulled conversation about nothing.

I looked across the table at Bud and thought: Could he really be my uncle? He'd told me he didn't have any brothers and sisters but he could have lied about that. I wanted to ask him directly who I was but I'd also promised to protect Nuffer. What if I just told him I'd heard a rumor that such and such was the case? Could he figure out somehow Nuffer was the rat?

Bud was telling us about some suits he'd just bought at a new men's store in Beverly Hills, then Nello said: " 'Member Wingy? And them fucking shirts?"

"Oh yeah," Bud grinned, then he looked at me. "Before your time, Danny. Wingy Nussbaum. They called him Wingy 'cause he had polio or some kinda shit when he was a kid and he had this funny little arm, it was like a little kid's arm stuck on this growed-up guy. So he had to have all his coats and shirts made special. One time he ordered fifty silk shirts at thirty bucks a pop. So he goes in to pick up the shirts, and the tailor's fucked up. He's made the wrong sleeve short. Well, the tailor's scared to death Wingy's gonna kill him or something, but I guess

Wingy's in a good mood 'cause he just says: 'Don't worry about it. Just make me some new shirts.' 'But what am I gonna do with all *these* shirts?' says the tailor. Well Wingy scratches his chin a minute, then says: 'Bring me some scissors.' So the tailor comes back with some scissors, and asks Wingy what's he gonna do. 'I'm gonna make you some short-sleeve shirts,' says Wingy, and he cuts the sleeves off all fifty of them fucking thirty-dollar shirts."

Everybody laughed and started telling Wingy Nussbaum stories: how he bought an oil well on La Cienega and whenever he went to visit it he'd wear high leather boots and puffy pants and a pith helmet like he was going on a safari, and how he once beat a guy to death with the hand crank of an old Ford, and then I saw Tommy walk in.

When he saw us he got a look on his face like maybe he wasn't expecting Bud to be here and he turned back around, but Bud saw him and called out: "Hey, Tommy! Where you going? Come here!"

Tommy looked panicky for about a half a second then put a smile on and walked toward us as carefully as a man walking on a tightrope; of course, that very carefulness was a dead giveaway that he was drunk, then he was at the table grinning and chuckling and blowing out boozy breaths all over everybody.

"Hey, fellas. What's the good word?"

Bud started wiping his hands off on a Kleenex. He was very slow about it. One finger at a time.

"Tell me something. Is the sun down yet?"

Tommy chuckled some more. "Nope. Not last time I looked."

"It's summertime, ain't it? The days last fucking forever, don't they? It ain't even close to sundown, is it?"

Tommy was sweating, and swaying a little; he put out his hand and touched the table to stop himself.

"No, Bud. It ain't close."

"Then what are you doing walking in here drunk at"—he checked his watch—"three twenty-two in the afternoon? You know it's against the rules. I don't want a bunch of lushes working for me. And don't try and tell me you ain't plastered."

Tommy hung his head, like a little kid in front of the school principal. "I'm sorry, Bud. It won't happen again."

"You're goddamn right it won't happen again."

Tommy looked as though he was about to cry.

"It's just that—nothing's been the same since Goodlooking Tommy got it. Poor bastard. Just 'cause he was reaching for a piece of bread."

"If he hadn't've been reaching for the bread, *I* woulda been the one that got it."

"Better him than you, Bud, that's for fucking sure. But I miss the son of a bitch. I can't help it."

"Goodlooking Tommy was a prick," Dick said.

"I thought you guys hated each other anyway," said Nello. "You was always fighting."

"Naw, Nello, we was like brothers. It was like brothers fighting."

Bud finished his last finger, and dumped the Kleenex on the Kleenex pile.

"It ain't easy losing somebody you care about. I know that. But that don't mean you just gotta fall to pieces. Right?"

Bud was speaking in such a kindly fashion that I could see in Tommy's eyes he was thinking he was going to get away with it.

"Right."

"Now let's go over to the bar."

"What for?"

But Bud didn't answer as we all piled out of the booth and followed Bud toward the bar. The little Chinaman that cleaned up around the club was pushing a broom over the dance floor, and he found himself in Bud's path. His name was Ching-wei, but everybody called him Chink-wei. Bud said: "Outa the way, monkey!" and Ching-wei jumped aside. His mouth hung open as he watched us pass. He had nubby brown teeth and melancholy seen-it-all eyes.

Bud went behind the bar. "Whatcha drinking, Tommy?"

"Nothing."

"I said what are you drinking."

"Scotch. That's what I *was* drinking."

"What kinda Scotch?"

"Glenfibbet."

Nello and Willie snickered as Bud grabbed a bottle of Glen-livet and set it down on the bar in front of Tommy.

"Drink it."

Tommy eyed the bottle. It was about three-quarters full.

"All of it?"

"Yeah."

"I can't drink that much."

"You got a puppydog craps in the house, you rub its nose in it. That's what I'm doing with you." He unscrewed the cap. "So let's go. Drink."

Never taking his eyes off the bottle, like he was looking at a mountain he had to climb, Tommy wiped off his mouth with the back of his hand, then raised the bottle to his lips. He took a long drink then, coughing, set the bottle back down. Nello and Willie were looking on with amusement.

"You know what they say, Tommy," said Willie. "Don't buy booze if the baby needs shoes."

"The baby don't need shoes," said Tommy hoarsely. "There ain't no baby."

"Bottoms up, Tommy," said Nello.

"This ain't fair. I ain't the only one around here ever took a drink during the day."

"Maybe so, but you're the one that got caught," said Bud.

"So keep drinking."

Tommy continued working his way through the bottle. He coughed and gagged and mumbled and laughed and his eyes watered and got glassier and glassier. He nearly made it too— only had about a golden inch of booze to go when he suddenly threw up all over on the bar. Some of it splashed on Bud's new suit.

Bud was enraged. "You filthy pig!" He took the bottle by the neck and swung it at Tommy's head. Tommy lifted up his left arm to block the blow and the bottle shattered against his forearm as his right hand dove into his pants pocket for his gun. But Nello and Willie were all over him and easily wrested the gun away.

Now Bud was incredulous. "You fucking see that? Son of a bitch was gonna shoot me!" His face was turning about eight shades of red. He grabbed handfuls of Tommy's coat at the shoulders and yanked him over the top of the bar.

Tommy's body went out of sight and I heard it thumping down on the floor. From one of the shining rows of bottles behind the bar that many a long summer afternoon Tommy had gazed at so longingly, Bud snatched a quart of Wild Turkey and started swinging. I heard a couple of dull-sounding thuds then peered over the bar just in time to see the bottle break over the back of Tommy's head.

He was on his hands and knees trying to crawl away like Wendell Nuffer. He was screaming and Bud was screaming. Bud was left with the jagged neck of the bottle in his fist and he drove it in Tommy's neck. Blood spurted and he grabbed one bottle after another and pounded away on Tommy's back and shoulders and neck and head. More puke came gushing out of Tommy's mouth. There were jets of blood and explosions of glass and booze as Tommy crawled through the tunnel-like space over the broken glass and the slippery floor.

I looked at Nello and Willie; they were leaning over the bar watching, fascinated, smiling. When I looked for Dick, all I saw was his back as he walked away.

"Stop it, Bud! Jesus Christ! Stop it!" I yelled, but Bud just shot me a lunatic look and kept whaling away.

"Mother, help me! Mother, he's hurting me!" screamed Tommy.

It was a bottle of dark rum that finally did the trick. It crunched into the back of Tommy's skull without breaking and Tommy dropped on the floor. A croaky sound came out of his throat, and then he was quiet.

The air stank of liquor. Bud was panting; for someone so particular that even when he went in a fancy joint like Perino's he'd spend two minutes wiping off the silverware with his napkin, it was interesting how often Bud wound up covered with awful stuff. Some slivers of glass were caught and sparkled in the blood on his face. He took out his handkerchief and began wiping at himself.

I saw the white hair and black-framed glasses of Stan Tinney. He was beholding with dismay the scene behind the bar; it looked like somebody had thrown a bomb back there.

"We open in two and a half hours. *Two and a half hours.*"

"More than enough time," said Bud, and he nudged the corpse of Tommy with his toe. "We just need to get this sack of shit outa here," and then he looked at me.

12

Fortunately I got Dick to help me out. We wrapped Tommy up in a tablecloth first then rolled him up in a rug from Stan's office. The rug was so if anybody happened to see us in the Peacock parking lot cramming the body in the rumble seat of Dick's car they wouldn't think anything about it. Just two guys with a rug. We brought along a couple of shovels too. Just two guys with a rug and a couple of shovels.

Dick had a Ford coupe painted a hideous orange. We went west on Sunset till we got to Sepulveda where we turned north. Then we crossed over the Sepulveda Pass and went down into the San Fernando Valley. It was beautiful there. Kind of like the Garden of Eden. Orange and walnut and avocado orchards, and wide green well-watered fields, and white farm houses set back from the road surrounded by shade trees. Three pretty teenage girls on horseback gave us sunny smiles and waved at us as we passed. If only, I thought, they knew what was riding in the rumble seat.

" 'Member Ginger Rogers?" said Dick wistfully. "When we seen her on that horse?"

"Yeah."

That's all either of us said for a long time. We listened to the car radio. Dick smoked. Every now and then he coughed. Finally he went in his pocket and pulled out a folded-up piece of paper, which he handed to me.

"What's this?" I said.

"Something I found in my mailbox."

I unfolded it, and read aloud: " 'My friend, you *can* have it all . . . more money than you've ever dreamed of, and the time and freedom to enjoy it! For a small initial fee, you can become a licensed dealer of J. R. Brinkley's Goat Gland Extract. This amazing new scientific discovery is GUARANTEED to restore sexual vigor within 24 hours, or the purchase price is cheerfully refunded in full!' "

"See, the deal is," said Dick, "you don't do none of the selling yourself. You get a bunch of other guys to do the legwork, and you get a cut of everything they make. While *them* poor slobs are walking around in the hot sun lugging around suitcases full of this crap and getting doors slammed in their pusses, *you're* drinking a beer in a bar someplace and sticking your hand up the skirt of some broad." He gave a cackling, triumphant laugh, as if he were already living such a delightful life.

I looked over the handbill. "I dunno, Dick. You think anybody's really gonna buy something like this?"

"You kidding me? Everybody ain't young and horny like you are, Danny. There's plenty of guys out there that can't get it up no more, and they got old ladies driving 'em nuts ever night, just begging for it."

"I have a friend named George. He says he can't get it up."

"See? What did I tell you?"

"He's glad about it though. He says women are more trouble than they're worth."

"Well, most guys, you give 'em the choice, they'd rather be able to get it up. Just so's they can jack off, if nothing else. So what do you say? You wanna go in partners with me in this?"

"Maybe. But how would Bud figure in?"

"I dunno. We could cut him in too, I guess." Although at first I heard: We could cut him in two.

"Lookit," said Dick, "I just want outa this racket. I don't wanna end up wrapped in a fucking rug like Tommy."

We got on a highway that led us out of the valley. The green fields and orchards gave way to brown, dried-up hills, and off to our left the sun seemed to get bigger and bigger as it drifted down. I didn't ask Dick where we were going. I just slumped down in the seat and let the hot dry air gush in through the window and dry the sweat off my face as fast as it formed and I tried not to think about Tommy hollering for his ma. The road rose and then the land began to flatten out, and I saw a few cactuses and knew we were in the desert.

We saw only a few other cars, and one truck filled up with stoves; "STEVE'S STOVES" was painted on the side, and it was traveling so fast you had to assume there was a desperate stove shortage somewhere. After about half an hour, Dick slowed down and turned off the highway onto a rutty dirt road.

We bumped and lurched along toward the setting sun. A wind had kicked up, and dust was blowing across the road, and then a swirl of white and brown feathers. Then I saw a dead chicken. Then I saw a live one, stumbling along the side of the road like it was drunk. It had blood on its feathers. Then we passed a chicken coop and a sagging tarpaper shack, with more chickens wandering around and pecking at the dust.

"Why would anybody," said Dick, "wanna live way out here and raise fucking chickens?"

The road got increasingly rough, then suddenly ended, as if the roadbuilders had come to their senses and realized the road was a bad idea. We got out of the car. We looked around. You couldn't see the highway from here. Off in the distance jumbles of bare mountains rose up. I felt like Dick and I didn't belong here. Like the desert didn't have the slightest use for us.

We took the shovels out of the car, then I followed Dick out into the desert. We cast long thin shadows as we walked past cactuses and scrubby bushes and strange little twisted trees.

"You been here before, I guess," I said.

He shrugged.

"Who's out here?"

"Well—Flumentino's around someplace."

"Emperatriz too?"

"I told you. She went back to Mexico, I think."

"I heard different."

He was silent; then he smiled a little.

"That Emperatriz was one cute dame. Did I tell you? She had a name for me. *El Flaco.* The Skinny One. 'Why you ain't got no girlfriend, *el Flaco?*' she'd say. 'You are such a handsome man!' "

A couple of hundred feet from the car, Dick looked around and said: "Guess this place is as good as any."

The ground was hard and dry. We'd already shed our coats in the car, and now we rolled up our shirt sleeves. The sweat was pouring off us, and I was unbearably thirsty. The wind blew over us, and dust stung our eyes. This was the second burial job I'd done with Dick. I remembered holding Doc's hand. The way he'd looked up at me so trustingly as I led him out into the garden.

"Poor Doc," I said.

"Quit talking about him. I mean it. You're always bringing him up. Just knock it off."

"Sorry."

"I guess that's deep enough," said Dick after a while.

It didn't look very deep, but I didn't argue with him. We went back to the car, and opened up the rumble seat. While he'd been getting murdered, Tommy had emptied his bladder and bowels. Add to that an hour or two in a hot car, and the smell was like a punch in the face.

Dick cursed as we took Tommy out. He wasn't a big guy, but

we struggled to carry him. He seemed all slack and loosey-goosey inside the tube of the rug and I was afraid he'd slither out one end or the other.

"They're a lot easier to carry when they're stiff," said Dick, red-faced and gasping. "He ain't been dead long enough to get stiff yet."

We plopped him down in the hole and quickly began to cover him up. When we finished, we leaned on our shovels and surveyed our handiwork.

"Adios, you rotten bastard," said Dick.

"Was he right?"

"About what?"

"About that bouncer's name. Was it Cairo Mary?"

Dick smiled. "Yeah. Yeah, he was right about that."

Suddenly a gust of wind blew his hat off. It rolled and tumbled along the ground as Dick chased after it. It finally came to rest near the base of one of the weird-looking trees. Dick bent over to get it, but then he yelled: "HOLY SHIT!" and came running back my way.

"Dick, what's the matter?"

"Snake! One of them *rattle*snakes!"

"Where?"

"Right there! By the tree!"

I looked toward where he was pointing, but didn't see anything. I was willing to take his word for it though.

"Come on, let's get outa here."

"I can't leave without my hat! It cost me ten bucks!"

Dick pulled his gun out and began blazing away in the direction of the tree. The bullets kicked up the dirt. I still couldn't see the snake. Now the hat somersaulted as one of the bullets hit it.

"Dick, you just shot your hat! It's no good anymore! Now let's get outa here!"

Dick was staring toward the tree, his eyes wide and wild and his lower lip trembling.

"You seen it, didn't you, Danny? You seen the snake?"

"Yeah, I saw it. Now let's go."

We walked quickly back to the car with a mounting sense of panic, as if we were being chased by the snake, or maybe the wrathful ghosts of Emperatriz and Flumentino. We threw our shovels in the coupe and jumped in and Dick got it turned around and headed back toward the highway. Then we gave each other relieved we-made-it looks.

"Fuck," said Dick.

"Yeah."

Pretty soon we saw feathers blowing across the road again.

"I'm thirsty as hell," I said. "You think maybe the chicken farmers would give us some water?"

"Good idea, kid. I'm pretty dry myself."

We stopped the car in front of the shack and the chicken coop. There were chickens everywhere, some alive, some dead, some somewhere in between. The smell was awful, and the air was full of flies. Now we saw a little kid sitting in the doorway of the shack with a rifle across his knees.

The dust had turned the sun red, and the horizon had cut it in half, and we walked warily through the bloody light toward the kid, who never took his eyes off us.

"What you fellers want?" he said.

He looked about nine or ten. All he was wearing was a filthy pair of shorts. At first I'd thought he must be a Mexican he was so brown, but now I saw the brown was a mixture of suntan and dirt.

"Just some water," said Dick. "That okay?"

The kid looked us over. "It'll cost ya."

"How much?" I said.

"Two bits. Apiece."

"That's fine." I went in my pocket and pulled out a shiny new half-dollar. I walked over and dropped it in the kid's grubby palm. He had extraordinary light-green eyes, the color of an empty Coke bottle.

"Water's over yunder," he said, nodding towards a rusting pump.

A bucket sat under the spout of the pump, and there was a tin cup next to the bucket. Dick and I looked into the bucket: it was half full of water, with a layer of feathers and dead flies floating on it. We looked at each other, then Dick grabbed the pump handle and began working it.

"I guess this is how you do it," he said.

At first the pump just made hoarse wheezing noises, but then water began to well up and flow. I filled up the cup and drank it. The water was very cool, with a mineral taste. I had another cup, then pumped for Dick.

Now I saw a floppy-eared brown and white hound lying on its stomach at the side of the shack. It was chomping on a live chicken that it was holding down with it paws. The chicken feebly beat its wings as the wind blew its feathers away.

The kid raised his rifle, pointed it at another chicken, and shot. Except it wasn't a rifle after all but a BB gun. The BB made a snapping noise as it hit the chicken, which jumped and squawked and flapped and staggered off.

The kid guffawed, and slapped his knee. "Right in the dang butt!"

Dick looked at me. "Want any more water?"

"Nah."

"Let's get outa here then."

The kid cocked his BB gun then shot another chicken.

"Why are you doing that?" I said. "Why are you shooting your chickens?"

The kid leveled his green gaze at me.

"It's just something to do, mister. You got any better ideas?"

"But you need your chickens, don't you? To make a living?"

"Ain't no living to be made. The bottom's plumb fell out of the fucking chicken market. We ain't even making enough money to buy chicken feed. They's all starving to death. Can't you see that?" The kid eyed us suspiciously. "What you fellers doing out cheer anyways? How come you're asking all these questions? Y'all ain't G-men, are ya? Daddy told me to keep a look-out for G-men."

"Naw, kid, we ain't G-men," said Dick. "We're just passing through. Come on, Danny."

But then a little girl came walking around the side of the shack. She was maybe six or seven, and was as filthy, and had the same bottle-green eyes, as her brother. She was holding by one arm a pinkish plastic baby doll missing a leg.

"Zeke, I seen a rabbit," she said. "A bunny rabbit. A-hopping around."

"Looky here, Ruby, at what I got!" said Zeke. "A fifty-cent piece!"

Ruby looked wonderingly at the bright coin. Green snot was oozing out of her nostrils, and she had a harsh, croupy cough.

"Golly, Zeke. Is that morn a nickel?"

"Damn right it is."

"Zeke, you better hurry up."

"Hurry up and what?"

"Shoot the bunny rabbit. 'Fore it goes a-hopping off. Hippity hop."

"Where's your daddy?" I said.

"Around," said Zeke, suspicious again. "What you wanna know fer?"

"I just want to make sure there's somebody to take care of you guys. Do you have enough to eat?"

"Sure, mister. We eat chickens."

"And aigs," said Ruby.

"But we ain't been eating aigs lately. They don't lay aigs lessun you feed 'em."

"I hate chickens," said Ruby. "They're mean. I had a pet bug once and the chicken et it."

Zeke shot another chicken. Through the neck this time. It went down in the dirt in a flurry of feathers and squawks.

"Kid, you're a hell of a shot," said Dick. "Let's go, Danny."

We turned and walked toward the road. I felt the luminous green eyes of the siblings on our backs. I braced myself for a BB popping me in the butt.

We passed by a handsome red rooster. He was stalking around arrogantly, like he wasn't aware of the unfolding catastrophe, didn't know or care all his wives were starving and being shot.

"What you limping fer, mister," Zeke called out, "you some kinda cripple?"

"Some kinda cripple!" Ruby shouted, then I heard her giggle and cough.

We walked through the dusty red feather-filled light, away from the stench of dead chickens and chicken shit. Got in the car and got to the highway and headed south toward the city, lickety split.

"I don't think I'll be eating chicken for a while," said Dick.

"Me neither."

13

It was the middle of July, and it was hot. I sat on the black davenport wearing only my undershorts. The sun was shining through the shrubbery outside my window, and throwing shadows on the hardwood floor.

I imagined taking my new yellow broom and briskly sweeping up all the shadows. They ended up in a tidy little heap of darkness in the corner, while the floor was filled with nothing but light.

14

"I don't get it," I said.

"Don't get what?" said Darla.

"Why you're moving in with him. I thought you wanted to get away from him."

"This doesn't have anything to do with what I want. I don't pay for my apartment, he does. And he doesn't want to pay for it anymore."

We were on our way to her apartment. She wanted me to help her pack a few things. She took out a Lucky Strike, leaned toward the dashboard, and pushed in the electric lighter.

"But that doesn't mean you have to move in with him," I said.

"Oh, it doesn't? Tell *him* that."

The lighter popped back out, and she applied it to her cigarette.

"What's up with Tommy?" she asked.

"What do you mean?"

"I heard Teddy and Nucky talking about him, but they clammed up when I walked in the room. Then I asked Bud about him, and he said he'd gone off to take care of his sick aunt in San Francisco."

"Yeah. That's what I heard."

"Hey, Danny? It'd be nice to have one person in my life I knew would never lie to me."

I thought about it a minute.

"Okay. I know where he's at. And it's not San Francisco."

She sighed out some smoke, said: "I get the picture," then stayed silent the rest of the way to her apartment house.

We took the elevator to the top floor.

When we got in her apartment, Darla said: "Whew! It's like an oven in here. Danny, would you be a darling and open some windows? I'm going to make a drink. Like one?"

"No thanks."

She went in the kitchen, as I spread out the curtains and lifted the front window. I had a pretty good view up and down the street. The red Buick was parked not too far off. I couldn't see inside, but I could see some smoke drifting up from the driver's-side window.

I'd never been in Darla's apartment before. I looked around the living room. Everything was nice enough, but except for a stack of unopened mail on a side table, there were no indications a particular person lived here. It was kind of a high-class version of where I lived.

I went in her bedroom and opened the window there.

Out of the corner of my eye I caught some movement, but then saw the movement was me: my reflection in a mirror over a bureau. A few weeks ago I'd gone out to Venice Beach with Dick, and we went to one of those places where you try to knock over wooden milk bottles with a baseball. There was this guy whose job it was to scurry around and re-set the milk bottles after they'd been knocked over. He looked like a monster. His skin wasn't anything but slick pink scars. I asked the guy that ran the game what had happened to him, and he said he'd been burned up in an oil-well fire in Signal Hill a few years back. So then I started wondering what he used to look like, and who he really was under the scars. And now, as I looked at myself in the mirror, I started wondering who I really was under Danny Landon.

Darla's reflection joined mine. She was holding a stubby tumbler full of ice and vodka. She looked at me, smiling a little.

"In love with your own reflection?"

"No."

Now her eyes moved to herself.

"I stand in front of the mirror sometimes. I take off all my clothes, and I look at every inch of myself, and I wonder how long it's going to last. 'Cause that's all I've got, is what I look like."

She took a gulp of her drink, and walked over to a closet. She started taking out pairs of shoes and putting them in a cardboard box.

"Need any help?" I said.

"No. Just relax."

I saw a stuffed lamb sitting on the bed. It had blue glass eyes and a simpering smile and a red bow around its neck.

"Where'd you get the lamb?"

"Mr. Bruff gave it to me. For Christmas." And then, after a moment: "He wants to marry me."

"Bud?"

"Yeah."

"But he's already married."

"He says that situation will be taken care of very soon."

"Just tell him no."

"*You* just tell him no."

"I heard a rumor. That there's some important people that aren't happy with him, and his future in this town is limited."

"What do you mean? They're gonna send him to visit his sick aunt in San Francisco?"

"I guess so. So maybe if you can just hold out a little longer, your problem will be solved for you."

"Just my luck, somebody'll plant a bomb in his car, and I'll be with him when it blows up."

"That's not gonna happen."

She finished off the vodka, then held out the glass to me.

"Danny, would you be a dear and get me some water?"

I was glad she wasn't asking for more vodka. In the kitchen, as I held the glass under the tap, I thought about her standing in front of the mirror without any clothes on. I thought about every inch of her.

When I went back in the bedroom, she was standing by the bureau, taking a medicine bottle out of her purse. She unscrewed the cap and tipped out three tablets into her palm.

"What's that?" I said.

"Veronal."

She took the glass from me and popped the tablets in her mouth.

"What's it for?"

"It's just a calmative. And don't give me that look. My *doctor* gives them to me. It's *medicine*. I'm not a dope fiend."

"Didn't say you were."

She started taking stuff out of the bureau drawers. Frilly, silky, filmy, fascinating stuff.

"Damn," she said. "I left my cigarettes in the car. Would you be a dear?"

Of course I would. I took the elevator down. The street was lined with palm trees, and a hot, dry wind rattled above me through the fronds.

The red Buick was still waiting, still spying. I suddenly felt mad. Like I'd had enough. I started walking toward it. I was behind it. Smoke was floating out of both sides. A shirt-sleeved elbow was sticking out of the passenger window. When I got to within about twenty feet, the engine started up, and the car took off, its tires making a brief screech.

I was surprised to find myself chasing it down the street and yelling: "Fuck you, you fucking bastards! Quit spying on me, goddamn it!"

The Buick sped away and was gone. Sweating and panting, I headed back toward my Packard. On the other side of the street, a woman and her two kids were looking at me fearfully; now they averted their eyes and hurried on.

I fetched the Lucky Strikes and went back up.

Darla was curled up on the bed, hugging the lamb, her eyes closed.

"I got your cigarettes."

"Oh thanks, honey," she said, not opening her eyes, and then: "Vodka and Veronal are *wo-o-on*derful together."

I stood above her, holding the pack of cigarettes she didn't seem to want now, not knowing what to do next.

"Did I hear you yelling at somebody?" she asked.

"No."

"I thought I heard you."

"No."

"You wanna lay down with me?"

Yes. I took off my hat and shoes. Her back was to me. I laid my head on the pillow right next to hers.

I breathed in her scent.

"Mitsuoko?"

"Yeah. You still like it?"

"Uh-huh."

I eased my nose tentatively into her golden hair.

"Jean Harlow hasn't got anything on you."

She laughed. "Oh, stop it."

"I mean it. You're ten times more beautiful than she is. No. *Twenty* times."

I lifted my head and with a finger pushed some damp locks of hair away from her neck and put my mouth there. Her flesh was very warm and was moist with perspiration. I slid my lips slowly back and forth.

She made a gentle, negative noise in her throat, and murmured: "Not now, Danny."

My head sagged back onto the pillow, and I sighed. She reached back and gave my knee an understanding pat.

"Imagine what he'd do to us if we did it and he found out."

"How would he find out?"

"Maybe I talk in my sleep."

So I lay there in the perfumy heat within inches of Darla. We were both quiet for a moment; and then Darla said: "I had a dream. About you and him."

"What happened?"

"We were on a ship. This big ocean liner, like the *Queen Mary*. We were on deck playing shuffleboard. We were all dressed in white, and we were all laughing, and having a good time, especially Bud, because he was winning. But then he turned his back on you, and you started hitting him with the shuffleboard stick. You hit him over the head, and he started staggering away, and there was blood everywhere, all over our white clothes, and you followed him and kept hitting him and hitting him. Bud was pleading with you, but your face, it was like a mask; it had no feeling in it."

"You know, Darla—I'm not a killer."

"Yes you are. You just don't remember. And I'll bet it's like riding a bicycle. You never forget how."

"What are you trying to say?"

"I'm trying to say . . . I wouldn't ask you to do it just for me. You'd be doing it for yourself too. You're his prisoner too. Anybody that gets close to him becomes his prisoner." Now she turned over, and looked at me. She moved some hair away from my forehead, and her fingers brushed over the dent in my skull; it seemed like such an intimate thing, as if she were touching my private parts. "And then you and me—we could go away together."

"Go away where?"

"Wherever you want." She was wearing her charm bracelet, and now she fingered the crescent moon. "How about the moon? Everything would be very clear and bright and clean and glowing. And nobody would ever bother us."

I could tell the vodka and Veronal were like a giant wave washing over her. Her eyes were becoming all dim and dreamy. She turned away from me, and snuggled up to the lamb.

"Life's so funny," she whispered to the lamb, and then, as her eyes closed: "Nobody's ever loved me like Mr. Bruff."

15

That night I was unpeeling one of the extraordinarily tasty oranges I'd plucked from the dwarf orange trees in the courtyard, when I heard from outside: "No, Jerry! Please!"

It was Sophie's voice. I went to the door.

Sophie and Jerry were on the sidewalk in front of Sophie's bungalow. Jerry was bending over something, and Sophie was yelling: "I'm sorry! Honest I am! Don't do it, Jerry!"

Then Sophie's trampish mother Lois came out the door, wearing only a full slip which her big sloppy breasts were in danger of spilling out of. "Go ahead, Jerry!" she slurred, obviously loaded. "Do it! Show the little bitch who's boss!"

I headed out the door and across the courtyard. To my left I saw Dulwich, wearing his many-colored silk smoking jacket and tasseled slippers, going in the same direction. Sophie was still yelling and she was pulling at Jerry's elbow and now I could see what he was up to: he was squirting a can of lighter fluid over Sophie's tap-dance shoes.

"Don't do it, old man!" said Dulwich, but Jerry already had his lighter out and now the red shoes went up in a whoosh of blue flame.

Sophie screamed.

Lois slapped her face and said: "Shut up!"

"Leave her alone, you bitch!" I yelled.

"I'll ask you to mind your tongue, Danny, especially where Lois is concerned," said Jerry haughtily; he was wearing pinstriped gray trousers and a stained undershirt. "This here is none of your affair. Nor yours neither, Mr. Dulwich, with all due respect. It's a family matter. Sophie is being punished because she was a bad girl."

"The filthy names she called us," said Lois. "I don't know where she ever learned such language."

"From you, you cunt!" said Sophie.

"Now that's enough!" said Jerry as he roughly seized her upper arm.

Sophie tried to jerk and twist out of his grasp. "Let go of me, you ugly ape! You're not my father! You're just some bum that lives off my mother!"

"You're gonna pay for that, Sophie!" said Jerry and now he started to drag her inside.

Dulwich stepped over the burning shoes and dispatched an elegant left cross into Jerry's ribcage and then a whistling right cross into Jerry's jaw right below his ear. His head snapped sideways and his knees buckled and he fell on his butt.

Dulwich stood over him, rubbing his knuckles and waiting for him to get up. Jerry massaged his jaw and gave Dulwich a look of bleary reproach.

"I'm surprised at you, Mr. Dulwich. I thought you was a gentleman."

"Assuming for the nonce that I am a gentleman, my only regret is to have sullied my knuckles with a man like you."

Sophie took the opportunity to dart inside and slam the door. Her mother was right behind her; she rattled the doorknob futilely.

"She locked us out, the little brat!" She began to pound on the door and shout: "Sophie, open the door! Sophie! Unlock the door *now!*"

Some of our neighbors had drifted out of their bungalows and were watching from a safe distance. Now Mrs. Dean came charging toward us, her pinched face furious and the dying flames from the tap-dancing shoes flashing in her glasses.

"Good gracious heavens alive! What on earth is going on here?!" She was wearing a ratty sky-blue quilted housecoat over a pink nightgown. "This is the Orange Blossom Bungalow Court, not some slum!"

"I'm sorry, Mrs. Dean," said Lois, who seemed to be sobering up fast. "It was just a little family spat. Sophie locked us out."

Jerry climbed back to his feet, and stuck his hand in his pocket. "I've got a key."

"Oh, that's swell, sugar." Lois took the key and unlocked the door. "Sorry again, Mrs. Dean. We won't be any more trouble."

"Well, you better not be. This is a respectable place, Lois. You're practically naked. I'll call the police if I have to."

Lois and Jerry headed inside.

"Jerry?" I said. "Keep your hands off Sophie."

Jerry stopped and looked back at me. "I know who you are, Danny. I know you're supposed to be some kinda hooligan or gangster. But you don't scare me none, Danny. I grew up in a pretty tough neighborhood. I can take care of myself."

"Keep your hands off her," I said, my voice rising, "or I'll tie you to a slot machine and throw you in the ocean!"

His attempt at a defiant sneer collapsed into a grimace of panic. He and Lois hurried inside and shut the door.

Mrs. Dean looked down at the charred, smoking remains of Sophie's shoes, and sadly shook her head.

"Look at the burn marks on the sidewalk! Well, I'll get Matilda over here to clean it up. Matilda can clean up anything."

"You're pretty good," I said. "With the fists."

Dulwich looked pleased. "Well, I did do a bit of boxing in my youth."

I was sipping scotch, while Dulwich was puffing on his opium pipe; now he looked at the photograph of Aubrey Joyce.

"Aubrey and I were actually the best boxers in our school. I could never beat Aubrey, however. I think it may have been because his features were so beautiful I would unconsciously hold back a little for fear of marring them. He obviously had no such compunctions in regards to me. He probably felt that any rearrangement of *my* features could only be for the better."

I laughed, and Dulwich grinned. His cat was on his lap; he scratched her head, and peered at her as if he'd never quite seen her before.

"What's it like to be Tinker, Tinker?"

"The day we gave the shoes to her? Something happened. With her and me, I mean."

Dulwich looked at me, and waited for me to go on.

"She came over later, and she was—very affectionate, I guess you could say. And then she put her hand on my crotch."

He took the pipe out of his mouth. "You don't say."

"So naturally I was pretty shocked. She told me she thought that's what I wanted; then I guess her feelings were hurt and she ran away. I haven't talked to her since."

Dulwich looked gloomy. "I wonder where she picked up *that* little trick."

"Jerry?"

"Perhaps. But there have been any number of Jerrys. Who knows what sorts of lascivious doings she's been exposed to?"

"What can we do about it?"

"I'm not sure there's anything we *can* do, Danny. Beyond being her friend." He smiled. "And making bloodcurdling threats against Jerry. Did that business with the slot machine ever really happen?"

"Yeah. To a guy named Sal Tagnoli."

"Were you there?"

I shook my head. "I just heard about it," then I added: "I just heard about everything that happened before about a year ago."

"What do you mean?"

"I've found out I wasn't here before a year ago. I didn't get beat up in Ocean Park. I got beat up somewhere else. Probably New York. I was taken here on a train."

If Dulwich was surprised by any of this, he didn't show it.

"Taken by whom?"

"Bud Seitz. I'm supposedly the son of an old friend of his or maybe even his nephew. My name's probably not Danny Landon. I'm probably not a gangster. Bud just made up all that stuff about me sinking the ship and everything and told everybody else to go along with it."

"To what purpose?"

"I don't know. But the thing is, I'm kind of like Steve Harrison."

"Who?"

"The guy in that story you read us. In *Super Detective Stories.*"

"Oh yes. But how are you like him?"

"I don't really *exist.*"

"Well, it's clear you exist. Otherwise, to whom am I talking?"

"I don't know. That's my point."

"How did you find out all this?"

"A guy close to Bud told me. But I can't tell you his name."

"Is his version of events to be trusted?"

"I think so. But listen to this. I saw Darla today. She wants to get away from Bud, but thinks if she tries, Bud will kill her. So she wants me to kill him for her; then she says she'll run away with me."

"My god."

"Of course she thinks it's no big deal for me to kill some-body—that I'm this dangerous gangster that's bumped off all these people in the past."

"Why don't you tell her the truth?"

"I thought about it. But what would it change? Darla would still want to escape from Bud, and she'd still think the only way to do that is for me to kill him. And I think she might be right."

"And you still fancy yourself in love with this girl."

I nodded. Dulwich gave me a keen look, as though he'd just figured out the solution to my problem. He leaned towards me, and tapped my knee.

"I'd say you're in a pickle, old boy. A definite pickle."

"Yeah, no kidding."

16

I was walking with no destination in mind. The sun was going down, and the pavement was giving up the heat of the day. I went through an alley. Two tramps were squatting on their heels against a wall, sharing a bottle. They looked at me as I passed like they were thinking about knifing me and taking my wallet then spitting on my body as they walked away. Farther down the alley, amid a cluster of overflowing garbage cans, was the corpse of a dog. Flies were crawling around on a sore on its leg; now I recognized it as the forlorn beagle I'd given my ice cream cone to a couple of weeks ago.

I found myself on Vine Street in front of Healy's Bar; maybe this was where I'd been heading all along. Inside at their usual spots in front of the Custer massacre were George, Sonny, and Kid McCoy.

"You arrived at an opportune moment," said George. "The Kid is buying."

"He's rolling in dough," said Sonny. "Just filthy with it."

The Kid nodded with an air of solemn pride.

"Congratulations, Kid," I said. "What happened?"

"Won a hunnerd fifty bucks in a Chinese lottery."

"Ain't you heard?" mumbled an old man a few stools down; he was looking at us with eyes every bit as full of life as the boiled eggs floating in the jar on the bar.

"Ain't I heard what?" McCoy said.

"They're tearing down Chinatown! Getting rid of the Chinks!

They're running away like shithouse rats! High time, if you ask me. Polluting white women with their little yellow peckers. And I've heard they eat cats! Boil 'em alive like lobsters! No, I'll be crying no tears for the poor Chinee."

"Oh, shut up, you old hooch-hister," said the Kid. "Nobody asked you a goddamn thing. What are you drinking, Danny?"

"Scotch. On the rocks."

"You heard him, Henry," he said to the bartender. "Glad to see you ain't still drinking that horse piss. That Russian crap. You get rid of that girl?"

"Nah."

"Why the hell not?"

"I don't know."

"Is she purty?" asked Sonny.

"Beautiful."

"Be you tee full," sighed Sonny.

"I was in love with a Jap girl once," said George. "She was beautiful. Just like Danny's girl. She was the daughter of my gardener. This was back when I had a big house on a hill in Echo Park, and I was still vice-president of the South Basin Oil Company. I told her I'd divorce my wife and marry her if she had eyelid surgery so she wouldn't look like a Jap. She agreed to it. I found her a doctor and paid for the operation."

George stopped, like the story was over.

"Well what the hell happened?" said McCoy.

"Didn't work. She still looked like a Jap. She ended up marrying a Jap. A fisherman. The last I heard, she was living on Terminal Island, eating raw fish and mending nets and raising a bunch of slanty-eyed Jap children."

"What ever happened to your wife?" I asked.

"She took it pretty hard when we lost everything. I had to put her in the state insanitarium."

"She went insane?"

"I'm afraid so. But she wasn't alone. Did you know there's twenty-nine private insanitariums in Southern California?" He gestured with the stem of his pipe as he talked. "Did you know that Los Angeles leads the nation in suicides, drug addiction, and bank robberies? People come here from all over to escape America, the nightmare of America. What they don't understand is that Los Angeles is the most American city in the world. They bask in the sinister sunlight and peel their oranges and grow golden and die."

"Oranges!" snarled Sonny. "Mountains of fat, juicy oranges! They spray 'em with tar so can't nobody eat 'em. Just to keep the dadblamed prices up when folks are sending their babies to bed hungry."

"Oh don't start that shit again," grumped Kid McCoy.

"The Kid's right," said George. "I think the Fish Committee should investigate this bar for possible Communist activity."

"Well, I ain't a Communist, but I'll tell you what I am. I just joined up with a outfit called Mankind United. Pretty soon, everybody that wants one is gonna have a job, and it's gonna pay at least 3000 bucks a year. And get this! Nobody's gonna have to work morn four hours a day and four days a week!"

"And how, pray tell," said George, "is this economic miracle going to come to pass?"

"Well, there's this race of all-powerful midgets that live in the middle of the earth. They got metal heads, and they got ray machines that knock out people's eyeballs a thousand miles away. We're in contact with 'em, and they're gonna help us out."

Kid McCoy began to laugh. He laughed so hard he started slapping the bar like he just couldn't stand it.

Sonny glared at him. "Yeah, Kid, you just go on and laugh. Let's see if you're still laughing one of these days when a ray machine knocks your fucking eyeballs out."

The Kid kept buying, and I circled down and down into a radiant whirlpool of cheap whiskey. Once I closed my eyes, and I saw a nurse dressed all in white with a lovely but cold face bending over me, and I could feel the vibrations of the train, and George said: "I got a new job."

I opened my eyes. "Yeah? Doing what?"

"Selling oil leases. I even have an office. Not much of an office. I share it with some other fellows. Some real estate salesmen. Plus a fortune teller. And a mail-order faith healer. But it's a start."

"Don't give him any money, kid," said the Kid. "Not a dime."

George looked hurt. "I wasn't going to ask him for money. Did I ask you for any of your Chinese lottery winnings?"

"No. 'Cause you knew I'd tell you to go fuck yourself."

"No, that's not the reason. It was because I knew you'd been hit in the head too many times to recognize a real opportunity when it came your way. In Santa Fe Springs the oil comes practically bubbling unbidden out of the ground. But no, I don't want Danny's money unless he's in the mood to double it in no time. All I wanted was to share with Danny the fact I've put one tentative foot on the bottom rung of a shaky ladder that I trust will lead me back to the man I used to be. Before I became a desperate drunk living in a retired P.E. streetcar without power or indoor plumbing or faith or hope or love."

Sonny was looking at George with tears in his eyes. "You can do it, George. I know you can. If I had any money I'd give it to you. Ever red cent of it."

"I'm deeply touched. You're a good man, Sonny."

"I'm deeply touched too," said Sonny.

He pulled a harmonica out of his pocket, blew a few experimental notes.

"This here song is called 'Run, Nigger, Run.' "

He launched into a rollicking tune. The old man down the

bar grinned and started clapping along.

Custer, surrounded by howling red Indians and dying blue-coated soldiers, brandished his sword over his head. He was dressed in golden buckskins, and a long red scarf streamed from his neck. He didn't look the least bit scared. Just defiant. In the foreground, one of his soldiers was getting his scalp peeled off by a terrifying Indian with a knife between his teeth.

"What if somebody saw somebody kill somebody?" I said. "He didn't have anything to do with the killing, but afterwards, he helped get rid of the body. Would he be guilty of a crime?"

George and Kid McCoy were both staring at me. Finally George said: "I believe he would be guilty, yes. 'Accessory to murder after the fact'—something of that nature." Then he laid a gentle hand on my shoulder. "What's the matter, Danny? You in some kind of trouble?"

"I don't even think I know my own name. Would you call that trouble?"

"You know, George isn't *my* real name. It's just a name I use in here."

"George ain't your real name?" McCoy said.

"Nope."

"What is it then?"

"Not telling."

"What other shit have you lied about?"

"Practically everything."

"Well, don't feel so bad, kid," said McCoy. "When I was your age, the whole world knew my name. And where'd it get me?" He addressed his ravaged reflection in the mirror behind the bar. "Bright lights go out the quickest. Kid McCoy knows."

17

Dulwich appeared at my door with the morning paper.

"There's something in here that might be of interest to you," he said as he handed it to me.

Above a photo of a lopsidedly smiling guy who looked like Humphrey Bogart was a huge headline: "DILLINGER SHOT DEAD BY FEDS OUTSIDE CHICAGO MOVIE THE-ATER."

"So they got Dillinger, huh?"

"No, I wasn't talking about that. Look at the bottom of the page."

A nattily dressed guy was walking out of a brick building. It took a moment to sink in that I was looking at Bud Seitz. Trailing a little behind him was his lawyer Arnold Dublinski.

"UNDERWORLD BOSS BUD SEITZ ARRESTED BY L.A. POLICE," read the headline.

"Did you know about this?" asked Dulwich.

I shook my head. He left the paper with me, and I sat down on the davenport and read the story.

"The Gangster Squad caught reputed crime kingpin Reuben 'Bud' Seitz not only with his pants down Sunday morning, but all the way off. Members of the elite crimebusting unit of the Los Angeles Police Department arrested Seitz in the steamroom of the Hollywood Y.M.C.A. Seitz was wearing only a towel at the time. 'He was mild as a kitten when we put the cuffs on him,' said Lt. Jack Otay, head of the Gangster Squad. 'He knew the jig was up.'

"Seitz was arrested for running a bookmaking operation that Los Angeles County District Attorney Buron Fitts called 'the biggest on the west coast. It's just the tip of the iceberg,' continued Fitts. 'Seitz has his fingers in every dirty pie in this part of the country, prostitution, gambling, drugs, you name it. This is just the latest example of how myself, Mayor Shaw, and Chief of Police Davis are taking our community back from those racketeers and crooked politicans that have preyed on the public for far too long.'

"Fitts also said he'd like to talk to Seitz about several unsolved homicides, including that of Clarence 'Doc' Travis, a bootlegger and known associate of Seitz's. The decapitated head of Travis was found in the waters of Lake Arrowhead in 1929 by a troop of Girl Scouts on a nature hike. 'I know some of those innocent young ladies are still having nightmares about their terrible discovery to this very day,' said Fitts, his voice filled with indignation.

"Seitz was released later in the day on $10,000 bail. When asked by reporters on the steps of the Central Police Station about the charges against him, he said, 'It's all a big frame job. I'm a businessman and sportsman, not a mobster. Fitts is barking up the wrong tree.' Queried about his involvement in the murder of Travis, Seitz answered, 'They say I killed everybody but Cock Robin. Doc Travis was a friend of mine. I don't kill my friends.'

" 'Or anybody else, for that matter,' his lawyer, well-known mob mouthpiece Arnold 'Blinky' Dublinski, quickly added."

I called Bud's house. Dick Prettie picked up.

"Dick, what's going on? I just read in the paper Bud got arrested."

"Yeah. Louie Vachaboski made a deal with the D.A. and ratted Bud out."

"Fay Wray?"

"Hey, I just remembered. I ain't supposed to be talking about none of this shit on the phone. Bud's scared it's being tapped. Anyway, I was just about to call you. Come on over. Bud wants to see you."

I drove to Bud's. Beeped my horn at the front gate. A grotesque, unfamiliar face glared out at me through the bars.

"Yeah? What do you want?"

He was young, probably even younger than me. It was like a giant raspberry had been smashed against one side of his face, and his nose was nothing but a big red lump. He was holding a shotgun, pointing it not quite at the ground and not quite at me.

"Who the fuck are you?" I said.

Now the shotgun began to point a little more definitely toward me. The side of his face that was normal started turning red like it was trying to catch up with the other side.

"Who the fuck are *you?*" he said.

Willie the Coon strolled up. "Take it easy, Bo. That's Danny. He's with us."

Bo lowered his shotgun with a look of deep regret. Willie hit a button and the gate opened.

I drove up to the house. Dick and Nello were standing outside, smoking.

"Who's the asshole with the thing on his face?" I said as I got out of the car.

"Bo Spiller," said Dick. "Some punk from Detroit."

"What's he doing here?"

"Bud brung him in," said Nello. "He's supposed to be some kinda mad-dog shotgun killer or something."

"What's he need with a mad-dog killer?"

"He's beefing up his pertection. He thinks everybody's out to get him."

"You hear about Teddy?" said Dick.

I shook my head. "What about him?"

"He went to work for Shitter."

"No kidding. How come?"

"Maybe Shitter's giving him more dough. Or maybe he's thinking it ain't healthy working for Bud Seitz no more."

"There ain't many of us old guys left," said Nello. "Me, and you, and Nucky, and Mo—"

"And me," I said.

Dick and Nello exchanged a look.

"That's right, kid," said Dick. "And you."

I went inside. Anatoly led me into the dining room. Bud was having lunch with Darla. He looked glad to see me.

"You hungry, Danny? We're having pheasants. Anatoly, get Danny a plate."

Darla gave me a searching look but didn't greet me as I sat down at the table. Anatoly brought me a plate with a honey-brown pheasant on it and roasted potatoes and green peas. I was starved, and I dug in.

Bud watched me eat. "How is it?"

"Delicious."

"I hadn't never even heard of a fucking pheasant when I was a kid. Now I can eat as many pheasants as I wanna. I could eat a dozen, two dozen a day if I didn't mind looking like Moe Davis. That's why this kinda shit really pisses me off." He held up the same newspaper Dulwich had shown me, and slapped the photo of himself with the back of his fingers. "You see this?"

"Yeah."

"You can't eat pheasants in prison. You can only eat the worst kind of slop. And that's what these sons of bitches wanna do to me. They wanna make it where I can't eat no more pheasants. It says here I got arrested for running a bookmaking operation that was 'the biggest on the west coast.' That's some joke. I'm only small potatoes in that racket, and everybody knows it. And the fucking Gangster Squad's 'an elite crimebusting unit'?!"

He pronounced elite "uh light." He laughed incredulously.

"I'm a law-abiding citizen compared to them crumbs. And that fucking Jack Otay. I *made* that prick. When I met up with him he was just a dumb detective in a cheap suit that couldn't have found a bull fiddle in a phone booth. Now he's driving around town in a sixteen-cylinder Cadillac and he's got a house in Palm Springs and he's fucking some movie star that don't speak any English. And him saying I was 'mild as a kitten'! All I know is his face went white as this fucking tablecloth when I told him what I was gonna do to him when this is all over with."

"Did Girl Scouts really find Doc Travis's head?"

"Buron Fitts deserves some kinda prize for being the biggest liar in America. It wasn't fucking Girl Scouts, it was this buncha whores from this cathouse in Big Bear. This old dame named Flo ran the cathouse. It was her seventieth birthday or some kinda shit, so her and all her whores got drunk and drove down to Arrowhead and stripped naked and took a midnight dip. That's when they found poor old Doc's head bobbing around. I heard they all run outa that lake and drove back to Big Bear so fucking fast they didn't even take the time to put their clothes back on."

He continued to eat as he looked over the story. "Now this ten G bail's an interesting thing. Ten G's is nothing. Maybe they *want* me to take it on the lam. Maybe that'd solve all their fucking problems for 'em. Maybe they don't want me going up on the stand and yapping about everything I know 'cause I'd take a lotta them down with me. I'd be like that blind guy in the Bible, Goliath. He brung down the temple on his fucking head but killed everybody else too."

"Samson," said Darla. We both looked at her; she wasn't really eating, just pushing around the peas.

"Samson brought down the temple. Goliath was this big giant that David killed."

"Oh yeah. With a fucking slingshot, right? How come you ain't eating nothing? You don't like pheasants?"

Darla shrugged. "It's not that. I just don't feel so hot."

"Whatsamatter?"

"I'm kinda sick at my stomach."

"You want I should call a doctor?"

"Nah." She took her napkin off her lap and put it on the table and stood up. "I'm gonna go sit out by the swimming pool. If anybody wants to join me later," and she meaningfully caught my eye as she walked past, "I'd love the company."

Bud waited till she was out of the room.

"You know what kinda doctor that dame needs? One of them head doctors. She's getting screwier ever day. She nearly killed me the other night."

"Oh yeah? How?"

Bud laughed. "With fucking perfume bottles. You know she's got about a million bottles of the same kind of perfume. She was throwing 'em at me and I was ducking and dodging and they was busting against the walls. It looked like there'd been an explosion in a fucking perfume factory when she got finished up."

"How come she was throwing them at you?"

"Same old story. She thinks the greatest thing in the world's singing in some saloon in front of a buncha drunks trying to imagine what she looks like without no clothes on. I keep telling her all she's gotta do is lift up one little pinkie and she can have anything she wants. She don't need to sing."

"Maybe it makes her happy."

"One thing I've learned, Danny, there ain't nothing ever gonna make a broad like that happy. I let her sing then two weeks later she's gonna be throwing perfume bottles at my head again 'cause of some other damn thing. Anyway. What was we talking about?"

"Taking it on the lam?"

"Yeah. I did that when I was a kid. I ain't doing it again. I like my life here," and he gestured to the room; it was a beautiful room, with a high ceiling and a crystal chandelier and a breeze coming in through the French doors that opened out on a patio and the green, blossoming garden. "I ain't gonna just walk away from it. I just gotta figure out how to turn the tables on these sons of bitches."

Anatoly came in and re-filled our water glasses. I stared as always at his three-fingered hand. When he left, I said: "There's this red Buick. It's been following me."

"Yeah?"

"It always has two guys in it, but I've never been able to get a good look at them. And they only follow me when I'm driving Darla around."

Bud nodded, put some peas in his mouth, and chewed.

"You don't seem too concerned about it," I said.

"That's 'cause I ain't concerned. They're my guys."

"But how come? You don't trust me with Darla?"

"That ain't it. This town's full of people with blood in their eye. I got you guarding Darla 'cause I don't want her to get hurt. And when you're guarding her, I got them two guys guarding you for the same reason."

"So have you got two more guys guarding *those* two guys?"

Bud laughed. "Naw, them two are on their own. If somebody was to knock 'em off, I wouldn't mind a bit. The world would be a better place without 'em."

I finally worked up the nerve to say what I'd been dying to say.

"I know all that Two Gun Danny Landon stuff is made up. I know you brought me here on a train about a year ago."

Bud wiped his mouth carefully with his napkin.

"Yeah? How do you know that?"

"Somebody told me."

"Who?"

"Tommy."

"Tommy told you? When?"

"A couple days before . . ."

I let my voice trail off discreetly. Bud smiled a little.

"He was playing a rib on you. That's how Tommy was. Always with the jokes. I can't believe you fell for it. You want another pheasant? Hey, Anatoly!" he yelled. "Get Danny another pheasant!"

As we were finishing lunch, Blinky showed up, lugging a thick briefcase; he was out of breath and mopping his face with a handkerchief like he'd come over here from his office on foot and at a dead run. I left him with Bud, and walked out to the swimming pool.

The seagull was sitting quietly on the sand under the shade of an umbrella. It cocked its head and watched me as I walked by it towards Darla.

She was sitting in a lounge chair, reading *House and Home*. She was wearing a light-green bathing suit and a white floppy hat and sunglasses. One leg was straight, the other bent; they were smooth and golden and a-shine with sweat and lotion.

"Feeling better?"

She lowered her magazine and peered up at me over her sunglasses.

"I always feel better as soon as I leave a room that has Bud in it."

I dragged over another lounge chair and sat down.

"What did you guys talk about?" she said. "After I left."

"About how you tried to kill him with Mitsuoko bottles."

She didn't deny it. She seemed amused. She picked up a tall

glass of lemonade with a straw sticking out of it. The glass probably had more than just lemonade in it. She took a suck on the
straw, then said delicately: "You thought any more about,
uh . . . ?"

"What?"

"What we talked about. In my apartment."

"Darla, if he goes to prison, everything's gonna be okay."

"Maybe he won't go to prison. And even if he does, that
won't change anything. He'll have his spies. They'll tell him
everything I do."

"Look, I'm not gonna kill him for you. You can forget that."

She looked at me without saying anything. She jabbed at the
ice in the glass with the straw. Finally she said: "Okay."

Now she returned to her magazine. She was doing her
Danny's-vanished-into-thin-air act.

"Darla?"

She continued slowly turning the pages. "What?"

But I didn't know what. I heard voices. Willie the Coon and
Bo Spiller were walking by. They were ogling Darla and giggling. Then Bo socked Willie in the arm and took off. Willie ran
after him. Bo got behind the trunk of a palm tree and jumped
this way and that as Willie tried to grab him. They were showing
off for Darla like schoolboys.

"I've got a gun," she said.

"You've got a gun?"

"Yeah."

"Where?"

"Hidden someplace. For when I need it."

The seagull started screeching. Darla and I looked over, and
saw Anatoly approaching. He had a plateful of table scraps. The
gull was beside itself with excitement, it flapped its wings and
rose into the air as Anatoly started tossing it chunks of potato
and crusts of bread and pieces of pheasant. Anatoly spoke softly

to the gull in Russian.

"He sure loves that bird," I said.

"That's good," said Darla. "It's good to love something."

18

All I really wanted to do was sleep. Over the next several days I would go to bed early and sleep late and then during the middle of the afternoon take a long nap. It was like my consciousness was an island in a sea of sleep and the waters were rising and threatening to overwhelm the island altogether.

I woke up from one nap, and saw Sophie standing at the dresser with her back to me, stealthily pulling a drawer open. She looked through it quickly, shut it, then eased the next drawer open.

She glanced over her shoulder at me. I snapped my eyes shut. Then I opened my eyes a crack, and peered out at her through the trembling shroud of my eyelashes.

She was counting the money in my wallet. Now she took out a few bills, and stuffed them in the pocket of her shorts. Then she put the wallet back in the drawer, and closed it.

She looked at me again, then tiptoed out of the room. I gave her enough time to get out of the house before I got up.

I remembered having a hundred fifty bucks or so in my wallet. Now I had about half that. I was glad for her to have the money if she felt like she needed it that bad, but I was sorry she hadn't just asked me for it.

It felt like there was another shoe that needed to drop, and it did so that night. I was in the kitchen making a sandwich when I heard a woman yelling for help out in the courtyard.

I ran outside. Mrs. Dean was in front of Sophie's bungalow.

"Fire!" she screamed. "Oh my lord! Fire!"

The front door was closed and no lights were on inside, but I could see an orange flickering glow through the window, and smoke was drifting out.

"Where's Sophie?" I said.

Mrs. Dean looked blankly at me, like I was a stranger. She screamed: "Fire!"

The door wasn't locked. I stepped into the smoky dark and called for Sophie. No answer. The bungalow was laid out just like mine. I saw the fire was in the back, in the bedroom. The door was half open, and I pushed through it.

A ferocious fire was consuming the bed.

"Sophie! Are you in here?"

I fumbled for the light switch, turned on the overhead light. The air was thick with acrid smoke. I started to cough. My eyes were burning and watering and I could hardly see.

I was afraid she was in here someplace. Maybe lying on the floor, overcome by the smoke. Maybe cowering in the closet.

I stumbled around the room, coughing and calling for her. I opened the closet and thrust my arms into a thicket of clothes.

Someone grabbed my elbow.

"She's not in there, old boy. Come on. Let's get out of here."

Dulwich was holding a handkerchief over his mouth and nose. I let him pull me out of the house.

The usual crowd of bungalow dwellers had gathered around to gawk. Mrs. Dean was still going nuts. Tears were streaming out of the eyes of Dulwich and me. Suddenly five red-hatted firemen came running up the seven steps from the street. They dragged a big brown hose into the house and had the fire put out in short order.

Mrs. Dean, who I never knew was so religious, repeatedly thanked the Lord when she found out the fire hadn't spread beyond the bed, and her bungalow, though smoky and scorched and waterlogged, was intact. The firemen were leaving as Lois and Jerry showed up. They were dressed up and drunk and seemed to be returning from a night on the town.

"Where's Sophie?" yelled Lois when she figured out the center of all the excitement was her own home. "Where's my little girl?"

But nobody knew. Mrs. Dean wanted to know how the fire had started. Had one of them been smoking in bed?

"We been gone for hours," said Lois, "how could we have been smoking in bed?"

"When was the last time you saw Sophie?" I said.

"Well, it was when we left here, what time was that, Jerry, a little after six?"

"It was her that done it!" said Jerry. "The little brat!"

"Oh, Jerry, you don't mean that—"

"The hell I don't! And now she's run away, to escape her proper punishment!"

"But why would she set the bed on fire?" said Dulwich.

Jerry glowered furiously at Dulwich, at the same time taking a step backwards.

"I'm not talking to you no more, Mr. Dulwich. Not after being the innocent victim of your fisticuffs. You caught me by surprise that time, Mr. Dulwich, but maybe next time you won't be so lucky!"

"Jerry," said Mrs. Dean, "I hope you understand that you and Lois will have to pay for the damages to my unit."

Jerry looked taken aback. "But don't you have insurance?"

"Not for this sort of thing."

"That little monster don't belong to me. I'm not responsible for what she does."

"Don't call her that! Don't call my daughter a monster!" said Lois, and then she took a swing at Jerry. It popped him right on the ear.

He yowled in pain. "Jumping Jesus! I think you broke my goddamn eardrum!"

"Oh, I'm sorry, baby, I didn't mean to," and she reached for his ear, but he batted her hand away.

"I've had it, Lois! You and your little brat haven't been nothing but trouble for me! I'm getting my stuff and I'm moving out! And don't try and stop me!"

Jerry stormed toward the bungalow as Lois wailingly tried to stop him. Their neighbors looked on, slackjawed with satisfaction, as though this had all been an especially good episode of *The Shadow* or *Amos 'n' Andy.*

I turned to Dulwich and said: "Where's the nearest bus station?"

19

The Greyhound depot was downtown, on South Los Angeles Street. A terrible beggar with some kind of shiny steel contraption in place of a lower jaw sat out front; he had a straw boater with a few pennies and nickels in it. Inside, in the waiting area, several sailors were sitting around chewing gum and drinking sodas and smoking cigarettes and reading magazines. A shabbily dressed woman in a Gilligan hat was stretched out on a bench asleep, using her suitcase as a hard pillow. A guy with thinning, slicked-back hair and a checkered vest was sitting with his legs stuck out and his fingers interlaced over a plump belly. He had a smug smile, and was gazing with beady, barely open eyes at Sophie, who was sitting directly across from him.

A little suitcase sat by her feet. She was reading a book. She looked up at me as I walked over. She seemed surprised.

"Hi, Sophie."

"Hi."

I gave the guy in the vest a hard look.

"I think your bus is about to leave."

He kept the smug smile. He checked his watch, said: "You're right, friend. Thanks," then stood up and sauntered away, taking his sweet time about it, melodiously whistling "Beautiful Dreamer."

"Can I sit down?"

She nodded.

"What are you reading?"

She showed me the cover of the book: *Kidnapped!* by Robert Louis Stevenson.

"Is it good?"

"Yeah. How'd you know I was here?"

"Lucky guess."

"Well—I'm not going back."

"Don't you wanna know if your house burned down?"

She looked away. "I didn't do it."

"You scared me to death, Sophie. I thought you were in there. I couldn't see anything because of the smoke."

She looked back at me. "You ran into a burning house . . . just to look for me?"

"Dulwich did too. It didn't burn down though. Just the bed."

Sophie gave me a sniff. "So that's what you smell like. Smoke."

"You already got your ticket?"

"Yeah."

"For New York?"

"Uh huh."

"Where'd you get the money?"

"I been saving up for it."

"I woke up today. When you were taking the money out of my wallet."

She regarded me with a mixture of guilt and puzzlement. "Then why didn't you stop me?"

I shrugged.

"Well, don't worry, I'll pay you back. When I get a job. Every penny."

"Look. Here's the deal. I can't let you go off to New York. Not now. Not by yourself."

"How you gonna stop me?"

"I'm bigger than you."

"But I can run faster."

"Sophie, you're just too young. I have a friend, she ran away from home when she was about your age. She couldn't protect herself. Horrible things happened to her on the road."

"Horrible things happen to me at home."

"I know. But Dulwich and me, we live right across the courtyard. From now on, anything happens, you just come to us. And anyway, Jerry said he's moving out."

"When did he say that?"

"Tonight. When he and your mom came home, and found out about the fire. They got in a big fight, and your mother punched him in the ear, then he said he was leaving."

"He always says that. Any time they fight. But he never does."

"Like I said. We're just across the courtyard. So what do you say we try and get a refund on your ticket? Then we'll see if we can find a drugstore that's still open, and I'll buy you a chocolate soda."

Sudden angry tears filled Sophie's eyes. "I'm not five years old! You think you can bribe me with a chocolate soda? Why should I go *any*where with you? You were so . . . *mean*. You made me feel . . . dirty. No good."

"Sophie, listen, I'm sorry. You're the last person in the world I'd ever want to hurt. I mean that."

Sophie's knuckles were pressed against her mouth, as she fought back tears and stared off bitterly at nothing.

I offered her my handkerchief. She wiped her nose with it, then handed it back to me. Then she stood up, and picked up her suitcase.

"Okay. Let's go."

The nice man at the ticket counter gave her back the thirty-two fifty with no problem. She made me put five bucks in the straw hat of the jawless beggar. As we walked to my car, a Greyhound bus moved past, its engine growling as it picked up speed, and I too felt the lure of leaving, of sitting in the rumbling dark with dozens of strangers, of venturing forth into the dreaming, star-lit nation, of breaking with the present and embracing the unknown—and then I felt Sophie's hand slip into mine.

"I'm glad you found me," she said.

"Yeah. Me too."

20

Turned out Sophie was wrong about Jerry. The next day the population of our bungalow court was minus one unemployed plaid-sports-coated door-to-door salesman.

To celebrate, Dulwich and I took Sophie to Capezio's and bought her some new tap-dancing shoes, then we wandered down Hollywood Boulevard. A store had signs in the window that said: "SOUVENIRS. PRACTICAL JOKES. LIVE BABY TURTLES." We declined to get her a baby turtle, but we agreed to buy her green trick dice that only rolled sevens and a metal ashtray in the shape of the state of Louisiana.

When we returned to La Vista Lane, a pair of workmen were taking a mattress out of a truck under the scrutiny of the grim eyeglasses of Mrs. Dean. Matilda was in Sophie's bungalow helping Sophie's mother clean things up, and Sophie got recruited to help; she pitched in immediately with all the cheerful enthusiasm of a shanghaied sailor.

"How about a nice glass of plonk?" said Dulwich, and though I didn't know what plonk was, I said sure. He took a bottle of French red wine out of the cupboard. We sat in his living room sipping the plonk, and Dulwich smoked some opium; then he said it was beastly hot in here and suggested we go outside.

It was late afternoon, and the courtyard was mostly in shadow. We sat cross-legged like Indians on the grass in front of his flower bed. Tinker sat with us. Dulwich absently scratched the back of her neck. Suddenly she began producing a strange clicky kind of sound in her throat.

Her tail twitched. Her emerald eyes were fixed on a flock of sparrows that had descended on Mrs. Dean's birdseed.

"Careful, Miss Tink," said Dulwich. "The redoubtable Mrs. Dean is about."

"Have you finished your story yet?"

"No. I gave it up."

"Why?"

"Because it wasn't any good. I really need to face the simple fact that I am not a writer. I'm not much of anything, really. I'm fortunate enough to have a modest monthly income that lets me live a very pleasant, very little sort of life. I thought when I was young that I was destined for some kind of greatness. Obviously I was absurdly mistaken."

I felt bad for Dulwich, but didn't know what to say. We sat there silently for a while. A cooling breeze blew across the grass. Then Dulwich said softly:

> You smug-faced crowds with kindling eye
> Who cheer when soldier lads march by,
> Sneak home and pray you'll never know
> The hell where youth and laughter go.

"What's that?" I said.

"A poem. By a soldier named Sassoon." A pause, and then: "I was reminded of the war."

I looked around the courtyard. "Reminded by what?"

"The sparrows. I used to watch flocks of sparrows and starlings feeding on the Turkish corpses hanging in the barbed wire. Outside the mud fort at Kut."

"What's Kut?"

"You don't really want to hear a lot of old war stories, do you?"

"Sure I would. If you wouldn't mind telling me."

"No. I wouldn't mind."

He took a thoughtful sip of plonk.

"Kut was a dreary little mud town on the banks of the Tigris River in Mesopotamia. We had come to Mesopotamia because the Turks had seized the facilities of the Anglo-Persian Oil Company at the port of Basra. The British Navy was in dire need of that oil, we were told, and by George we were the ones that would get it back!

"Well, Danny, the Turks made such a poor show of it at Basra that our brilliant brass hats decided it would be a good idea to push inland and capture Baghdad. So an army of 10,000 went marching forth from Basra, and the cry was: 'Baghdad by Christmas!'

"Mesopotamia was a featureless brown immensity, and we were 10,000 specks crawling across it, and it swallowed us up. We actually made it to within sight of the fabled city of Sinbad; I can see as though they were in front of me now its turquoise minarets shining in the sun. But then we were met by a force of 20,000 Turks, they had yellow uniforms and barbarically long bayonets, whereupon the brass hats decided it would be a good idea for the British Indian Expeditionary Force to retrace its steps.

"We fell back on Kut. There it was decided we would make a stand, and await reinforcements. We were swiftly encircled by the Turks.

"A mud fort was erected northeast of the town, to serve as an observation post for our guns. I was a lieutenant in the 17th Brigade, which was given the task of defending the fort.

"The Turks shelled the fort relentlessly day after day. And then at 8:30, on Christmas Eve morning, the biggest bombardment to date began. It lasted for three hours, then all became silent. Then we began to hear something outside the fort. We looked through the loopholes in the walls, we could see nothing through the smoke and dust, but we heard the thudding of boots, and then we saw the glint of the long bayonets through the smoke and then we could see clearly the Turkish infantry running towards us.

"Our machine guns shot them down and they became tangled in the barbed wire and the future food of birds but they were wonderfully brave and they kept coming, kept coming. The bombardment had blown a hole in the northeast wall, and finally the Turks fought through the breach and were inside the fort and amongst us.

"It was quite terrifying, Danny, fighting your enemy face to face like that, but it was also exhilarating. For as long as it lasted, I don't think I ever had a thought in my head, it was all animal instinct and action. There was no time to reload your rifle or pistol, your weapons were bombs and bayonets and rifle butts; I even bashed in a man's head with a cooking pot! So much for any lingering schoolboy notions I might have had about the nobility of man, his supposed superiority to the rest of the creation. By far, *Homo sapiens* is the most violent species. As a lamb is to a lion, so a lion is to a man.

"Eventually the Turks withdrew, but that night they came back. Again they entered the fort through the breach in the northeast wall. Fighting by night is a different experience than fighting by day. The infernal flashes of light leaping out of the darkness, the silhouettes and shadows, the confusion of friend and foe, the clawing lunatic flames. Even the shouts and the screams of the combatants sounded different at night, more mysterious, more terrible.

"During the early hours of Christmas Day, the Turks retired for good. They left behind hundreds of their dead and wounded in and around the fort. Most of my men, too, had been either killed or wounded. Astonishingly, though, I'd made it through unscathed.

"General Townshend sent word from his headquarters in the town that the defense of the fort by the 17th Brigade would be remembered in the annals of British military history for as long as the et cetera et-cetera'd and the so on so-on'd, but he was wrong, of course. The siege of Kut is only an obscure and embarrassing footnote now. The Middle East was always just a sideshow next to France."

"When were you taken prisoner?"

"Not for several months. The Relief Force was perpetually expected but it never arrived, for it, too, was attacked by the Turks. Our rations dwindled rapidly. I discovered that mules are better to eat than horses. But I drew the line at dogs and, of course," and he glanced at Tinker and whispered, "cats. Most of our Indian troops refused to eat horse flesh for religious reasons, and so the poor devils calmly settled in to starve to death.

"Several thousand Arabs were trapped in the town with us. It was just their unlucky fate we had chosen their town to make our stand. Some tried to escape across the river by boat or raft, but they were shot by the Turks, and their bodies floated away down the river or washed up on the banks.

"The river became a place of horror. During the winter it was cold and rainy, and the banks of the river turned into mud. By April it had become extremely hot again, and steam curled up from the mud. The banks were littered with the rotting bodies of Turks and Arabs. The decaying flesh and the mud seemed to merge into a single substance, a corrupt slime which sucked at your boots, which wanted you to join it, to become slime yourself.

"Our position became untenable. We were starving, and racked with diseases. What was left of us surrendered on April 29, 1916.

"The Arabs were in a panic. They feared the Turks would wreak a gruesome revenge on them for cooperating with us, and they were right. The Turks immediately set up makeshift gibbets by the river, and began hanging people; others were murdered by firing squads.

"We officers were separated from our men. We were put aboard a river steamer, which would take us up the Tigris to Baghdad and beyond. A column of our soldiers were walking along the bank under Turkish guard. I heard someone calling my name. It was Private Pilditch, one of my favorites. A cheerful, rosy-cheeked lad, and a stalwart soldier. He was barely literate, and I used to help him write letters to his fiancée, Mary. 'Mr. Dulwich!' he called. ''Ow in 'oly 'ell did we lose the 'ole blooming army?!' I didn't have an answer for him. He wasn't cheerful or rosy-cheeked any longer; he was skeletally thin; he had pneumonia, and an oozing, festering sore on his leg. I waved farewell to Pilditch, and he waved forlornly back, and I watched him limp away up the river.

"So we all went into our captivity. As it turned out, the officers were treated tolerably well, but our men suffered abominably. Few returned. Pilditch didn't.

"My men meant so much to me, Danny. I call them men, but they were boys, really. I was in love with them, collectively. I loved them as if they were one soldier, handsome, smiling, sturdy, youthful, brave, and afraid. And I wanted to protect my soldier, do my best for my soldier, for my brave lad, my smiling lad. But he was shot, bayonetted, blown to bits, bludgeoned, starved, drowned in irrigation ditches, blinded, emasculated, tortured, made mad. And of course Dulwich never got a scratch. Lieutenants in the Great War were expected to lead ephemeral lives, like insects hatching and mating and dying all in a day. But Dulwich just went on and on. On and on . . ."

Something startled the sparrows, and they whooshed away. Dulwich gave me a wan smile.

"More plonk?"

21

Dick and I drove out Sunset to the ocean then up the Coast Highway to Malibu then onto a little dirt road that took us up into the brown hills. It was hot but we were drinking cold beers and listening to the radio and it was a pleasant ride. We passed some dilapidated cottages and a couple of house trailers and a viciously barking dog chased us for a while till Dick threw his bottle of beer at it, then he pulled over and parked in the shade of a stunted oak tree.

You had some view from up there; the ocean was wrinkled near the shore then got smoother and smoother and you wished you were an arrow shot from the bow of an infinitely strong archer and you were flying away from Malibu into the endless blue.

We walked away from the road and up a little draw. We took some beer with us plus a paper sack filled with empty beer bottles.

Dick unzipped his fly then delivered himself of such a massive amount of piss it was a wonder his skinny frame had had the space to store it. Then he took six of the beer bottles and lined them up in a row. Then we took a position about twenty-five feet away.

I'd gone to a store on Alvarado called Andy's Guns & Ammo and got a new Smith & Wesson .38 to replace the one the Mexicans stole; we'd come up here so I could try it out.

"I'll take the three on the left," said Dick.

"Okay."

Dick took his own pistol out of his waistband, then we took turns firing. The noise disturbed a crow that flapped away, peevishly cawing, and I didn't blame it a bit. It would've been ideal to have three arms so I could've put a finger in each ear as we blazed away.

It took Dick four shots to shatter his three bottles, but after I'd emptied my gun of bullets my three bottles still stood sassily upright, gleaming in the sun.

"Hard to believe I was ever any good at this," I said as I reloaded.

Dick coughed, and lit up a cigarette.

"You're right, kid. It is hard to believe."

★ ★ ★ ★ ★

3

★ ★ ★ ★ ★

1

Bud called. He said Darla had a pain in her back, and he wanted me to pick her up in the morning and take her to a chiropractor.

"Okay," I said. "What time?"

"Her appointment's at six-thirty. Address is 418 Grand. The doc's name is Brunder."

It seemed like a strange time to see a chiropractor, but I didn't ask any questions. I was at Bud's house about a quarter to six. Bo Spiller's shotgun and smashed-raspberry face greeted me at the gate.

Darla came out of the house, a scarf over her hair and her eyes hidden behind her sunglasses. She managed to look pale even through her tan. She didn't say anything to me when I said good morning. As he opened the gate for us, Spiller gave her his best imitation of a suave grin, but unfortunately it turned into the leer of a maniac.

We drove south on La Brea through the slowly awakening city. Darla lit up a cigarette. I said: "How's your back?"

"It's fine," she sighed. "There's nothing wrong with my back."

"But—Bud said—"

"Oh Danny, can you really be that dumb? Maybe the fellas are right about you." She was silent, and then: "Look, I'm sorry. I didn't mean that. I feel lousy. This is a lousy day. I'm having a baby. Except I'm not."

She looked at me for the first time; at least I assumed that behind the black glasses pointing at me her eyes were looking at me.

"Well—say something."

"Like what?"

"Like I'm a cheap tramp and I'm going to hell."

"Whose idea is this? His?"

"It's mine too. We agree on something for once. He doesn't want a kid 'cause he says two's company and three's a crowd. And I don't want a kid 'cause, well, what girl in her right mind would wanna have Bud Seitz's baby? It'd probably be a monster, just like him. It'd probably have two heads."

"But Darla, isn't it wrong? Isn't it just like killing?"

"You *are* a killer, Danny. That's what you do. So you don't get to judge me."

I checked my rearview mirror. Didn't see any sign of my buddies in the red Buick.

"Look, let's just go. Now. You and me. I'll be its father. It won't have two heads. We'll be happy."

Darla exhaled a weary plume of smoke.

"We'd be lucky to make it to the city limits."

"This car goes fast. Real fast."

"Forget it. I told you. He's gotta be dead first."

"What do you expect me to do? Turn around and go back to the house and kill him? What about all the guys he's always got all around him? You expect me to kill Nucky and Nello and Willie the Coon and that new guy with the thing on his face too?"

"I don't expect you to do anything anymore, Danny. Except to shut up. And leave me alone."

Grand was downtown. It wasn't much of a downtown; none of the buildings were more than ten or twelve stories high. The directory in the lobby of 418 Grand said Dr. Rudolph Brunder's office was on the eighth floor. The eighth-floor hallway was empty. The pebbled-glass door to Brunder's office was locked. I looked at my watch. We were a few minutes early.

There wasn't any place to sit down. Darla smoked. I leaned against the wall with my hands in my trouser pockets—rattled the change there until Darla gave me a dirty look and stopped me.

In a little while the elevator down the hall opened, and a short, dark man headed our way. He had a carefully trimmed red moustache and was wearing a black homburg hat. He glanced at us as he unlocked the door and his mouth twitched in a smile-like fashion.

"Good morning," he said, with some kind of foreign accent. "I hope I am not late?"

I didn't like him. I shrugged. He ushered us into a small, stuffy waiting room; there was a sofa in a putrid-green color and a coffee table with some magazines and a glass jar of lollipops on it and a tall potted plant in the corner that looked like it was hanging on to life by its fingernails.

"Please have a seat," said Dr. Brunder. "Help yourself to the lollipops. My assistant should be here shortly, and then we will get started."

Brunder twitched his lips at us again then disappeared through another door. We neither had a seat nor helped ourselves to the lollipops. Darla lit up another cigarette and walked over to the window, while I just stood there in the middle of the room, a sort of human version of the potted plant.

The door to the hallway opened, and a woman came in. She was very fat in a particular kind of way, fairly normal at the top but getting fatter the farther down you went. Either one of her thighs was bigger around than all of Dick Prettie.

"Hi, I'm Polly," she said with a warm smile. She waddled over to the window Darla was standing at and lifted it open. "It's going to be another hot one," then she looked at Darla.

"You ready, honey?"

I saw Darla's gaze move from Polly back to the open window, and my heart gave a sickening lurch as for a fraction of a second I thought she was about to jump, but all she did was toss out her cigarette; then she followed Polly.

Polly held the door open for her, and she passed through it and out of sight. Now Polly smiled back at me.

"Help yourself to those lollipops, honey. That's what they're there for."

I wanted to say who cares about your fucking lollipops and you oughta be in a circus you're so fat but I didn't say anything and went over to the sofa and sat down; it was very soft, and I sank down into its putrid-green embrace and closed my eyes. It wasn't that I was sleepy; I just wanted to block from sight the dog-eared magazines from last year and the year before that and the poisonously orange and yellow and red and green lollipops and the dying plant. But the problem with closing your eyes is, it tends to awaken your mind's eye. I saw Doc Travis standing on the balcony during a rain storm and sticking his hand out and watching the rain patter into his wrinkled black palm, and Sophie waiting all by herself to board a bus to nowhere, and Vera Vermillion's glowing blue moon, and Bud killing Tommy with a bottle of Bacardi rum, and Dulwich's gappy grin under his Mexican hat, and the cold eyes of the nurse on the train, and Darla standing by the lake under the moon and looking up at me as I thought we were about to kiss, like any regular guy and girl might kiss in such circumstances. By a lake. Under the moon.

I heard a pleasant soft burbling—opened my eyes and saw two pigeons on the ledge outside the window. I wondered if the pigeons ever flew inside, then I had a sudden memory: a panicked bird flying around inside a room, and my mother laughingly chasing it with a broom. She wasn't trying to hurt it, was just trying to guide it back toward the window it had come in through. Lacy curtains hung in the window, they billowed in a luminous breeze—

The door to the hallway opened a foot or two, and a girl peered in. She saw me—looked alarmed—but came in anyway.

She sat down on the sofa as far away from me as possible. I suppose to her I was just part of the awfulness of it all. She had a small, turned-up nose, and looked sweet and pretty and not more than eighteen. I wondered who the cad was who got her in trouble and why he wasn't here with her.

I tried to get back to the memory of my mother with the broom, but it was all gone now, as if it had escaped back out the window with the bird.

I'd heard that when women got abortions it was like torture and they screamed like damned souls and I was straining my ears for any sign of that but, except for the cooing of the pigeons and the crinkling of the cellophane that the girl removed from one of the lollipops, everything was quiet as a tomb.

At last the door opened and Polly came out. She beamed at us.

"Susannah? We're ready for you now."

Susannah put down her magazine and left the sofa.

"What about Darla?" I said.

"She's doing just fine, honey. It's all over. She's resting now. She'll be out soon."

I tried reading one of the magazines, but the world it described of movie stars and politicians and sports heroes and kings and queens seemed unreal and boring. I went over to the window. The pigeons, heads bobbing, walked away from me down the ledge. Traffic noise floated up. The building across the street was being increasingly lit up by the rising sun.

I had one of my headaches, for the first time in a while. I went out to a water fountain in the hallway, but then discovered

I hadn't brought my aspirins. I was about to drink some water anyway, but only the barest trickle was coming out. I thought of all the germy horrible mouths that must have been down there. I hesitated.

"Danny?"

Darla was standing just outside the chiropractor's office, leaning against the door frame.

"I thought you'd left," she said. "Without me."

I hurried down the hallway to her.

"Course not. How do you feel?"

"Like shit."

She looked like it too. We walked slowly toward the elevator. She seemed a little woozy. Then she put her hand over her mouth.

"I think I'm gonna be sick."

"I saw a ladies' room. Down this way."

We started moving fast. We got to the ladies' room and she tried the door. It was locked. She rattled the glass door knob and wailed: "Oh fuck!" Then she leaned over and threw up.

I watched her helplessly as spasm followed spasm. The elevator opened, and two well-dressed guys with briefcases came out. They stopped and gaped at the sight of the beautiful vomiting girl.

"Get the fuck outa here!" I yelled.

They looked scared, and headed the other way.

Darla seemed through now. I handed her my handkerchief, and she wiped her mouth off.

"You okay?" I said. "You wanna go back and see Dr. Brunder?"

"You kidding me? Just get me outa here."

We took the elevator down. It was already hot, even down at the bottom of the shady canyon between the tall buildings. As I helped her in the car, she winced and sucked her breath in.

"You okay?"

"Quit asking me that."

I got in the car and drove her out of downtown. She curled up in the seat with her back to me. I was wondering what Dr. Brunder had done to her. I saw other people in their cars on their way to work and I envied them because their faces seemed normal and calm like this was just another morning and their lives weren't all screwed up and everything wasn't falling apart.

"It hurts," said Darla in a small, tight voice, and then I saw the blood. It was very red against the black leather of the seat. It was like somebody had tossed a bucket of it on Darla's lap.

Darla sat up and took off her sunglasses and looked at her lap and then looked at me.

"Oh god!" she screamed. "Am I dying?"

2

We weren't far from Cedars of Lebanon Hospital. I drove up Vermont honking my horn and running red lights then turned left on Fountain and went a couple of blocks and we were there.

By now, Darla's head was lolling around and her eyes were rolling up and showing white. "I'll be right back," I said, but she didn't answer me; she'd passed out or was on the verge of it. I jumped out of the car and ran inside the hospital, yelling for help. Two orderlies grabbed a stretcher on wheels and rolled it out. A Polly-sized nurse lumbered along behind them.

A black Pontiac had pulled up behind my Packard. Two guys were inside. They watched as the nurse and the orderlies got Darla out of the car and on the stretcher. Their white uniforms got splotched by Darla's blood; it occurred to me people in their line of work should dress in red. As they trundled her inside, the nurse asked me what had happened to her. I figured the best thing for Darla was just to tell the truth.

Darla disappeared behind swinging double doors. The nurse wouldn't let me go with her. I realized I was shaking all over; I tried to stop myself, but couldn't.

The two guys from the Pontiac came in. Both squat, blubbery-lipped, and ugly. They walked up to me like they knew me.

"What's going on?" said one of them.

"What's going on with what?"

"The broad. Darla. What's the matter with her?"

"What's it to you?"

"We work for Seitz," the other said. "Like you. So what's up with the broad?"

"You guys must be the assholes in the red Buick."

"We're in a black Pontiac, moron."

I walked away.

"Hey!" said the first guy. "Where you going?"

I ignored him. They followed me. I found a phone booth and called Bud. He came walking in fast ten minutes later, with Nucky and Willie hurrying along with him.

"Where is she?" he said.

"They took her through there," and I pointed toward the swinging doors.

Bud headed that way.

"I don't think we're allowed back there," I said.

"Fuck that," and he shoved through the doors. Nucky and Willie and I were right behind him.

We moved down a short hallway then into a room with a lot of beds with curtains around them. Bud went over to the first bed and jerked the curtains back. A nurse was putting a thermometer in the mouth of an old lady. They stared at us in surprise and horror like they thought we were about to murder them.

"Who are you?" said the nurse. "What do you want?"

"Sorry," muttered Bud, "I'm looking for somebody," then the nurse with Darla's blood on her uniform came running up.

"You're not allowed back here! *Not allowed!*"

"I'm allowed any fucking place I wanna go, you fat cunt! You know how much dough I give this joint?"

"Nurse! Nurse! Everything's all right. I'll take care of it."

A middle-aged doctor came walking up. He was short, with broad shoulders, an unnaturally large head, and a handsome mass of wavy, prematurely gray hair. He looked familiar.

"Dr. Swan," said Bud. He seemed relieved to see him. He even shook his hand.

"Good morning, Mr. Seitz. I know why you're here. I recognized your friend as soon as they brought her in. I saw her sing once at your club. She was unforgettable."

"Yeah, doc, that's great, but how's she doing?"

"Dr. Zamsky has located the source of the bleeding and stopped it. You remember Bernie Zamsky, don't you? She couldn't be in better hands."

"So she's gonna be okay?"

"Barring infection, which is always a risk in this kind of case, she ought to be just fine."

Bud let loose a big sigh. "Thank god, doc. That's great news. See that she gets anything she needs. The best of everything."

Dr. Swan was looking at me curiously. "Don't I know you?"

Bud laughed, and clapped me on the shoulder.

"That's Danny, doc. Remember? He got beat up by them guys at Ocean Park last year."

"Danny. Of course. Well, you've certainly changed. What a tremendous recovery."

"That's 'cause of the great doctoring you guys gave him. So when can I see her?"

"It shouldn't be too long. Why don't you wait in the lobby? I'll come get you when it's time."

Out in the lobby, I filled Bud in on what had happened with Darla.

"I don't get it," he said. "I've sent girls to this Brunder guy before and there hadn't ever been no problems. Then when I send him over a girl I really give a shit about, he carves her up like a Thanksgiving turkey."

"You want me and Willie to pay him a visit?" said Nucky.

"Yeah," said Willie. "We'll get you a fucking refund."

"That's a good idea," said Bud.

I watched Willie and Nucky strut their way out the door.

"What are they gonna do to him? Throw him out the window?"

Bud laughed. "I gotta be careful these days, Danny. They'll throw me in the sleazer for spitting on the sidewalk. Nah, they'll just do like Willie said. Get a refund."

He took out a Kleenex and wiped his hands off.

"I hate hospitals. Full of fucking germs."

"You really give money to this place?"

"Sure. Jews make the best damn doctors in the world. A joint like this makes you proud to be a Jew. I give money to a lot of Jewish stuff. The Jewish Home for the Aged. The Hamburger Home for Young Women. Things like that."

"I didn't know that."

"Yeah, you see, I ain't a total crumb."

I saw my shadows in the red Buick/black Pontiac standing on the other side of the lobby, smoking and casting sheepish looks in our direction.

"Who are those guys?" I said.

"Them? That's Freddie Kornblum on the left. The other guy's his brother Mousie. They call him that 'cause of the way he eats. Kinda nibbles his food real fast, like a mouse. I'm really scraping the bottom of the barrel when I got dumb cocksuckers like the Kornblum brothers working for me, but I ain't got no choice. All my best guys is getting killed or going over to work for my enemies. That's why I'm lucky I got you. When you called me up and told me about Darla, I felt like my balls had turned into lead and they was dropping right through the fucking floor. I'm so stuck on that broad it ain't even funny. But I can see now everything's gonna be okay. You handled things real good, Danny. You took care of Darla. I can always count on you."

Now he put his hand on my shoulder.

"Hey, you look beat. Why don't you go on home. Get a little shut-eye. Take the rest of the day off."

I was reluctant to leave Darla.

"I'll be glad to stick around, Bud. Keep you company."

"Beat it, kid," he said, taking out a Kleenex to wipe his fingers off after touching me. "That's an order."

My car looked like a crime scene. I drove into the nearest gas station. The owner, looking disgusted, said it was gonna cost me. I said fine. While they cleaned up the car I drank a Coke, and watched the traffic go by.

3

The next morning I went to a building in the shape of a flower pot on Melrose Avenue that sold plants and flowers. I bought a bouquet of white and red and yellow snapdragons, then went to the hospital.

Nucky Williams was out in the hallway guarding Darla's room. He grinned at the flowers.

"Aw, how'd you know it was my birthday?"

I reached for the doorknob. He stepped in between the door and me. His mashed-in face and flat chicken eyes were just a few inches away.

"Get outa my way, Nucky."

But he didn't budge.

"All us guys been trying to figure out what your secret is. You got one of them foot-long peckers? Or maybe it's just that Darla's hot for gimps. What do you say, Limpy? If I was to shoot myself in the foot, would Darla let me fuck her too?"

I grabbed his right shoulder with my right hand and forearmed him out of the way. He pretended to stumble and be afraid.

"Easy there, Danny! Don't hurt me! Please don't hurt me!"

Darla looked up from a magazine as I came in. She was lying in bed in a white hospital gown with her blue-eyed, red-bowed lamb beside her. She smiled faintly.

"Hi, Danny."

"Hi. How you feeling?"

She shrugged. I handed her the flowers. She sniffed them dutifully.

"They're nice. Thanks."

"They're snapdragons."

"I like snapdragons."

The room was filled with flowers, red roses mostly. It was big and airy, with nice furniture, and watercolors of sailboats and sunsets and misty mountain ranges on the wall. I dropped my hat on a gleaming mahogany table.

"This is a pretty ritzy room for a hospital," I said.

"You know who stayed in this room?"

"Who?"

"Guess."

"Eleanor Roosevelt?"

"Clark Gable."

"Yeah? When?"

"Last summer. He got his gallbladder taken out."

"No kidding."

"This nurse told me about it. And she said this other nurse was such a big fan of Clark Gable that she didn't throw his gallbladder away like she was supposed to."

"What did she do with it?"

"She put it in a jar filled with formaldehyde. She keeps it in a drawer at home. Every now and then she takes it out of the drawer just to look at it."

"Jesus. What a nut."

"Yeah."

We both laughed a little. Then it became quiet. The room smelled like roses and disinfectant. Darla looked at the lamb. Plucked at the red bow around its neck. Her eyes filled up with tears.

"Darla?"

I sat down on the bed and she leaned into me and I put my

arms around her and she began to cry.

"It was so awful," she whispered.

"I know."

"He gave me laughing gas. I don't know why they call it that. I didn't laugh. The light from the window started spinning around. It got smaller and smaller till it was just this teensy little point of light, and I knew that when that little bit of light disappeared, I would disappear, and I ripped the mask off. The doctor said, 'Calm down, you stupid girl,' and he put the mask back on and he held it there. And then it was like I went on this trip through the universe, and this voice was telling me that everything you've ever been told is a pack of lies. And the voice was saying, *look*, this is how things really are! And it was like I was passing from one hell to another, from hell to hell to hell to hell. And everything was hopelessness and pain. Anger and evil. And then it was like I was falling into a giant volcano. I saw the lava below me, it was red and bubbling, and I could feel the heat and my skin started burning, then I heard the doctor say, 'You can stop squirming, you stupid girl, I'm done now.' "

The door opened. I looked around and saw Bud. He said: "What's going on?"

I stood up. I could see Nucky in the hallway behind Bud; he grinned at me then shut the door. Bud walked toward us, as Darla looked at him, sniffling and wiping her swollen eyes.

"Whatsamatter?" he said.

"I'm just feeling kinda blue, Bud."

"Aw, baby, I'm sorry. Maybe this'll make you feel better."

He handed her a heart-shaped box of Whitman's chocolates.

"Thanks."

"How you doing, Danny?"

"Okay."

"Lookit, I got a thing or two to talk over with Darla. You mind, uh . . . ?"

"Sure, Bud," I said, and picked up my hat.

"But don't go far. I wanna talk to you too," then he turned to Darla. "Hey baby, open the box up. Give Danny some candy before he goes."

Still sniffling, Darla glanced at me, then pulled the ribbon off the box. She took its top off reluctantly, like it might be filled with spiders or dead mice.

Not that I really wanted one, but I selected a dark rectangular chocolate, and bit it in half. Bud watched me chew.

"What kind you get?"

I showed him the half I was still holding. "Kind of an orange cream."

Bud looked pleased. "You're lucky, kid. That's a good one."

4

Bud and I sat in the back of his black Lincoln as it glided down Santa Monica Boulevard. Nello and Bo Spiller were up front. I had no idea where we were going. All Bud had said when we left the hospital was he wanted to show me something.

He was very quiet, and kept casting thoughtful glances at me. Maybe he'd finally caught on to how I really felt about Darla, and seeing me hugging her was just the last straw. Maybe they were taking me out in the desert like I took Doc out in the garden.

Nello and Bo weren't saying a word either. I stared at the blank backs of their heads and hats, and wondered which one would do it. Bo, probably. The mad-dog killer.

To break the silence, I said: "You know when your trial's gonna be?"

"I got a hearing next week. That's when they'll set the date for the trial. Blinky's feeling pretty good about it. He says the D.A. ain't got a leg to stand on but Fay Wray, and he'll tear him to pieces once he gets him up on the stand."

"You shoulda put both his fucking eyes out," said Nello.

"Maybe I still will."

Bo laughed loudly. Now Nello slowed down and turned off Santa Monica, and I saw a sign that said: HOLLYWOOD MEMORIAL PARK. We passed through a gate. It was a pretty place to spend forever. Acres of well-tended green lawns with gray and brown tombstones sprouting out of them. A little lake.

Palm trees and evergreens.

Nello drove down a blacktopped lane that took us along the western edge of the cemetery. "Stop here," said Bud. He and I got out, while Nello and Bo stayed in the car.

We strolled along the lane. I started feeling more relaxed, since it was clear I wasn't about to be knocked off.

"This here's for Jews," said Bud. "It's called the Beth Olam Cemetery."

I looked at the names on some of the stones. Laskowitz. Rosen. Meltzer. Bloom.

"Why'd you bring me here?"

"Like I said. To show you something."

The sun was nearly straight overhead in another cloudless sky. I could feel sweat trickling down the middle of my back.

"I been thinking about my ma a lot lately," said Bud. "She had a cancer. It started in her mouth and then it started eating up her whole face. So here she is dying at the end of a lousy, fucked-up life, but all she keeps saying is: 'I just want to live.' At the end she couldn't talk no more, all she could do was write notes. And the last note she wrote was: 'I just want to live.' "

I saw that his eyes had welled up. I'd never seen that before.

"So the city took her body off and buried it where they bury winos and bums and other people without no money. I tried visiting her once, but I couldn't find no tombstone, no nothing. She shoulda had a nice grave, with lots of flowers. But instead she just got dumped in some hole in the ground like she was some kinda animal.

"Then I didn't have nobody. Now I'm starting to realize how much I've missed not having a family. Who can you count on but your own family? It's more important than anything. I believe in God, but I think He ain't as important as your family is. It's like that story in the Bible, where God tells that guy to sacrifice his son. He was just testing his faith and shit, seeing if that guy would really go through with it. And when God seen the guy was actually gonna do it, He called it off, right at the last second. Well, I never woulda gone along with it. If God ever told me to sacrifice my son, I'd just tell God to go fuck Hisself."

"But I don't get it," I said, then stopped myself.

"You don't get what?"

"Well, if you want a family, I don't get how come you sent Darla to that chiropractor."

"That was all *her* idea. I told her I was all for having a kid with her, but she said if I didn't help her get rid of it she was gonna throw herself down the stairs and get rid of it that way. So what's the deal, Danny? She tell you it was *my* idea? Broads," he snorted. "They're just good for two things: fucking, and fucking things up."

At the end of the lane, in the southwest corner of the cemetery, was a long, low mausoleum. A row of thin cypress trees stood in front of it. Behind it rose the huge sound stages of Paramount Pictures.

We went inside. You might think of mausoleums as being dark creepy places, but this one was bright and beautiful. We walked slowly down a polished marble floor between rows of crypts that went all the way up to the ceiling. Sunlight poured in through stained-glass skylights.

"Nice, huh?" said Bud.

I nodded. We passed Glasbands, Schinagels, Ginsburgs, and Fishes.

"Hey, here's a guy named Hamburger," I said. "You think maybe he had something to do with the Home for Young Women?"

"I dunno. Maybe."

After a while we stopped, and Bud pointed up at a crypt with no name on it on the top row.

"That's gonna be mine. Number 656."

We craned our necks as we stared up at it.

"Not that I'm planning on kicking the bucket any time soon. But a guy in my line of business, you never know."

"How come you wanna be in here and not outside? With the grass and the trees and everything?"

"I hate dirt. Why would I wanna be buried in the fucking dirt?"

"Why so high?"

"When I was a kid, I loved climbing on fire escapes and up on the roofs of buildings and looking down at everybody. So I guess it's the same kinda thing.

"The one next to it," he said, pointing. "Six fifty-four. I bought that one too."

"For somebody in particular?"

"Well, at first I was thinking I'd put Darla in it. But that's not gonna work 'cause she ain't Jewish. They won't let you in a Jew cemetery if you ain't a Jew. But now I'm thinking," and then he stopped. He looked at me for a long moment.

"I'm thinking now—I mean, if you wanna—*you* can have it."

I was taken aback.

"You're saying I'm Jewish?"

He nodded.

"But 'Danny Landon''s not a Jewish name, is it?"

"No. But that ain't your name."

5

Bud and I turned away from 656 and 654, and started walking back the way we had come. Over the polished marble, under the radiant glass.

"I figure the time has come to level with you. I don't know why he done it, but Tommy told you the straight truth. I did bring you back here on a train. I brung you back from New York. That was after your ma wrote me a letter and told me how you'd got beat up. How your head was hurt."

"Who was she? My mother?"

" 'Member me telling you about heisting them anchovies? And how I got hot and had to get outa town? And how I had a girlfriend and she gave me some dough and then I never seen her again? Well, that was your ma. I didn't know she was gonna have a baby when I left. She didn't know neither. I didn't know nothing about you until last summer.

"You coulda knocked me over with a fucking feather when I opened up that letter and it was from her. She said she'd read about me in the papers, that's how she tracked me down. She was in a real jam, she said. They was trying to throw you outa the hospital 'cause you didn't have any dough. And she was real sick and she couldn't work no more and she didn't have any money neither. And so she didn't have no place else to turn to but me. The next train to New York, I was on it."

"What happened to me? How'd I wind up in the hospital?"

"Well, you got beat up by some guys, just like I always told you. 'Cept it happened in New York. There was this old Greek guy, he had a dry cleaners. One day these guys jumped him, they was beating him up and was gonna rob him, but then you happened along. You tried to help him out. That's when you got knocked in the head with a lead pipe."

We came to the mausoleum entrance, and went out. Looking directly down the lane you could see in the hills the Hollywood-land sign. We turned right, and walked along the southern edge of the cemetery.

"Your ma said that trying to help out that old man, that was just the kinda guy you was. You was the prince of the neighbor-hood, she said. Everybody liked you, everybody looked up to you. Everybody thought you was really gonna go places. You was going to college, you was planning on being a lawyer. You talked about being the mayor of New York someday. But then when your mother got sick you had to quit college and get a job."

"You know what kind of job?"

"Yeah. In a shoe-polish factory."

I was quiet a moment, letting it all sink in. The prince of the neighborhood. A shoe-polish factory.

"Did she have any family? I mean, besides me?"

Bud shook his head.

"Her mother and father, when she told 'em she was having a baby, they wanted her to go to one of them home for unwed mother places. You woulda ended up in an orphanage. But she wanted to keep you. So they just threw her out on her fucking ear.

"No telling what woulda happened to her, but she ran into this guy. This little mick. He was eating a hot dog in the park. He seen her watching him, and seen how hungry she was, so he bought her a hot dog too.

"He was a lot older than her. He was a bookkeeper. When he

found out what the deal was, he said he'd marry her and he'd raise the kid as his own. And that's what happened.

"Your ma said he treated her like gold, and he was a real good father to you. She said you never knew the truth about who your real pa was. She said the three of yuz was all real happy together. But then when you was five or six, he was just walking down the street and this big chunk of limestone fell off a fucking building and killed him.

"So it was just your ma and you. She got a job working as a salesgirl in a ladies' hat store. And she stayed there till she got sick."

"What was the matter with her?"

"Consumption. Her lungs was rotting out. When we was both kids and she was my girl she was gorgeous. But when I first seen her last summer I didn't hardly recognize her. She was so skinny she was like a skeleton."

"What did she look like? When she was young."

"Well, she had blue eyes. Light-brown hair. A little nose. She didn't really look like a Jew, if you know what I mean." He smiled a little. "You look like her, not me. Lucky for you."

"Did she have a scar?" I said, and I touched my left cheek. "About here?"

"Yeah. She said she got hit in the face with a seesaw or something when she was a kid." He eyed me curiously. "So you're starting to remember stuff?"

"Some stuff." And then I said: "She's dead, isn't she?"

"Yeah, kid. Sorry. Couple weeks after I got there she started coughing up blood. Lots of blood. Then she passed out. She never did wake up again. She died that night. I was there with her. Then it was just you and me.

"The first time I seen you, you was like a baby in the body of a growed-up man. You couldn't talk, you couldn't feed yourself, you had to wear diapers. You was in that same crummy hospital

I was in after I got plugged heisting the anchovies. So I got you outa there and into a real good hospital and I got you the best fucking doctors in New York. Then after your mother died I decided to bring you out here.

"I think you musta liked California. You started getting better real fast. But you couldn't remember nothing. You had that amnesia thing. So I figured I'd just give you a fresh start. I used to know this guy in the old days, Danny Landon. He was a real good friend of mine. He got drunk one night and fell asleep on the trolley tracks and a trolley run over him. Cut him right in half. So anyway, I named you after him."

"Did you ever hear of a girl named Gwynnie?"

He frowned. "Yeah. Your ma told me about her."

"Who was she?"

"Her and you was gonna get married. Your ma said after you got hurt, she come to the hospital a few times, then she quit coming around. Your ma said she'd heard she took up with this other guy that'd been your best pal. She was a cunt. You shouldn't worry about her. All them people in that neighborhood of yours, you shouldn't worry about 'em. When you and your ma needed help, none of 'em lifted a fucking finger. Your ma tried to make excuses for 'em, she said it was 'cause of the Depression, nobody had any extra dough, but that ain't no excuse. You helped that old man out, but nobody helped you. Even the old man didn't help you! Fuck all of 'em.

"See, that's why I thought it'd be better if you just started over out here. I told all the boys to just act like you was one of them. That way you wouldn't have to lose any sleep over all that shit that happened in New York that didn't matter no more."

"What was my mother's name?"

"Rachel."

"What's my name? My *real* name?"

"I'll tell you someday. Now ain't the time."

"Why not?"

" 'Danny''s good enough for now."

"Why couldn't you have just told me who you really were? Right from the beginning?"

"I dunno." He thought about it. "It's a big thing telling somebody that. That you're their father. I thought I'd see how it went with us. And in my book, it's gone pretty damn good."

I noticed Bud's Lincoln behind us, creeping along, keeping its distance. We were approaching the lake. Next to it was another mausoleum, which Bud gestured at.

"Guess who's in there."

"Who?"

"Rudolph Valentino. We're gonna have a pretty famous neighbor, huh?"

I felt terribly tired all of a sudden. It was hard to walk, as if the asphalt of the road were melting and sticking to my shoes.

"Lots of famous people buried here," said Bud.

A black crow winged over the blue lake, its shadow skimming along beneath it.

"It's great to finally get that off my fucking chest," said Bud.

He regarded the world with a relieved smile. He slapped me on the back.

"Well, how you feel, now you know I'm your old man?"

As often happened when I was talking with Bud, I couldn't think of a thing to say.

6

Bud dropped me off at my car in the hospital parking lot, but I didn't feel like going home. So I went to the movies.

Mickey Rooney was an orphan name Blackie Gallagher and he became best pals with another orphan and then he grew up to become Clark Gable. And Clark Gable was a charming gangster and the other orphan was the D.A. but even though they were on opposite sides of the law they were still best pals but then they both fell in love with Myrna Loy.

It was a good movie, but I had trouble keeping my mind on it. I started thinking about Clark Gable and his gallbladder, and how we must have been at Cedars of Lebanon at about the same time. Maybe we'd even encountered each other at some point; maybe buried somewhere in my battered brain was a memory of his big ears and cocky grin as he wisecracked with a nurse, and maybe he remembered how the sight of me being rolled down a hallway, drooling and glassy-eyed, had made him feel lucky all he had was a bum gallbladder.

I sat there in the theater's semi-dark, and thought about how I'd been practically kidnapped by Bud Seitz. He hadn't created a fictitious life for me because he wanted to spare me any troubling truths about my real life, but because he knew the natural thing for me, as soon as I was well enough to travel, would be just to go back home. To try to pick the pieces up of who I used to be.

"Young man?" I heard, then I felt a gentle touch on my

shoulder. "Are you all right?"

I turned around. A middle-aged woman was sitting behind me. The gigantic images of Clark Gable and William Powell were miniaturized in her spectacles. She and her husband were looking at me with concern, and I realized, to my embarrassment, that I was crying.

"I'm okay. Sorry."

I turned back around, and tried to stop crying, and tried to figure out why I *was* crying. Because my mother was dead? Because my fiancée was lost? Or because *he* was dead, *he* was lost? That absurd young man working in the shoe-polish factory who thought he might be the mayor of New York someday.

I got up and stumbled toward the aisle, stepping on the toes of a sailor who had his arm around the shoulders of a girl. "Hey, watch it, mac!" he said, as up on the screen Blackie Gallagher said: "Say, everything's just hotsy totsy!"

It was all too much. As I'd gotten out of Bud's car back at the hospital, he had said to me: "By the way, them guys? That beat you up? There was four of 'em. Now there ain't any of 'em."

7

That night I barely slept. When occasionally I did begin to drift off, it was like the air around me became filled with swirling whispering ghosts that would vanish when I opened my eyes. About two a.m. a violent-sounding cat fight broke out right under my window. I hoped Dulwich's cat wasn't involved.

Finally daylight began to filter into my bedroom. I felt a little hungry. All I'd eaten yesterday was the chocolate at the hospital. I went in the kitchen and had a bowl of stale corn flakes. Then I went in the living room and sat down on the davenport and turned on the radio.

At some point Mrs. Dean came over with a slice of coconut-cream pie. I asked her how she knew it was my favorite, but all she did was smile at me. She wasn't wearing her false teeth, so it was a gaping empty jack-o'-lantern kind of smile. I felt bad that I hadn't ever played checkers with her housebound husband, and I tried to apologize, but she just kept smiling bigger and bigger, she was scaring me to death, and then I woke up.

I was soaked in sweat. I got up to turn on the fan. The radio was still playing and the news came on. The newscaster announced that Bernice Seitz, wife of mobster Bud Seitz, had drowned in the swimming pool of her house on Bedford Drive in Beverly Hills.

"According to Captain Chuck McCumber of the Beverly Hills Police Department," said the newscaster, "the body was discovered last night by the maid. It was her night off. When she came back to the house at about eleven o'clock, she found Mrs. Seitz's body floating facedown in the swimming pool, clad in a bathing suit. McCumber said the death appeared to be accidental. When asked if foul play was a possibility, he replied: 'Are you talking about murder? This is Beverly Hills. We don't have murders in Beverly Hills.' "

I knew I had to see Darla. I got dressed and got in my car and drove to the hospital.

Her room was empty. A Negro woman with a polka-dot scarf over her hair was mopping the floor. I asked her if she knew where Darla was.

"Who?"

"Darla. She's a blonde girl. This is her room."

She shook her head and kept mopping. "Don't know nothing about no blonde girl."

I went to the nurses' desk. They told me Darla had checked out that morning.

I headed up La Brea toward Bud's house. I tried to fight down the panicked sense that Darla was slipping beyond my grasp. That she had fallen through the ice, or was dispersing like smoke, or had never been real to begin with.

I tooted my horn at the front gate. I was relieved to see Dick Prettie in his usual cheap suit and silly tie waving at me and opening the gate.

"Hi ya, Danny," he coughed.

"Is Darla here?"

"Yeah. Bud brung her back this morning."

"How is she?"

"She wasn't doing so hot when I seen her. Nello and me nearly had to carry her up the stairs."

"Is Bud here?"

Dick shook his head. "He had to go and make plans for the

293

funeral. For his wife. You heard about that, right?"

"Yeah. So what happened to her?"

"She drowneded to death."

"Yeah, I know. But the radio said it was an accident. Is that what you think?"

Dick took a drag on his cigarette.

"I dunno. What do you think?"

"Probably same as you."

"Lookit. Here's all I know. Around eight last night, Willie and Nucky and Bo come driving through here. Nucky and Bo was soaked to the skin. There was puddles around their fucking shoes. And Nucky's face was all scratched up."

"How come you think Willie wasn't wet?"

"Maybe he was the lookout. While Nucky and Bo drowneded that poor bitch to death." He flicked his cigarette through the gate. Watched it roll down the drive. "I've had it, Danny. I'm getting out for sure. I'm just looking for the right time."

I drove up to the house. Anatoly met me at the front door.

"The boss, he is not here, Danny."

"I know. I came to see Darla."

"Sorry. The boss says no visitors."

"I just want to see her a minute."

Bo Spiller appeared behind Anatoly.

"You heard him, Danny. Get outa here."

"Please, Danny," said Anatoly. "She is very tired. She is sleeping. Let her rest."

Now Anatoly closed the door.

I went back to my car. Started to get in. Then changed my mind, and walked around to the back of the house.

The sun wasn't far from setting; it was flooding the garden with golden light. I looked up at the second-story balconied bedroom of Bud and Darla. The curtains were drawn. She seemed like a princess imprisoned in a tower.

"What are you doing, Danny?"

It was Nucky.

"Nothing."

Four vivid scratches diagonally crossed his cheek. He strolled up beside me then put his hands on his hips and gazed up at the bedroom, as though we were trying to puzzle through a common problem.

"I seen this movie once. This guy was gonna elope with this dame. So it's the middle of the night, right? And he's throwing little rocks up at the dame's window to let her know he's there." He giggled. "But he's got the wrong fucking window! Her old man sticks his head out and gets a fucking rock right in the eye. I'm telling you, Danny, I nearly laughed myself sick." Then he looked me over with his lifeless eyes. "Now beat it, kid. Before I fucking kill you."

I stopped off at Healy's Bar on the way home. I always found something comforting in the befuddled company of George and Sonny and the Kid; maybe it was the feeling they gave you that life was something that had happened to them a long time ago and thus was no longer a source of fear or worry. But they weren't here tonight. Neither was Henry, the regular bartender.

I climbed on my usual stool and ordered a beer from the new bartender, a skinny guy with a nervous, rabbity mouth.

"Where is everybody?" I said.

He looked around and sniffed: "I don't know who you mean by 'everybody,' " like I was belittling both him and his two or three seedy-looking customers.

I drank that beer and then, as I pondered the lessons of the Custer massacre, had a couple more. When I went back out on Vine Street it was dark.

Searchlights swept the sky, advertising the grand opening of a hot dog stand.

I drove down La Vista Lane, and parked. Went up the seven

steps. As I opened my door and reached for the light switch, I smelled cigarette smoke.

Teddy Bump was sitting on the davenport, blinking mildly at me in the sudden light. He was holding a gun in his lap, which he didn't bother to point at me.

Beside Teddy was Vic Lester. The guy I saw at the lake with Teddy's dick in his mouth. Vic was obviously just waking up. He looked confused. "What's going on?" he mumbled.

"Asshole's here."

Vic yawned at me. "Hello, asshole."

"You got a piece?" Teddy said to me.

I nodded.

"Get rid of it."

His gun drifted in my direction now. I took my gun out and placed it on the coffee table in front of them.

They stood up.

"Okay, Danny-boy," said Teddy. "Let's go."

"Where we going?"

"No place special."

8

My head banged on the roof as I was shoved into a maroon Hudson. Teddy got behind the wheel. I was jammed in between him and Vic as we pulled away from the curb.

The headlights lit up Dulwich walking down the sidewalk. He wasn't paying any attention to us. I wanted to yell out to him but didn't, and he was swiftly left behind in the darkness.

Vic pushed in the electric lighter on the dashboard. Teddy started fiddling with the radio dial. The lighter popped back out, and Vic puffed a cigarette into life.

"What's this all about?" I said.

I didn't get an answer. I wondered if Teddy knew it was me that had ripped his false eyebrow off and dropped it in his mouth and now he was about to get even with me.

"I've saved up some money. A whole lot of money. If you guys let me go, it's yours."

"Shut up," said Teddy. "I love this song."

It was "The Carioca." He started singing along with it in a cracked falsetto—

Now that you've done the Carioca
You'll never care to do the Polka . . .

We went south then headed east on Beverly. Vic put his hand on my knee. I stared at it. Now it started sliding up my thigh. When it neared my crotch, I jerked my leg away and slapped at it. He giggled, and blew some smoke in my face. He put his hand back on my knee. I slapped it away again.

"Give it up, kid," said Teddy. "Trying to keep this guy away from your dick's like trying to keep a mouse away from a piece of cheese." Then he let loose with his hyena laugh and Vic joined in.

I considered making a desperate lunge for the door handle and throwing myself out of the car. But then Teddy turned onto Alvarado then a short distance later pulled off the street. In the sweep of the headlights I saw THE PINK RAT painted in peeling pink letters on the side of a deserted-looking brick building.

Behind the building in a small parking lot two fancy cars were parked: a sky-blue Cadillac and some kind of long black limousine. Teddy stopped his car. He and Vic got out. I stayed put. Teddy reached in and grabbed my arm and dragged me out.

The night was loud with crickets. There was a vacant lot behind the parking lot filled with high weeds, and I wondered if I was about to be marched into it and murdered, but Teddy led me over to the limousine instead. The windows were tinted and I couldn't see inside. He opened the back door and said: "Get in."

I ducked my head and entered. Teddy shut the door behind me. I found myself in a spacious rear compartment with seats facing each other at either end. I saw two shadowy shapes on the back seat and one on the front. I crouched in the middle like a captured, frightened animal. Nobody said anything. Somebody coughed. Then a dome light came on.

On the back seat were Max Schnitter and Loy Hanley; on the front was Jack Otay. Past Otay, on the other side of a glass partition, I could see the backs of the heads of two guys in the driver's compartment.

Everybody was looking at me in a friendly, interested fashion.

"Come on over here, Danny," said Otay.

I sat down beside him on the gleaming red leather seat; the whole interior of the car was red.

"Would you like a drink?" asked Schnitter.

"Yeah. I could use one."

Schnitter smiled, showing his sharp eye teeth. "Jack, pour Danny a drink."

"Scotch all right?" said Otay.

I nodded. He poured some scotch out of a crystal decanter into a glass. I saw they all had their own glasses of scotch already. They watched me as I took a drink. They noticed how my hand was shaking.

Schnitter and Loy Hanley were like Mutt and Jeff sitting together. Schnitter's little two-toned shoes barely reached the floor, while Hanley's long, cowboy-booted legs were stuck out straight in front of him.

Hanley started handrolling a Bull Durham cigarette.

"So how's life been treating you, son?"

"Fine. And you?"

"Got no complaints."

"How's Violet?"

He gave a disgusted snort. "That crazy bitch. I kicked her out on her fat ass. And I do mean kicked."

Schnitter gestured vaguely out the window. "Is this your first visit to the Pink Rat?"

"Yes sir."

"It was a wonderful place, before they closed it down. A Presbyterian minister named Gustave Briegleb led a campaign against it. He called it a 'den of iniquity.' A place that had been given over to 'the world, the flesh, and the devil.' All true, of course. That's why it was so wonderful. But now Loy and I are making plans to re-open it. Restore it to its former glory."

"Yeah," said Hanley, "the Pink Rat'll be giving the Peacock

Club a run for its fucking money."

"But I thought you guys weren't getting along," I said.

Schnitter raised an eyebrow. "Oh?"

"Well—that's what I heard up at the lake."

"Hell, Max and me are like dadgum blood brothers," said Hanley. "Ain't that right, Max?"

Hanley slapped Schnitter's knee; Schnitter winced a little through his smile.

"That's true, Loy. We had our differences, but they're in the past. Just like my friendship with Bud Seitz is in the past."

"Mr. Schnitter, what happened with that girl at your birthday party—I hope you don't think it was some kind of practical joke or something. It was an accident. I know Bud felt really bad about it."

"Loyalty's a virtue, Danny. Up to a point." Then he said, very slowly: "And then self-preservation begins to set in."

I took another gulp of whiskey. Hanley lit his cigarette with a kitchen match that he struck off the bottom of his boot. Looked at me through the smoke with his hard, gunmetal gray eyes as he waved the match out.

"We're offering you a job."

"Doing what?"

"Helping us get rid of your boss."

"But in a strictly legit kinda way," said Otay. "Like they done in Chicago with Capone."

"That's how the mayor wants it," said Schnitter. "He's been getting a lot of heat from the Reverend Briegleb and some of the papers to 'clean up the city.' And so Seitz becomes our sacrificial lamb. It was an easy choice to make. Repeal changed everything, Danny. The competition for new business is ferocious. But Seitz is stuck in the past. In the old ways of doing things."

With its windows closed, the car was already smotheringly

hot, and now it was filling up with Hanley's smoke. I could barely breathe, but the others seemed like creatures that loved the smoke and the heat. I resolved that I would say or do anything that would contribute to me getting out of the parking lot of the Pink Rat alive.

"I see what you mean. But what do you need me for? You already got Louie Vachaboski."

Schnitter frowned. "Not anymore."

"Louie's skedaddled," said Hanley.

"To Old Mexico," said Otay.

"Which means," said Schnitter, "we have to start over. With a new case."

"What do you know about Bud's wife?" said Otay.

"Nothing. I never even met her."

"But you know Bud had her knocked off, right?"

"I don't really know anything about it."

"Everybody knows Bud wanted a divorce and she wouldn't give it to him. So don't it stand to reason that he knocked her off?"

"I don't know. Maybe it was an accident. Or suicide."

Schnitter tugged pensively at the lobe of one of his pointy elfin ears.

"I've never quite understood the relationship between you and Bud. You show up out of nowhere, and suddenly you're his best friend. But it's none of my business. I have secrets too. We all have secrets. We're just hoping you can find out the truth about his wife. After all, if she was murdered, her killer should be brought to justice. Wouldn't that be the right thing to do?"

I nodded. I started to take a drink of scotch, but my glass was already empty. Otay obligingly refilled it.

"Look," he said, "we're setting things up all sweet and pretty for you. Everybody knows you got the hot nuts for his girlfriend. Everybody but him, anyways. Help us put him away and you'll have her all to yourself."

"Of course, we'll also pay you well," said Schnitter.

"So what do you say, boy?" said Hanley. "You on board?"

"Sure. Sure I'm on board."

Schnitter cocked his head a little to the side and gave me a quizzical look.

"Why am I not convinced you're sincere?"

"I don't know why. I'm very sincere."

"Used to know this feller named Herbert Stittmatter from up around San Joaquin," said Hanley. "I thought he might be stealing from me, but he swore up and down he wasn't doing no such of a thing. So I buttered up the barrel of a twelve-gauge shotgun and shoved it up his ass. Told him I was pulling the trigger if he didn't convince me he was sincere."

"What happened?" I said.

Hanley shrugged. "Son of a bitch didn't convince me."

"Danny?" said Schnitter. "Finish your drink."

"Why?"

"Just do it," he said gently.

The glass was nearly full. I swallowed it all down. It burned my gullet. I coughed and shuddered.

Now Schnitter said to Otay: "Danny has a nice face. Leave it alone."

9

The limousine pulled out of the parking lot, leaving me alone with Otay, Teddy, and Vic. My head was spinning with the whiskey. It was very dark. The crickets sounded about twice as loud as when we arrived.

Otay walked over to the edge of the weedy lot and unzipped his pants. In a moment we heard the patter of pee, and Otay making noises like: *"Arrrg! Oohhh! Ooook!"*

"What's the matter with him?" said Vic.

"He's got the clap," said Teddy. "Said he got it from that movie star he's been screwing."

"Poor bastard," said Vic, and they both snickered.

Otay zipped up, and came back. In the starlight I could see a sheen of sweat on his ugly-handsome face. "Let's go," he said weakly.

We walked to the back door of the Pink Rat. There was a padlock. Teddy had a key. "What are you gonna do?" I said.

Nobody answered. Teddy lifted the padlock out of the hasp. Then he opened the door, and Vic shoved me into a foul-smelling darkness.

Somebody turned on a light. I was in what used to be the kitchen. It was empty now, except for a few panicky roaches running for cover and a dried-up pile of human shit in the corner near the mummified corpse of a mouse in a trap. Swinging doors on the other side of the room led into the public part of the Pink Rat.

I heard the door shutting behind me, and I turned around and saw the three of them standing together and looking at me. Otay took out a pair of handcuffs from under his jacket. I took a few faltering backward steps. Otay said: "Grab him, boys."

I turned and broke for the swinging doors, but Teddy and Vic caught up with me easily and, each taking an arm, they dragged me back.

"Poor old Limpy," laughed Teddy. "He just can't run worth a shit."

Otay cuffed my hands behind my back; then he took a pair of soft brown gloves out of his pocket and began to tug them on.

"Jack," I said, talking fast, "I don't know why you're doing this. It's not necessary. I meant it when I said I'd go along with you guys. Bud's a bad guy. He needs to be put away. And you're right, I want his girlfriend. You nailed it, Jack. I'll be sitting pretty—"

Otay's fist whumped into my stomach. My shoulders hunched and my knees sagged and my eyes scrunched shut and out of my mouth came an explosive moan. He might as well have been Kid McCoy in his prime and myself his canvas punching bag as he alternated lefts and rights into my stomach and ribs and sternum. Once he hit me smack on my heart and darkness flashed in my eyes and I was like a tiny barrel tumbling over some vast black waterfall. When I came back to my senses and the Pink Rat, Teddy and Vic were still holding me up, and Otay was standing in front of me, red-faced and sweating, catching his breath, one gloved hand rubbing the knuckles of his other.

"Stop it," I said. "Please."

"Turn him around," he said to Vic and Teddy.

Now he went to work on my back. Rabbit-punched me until I blacked out.

When I came to, I was sitting on the filthy floor in a little puddle of my pee. My back was against a cabinet and my legs were splayed out in front of me. The three of them were looking down at me. Otay was peeling his gloves off like a weary surgeon who'd finished an operation.

"This isn't nothing personal, Danny. Far as I can tell, you're a nice enough kid, and I hadn't got nothing against you. This is just so's you'll know what'll happen if you ever fuck with us. 'Cept it'll be about a hundred times worse. And you won't live through it."

"Anything you want," I gasped. "I'll do anything."

"Your turn," Otay said to Teddy.

I'd thought it was over.

"Wait," I said.

But Otay walked away. Teddy grinned down at me.

"Wait," I said. "Wait."

Teddy pulled out of his pocket a pair of wire pliers.

"*Wait!*"

10

"Drink this."

It was a murky brown liquid steaming in a teacup.

"What's in it?" I said.

"A drop of dragon's blood," said Dulwich. "A pinch of dirt from the Lone Sod. A sprinkling of dust from the dark side of the moon."

I took a sip. It tasted lousy. I coughed, which hurt my ribs. I winced.

Dulwich frowned down at me.

"Perhaps we should take you to the hospital, and have your ribs X-rayed. Make certain there aren't any fractures."

"I hate hospitals. I wanna stay here."

I was in Dulwich's bed, wearing a pair of his pajamas. I'd stumbled to his door after Teddy and Vic had brought me back. He'd already cleaned me up and bandaged my toes and wrapped my ribs, all without asking a single question.

I choked down some more of the vile stuff in the cup.

"No kidding. What is this?"

"A tea I got from an herb doctor in Chinatown. It will help you sleep."

It did, though I didn't realize it till I found myself waking up. The bedside lamp was still on. I heard the rustle of a turning page. Dulwich had pulled up a chair beside the bed. He was reading a book called *The Well at the World's End*.

He didn't notice I had awaked. He seemed a fatherly, reassuring presence. It felt safe to go back to sleep.

It wasn't, though. I found myself being tortured back at the Pink Rat. But everything looked different, there was a big picture window with tatters of fog floating past it, and my torturers were different too. Tommy and Goodlooking Tommy were holding me down, and Ching-wei, the Chinaman who worked at the Peacock Club, was wielding the pliers. He seemed to want me to confess to something, but since he was questioning me in Chinese, I didn't know how to reply.

At a table in the corner, Darla was playing cards with Vera Vermillion.

"You got any elevens?" said Darla.

Vera was naked, and her skin was turning blue.

"No way, honey. Go fish."

Neither paid any attention to my screaming.

"Wake up, Danny. Everything is all right."

I opened my eyes. Dulwich was bending over me.

"They can't hurt you now."

My, Dulwich's, pajamas were soaked in sweat, and my mouth was bone-dry. "I'm thirsty," I croaked.

He was back a moment later with a glass of water. With one hand he supported the back of my head, and with the other he held the glass to my lips.

I drank my fill; then I started getting drowsy again. As my eyelids drooped, I saw Dulwich looking down at me.

"Poor boy," he murmured, then he bent and kissed my forehead. "Dear boy.

"Sleep."

Over breakfast in bed the next morning—scrambled eggs, buttered toast, raspberry jam, and orange juice—I told Dulwich everything.

"I always wondered how I would stand up to torture," Dulwich said as he munched on his toast. "Fortunately, I was never in a position to find out."

"I was pathetic. I cried. I yelled. I begged."

"But Danny, you're not giving yourself enough credit. You already had the information about Mr. Seitz and his late wife that they wanted you to obtain. And yet you withheld it from them. The question, of course, is: why? Why did you protect him?"

"Well—he *is* my father. And he's always been nice to me. Even though everybody says he's a monster."

Dulwich wiped a glistening smear of jam off his thick lips with his napkin.

"I suppose," he said, "if you were to rake over the ashes of what remains of Seitz's soul, and you were to find a few glowing embers of decency left, probably those embers would have to do with you."

After breakfast, Dulwich put his cat in a wire cage, then left in his ancient, barely running Franklin convertible for the dog and cat hospital. It turned out it *had* been Tinker that had been involved in the fight the other night; she'd suffered a nasty scratch behind her ear, and Dulwich was concerned it was getting infected.

He left me with the morning paper. The first story my eyes fell on began: "Out of work for months, W. E. Main, 50, engineer, ended his life yesterday in a rooming house at 142 West Jefferson Street by sending a bullet through his heart." I sighed, and tossed the paper down. Thought about W. E. Main for a while. It seemed like a curtain of crumminess was descending on the whole world.

I got out of bed, and tottered to the bathroom. I was appalled to see what looked like strawberry Kool-Aid streaming into the toilet. I finished up and flushed; then I heard somebody knocking at the front door.

It was Sophie.

"I just ran into Mr. Dulwich, and he said you were here. Can I come in?"

"Maybe now's not the best time."

"Please? There's something I have to tell you."

I let her in, then limped over to the sofa. She watched me ease myself down like an old man.

"Mr. Dulwich said you'd been in some kind of accident, but you were going to be fine and I shouldn't ask you about it."

"He's a smart fella, Mr. Dulwich. You should always listen to him."

Sophie perched awkwardly on the edge of the sofa, her hands clasped in her lap.

"So what did you want to tell me?"

She looked away, towards the door, like somebody had suddenly arrived there. Her eyes filled up with tears.

"Sophie? What's the matter?"

"My mom's sending me away. To some kind of reform school."

"You're kidding. When?"

"Next week."

"But—how come? When did all this happen?"

"My mom lost her job at the department store. She said it was because her boss didn't like her, but I think it was because she was drinking. She drinks all the time now. Anyway, Jerry's been coming around again. He's got some kind of job now, selling carpet cleaner or something. And one night, they thought I was asleep, but I could hear them talking. And she was trying to talk him into coming back, but he said he wouldn't as long as she had that little brat living with her. Me—I'm the brat. And she said don't worry, they've got places for crazy kids like her, kids that try to burn down houses.

"Then a few days later a policeman came to see me, and he

had a man and woman with him. Mr. McNamara and Miss Hazeltine. Mr. McNamara seemed kind of like a preacher, he was dressed in black and he was really old and he wore glasses. Miss Hazeltine was younger and kind of fat, but she wore glasses too. They said they were from the Sonoma State Home in Eldridge. They said they'd come to see me because they'd heard I was a troubled little girl and they thought they could help me. I said I wasn't a troubled little girl, and they asked me then why did I set fire to the house, and I said I didn't. Then they gave me a written test with a lot of crazy questions."

"What kind of questions?"

"Well, like, how many boys have you kissed, and have you ever dreamed you went to school in your underwear, and if you were an animal, what kind of animal would you like to be, and why? I wrote I'd like to be a bat, 'cause if I was a bat I'd be blind, and I wouldn't be able to take this dumb test.

"I don't know whether I passed the test or not. All I know is Mr. McNamara called my mother yesterday and said they'd be coming back on Monday. To take me to Eldridge."

She sniffled, and swiped at her nose with the back of her hand.

"I've seen lots of movies about reform schools. They make you wear dopey uniforms and they feed you something called 'gruel' and they make you stand out in the rain for punishment. You should've just let me run away."

"Oh, it might not be so bad," I said without much conviction.

"I'll probably never see you again."

"You'll see me again. I'll come visit. Dulwich and I both will."

"Promise?"

"Promise." Then I tapped the tip of her nose with my finger and said: "Did you know you have exactly eleven freckles?"

The droopy corners of her mouth turned up in a smile, and then we heard: "I'm gonna have to put you on a leash, honey!"

Lois Gubler barged through the door, looking awfully happy for ten o'clock in the morning. Her platinum-blonde hair looked as stiff and dry as straw. She didn't seem to be wearing any underwear under her sloppy dress; I could see her nipples, along with some sort of yellow substance dripping down the front.

"I made us some breakfast. French toast. Your favorite!"

"So that's why you got egg all over you," said Sophie.

"Where?" she said, then she saw the yolk and laughed. "Oops! Betty Crocker I ain't! Come on, Sophie. It's gonna get cold."

"I'm not hungry."

"But I made it just the way you like it."

"She said she's not hungry," I said.

Lois turned her unsteady attention on me and my red silk pajamas.

"Nice peejays," she sneered. "So you living here now?"

"He had an accident," said Sophie, "and Mr. Dulwich is taking care of him."

"What kinda accident?"

"None of your business," I said.

"You know, Jerry always thought there was something funny about Mr. Dulwich. Maybe there's something funny about you too. I've got a good mind to call the cops. They got laws against guys like you."

"They oughta have laws against mothers like *you*."

"Yeah? What do you mean by that?"

"A mother oughta raise her kid—not ship her off someplace just so she can shack up with a bum like Jerry."

Lois was looming over us now, her different scents billowing over us like a cloud: booze and perfume, tobacco and B.O.

"Oh, I get the picture. Sophie's been giving you an earful. But she probably didn't tell you this is all for her own good.

See, my daughter's got this problem. I mean, besides being a firebug. She's boy-crazy. Just can't control herself. She's always shaking her skinny little fanny in the faces of my fellers. But probably I ain't telling you nothing you don't already know. No telling what you two have been up to. But this new place she's going, they're gonna take care of all that. She won't be acting like a little whore no more 'cause they won't put up with it."

Sophie stood up indignantly. "I hate you! *You're* the whore!"

Lois slapped her. She lifted her arm to slap her again, but I lunged up off the sofa and grabbed her by the wrist. She spit in my face.

I felt the warm sticky wetness oozing down.

"If you weren't a girl, I'd deck you."

"And if you weren't a crummy little cripple, I'd be *scared* of ya!"

Sophie had had enough. She ran out the door. Lois stumbled after her, yelling: "Sophie Gubler, you come back here! You run away again, I'll call the cops!"

I went in the bathroom to wash off my face. Needed to wash it several times before I was satisfied.

11

"Some of these state places can be pretty bad," I said.

"Unfortunately," said Dulwich, "I don't think there's anything we can do. Except, as you promised, visit her. Write her. Remain her friend."

I'd slept most of the day; now I was having dinner with Dulwich. Spaghetti and tomato sauce, broccoli, French bread, and plonk.

"This is great," I said. "I didn't know you were such a good cook."

"Spaghetti's easy. But thank you. I do enjoy cooking, I admit."

Tinker Bell walked over to the table. The veterinarian had given her some medicine to put on her battle wounds and said she ought to be fine. Now she meowed up at us.

"There's nothing here you'd like, old girl. Sorry."

"How come you've never been married, Dulwich?"

"Oh, I'm a confirmed bachelor, Danny. I've discovered that romance roils my soul intolerably."

"Maybe *I* oughta be a confirmed bachelor," I said gloomily.

"So let's talk about this."

"About what?"

"About what on earth you plan to do?"

I pushed at a strand of spaghetti with a tine of my fork.

"I plan to live a long, happy life. And to pass away peacefully in my sleep in the year 1999."

"Do you have any interest in what I think?"

"Sure."

"You're a decent young man who has fallen into a nest of vipers. Your position's becoming increasingly untenable. I've grown quite fond of you, Danny, and for selfish reasons, I would hate to see you leave. But I do think it would be for the best."

"Not without Darla."

"Then take her with you."

"But Bud'll hunt us down. And those other guys, Schnitter and them—they said they'd hunt me down too if I took off. Guys like that, they never give up."

"Oh, that's just a lot of rot. That's what they *want* you to think. In reality, they're just stupid, brutal thugs who aren't half as smart as you. *They're* the dull-witted hounds. *You're* the sly, quick fox."

"You make it sound easy."

"No. I think it will be desperately difficult. And I think you have no choice."

It was dusk. Outside, we could hear a noisy cawing of crows. Every day about this time, dozens of them would pass overhead, in a hurry to find a place to roost before night fell.

" 'Crows make wing to the rooky wood,' " said Dulwich.

12

By the next morning, I was peeing yellow again, and I felt well enough to go back to my own bungalow. I took a long hot bath, then inspected myself in the mirror. It was fascinating to look at the blue and black imprints of Otay's pigskinned knuckles that covered my torso, front and back. Then I got dressed, went out in the living room, and called Wendell Nuffer.

I told him I was trying to find out some information about a reform school: the Sonoma State Home in Eldridge.

"I believe I've heard of it, Danny, but that's all. Why are you interested?"

"There's this little girl I know, she's a neighbor of mine. She's being sent there."

"For what reason?"

"Her mother's a bitch and wants to get rid of her. Anyway, she's a good kid, and I'm concerned about her."

"Tell you what. I'll make some calls, find out what I can, and call you back."

"Thanks, Mr. Nuffer. I appreciate it."

"Always glad to do whatever I can for a friend, my boy."

Nuffer was acting as happy as if I'd called him up to tell him he'd just won a million dollar jackpot.

"Sounds like you're in a good mood," I said.

Nuffer laughed. "I'm in the best of all moods in the best of all possible worlds."

"How come?"

"My Violet has come back to me. It's been eleven magical days now. She told me she'd only been with Loy Hanley a short time when she realized she'd made a dreadful mistake. That it was me that she loved. When she told Hanley she was leaving him, he wept, he pleaded, he begged her to stay. All to no avail. But don't think I was just a pushover when she came back, my boy, oh no! I was hard as stone. Cold as ice. But gradually I melted in the warmth of her obvious repentance and affection."

"I'm glad you're happy, Mr. Nuffer, but—are you sure this is a good idea? I mean, the last time things didn't work out so great."

"Time will tell, time will tell. But think of it this way. I'm sure you've had the bittersweet experience of seeing some unbearably beautiful girl in a crowd, and watching her for a few moments, and knowing you're never going to see her again. But I *am* going to see that girl again, Danny! In a little less than three hours, I'll be in her adorable arms again! No joy matches that! It's *worth* risking everything for!"

After I hung up with Nuffer, I called Bud's house. Anatoly picked up. I asked to speak to Darla.

"She is resting now, Danny. Probably better not to disturb her."

I heard somebody in the background say: "Hey, is that Danny?," then suddenly I found myself on the phone with Bud.

"Hi ya, kid! How's things?"

"I'm fine. I was just calling to see how Darla was doing."

"Well, that's real thoughtful of you, Danny. She's been kinda down in the dumps, but she'll be okay. It's funny, I was just thinking about you."

"Yeah?"

"Yeah. You and me, we need to get together. We gotta make some plans. Wait a minute. Maybe you ain't heard the news."

"What news?"

"Fay Wray went on the lam. They dropped the fucking charges. I beat the bastards!"

"Gee, that's great, Bud."

"I'm gonna be busy all day, but why don't you come over tonight. Maybe around eight o'clock."

My cretinous shadows, the Kornblum brothers, were manning the front gate.

"What do you want, kid?" said either Freddie or Mousie; I wasn't sure which was which.

"It's okay," said the other one, Mousie or Freddie. "The boss is suspecting him."

I assumed he meant *ex*pecting. I headed up the driveway. Several powerful floodlamps had been installed since I was last here at night, and the grounds were awash in harsh light. I parked and got out. Anatoly in his red velvet vest was standing in front of the house, staring towards the swimming pool.

Bo Spiller and Willie the Coon were there, laughing and clowning around. Bo had his shotgun. He pointed it at the seagull, then yelled: "BLAM!" The gull squawked and flapped at the end of its tether, as Bo and Willie yukked it up.

Anatoly's lips curled in contempt.

"Muzjiki," he said.

"What's that mean?"

"Peasants." He looked at me, and sighed. "This job is not any good anymore. I think I am leaving soon. I take the bird and go. To Papeete, maybe."

"Would you tell me something, Anatoly? What happened to your fingers? Did you really get them shot off in the Russian Revolution?"

He nodded.

"How did it happen?"

"It was cavalry charge. Across open field. The Bolsheviks

were waiting for us in the trees. I was holding sword, I was waving it like this," and he circled his three-fingered hand over his head. "I feel very happy at that moment, Danny. I feel like I am Cossack. I feel like I am *Bog*. God! But the Bolsheviks have machine guns. They shoot sword out of my hand, shoot my fingers away. Shoot my horse. My poor horse. Horses no good against machine guns.

"He is waiting for you, Danny. In billiard room."

He and Dick were playing eight ball. Dick was lining up a shot, a cigarette with an inch of ash hanging from his lips. Bud was puffing on a cigar. His face lit up when he saw me.

"Hey, Danny! How's it going? Want a drink? You take over for Dick. Dick, get outa here. Give Danny your stick. Scotch all right?"

"Sure."

"Beat his ass, kid," said Dick as he handed me his stick and sauntered toward the door.

Bud brought over a glass of scotch. He had one too. "Here's mud in your eye," he said, and we both took a drink.

I eyed the table. There were five stripes left and three solids.

"What am I?"

"Stripes."

I decided to knock the nine in the side, which ought to set me up for the fourteen in the corner. But as I leaned over the table, pain ripped through my ribs. I sucked in my breath and winced.

"Jesus Christ, Danny. What's the matter?"

"I was moving some furniture around and threw my back out. It's no big deal."

I took the shot, and missed. Bud was looking at me with concern.

"I got a bum back too, it's nothing to fuck around with. I got a great chiropractor. Why don't you go and see him tomorrow?"

"Dr. Brunder?"

Bud grinned. "Nah, not Brunder. I hear he just went outa business."

He sank the three, but missed the six. I put the twelve into the corner.

"So how come Darla's down in the dumps?"

"Aw, it's always something with that broad. Now she's acting sorry about what she done. So the stork ain't gonna be paying her a visit after all. Well, that's life. You make a choice, you gotta live with it."

Evidently I'd misspent a significant part of my youth in pool halls, because I was a pretty good player. Now as I chalked my stick, I saw I could run the table on Bud if I didn't screw up.

"Sorry to hear about your wife."

"Yeah. What a terrible accident."

He said it with a straight face.

"You really think it was an accident?"

"Who the hell knows? All I know is, some people deserve what happens to 'em. Bernice deserved to drown like a rat in a fucking sewer. You don't know what kinda hell she put me through. Aw, nice shot. Hey, I got good news for you. I'm giving you another raise. To a yard and a half a week. How does that sound?"

A yard and a half was a hundred fifty bucks.

"It sounds great, Bud. Thanks."

I lined up another shot. A tricky bank.

"Ten bucks says you miss it."

"You're on."

"Shit! You're on fucking fire, kid. So I'm gonna have a party. It's been a while since I throwed one. But since things is starting to look up for me again, it seems like a good time. And I'm gonna make a couple of announcements."

"What kind of announcements?"

"That I'm your old man, for one thing. That way, people'll start treating you with the proper respect."

I knocked in the ten.

"What's the other announcement?"

"That Darla and me's getting married." He went in his pocket, pulled out a little box. Opened it to reveal a diamond ring, one big stone set in a twinkling constellation of smaller ones. "Wait'll she gets a gander at this, huh? I got it today at Lackritz. That's the fanciest jewelry joint in Beverly Hills."

"It's some ring, all right."

"So Darla's gonna be your stepmom. What do you think of that?"

I tapped the thirteen, watched its orange stripe wobbling across the table till it dropped into a pocket. I'd left myself an easy shot on the eight.

"Geez, kid. You oughta have some mercy on your old man."

But there was a glint in his eye of paternal pride as I finished him off.

"Double or nothing on the sawbuck?"

"Sure."

I got the balls out of the pockets and rolled them to Bud as he racked them up. I sensed Darla's presence in the house. Something more fundamental than my physical body could see the glow of her golden hair, could smell her Jean Harlow perfume. I had my gun on me. I could break my cue stick over Bud's head and knock him out and rush upstairs and grab Darla and we'd run outside and jump in my car and I'd gun down anybody that got in my way. We'd highball it out of this insane city into freedom, into the future. And then in a little cabin in a tourist camp out in the desert we'd do what Adam and Eve did, what guys and girls do. And she'd murmur and grow sad over my bruises and my tortured toes and the dent in my head and I'd say are you kidding? No man could be happier than I am at this moment.

"I want you to go out to Palm Springs with me this weekend. I got a very important business meeting."

"Yeah? Who with?"

"Some guys I know from Chicago. I'm looking for 'em to be my new partners. Since my old partners stabbed me in the fucking back. But I want you right there with me in the meeting. From now on I'm including you in everything."

He positioned the balls properly then lifted up the rack.

"Break."

I exploded the bumpy bright pyramid of balls. The two and eleven dropped in.

Bud drank some scotch and shook his head. "Geez. I might never get another shot."

But I missed the next shot, even though it was easy. Bud looked at me suspiciously. "You do that on purpose?"

"Course not."

" 'Cause when you got your foot on somebody's neck, you don't ever let 'em up."

He walked around the table, cleaning his cue with a Kleenex as he examined the angles.

"You know, I had the goddamnest thing happen to me the other night."

"What?"

"I was in here by myself just knocking the balls around. I do that sometimes when I can't sleep. And guess who comes strolling in the door."

I shrugged.

"Doc Travis! That's who."

"The bootlegger or the monkey?"

"The bootlegger!"

"Did he still have his head?"

"Oh yeah. I woulda fucking fainted if he'd come walking in

here without a head. He was just like he always was. But he was real mad at me 'cause he thought I had something to do with what happened to him. He said when that stripper died up at the lake, what was her name?"

"Vera."

"Yeah. He said it wasn't no accident. He killed her 'cause he knew it'd make trouble for me."

"Doc said he murdered Vera?"

"Yeah. And you know ever since I come back from the lake I been feeling fucking hoodooed."

"Then what happened?"

"Nothing. He just turned around and walked back out the door. So either I'm losing my marbles or I seen a ghost."

"Well, I don't believe in ghosts."

"So you're saying I'm losing my marbles."

"No." I stared down into my glass, swishing the scotch around in it. "Maybe you were dreaming."

"Danny, I was as wide awake as I am right now."

I couldn't help but jump a little as out of the corner of my eye I saw somebody walking through the door. But it wasn't a ghost, it was just Darla. Though she looked a little like a ghost.

She was wearing a fluffy white robe over a pink nightgown. One hand clutched the robe shut over her throat. The strange thing was, she had on sunglasses, which stood out starkly against the pallor of her face.

Bud started towards her.

"Baby, what are you doing out of bed?"

"Don't touch me!" she hissed.

"Why are you wearing sunglasses?" I said.

She took them off. I expected to see that one or both of her eyes had been blackened, but that wasn't it. They were blue and red. The irises blue, the whites shockingly blood-red.

"What happened to your eyes?"

"They turned this way last night. After he tried to choke me to death. See?"

She let her robe fall open so I could see her throat. It was covered with bruises.

I turned to Bud.

"You bastard."

He looked at me warily. "This ain't none of your business, Danny."

"Why'd you do it?"

"I'll say it again. It ain't none of your business."

"I'll tell you why he did it," said Darla. " 'Cause I told him I couldn't stand him anymore. That I'd rather be dead than stay with him."

"It didn't happen like she said. I wasn't trying to choke her to death. I just flew off the handle a little bit, that's all. I told her already I was sorry."

Darla was looking at me with her unsettling blue and red eyes.

"Can she leave if she wants to?" I said. "Is she a prisoner here?"

Bud gave an exasperated sigh, ran his fingers through his thinning grey-goned hair.

"Come on, Danny. What are you talking about 'prisoner'? Can't you see she's a fucking basketcase? She don't know what she's doing. I'm looking after her, that's all. So she don't hurt herself.

"Hey, let's don't fight no more," he said to Darla, then he went in his pocket and pulled the little box back out.

"Lookit, baby. Look at what I bought you."

He took the ring out and held it out to her.

"It's from Lackritz, baby. Seven and a half carots! And that ain't even counting all the little ones."

She slapped it out of his hand. It bounced across the red

carpet and rolled under the pool table.

Something changed instantly in his eyes, like a light going on or a light going off. He bent down and reached under the table and got the ring, then he grabbed Darla's wrist and tried to force the ring on her finger.

"Put it on, you bitch!" he shouted, and she tried to jerk her hand free then slapped at his face then dug her fingernails into his cheek. He yelled then whacked her across the side of her face and sent her reeling and stumbling over the carpet. He never saw the punch I launched; it caught him in the left temple, and he grunted and dropped to all fours. He swung his head groggily back and forth, a glistening string of saliva dangling from his jaws. I took Darla by the elbow and said: "Come on, let's get outa here." We started toward the door, and then my fantasy of whacking Bud with my pool cue came true except in reverse: the stick came down where my neck met my right shoulder, and broke in half. The pain was paralyzing, and I fell to my knees. Then Bud knocked me on my face, and his knee was in my back as he crouched atop me and shoved the broken end of the pool cue against the back of my neck. He roared hoarsely: "I'M GONNA KILL YOU, YOU BASTARD!"

"Bud, don't!" screamed Darla as she tried to pull him off, then Dick and Anatoly came running into the room.

"Bud, are you nuts? That's *Danny!*" said Dick. Since they both knew the kind of man Bud Seitz was, it took a lot of guts for Dick and Anatoly to drag him off of me.

I sat up slowly, rubbing my neck and trying to catch my breath. I saw that a smidgen of sanity seemed to be returning to Bud's eyes.

"Get him outa here," he said. "Get him outa my fucking sight."

"Come on, Danny," said Dick as he helped me up, and then Willie and Bo Spiller joined the party. They weren't as gentle as

Dick. They grabbed me under the arms and proceeded to give me the bum's rush out of the house. I was looking around for Darla but she'd already disappeared.

I hadn't been home long when the phone rang. It was Bud.

"What the hell happened, Danny?"

His voice sounded different than I'd ever heard it before: kind of shaky, and small, and baffled.

"You need to let Darla go, Bud. She doesn't wanna be with you anymore."

"I guess it's true, then."

"What?"

"What I heard about you two. About her sucking your dick by the lake."

"No. That's not true."

"You swear?"

"Yeah. But there's something you need to know. I love Darla. I wanna be with her. I wanna marry her."

"Aw, shit," he said, and then came silence.

"You still there?"

"Yeah, kid. I'm still here. Listen. If you and her think you're gonna go skipping off hand in hand into the sunset together, well it ain't gonna happen. I mean, what kinda example would I be setting for you if I let you push me around over some broad?"

"I can't help the way I feel. And Darla can't help the way she feels."

Bud gave a humorless laugh.

"She's using you, kid. You ain't her type. You're too nice. She likes crumbs. Like me. Rich crumbs. Then when she gets sick of one rich crumb she goes on to the next one. If they don't get sick of her first."

"I don't think you really understand her."

"Aw, I understand her all right. Believe me, I'm doing you a favor by keeping her away from you."

"If you think she's such a rotten person, why do you even wanna be with her?"

"Broads are like a disease. It's like in the movies, where Clark Gable or somebody's going into the fucking jungle. And then he gets bit by a mosquito, and he gets real sick, and he's laying in some fucking hut sweating and moaning and talking out of his head, and the jungle drums are beating, and the cannibals are getting ready to come get him and cook him in a big pot, and it's all 'cause that fucking little mosquito bit him."

"I guess I got bit too, Bud."

Silence, and then a sigh.

"This stinks."

"Yeah."

"You know, I'd sooner cut off my right fucking arm than hurt you. And to think about what I almost done tonight . . . I got plans for us, kid. Big plans. But Darla's standing in the way. She's got in between us. So what are we gonna do?"

"I don't know."

"It ain't gonna work, you going to Palm Springs with me. But we'll talk when I get back. All right?"

"Yeah. Sure."

"See ya around, kid."

"See ya."

Then his end of the line went dead.

13

About eleven the next morning, Nuffer called.

"I've found out some information about the Sonoma State Home. I don't think you're going to like it, Danny."

"Let's hear it."

"To begin with, it's not a reform school at all. It's a mental hospital."

"But—that doesn't make any sense, Mr. Nuffer. There's nothing wrong with Sophie."

"I'm afraid there's more. The doctors there work hand in glove with an organization called the Human Betterment Foundation. It's based in Pasadena. A lot of prominent scientists and educators are members. My good friend Harry Chandler, the publisher of the *Los Angeles Times*—he's on the board. Their purpose is the betterment of the human race through the science of eugenics."

"What does that mean?"

"It means keeping the unfit from breeding excessively. According to California law, the state can sterilize the feeble-minded and insane."

"Wait a second. You're not saying they might sterilize Sophie, are you?"

"No, Danny, I'm not saying they *might*. I'm saying they *will*. *All* patients, male and female, who are committed to the Sonoma State Home are sterilized as a matter of course."

I thanked Nuffer, hung up, and crossed the courtyard to

Sophie's house. I had to knock awhile before Lois finally opened the door.

She looked at me blearily. "Yeah? What do you want?"

"Is Sophie here?"

"Unh unh."

"Where is she?"

"How the hell should I know? Out running wild, probably. Now get outa here. 'Fore I call the cops."

She shut the door. Her smell lingered. I walked out to the street. Looked up and down it. No sign of Sophie running wild, or doing anything else. I half hoped she had run away.

I sat down on the steps to wait for her. It was a hot day, and the sun was shining nearly straight down, and there wasn't any shade. I was sick of the sunlight and wished I was sitting here cold and shivering in the rain. I knew for a fact that I was living my final few days in sunny California. I wanted to get away from here like Darla had wanted to get away from Nebraska City, Nebraska, and Elwood, Indiana.

Tinker Bell joined me for a while, but the sun became too much for her and she retired to the shade of a nearby bush. She lay on her side and gazed at me with her calm green eyes.

After a while I checked my watch. I had to leave. I had to meet Dick at noon.

"I love fucking fried oysters," said Dick.

He was on his second plate of them. He could eat a lot for a skinny person.

We were at a restaurant called Eddie's on the Santa Monica Pier. I was having the seafood platter. A melancholy-looking stork was sitting on a railing outside the window watching us eat.

"Has Bud said anything about me?" I asked.

"Yeah. He said if you was to come around again, not to let

you in. But not to rough you up or nothing." Dick shook his head. "Geez, Danny. You and Darla. What was in your fucking head? You must wanna die young or something."

"Are you going to Palm Springs with him?"

"Nah. He wants me and the Kornblum brothers to stay at his house."

"And guard Darla?"

"Yeah, I guess so."

Camilla, our slinky, sloe-eyed waitress, brought us over two more mugs of beer. Dick slurped some down, getting foam on his moustache, as he watched her sway away.

"When's he leaving?"

"Tomorrow."

Which was Saturday.

"And when's he coming back?"

"Sunday. You're making me nervous, kid. What's with all the questions?"

"Don't you think it's time?"

"Time for what?"

"To get outa this racket. Like you're always talking about. And sell goat-gland extract. Or whatever."

"Yeah, it's probably about time."

"How about tomorrow night? Around midnight. Or whenever the Kornblum brothers fall asleep."

Dick chewed grimly on a french fry. "I don't think I wanna hear this."

"All you gotta do is get a message to Darla. Tell her I'll be waiting outside the gate for her at midnight. And then she sneaks outa the house, and you open the gate for us, and then we all get outa town."

"And then they catch us, and then we wind up keeping Tommy company. Out in the desert, by that fucking chicken ranch."

"They're not gonna catch us. The Bud Seitz gang's a sinking ship, Dick. It's like the *Monfalcone*. Everybody's ganging up on Bud. He's gonna be too busy trying to save his own neck to worry abut what we're doing."

"Even if I was thinking about maybe going along with this, I only got about fifty bucks. How far's that gonna take me?"

I went in my pocket and pulled out a wad of bills and put them on the table between us.

"That's 500 dollars. It's yours now. And I'll give you another grand tomorrow night."

Dick gave a soft whistle. "That's a lotta jack," he said. But the money remained on the table at the end of the meal. I re-pocketed it, and we left Eddie's.

Dick lit up a cigarette, and we walked down the pier. The ocean breeze felt nice after the relentless heat of Hollywood. Far to the north I could see Point Dume. I remembered being there with Darla. Watching the sea lion on the rock as she told me about Beau Jack. All of a sudden it struck me that, though I had lost my past, I was building up a new past. Every day I was becoming more solid, less ghost-like. And I felt a surge of energy, an optimistic tingle down my spine, a conviction that I'd be able to pull everything off, make the world right for Darla and Sophie and me.

We reached the amusement-park part of the pier. It was aswarm with kids. We stopped in front of the Ferris wheel. It was taking on new passengers.

Dick blew out some smoke, and smiled a little.

"Fucking Ferris wheel," he said.

"Yeah."

"I loved going to Coney Island when I was a kid. There was this place called Dreamland. It was only open a few years, and then it burned down. They had the greatest rides. The Shoot-the-Chutes. The Fighting Flames. The fucking Haunted Swing.

The Giant Racer Roller Coaster. I met this girl there once. Her name was Mildred Beasley. She was real pretty, and she wore real nice clothes. She said her old man was a watchmaker. I didn't wanna tell her my old man was dead, so I said he was a shoemaker, and owned his own shop. Then I seen her looking down at my shoes. Well, my shoes was fucking falling offa my feet, they was so old, and I could tell she knew I was lying, but she didn't say nothing about it. She just smiled. She was always smiling.

"Anyway. I end up spending ever fucking cent I got on her. I'm buying her cotton candy, and hot dogs, and teddy bears, and then we go for a ride on the Ferris wheel. So we're going around and around together, and she tells me I'm the nicest boy she's met all summer, and she kisses me right on the cheek. I'm telling you, Danny, I ain't never been so happy before or since.

"We made plans to meet up again exactly one week later, right there at the Ferris wheel." He smiled again, a little bitterly this time. "I'll give you three guesses whether she showed up or not. I'm still waiting for fucking Mildred Beasley."

It was quiet a minute, and then I said: "Wanna get on?"

"The Ferris wheel?"

"Yeah."

"With you?"

"Yeah."

He seemed to consider it for a moment, then: "Nah. People'd think we was fairies."

We walked on, towards the rumbling roller coaster. Kids screamed as they were swept past us, as though caught up in a catastrophe. "You really good for another G?" said Dick.

I nodded. Took the roll of bills out of my pocket and handed it over to him.

"I ain't never been to Florida," he said. "I hear you can pick

331

oranges right off the fucking trees."

I was still a few blocks away from the bungalow court when I saw Sophie roller-skating down the sidewalk. I pulled up beside her, tooted my horn. She looked over and smiled and waved.

"You're just the person I wanted to see," I said.

She seemed delighted. "Really?"

"Yeah. Get in."

She clomped on her roller skates over to the car and climbed in. Her cheeks were flushed, and her face and her skinny arms were filmed with sweat. She was working on a big wad of bubblegum. She looked up at me expectantly.

"I want to have a very serious talk with you, Sophie."

"Okay."

"I've found out some things about the Sonoma State Home. It's not a very nice place. In fact, it's a really bad place. I don't think you oughta go there."

"I don't think I oughta go either. But Mom says I have to."

"No. You don't."

"But what should I do? You mean I should run away again?"

"I'm leaving Los Angeles. Tomorrow night. I'm going to New York. You wanna come?"

Sophie looked as though she could barely believe her ears. Her jaws worked even faster on her gum.

"Come to *New York?*"

I nodded.

"With *you?*"

I nodded again. Now she nodded too. Vigorously.

"Now this is gonna have to be a big secret. We're gonna have to sneak away. You can't tell anybody."

"It's a secret," she said solemnly. "I promise," and she crossed her heart. "Cross my heart and hope to die."

"Somebody else'll be going with us."

"Who?"

"Her name's Darla."

"Is she your girlfriend?"

I shrugged. "She's nice. You'll like her."

She blew a pink bubble till it popped.

"I doubt it."

14

As I told Dulwich my plan that night, he listened quietly, puffing on his pipe. Tobacco tonight, not opium. Tinker, on his lap, seemed to be listening too. When I finished, all Dulwich did was murmur: "Good old Danny." His pipe had gone out, and he began fiddling around with it, trying to get it re-lit. Tinker jumped off his lap, walked over to the front door, and began lovingly licking herself.

"Well," I said. "What do you think?"

"Morally, I think you're on solid ground in taking Sophie away with you. Legally, I think it's possible you could be charged with kidnapping, and if apprehended, could spend a very long time in prison. As for Darla . . ." His eyes wandered up to the painting—the yellow-haired girl on the windy cliff. "I would like to see you and your Darla be happy together. But I wonder if getting her out of the house might not prove trickier than you think. For instance, how far can you trust this Dick fellow? How do you know, after taking your money, he might not simply shoot you in the back?"

"I trust Dick. He'd never do that."

"And what about the charmingly named Mousie Kornblum and his brother?"

"Everybody says they're morons. I'm not worried about them."

"They may be morons, but they're morons with guns, which makes them dangerous. It's a common, and often fatal mistake to underestimate your enemy. Let me give you some advice, Danny: Worry about everything. Expect things to go wrong. Bring extra ammunition. Prepare to adjust."

"Okay."

Dulwich smiled sadly at me.

"Can it really be you're leaving tomorrow?"

"I'll miss you, Dulwich. It's been great knowing you. You've been a real friend."

Dulwich set down his pipe and walked over to his desk and opened a drawer. He pulled out a small silver cross attached to a short white ribbon with a purple stripe.

"What's that?" I said.

"It's the Military Cross. I'd forgotten all about it till I ran across it recently at the bottom of a dusty box. A forgotten medal awarded to a forgotten soldier for a forgotten action in a forgotten war."

"What happened?"

"It had to do with a bridge. Over the Tigris River, at Kut. It had just been built by our engineers, for obscure reasons; but when the Turks arrived, the brass hats, in their infinite wisdom, realized it could be used as easily by them as by us, and ordered it destroyed. It was one of those death-or-glory jobs. One would have had to have been a fool to volunteer for it. I volunteered."

Dulwich picked up the photograph of the noble-chinned Aubrey Joyce off the cabinet radio, looked fondly at it.

"I was in competition with Aubrey, you see. I knew he had already won the Victoria Cross in France. And even as I was volunteering I was already imagining telling him about my exploit after the war. In a wry, self-deprecating manner, of course, where he would have to read my bravery between the lines.

"In the event, it was a nasty business. It went off a little after midnight. I led a small raiding party across the bridge. I had to kill a Turkish sentry with my knife. A dear friend, Taff Bickerton, was killed. Poor Bickerton. He was such a gentle soul. He had no business being in a war. But the dual mission was accomplished: the bridge was blown up, and I won my medal. My glittering bit of metal."

"So did you tell Aubrey all about it? After the war?"

Dulwich smiled, as he sat back down. "Oh yes. It was all more or less as I imagined. He wasn't the type to say so, you know, but—I could tell that he was proud of me." He looked at the medal, then held it out to me. "I'd like for you to have it."

"Oh no. I couldn't take it—"

"Please. To remember me by."

I was surprised to see tears in Dulwich's eyes. I took it.

"Consider it a talisman of good luck," he said. "To keep you safe tomorrow night, and in the days to come."

"Thanks, Dulwich. This means a lot to me."

"I rather envy you, really."

"Oh yeah? Why?"

"Off on an adventure! I've done a bit of tramping about in my time. I recall the pleasures of wandering in a new place without a penny in your pockets. Not knowing what's to become of you. Knowing only that each step is a step into the new."

"Come with us."

"Oh, I think four would be a crowd, Danny. Five, counting Miss Tinker. But we'll come visit you when you're settled. Unlike most cats, Miss Tinker loves to travel."

"Okay. I'd like that."

Dulwich picked his pipe back up, struck a match, and put it to the bowl. "It's interesting. I've been having traveling dreams lately. Just last night, for instance. I was in a motorcar with Aubrey. We were traveling across a lush green countryside. Neither of us said anything; it was perfectly pleasurable just being together."

We heard a soft thud at the front door.

Tinker Bell was swatting at a pale-white moth fluttering against the other side of the screen.

15

The next morning, I drove to Drucker's Barbershop in Beverly Hills. Bud had introduced me to it. I got a haircut, a shave, a neck and shoulder rub, and a shoeshine.

Traffic was light for a Saturday as I drove back. The city seemed exhausted, like it had had enough of summer. I stopped at a filling station and got a full tank of gas, and had the oil, water, and air in my tires checked.

While I'd been gone the postman had come. I had one piece of mail. It began: "Dear Friend: To become independent you MUST invest! Line up with a REAL professional for REAL profits in the REAL ESTATE business!!!"

I wasn't hungry, but I forced myself to eat a bowl of Campbell's tomato soup with some crackers crumbled up in it.

Around two Dick called. Everything was set. Bud and the boys had left for Palm Springs. He'd talked to Darla, and she was eagerly awaiting my arrival. He suggested I show up around one in the morning. That would give Mousie and Freddie plenty of time to get drunk and pass out as was their habit.

I went outside around three and sat on the stoop and drank a lemon soda. The day was passing with agonizing slowness. It felt like I'd gone to get a haircut *last* Saturday instead of this morning.

For five minutes I watched a single strand of a spider's web moving a little in a breeze, the sunlight running up and down it. Then Lois and Jerry came out of Sophie's bungalow. Lois looked a little soberer and more presentable than she had recently. They gave me dirty looks as they walked toward the street but didn't say anything. Then a couple of minutes later Sophie came out.

"Are we still going?" she asked in a whisper.

I nodded. "I gotta go pick up Darla first. So I'll meet you out front a little after one."

"Can't I go with you to pick up Darla?"

"No, it's better we do it this way."

She couldn't keep the grin off her face.

"I'm so excited. I couldn't hardly sleep last night."

"You're not worried about missing your mom?"

She rolled her eyes in an exaggerated way.

"Oh, brother. You got any other funny jokes? Well, I better go pack. Before Mom and the creep get back. Hey, that rhymes!"

"Don't let her see the suitcase."

"Don't worry, I got a good hiding place. That rhymes too! See ya later!"

I finished my soda, then also went in and packed.

I wrote a note to Mrs. Dean apologizing for my sudden departure and put it in an envelope, accompanied by an extra month's rent.

I got another soda from the fridge, turned on the radio, and sat down on the davenport.

At dusk, the crows passed over.

Then I awoke with a start to darkness. I was sure that many hours had to have passed, that everyone was waiting, that everything was lost, and I groped in panic for the light switch, but it was only about ten fifteen.

I went in the bathroom and splashed water on my face. Looked at myself in the mirror. Felt for a half of a half of a second that I was about to remember my real name.

I was in the kitchen spooning Folger's coffee into my coffee pot when I heard somebody knocking at the front door, and hulloing softly.

Dulwich was standing there with a crooked, half-apologetic grin. "Hope I'm not disturbing you."

"No, come in."

As he walked in past me, I caught a whiff of cologne. He was wearing a light-brown linen jacket and matching trousers and a crisp white shirt. His hair was carefully combed, agleam with oil.

"You look like you're going out," I said.

"I am, Danny. I'm going out with you."

"Thanks, Dulwich. I appreciate the offer. But I'll be fine."

"But what if you're not fine? What if something goes wrong? Have you ever even been hunting, Danny? Have you ever killed even an animal with a gun?"

"I don't know. I don't think so."

"This is my kind of show, old boy. And besides—I know if I don't go with you, I shan't sleep a wink all night for worrying about you."

Dulwich and I looked at each other. I think a part of me had been hoping that he would come. Had somehow *known* that he would come.

"You got a gun?" I said.

He pulled back his coat to reveal a pistol stuck in his belt.

"I have a Smith & Wesson, like you. But mine's a semiautomatic, as you see. I prefer it to a revolver. One can both fire and reload more quickly. Which, in a tight spot, can make all the difference."

"I'm making coffee. Want some?"

"I'd love some."

16

Even on Saturday night, Los Angeles wasn't a town that stayed up late, so we pretty much had the streets to ourselves as we drove north toward Bud's. We saw a few bums and drunks and unappealing hookers and a very fat Negro man on a tiny bicycle kicking at a stray dog that was trying to bite him. Ahead of us, neon signs glowed atop hotels and stores on Sunset and Hollywood Boulevards, and beyond the signs, the dark mass of the Hollywood hills rose up, with pinpricks of lonely light scattered across them.

A police prowl car pulled up next to us at a red light. The two cops inside looked us over as if they sensed we were up to something questionable, but when the light went green they pulled away.

I reached Franklin then drove across it and up the little hill. I was hoping to see in the glare of the headlights Darla standing there with her suitcase waiting for me but there wasn't any Darla, or Dick either, just the stark iron bars of the gate.

I switched the engine off and turned off the lights. Dulwich and I looked at each other, then I looked at my watch.

"We're a little early," I said. "I'm sure she'll be along any minute now."

The first minute was okay, the second uncomfortable, the third intolerable.

"I say," said Dulwich, "I'm feeling a bit exposed here. Like a sitting duck."

"What should we do?"

"Why don't we just hop out and have a squint at things?"

We shut the car doors as quietly as we could. Walked up to the gate, peered through.

The grounds of the house were lit up by the floodlamps. The driveway curved up and around and disappeared behind some trees. I could see only a small part of the second story of the house from here; it was dark and still.

"Whose car is that?" said Dulwich.

Now I saw the orange Ford coupe off to the side of the driveway, parked close to the wall.

"Dick's."

"And he was supposed to meet you here? With Darla?"

"Yeah."

"Could there have been a misunderstanding about the time?"

"I don't think so."

Then we heard the crisp sounds of footsteps. Someone was walking rapidly towards us down the driveway.

Dulwich put a finger to his lips, motioned that we should step away from the gate. We concealed ourselves behind the stone wall.

I noticed Dulwich had his pistol out. The footsteps were getting louder. We peeked around the wall.

Dick emerged from behind the trees, swinging his arms briskly as he came down the drive.

"It's okay," I said. "It's Dick."

I stepped out and Dick saw me and waved. "Hey, kid. So you're here already." He hit the gate button, and it rattled open. But he got suspicious when he saw Dulwich. "Who's that?"

"Relax, it's Dulwich, he's a friend of mine. Where's Darla?"

Dick shook his head and coughed and lit an Old Gold.

"Ah, it's all fucked up, Danny. They got her locked up in her fucking room."

Expect things to go wrong, Dulwich had said. I tried to stay calm.

"So what happened?"

"Well, Mousie and Freddie was glad to let me guard the gate, 'cause nobody likes staying down here the whole fucking night. So I'm expecting Darla to show but she don't never show. So I go up there. Mousie's got drunk and passed out all right, just like he was supposed to. But he's passed out in a chair right in front of her fucking door. So I wonder where Freddie's at. I walk around looking for him, then I hear music coming from outside. This Guy Lombardo kinda shit. I go around the house, and I find Freddie camping out like some fucking cowboy under the room where Darla's at. He's drug one of them lounging chairs over from the swimming pool and he's hooked up a radio to an extension cord and he's sitting out there drinking a beer and eating some kinda big fucking sandwich. Bud musta told 'em to do that. Maybe he smelled a rat or something."

Sweat was pouring down Dick's face, even though the night was cooling off; now he took a rumpled handkerchief out of his pocket and mopped his forehead.

"I don't know, kid. Maybe tonight ain't the night. Maybe we oughta take a raincheck."

"I think Dick may be right," said Dulwich. "No point in taking unnecessary risks."

"But what about Sophie?" I said. "They're coming for her on Monday. I need to get her out of town. And tomorrow night'll be worse 'cause Bud and the guys'll be back."

"I don't know who this Sophie broad is," said Dick, "and I don't fucking care. All I know is it's making me nervous, us all just standing around here flapping our yaps."

"Is the door to the house unlocked?" asked Dulwich.

"Yeah. You can just walk in like you own the joint."

"If we can deal with Mousie quietly," Dulwich said to me,

"we probably won't have to deal with his brother at all."

I reached inside my jacket, pulled out an envelope. "Here's the G," I said, handing it over to Dick.

He opened it up and glanced at its contents, then stuck it in his pocket.

"Thanks, kid. Well—it's been nice knowing you. I mean that."

We shook hands.

"I feel the same way, Dick. I'll miss you."

Dick slapped me on the shoulder, then walked over to his car. Got in, started it up, hit the headlights, and rolled out the gate.

"Send me a postcard from Florida," I said to Dick as he passed by. He waved and went down the hill and was gone.

Dulwich was biting his lower lip thoughtfully as he gazed through the gate.

"We should move your car, Danny. To an inconspicuous spot inside the walls."

I got in my Packard and drove through the gate and off the driveway thirty or so feet over the grass and behind some azalea bushes, where I parked and got out.

Dulwich had hit the gate button, and it was sliding shut as I walked back to him.

He smiled faintly at me.

"So how do you feel, old boy?"

Sick inside. Like my soul was melting and flowing out of my body through the soles of my feet.

"I feel fine. Let's go get Darla."

17

We cast long shadows in the light of the floodlamps as we walked up the driveway. The bushes and trees and flowers we passed seemed unreal somehow, as if they were made of plastic or wax. The shaggy heads of the palm trees were perfectly still in the breezeless air.

The Kornblum brothers' black Pontiac was parked in front of the house. All the windows in the house were dark. Dulwich and I paused at the front door, then took our Smith & Wessons out from under our jackets. I opened the door, and we slipped in.

Dulwich eased the door shut behind us. Enough light came in the windows to make a dark twilight within the house. We passed through an anteroom. To our right was the room where in April we'd had the party, where Darla had eaten a cupcake and worn a gold lamé gown and Nuffer's face had got redder and redder as he looked at Violet Gilbertson. Straight ahead was the living room. We went straight and I led Dulwich to the bottom of the staircase that led up to the second floor. There was a glow at the top of the stairs indicating a light was on up there.

"Listen," whispered Dulwich.

I heard it too now: the rough rhythm of snoring rumbling down the stairs. Now Dulwich whispered: "Let's locate Freddie. Just to make certain he's where he's supposed to be."

We went into the dining room. The crystal chandelier was an

icy glistening above us in the half-dark. As we approached the French doors we could hear the smooth dance music Dick had talked about.

Freddie Kornblum was stretched out on the lounge chair under the balcony of Bud and Darla's room, his chin on his chest, his hat tilted down over his eyes, and his fingers interlaced over his stomach. Taking a little nap, it looked like, after his big sandwich.

We retraced our steps to the foot of the stairs. Listened to the snores and looked up at the glow.

"I don't suppose you have a knife on you, do you?" Dulwich whispered.

"No. Why?"

"Why do you think? We could get a knife from the kitchen. Where is it?"

"Do we really have to kill him?"

"What did *you* have in mind?"

"Well—sneak up on him. Get the drop on him. Take his gun away."

"And what if he decides to try to shoot us with his gun before we can take it away? Or what if he cries out for his brother? No, Danny. The safest thing is to silence him while he sleeps."

"Can't we just hit him over the head with something? Knock him out?"

I could see a hint of exasperation on his face; then he looked around.

Across the room was a fireplace. Next to it a shovel, a broom, coal tongs, and a poker hung off an iron stand. I followed Dulwich over there. He picked the poker up. Hefted it. "This should do," he said, and then the light came on.

It was like the light switch was hooked up to my heart too and had sent an electric surge through it. I looked around. Anatoly was standing near the arched entranceway, barechested and barefooted, wearing only a pair of white trousers. We stared at each other in mutual surprise.

I saw Dulwich had his pistol pointed at him, and I put a hand on his arm. "It's okay," I said.

Anatoly blinked at us. Smiled tentatively. "I think I hear something, Danny," he said in a soft voice. "But I see nothing here. Only empty room. Maybe it is mice. I am going back to bed now. Okay?"

I nodded. Anatoly turned the light off, and left.

"Who the devil was that?" said Dulwich.

"Anatoly. The butler."

"How do you know he won't give us away?"

"He won't. He likes me."

"Are there any other occupants of the house I should know about? Cooks? Maids? Filipino houseboys?"

"No. Only Anatoly."

"This is the point of no return, Danny. Shall we continue?"

I nodded.

We stole up the stairs. Peeked around the corner, down a long hallway.

Twenty-five feet or so of creaky hardwood floor separated us from Mousie Kornblum. He was sitting in a straight-backed chair, in front of Darla's door, his feet propped up on a footstool. His posture was nearly identical to his brother's, except his head was leaning back instead of forward and his mouth was open. He continued to snore heavily, his chest rising and falling. A tan fedora sat on the floor near a half-empty quart of Old Log Cabin bourbon.

Dulwich started to take off his shoes, and indicated I should do the same. Then: "Ready?" he asked in the faintest of whispers, and I gave him the slightest of nods, then we were gliding down the hallway in our stocking feet toward Mousie. Dulwich, in the lead, had his pistol in his left hand and the poker in his right. Mousie seemed so profoundly lost in drunken slumber you'd have thought he would sleep through an earthquake but when the floor beneath my right foot emitted a tiny squeak, he awoke with a startled wide-eyed snort. Dulwich closed the remaining distance in a rush, lifting the poker above his head. Mousie saw him coming out of the corner of his eye, and his head started turning as he raised his left arm, the arm closest to Dulwich, but the poker came in over it and struck the top of his head. It made a terrible sound, like a squishy crunch, like the sound the lead pipe must have made when it connected with my head. He grunted and began to slump sideways as blood began to squirt through his hair and Dulwich hit him again, on the side of his head this time. He toppled off the chair and the chair fell over too. He lay on the floor with one leg twisted under him and the other still up on the footstool and a pool of blood growing around his head and then, horribly, he began to snore again.

I tried the door but it was locked. Now I heard Darla through the door. "Who's out there? What's going on?"

"It's me. Danny."

"Danny? Open the door!"

"I will. Just hold on."

Dulwich was bent over Mousie and going through his pockets. He found a revolver and put it in his own pocket then held up a key and I unlocked the door then Darla was in my arms.

"Oh Danny," she said, "I was scared you weren't coming."

"Darla, this is Dulwich—"

"Hello," said Dulwich. "I suggest we move rather quickly now."

As Darla grabbed a suitcase and her purse the sock on my left foot became wet and warm, and I looked down and saw I was standing in Mousie's blood. It seemed like the poker had been hardly less lethal than a knife, though he was still snoring as we hurried away. I left a fading trail of bloody sockprints down the hall.

I was hoping the racket we'd made silencing Mousie hadn't awakened his brother under the balcony. Dulwich and I put our shoes back on and I took the suitcase from Darla and then the three of us scurried down the staircase then through the dark house. I felt elated. In a moment we would be out the door, then nothing remained but a breathless dash down the driveway to my Packard and then out the gate.

Dulwich moved to a window and twitched back the curtain and checked out front. Then he went out the door, and Darla and I followed.

We'd taken only a few steps away from the house when I saw down the hill through the foliage the glitter of headlights.

"Somebody's coming!" I said.

"Go back!" said Dulwich, and we raced back into the house and shut the door.

We went to the window. Two cars were pulling up out front: Bud's black Lincoln and Bo Spiller's red Ford.

"Shit," I said.

"Who are they?" said Dulwich.

"Bud. And the guys."

"What are they doing back already?" wailed Darla.

Bud and Nucky and Nello got out of the Lincoln, and Bo and Willie got out of the Ford. They began removing some luggage; I saw Bo taking his shotgun out.

"Let's go out the back," said Darla.

"No, Freddie's there," I said.

"Oh god," said Darla, "we're trapped!"

Dulwich was regarding the Bud Seitz gang with a look of no more than mild concern, as if they were rowdy interlopers at a genteel family picnic.

"We're not trapped, Darla," he said. "But it's important that we all keep a cool head and that you and Danny do exactly as I say."

Bud was looking especially spiffy tonight, in a silvery three-piece suit with a red carnation in his buttonhole. His face was scratched up like Nucky's. He was looking unhappily at the house. "Where the fuck is everybody?" he said, then he leaned inside the Lincoln and started honking the horn. "Dick! Freddie! Mousie!" he yelled.

In a few moments, Freddie came wandering around the side of the house with a confused look on his face.

"Hey, fellas," he said.

"Let's go," I said.

Dulwich shook his head. "Not yet. As they enter the house, we'll exit. That way we can proceed unobserved down the hill to the car."

"What are you doing back already?" said Freddie, yawning and scratching his neck.

"Ah, them Chicago cocksuckers was coming in like they was trying to take over," said Nucky. "So Bud told 'em to go fuck theirselves."

"How come there ain't nobody down by the gate?" said Bud. "What the hell's going on here, Freddie?"

"Dick ain't down there? He was down there just a minute ago."

"Yeah, and I don't see his car no place neither," said Nello.

"That's funny. It was here a minute ago."

Bud glowered at Freddie. Took a Kleenex out of his pocket and wiped off his hands. "Where's Mousie?"

"Upstairs. Outside Darla's room. Just like you said."

I saw Bud looking at the house suspiciously again; in fact, he seemed to be looking through the crack in the curtains right into my own blinking, terrified eye.

"Let's go check on Darla," he said, as Dulwich announced cheerfully: "All right, chums. It's time to leg it!"

18

We made for the back of the house, for the dining room, for the French doors beyond the glimmering chandelier. The house seemed to have gotten twice as big and twice as dark, and then in the living room I tripped over a footstool and took a tumble and Darla's suitcase went sliding over the floor. Dulwich grabbed the suitcase and Darla helped me up. "Hurry, Danny!" hissed Dulwich, then we were through the dining room door and moving around the big mahogany table.

We could see the floodlamped patio through the glass panes of the doors. Dulwich opened one of the doors and started to step through it then suddenly slammed it shut and flung himself backwards into Darla and me as the door exploded in front of us, glass shattering and wood splintering. Darla screamed, and as we fell back into the darkness of the dining room, I saw Bo Spiller and Willie the Coon out on the patio. Spiller's disfigured face was smiling as he pumped his shotgun, ejecting a red shell casing, and then there was a flash of orange light as he fired again into the room. Dulwich and I dived behind the table. I heard Darla screaming *no, stop,* then Spiller and Willie were advancing into the room like unstoppable forces of nature, Spiller pumping and firing his shotgun and Willie shooting his pistol. I could see under the table through the legs of the chairs their legs coming toward us, silhouetted against the outer brightness. Dulwich saw them too. He fired twice, and one of the bullets struck Willie in the kneecap. He hollered and clutched his knee and fell down as Dulwich popped up and put four quick slugs into Spiller's chest. As he was going down, virtually dead already, his finger jerked the trigger again; unfortunately for Willie, he was on the floor in front of the barrel and took the blast in his stomach. It didn't kill him outright. He howled and moaned and blabbered. Till Dulwich walked around the table and, as casually as if he were stubbing out a cigarette under his shoe, shot him in the head.

My ears were ringing, and the air smelt of gunsmoke. Dulwich took a fresh clip out of his jacket and shoved it in his .38. It wasn't necessary for me to reload since I hadn't fired a shot.

"You all right, Danny?"

"Yeah."

"Where's Darla?"

I looked around.

"I don't know. I guess she ran out."

"Oh bloody hell," he growled, then he raised his gun and seeming to point it directly at my head as if he'd had enough of my incompetence, he fired. I heard the bullet whistle past my ear like the time I'd nearly been killed by Janet Van der Eb, although it wasn't really a whistle, it was more like the air was being ripped. Then I heard a second bang and another bullet zipped past, but this time headed in the opposite direction.

I dove once more to my friend the floor. I saw a shadowy form in the doorway firing at Dulwich, Dulwich continued to fire back, then the guy at the door began to stumble forward like a man who was trying to keep his balance on ice, his arms swinging more and more wildly, till finally he took a nosedive and skidded to a stop just a couple of feet from me.

It was Freddie Kornblum. Blood, black in the dark, was pouring out of his mouth.

"Mousie," he croaked. "Where's Mousie?"

Then that Vera Vermillion stillness settled down upon him.

"I'm afraid I'm hit, old man."

Dulwich was holding his left side. I hurried around the table, stepping over Bo's body and slipping in Willie's blood. I helped Dulwich sit down on one of the dining room chairs. I saw a spreading dark blotch on his white shirt.

"Is it bad?" I said.

"I rather think not. Perhaps a broken rib. But it hurts a bit."

"I have to go find Darla."

"Yes."

"I'll be right back."

"Beware, Danny. Three are left."

Bud, Nucky, and Nello. I didn't know whether they were creeping around in the dark like me, or were still outside, waiting for us to leave so they could cut us down.

I felt like I knew what had happened to Darla. I felt like she had run away from the guns as she'd run away as a kid from her lunatic father in frozen Nebraska, and now she'd hid herself away in some nook or cranny of the big house. But how should I find her? Should I call out to her? But then mightn't someone other than Darla hear me calling out? And then shoot me dead as a doornail? Dead as a Willie, a Bo, or a Freddie? Their corpses stank and I knew now that's how it was, you pissed and shat yourself and squealed like a pig and died. The truth was, I had no idea what I was doing. The unshot gun hung heavy in my hand, and I was shaking all over and my heart was beating violently and I couldn't catch my breath. But whatever I was doing, I needed to do it fast, before Dulwich bled to death in the dining room.

I moved down a narrow hallway that led to the kitchen. I passed a closed door. It was Anatoly's room. I supposed he was in there now, listening to the madness, hoping it would pass him by.

I entered the kitchen. It was spacious, with lots of cabinets and cupboards, and a long counter in the middle, with pots and pans hanging above it on hooks.

"Darla?" I whispered.

Light jumped out of the darkness and there was the thunderous clang of a bullet striking a copper pot not far from my head. I crouched behind the counter, fired toward where the light had been. Now by the flashes of their pistols I saw two dark shapes near the door on the other side of the room. Their bullets ripped and whipped and whanged all around me, and one plucked at the sleeve of my jacket as if trying to get my attention, and it was like I was walking through a hailstorm but not getting hit by any of the hail. I emptied my revolver at them, and must have got lucky with one of my shots as the shooter on the left cried out and crumpled.

I ducked out of the kitchen and ran back down the hall. I shouted: "Darla, goddamn you, come out!"

I'd followed Dulwich's advice and brought extra ammo, and I could feel the cartridges rattling in my pocket like loose change. I reached the end of the hall and turned toward the front of the house, yelling: "Darla, come on!"

I saw the door to the billiard room and dodged through it. I shut the door and moved over to the pool table so I was facing the door and popped out the cylinder of my revolver and shook out the empty brass casings and went in my pocket and dropped a handful of cartridges on the table and then tried to reload. But my hands were shaking and as in a banal nightmare I couldn't seem to get the bullets into the gun, then the door opened and the light came on.

It was Nucky. He had his gun pointed at me. He was splattered with blood but didn't seem to be hit himself. "Put it down on the table," he said, talking about my gun. I did so.

Nucky edged down the room, keeping his gun on me, till he was standing across the table. He was smiling at me in a way I didn't completely like.

"I been waiting for this, asshole. I been waiting a long time."

And then I saw Bud. He had his own gun up as he came through the door. But when he saw me he stopped dead in his tracks and his gun dropped to his side. On his face was a look of shock, and it was clear he hadn't known till now who it was that had been rampaging through his house shooting down his men and clobbering them with pokers.

"Danny," he said.

"Yeah, fucking Danny," sneered Nucky. "I could hear him running around hollering for Darla. I told you you couldn't fucking trust him."

Bud saw the look on Nucky's face.

"Take it easy, Nucky."

"You kidding me? He just killed Nello. Plugged him right through the fucking heart."

"I said take it easy," Bud said more sharply.

I was looking back and forth between them, a fascinated spectator at my own life or death. Nucky seemed to waver a little, his gun lowering; then suddenly and swiftly he lifted the gun back up.

"Fuck it," he said.

Bud shot Nucky through the cheek. The bullet went out the other cheek in a spray of blood and flesh and a couple of Nucky's teeth went tumbling over the floor. It didn't knock Nucky down though, he was swinging his gun around toward Bud, but now Bud shot him several times, the bullets hitting him all over.

Nucky lay quivering on the floor; then a long, poignant-sounding sigh came out of him, and the story of Nucky Williams ended.

Bud turned back towards me. He gave me a puzzled half smile.

"Danny?" he said softly. "What's the deal?"

Out of the shadows of the hallway, Darla appeared in the doorway behind him. Something gleamed in her hand as she lifted it up. There was maybe one second where I could have said something like Bud look out but instead Darla fired and he pitched forward facedown on the red carpet, blood spurting up out of the back of his skull.

She was holding a little silver gun hardly bigger than the palm of her hand. She was looking blankly down at Bud. Now she looked blankly up at me.

We went to get Dulwich. Found him outside the dining room leaning against the wall.

"It's us," I said so he wouldn't shoot us. I turned on a light. I didn't like the way he looked. Chalk white, with bluish lips.

"I was trying to come, Danny. What happened?"

"They're all dead. Let's get you to a hospital. Can you walk?"

"I'll give it a go."

I took his gun from him and pocketed it as Darla retrieved her suitcase. Then he walked along slowly like a very old man as Darla and I guided him along by his elbows like his two grown grandchildren. We passed through the carnage we'd made and out the front door of the house.

I saw Anatoly by the swimming pool. He was fully dressed now. He was untethering the seagull. It perched on his arm and flapped its wings as he talked to it.

We walked by the Pontiac and the Lincoln and the Ford, all in need of new owners now.

"Why don't you wait here?" I said to Dulwich. "I'll walk down and get the car and drive back up."

"All right, Danny," he said, then a bullet hit the back of his neck and passed through and blew a hole in his throat.

Both his hands went to his throat and he looked like he was trying to choke himself.

I heard more shots, and looked around and saw Mousie Kornblum staggering toward us. It looked like somebody had dumped a pail of red paint over his head. Dulwich had taken his gun but now there were plenty of other guns lying around that nobody was using anymore and he must have picked up one of them. Or maybe he'd had two guns all along. Two Gun Mousie Kornblum.

I fired at Mousie with Dulwich's gun. I fired as many times as there were bullets in the clip and Mousie went down, for good this time.

When I turned back around, Dulwich was sitting next to the driveway with his back propped up against the trunk of a palm tree. His hands were still on his throat, and he was making choking noises. Darla was bending over him, looking as though she was about to burst into hysterical screams.

"What do we do?" she said.

"Gotta stop the bleeding," and I knelt in front of him and pried loose his hands. I was immediately hit by rhythmic jets of his blood. I took out my handkerchief and tried to cram it into the hole in his throat.

"You're gonna be all right, Dulwich," I said.

He couldn't talk. But I could feel his hazel eyes burning into me.

"We'll get the bleeding stopped. Then we'll call a hospital, and they'll send an ambulance. You'll be all right."

But the bleeding wouldn't stop, and the handkerchief was soaked through, and my fingers were slippery with the blood.

"You'll be all right," I said, and I could feel his burning eyes. Then he smiled a little, and reached for my hand and squeezed it, and then his eyes went dead and he was dead.

Darla said that we had to go. Said that we couldn't do Dulwich any good by staying here any longer.

She was right. We went down the hill to my car.

19

I drove south through the empty, dreamless streets. Darla said: "I forgot something."

"What?"

"My lamb. The one Mr. Bruff gave me."

"Well, we're not going back."

After that, we could have been department store dummies for all the talking we did to each other.

It didn't take long to get to La Vista Lane. I pulled over and parked. Darla looked around like she was coming out of a trance.

"Why are we stopping? Where are we?"

"This is where I live."

Now I saw Sophie with a suitcase coming down the steps.

"Who's that?" said Darla.

"Sophie. She's my neighbor. She's coming with us."

Darla looked at me.

"You're kidding."

"No."

I got out. Sophie's smile faded as I walked towards her.

"What's that on your clothes?" she said.

I put my hand on her shoulder.

"Sophie. Listen to me. Something terrible has happened."

Her eyes got scared. "What?"

"Mr. Dulwich went with me. To pick up Darla. Some men tried to stop her from leaving. Bad men. They—they shot Mr. Dulwich."

"He's dead?"

"Yeah. But you and me and Darla—we're gonna be just fine. I don't want you worrying about anything. Okay?"

Sophie looked over at Darla in the car, then back at me. She nodded.

"Here, I'll put that in the trunk," I said, taking her suitcase. It was little, and light. I took mine and Darla's suitcases out of the trunk.

"Darla? We need to wash up and change clothes."

Darla had blood on her too. She nodded, and got out. She and Sophie looked each other over.

"Hello," said Darla.

"Hi."

"We'll be back in a few minutes," I said to Sophie. "You wanna just wait here for us?"

"Okay." But then as Darla and I started away, she said: "Danny?"

"Yeah?"

"What about Tinker Bell?"

"Who's Tinker Bell?" said Darla.

"Dulwich's cat," I said.

"Who's gonna take care of her?" said Sophie. "What's gonna happen to her?"

I thought about it a minute, then said: "We'll take her with us."

We left Los Angeles on Route 66—the same highway Dick Prettie and I had taken to Lake Arrowhead.

Sophie was in the back seat with Dulwich's cat, who was in her cage. Sophie had brought along her cat food and food dish and water dish and cat toys, but understandably Tinker seemed pretty unhappy, meowing loudly every second or two.

"Where are we going, by the way?" asked Darla.

"New York," I said.

"Is that cat going to be doing that all the way to New York?"

"She's just scared, is all," said Sophie. "She'll be better soon."

"You know, Darla," I said, somewhat coldly, "we wouldn't be here right now if it wasn't for Dulwich. The least we can do is take care of his cat."

"Okay, I'm sorry. Geez."

The rabbit ranches and avocado orchards Dick and I had seen were lost in the darkness. There wasn't much traffic. I drove pretty fast. We listened to the radio and Darla smoked and Tinker meowed and Sophie talked.

"I made sandwiches for us, is anybody hungry?"

"I'm not," I said, and Darla shook her head.

"I'm not either. We can eat 'em later. See my lunchbox? It's a Jackie Coogan lunchbox."

She handed it up to Darla. A picture of the adorable waif as "The Kid" covered the front of it.

"Cute," said Darla, and handed it back.

"Jackie Coogan's gotten too old to play kid parts now. I don't even think he's been in a movie since *Huckleberry Finn*. I was in the third grade then. He played Tom Sawyer in *Huckleberry Finn*. He also played Tom Sawyer in *Tom Sawyer*."

She wasn't acting all that downcast about what had happened to Dulwich. It probably didn't seem real to her. I guessed it would sink in later.

We passed the turn-off for Lake Arrowhead in San Bernardino and the road jogged north and then we were in new territory as far as I was concerned. In the back seat, Dulwich's cat had calmed down, or just exhausted herself, and Sophie was finally running out of steam too.

"I think Tinker's sleeping," she said.

"Good," I said. "I think she'll be all right. Dulwich told me she loved to travel."

A minute or two passed, then Sophie said: "It's kinda lonely back here."

"Wanna come up here with us?"

Sophie eagerly scrambled over the seat, kicking me in the head in the process.

"Oops! Sorry."

Now she settled down between Darla and me. Within five minutes, she was asleep, her head on Darla's shoulder.

"What's her story?" said Darla quietly.

"Kind of like the story you told me about yourself. She's leaving home because she has to."

"Poor kid."

And in a sort of flash I could see that it was all going to work out, that we were going to become a family, man, woman, kid, and cat.

The road began to rise, then in a series of switchbacks it climbed the face of the Sierra Madre Mountains. We passed over the mountain range at the Cajon Pass, then began a winding descent through an evergreen forest.

Darla had been silent for so long I thought she was asleep too. I thought I had the night to myself. But then I heard her say: "Why are you crying?"

"Dulwich, I guess. I guess I was crying about Dulwich."

"I'm sorry, Danny."

"You know, it was my fault."

"What was?"

"Him getting killed."

"How do you figure that?"

"He wanted to kill Mousie, but I talked him out of it. Then Mousie wound up killing him."

"You're not to blame. Things just happen." She lit a cigarette, moving carefully so as not to awake Sophie. "You shouldn't feel so bad. In a way, I think Dulwich died happy."

"What do you mean?"

"Well, the last word he ever said was 'Danny.' And the last thing he ever saw was you."

"What are you talking about?"

"I think he was probably in love with you. From everything you told me."

"In love with—? That's crazy."

She shrugged. "Is it?"

"Who turned off the bathwater?" Sophie mumbled fretfully in her sleep, then her face began to twitch, then she turned over and leaned against me and was quiet again. Headlights flared into the car, as a vehicle came up fast behind us. When it pulled out in the other lane to pass, I saw it was a truck. STEVE'S STOVES was painted on the side. That Steve sure got around. The truck roared by, then its taillights dwindled as it left us behind. Steve was in a hurry. As long as there was anybody in the world that still needed a stove, Steve would be on the job.

"How much money you got?" said Darla.

"About 400 bucks. How about you?"

"A lot less. Bud never liked me to have much cash. He wanted me to have to depend on him for everything. But he gave me all this jewelry that must be worth a mint." She opened her purse, dug into it, pulled out her diamond engagement ring. "Like this," she said, and then she pulled out her ruby ring. "And this. We can sell this stuff off whenever we need to. We can live in style. For a while, anyway."

I liked the "we."

"And I'll get some kind of job."

"And I can start singing again," she said dreamily, then dropped the rings back in her purse.

"Why'd you shoot him?" I said.

" 'Cause he was about to shoot *you*."

"No he wasn't."

"Well, I thought he was."

"He wouldn't ever have shot me. Not in a million years."

"No? What makes you so special?"

I didn't answer. We passed through Victorville. It was starting to get light.

Just outside Barstow, a billboard showed a picture of an evilly smiling hobo holding up a sign that said: CALIFORNIA OR BUST. Under the picture it said, in lurid black and red letters: "UPTON SINCLAIR—AN EPIC FRAUD! HE'LL TURN CALIFORNIA INTO A HAVEN FOR RADICALS, FLOAT-ERS, AND BOXCAR TOURISTS! VOTE FOR FRANK MERRIAM FOR GOVERNOR!"

We stopped at a Standard Oil station to gas up and use the restrooms. Sophie took Tinker around the back of the station to a weedy area where she used the restroom too.

I went in the office to pay for the gas and buy a road map and some bottles of soda. The owner had a pockmarked face and wispy red hair that went every which way. He looked mean, but had a kindly manner.

"Which way you folks headed?" he said.

"Towards Arizona."

"Well, sody pop's just fine and dandy, but if I was you, I'd buy me some water too. You'll need it. It ain't gonna be no church picnic out there. Not in August, it ain't."

I bought three gallons, and we got back on the road. Route 66 turned due east here, straight into the heart of the Mojave Desert. The sun was floating up in front of us; I lowered the sun visor and Darla donned her sunglasses.

We were all getting hungry. Sophie opened up her Jackie Coogan lunchbox.

"I have three sandwiches. Delicious grape jelly and peanut butter, scrumptious butter and sugar, and boring Spam. Who wants what?"

"What do *you* want, honey?" said Darla.

"Well—grape jelly and peanut butter's my favorite."

"Okay. I'll have the butter and sugar. Danny?"

"Guess I'll have the Spam."

Soon it got hotter than I thought it possible to get. Heat mirages lay like puddles of water on the shimmering road. The landscape was unearthly and blasted-looking. What vegetation there was seemed primitive and savage: thorny cacti and twisted little trees with clumps of spiky leaves. You couldn't imagine even bugs or lizards living out here. Off in the molten-blue distance, mountain ranges jutted up like giant slag heaps. It was hard to see how the pioneers in the olden days had ever made it.

A railroad ran parallel to 66. Sophie leaned out the window and waved wildly at a freight train coming toward us. The red-capped engineer saw her and waved back and, much to her delight, gave a long, mournful toot on his whistle.

About an hour out of Barstow I saw an old jalopy pulled off on the side of the road, its radiator geysering steam. Two guys in shabby clothes were standing by it, one fanning forlornly at the steam with his hat. When I suggested that maybe we ought to pull over and give them some of our water, Darla said: "Keep driving, Danny. We need that water for us."

We did need it. We drank and drank it and still it didn't seem to be enough, it was like it was evaporating right out of us without even taking the time to turn into sweat first. Our lips burnt and cracked. I felt like I was drying up, becoming a mummy. The tongue of Dulwich's cat hung out as she panted like a dog. I wondered what she thought about all this. Snatched away from her peaceful, bird-filled bungalow court, encaged now in a baking Packard speeding over a dismal wasteland.

We passed through towns. It wasn't like the desert didn't have any towns. But Daggett, Ludlow, Siberia, Bagdad, Amboy, Chambliss, Summit, Danby, Essex, Java, were towns in name only, usually consisting of no more than a gas station and cafe and some woebegone tourist cabins, and sometimes not even that, just a deserted train station by the railroad tracks. When the sun was at its highest and hottest, we reached our first genuine town, Needles.

It felt like an oasis. Real trees were growing here, with actual green leaves on them, not thorns or spines. We drove slowly down the main street, looking for a place to eat, but everything seemed closed.

"How come nothing's open?" I said.

" 'Cause it's Sunday," said Darla.

It seemed strange, that it was Sunday. Days of the week, months of the year, seemed so regular and normal; they oughtn't to exist in a world that had lost its moorings, a world of murder and screaming, of shame and grief. Where a man's teeth could roll across the floor like dice.

"Look!" said Sophie. "Indians!"

Indeed, four Indians, a man and a woman and two little ones, were walking down the street. They were dressed gaily, in red and yellow and blue.

"Maybe they'll know a place to eat," said Darla.

But when I slowed up beside them, they looked at us so sternly I decided to drive on.

A little further along we found the Black Cat Cafe.

A sign over the lunch counter said: "CUP OF COFFEE, CIGARETTE, & TOOTHPICK—6¢." It was kind of a dumpy joint, but the food was okay. Darla had the fried chicken dinner and Sophie and I had hamburgers and french fries, and all of us gulped down glass after glass of iced tea.

A radio was playing; when the news came on, the announcer reported that a sensational crime had occurred Saturday night in Los Angeles. Eight people, including notorious gangster Bud Seitz, had been murdered at Seitz's home in Hollywood. Police said so far they had no witnesses or suspects.

Darla and I locked eyes across the table. The waitress sighed and shook her head as she poured us more tea. "Big cities! You can have 'em! Me, I like a place that's nice and slow. Like Needles."

We left the cafe and continued east. It was only a few miles to the Colorado River and the Arizona state line. The hell of the Mojave ended at the green river. As we drove over the bridge, we could see a cluster of tents and makeshift shacks and old cars and pickup trucks on the river bank—a Hooverville in the middle of the desert.

Next we had to climb over the ominously named Black Mountains. It was rough going for a while, in places the road wasn't even paved, but when we came down the other side of the mountains it was with the feeling that the worst part of the journey was behind us.

We were in Arizona now, and we could see a long way, and what we saw was beautiful. Sophie suggested we ought to sing a song like the people traveling to New York on the bus did in the Clark Gable movie.

"Did you know Darla's a professional singer?" I said.

Sophie looked at Darla, wide-eyed. "You are?"

"Yeah. Sometimes."

"I'm going to be a professional dancer someday. I've got swell dancing shoes. They're in my suitcase. Danny and Mr. Dulwich gave them to me."

It took awhile before we could settle on a song that we all more or less knew the words to. It was "The Animal Fair"—

The Kind One

I went to the animal fair,
The birds and the beasts were there.
The big baboon by the light of the moon
Was combing his auburn hair.
The monkey bumped the skunk,
And sat on the elephant's trunk.
The elephant sneezed and fell to his knees,
And that was the end of the monk, the monk, the
monk, the monk . . .

21

We gassed up the car at Oatman (POP. 500), and Sophie took Dulwich's cat out again, and she scratched in the dirt and squatted and peed, and then we kept going. There was plenty of light still left in the day and though I'd hardly slept for the last two days I felt like I was getting my second wind and could drive forever.

Sophie had the road map spread out, and it nearly covered her like a tent. "If we stay on Route 66 all the way, we'll end up in Chicago. Can we go to Chicago?"

"We can go anywhere we want," I said.

"But on the way to New York. We're still going to New York."

"Of course."

"Darla, have you ever been to New York?"

"Sure, I been there," Darla said, with little enthusiasm.

A billboard informed us the Tomahawk Trading Post and Restaurant was just three miles down the road and one could see the Amazing Indian Mummy there.

"Oh, I wanna see the mummy!" said Sophie.

"Wanna see the mummy?" I asked Darla.

She shrugged. "Why not?"

I parked in the shade at the side of the trading post, so Dulwich's cat could stay cool while we were inside. There was a hitching post out front; no horses were tied up to it, but several cars were parked there, including a sleek silver Zephyr, which Sophie oohed and ahhed at.

The trading post sold all manner of things Indian: pottery and turquoise jewelry and blankets and rugs and beadword and baskets and buffalo-hide shields and arrowheads and toma- hawks. I asked the pimply teenaged girl behind the cash register where the mummy was.

"Right over yonder," she said, pointing. "In that corner there."

It was a mummy, all right, in a glass case. A little mummy, curled up on its side, its arms holding its legs and its face tucked into its knees. Sophie began reading from a typewritten card scotchtaped to the glass: " 'The mummy of this little Indian girl'—oh, it's a little girl!—'was found in a cave by Bill Miller on his ranch near Kingman in 1912. She is believed to have been a member of the Walapai Indian tribe, and to have lived many hundreds of years ago.' Many hundreds of years ago," Sophie repeated as she stared in awe at the grayish-brown brittle-looking thing behind the dusty glass.

We wandered awhile through the trading post with the other tourists—Darla bought some postcards, Sophie an Indian doll called a *kachina*—then we passed through a little hallway to the restaurant. We sat down at the counter, and a fat, jolly waitress named Ruthana served us up ice cream sodas.

"I like your bracelet," said Sophie.

Darla was wearing her charm bracelet—the one Bud had given her, with the star, the crescent moon, the heart, the man's hat, the Scottish terrier, the owl, the mermaid, and the lightning bolt.

"Do you?" said Darla, looking at it; and then she began to take it off.

"Here, honey. I want you to have it."

"Really? No kidding?"

"Really and no kidding. Hold your hand out."

She fastened the bracelet around Sophie's wrist. Sophie held her arm up, and gazed blissfully at the dangling charms. She tapped the crescent moon with her fingertip, and it rocked back and forth.

"Gee, thanks, Darla."

"You're welcome."

Soon Sophie's straw was making slurping noises in the bottom of her glass.

"Can I go back and look at the mummy?" she said.

"All right," I said. "But don't wander off."

"I won't."

She hopped off her stool and ran through the door, as Ruthana watched her approvingly.

"You sure do have a cute daughter," she said to Darla and me.

Darla and I exchanged a look. She opened her purse, took out her cigarettes. Lit up.

She looked exhausted. It seemed like a long time ago that she had been butchered by Dr. Brunder, but it had actually only been a few days.

"That was nice," I said. "Giving Sophie the bracelet."

She blew out a thin, fluttering stream of smoke.

"She's a good kid. A little trouper. She never once complained, going across the desert. She deserves a lot more in life than just some crummy bracelet."

"She'll get it. She'll get everything she deserves."

Darla looked at me musingly. "You'll see to it, huh?"

"Well—maybe *we'll* see to it."

She tapped her cigarette on the edge of the ashtray, even though she hadn't been smoking it long enough to make any ash. Then she opened her purse again and took out her compact and looked at herself in the little round mirror, tugging at her hair, fiddling with an eyebrow.

"Jesus. I look a fright. I'm gonna go powder my nose."

"Okay."

She slid off her stool and walked off, toward the restrooms in the hall. But then a moment or two later I felt a hand on my neck, and looked around and Darla's face was just inches away, and she smelled like Jean Harlow and then her lips were on mine. This was a real kiss, a lingering kiss, a moist kiss. Then she pulled away a little, and looked at my face all over, and smoothed out the hair on the side of my head with her long fingers; then she turned and walked away.

I wasn't sitting any longer on a red leather stool, but on Cloud Number Nine.

I ordered a cup of coffee from Ruthana.

Half a chocolate cake sat on the counter under a glass cover. A fly landed on the cover, crawled around on it for a while, then just settled down to stare at the cake.

Several minutes passed. Neither Darla nor Sophie came back. I got a check from Ruthana, paid up, and went into the trading post.

Immediately, Sophie came running up to me with a can in her hand.

"Could I get this?"

I looked at the label.

"Rattlesnake eggs? What do you need rattlesnake eggs for?"

She rolled her eyes as if the answer was obvious.

"Please?"

"Okay." I looked around. Didn't see Darla anywhere. "Do me a favor? I think Darla's in the ladies' room. Would you go in there and check on her? Just make sure she's all right? In the meantime, I'll pay for . . . this."

"Okay."

Sophie took off. I gave the can to the pimply girl at the cash register.

"That'll be fifty-nine cents."

I dug in my pocket for some change.

"The last place I got rattlesnake eggs, it wasn't nearly that much."

"Oh really?" and then she saw I was kidding and she laughed. She took my money and gave me a penny back.

"That lady you was with?"

"Yeah?"

"She asked me to give you this."

She handed me a postcard. On it was a picture of the Petrified Forest. I stared at it, mystified, then turned it over.

Dear Danny—

The best thing I can do for you is just get out of your hair. I mean it. I'm bad news for you. Take care of the kid. She's swell. And the cat too.

I can't believe what you did for me. I'll always remember you. But I hope you forget me.

Love,
Darla

"Did you see where she went?" I asked the girl.

"Yeah." She motioned toward the window. Toward the road. "She went off with that fella that had the Zephyr."

"What fella?"

"He was in here earlier. When you was over there looking at the mummy, he was looking at it too. Nearly standing right next to you. You didn't see him?"

I shook my head. Sophie came back. "I can't find her anywhere," she said.

"I know." I handed her the rattlesnake eggs. "Let's go."

We walked outside. The spot where the Zephyr had been parked was empty. I looked at Route 66. I wondered which way they had gone. I could have asked the girl. But I decided not to.

"Darla's gone, Sophie. She's not coming back."

"Gone? What do you mean?"

"She got a ride with somebody. She's decided to go off on her own. So it's just you and me now."

Sophie stood there, and thought about it, and then said: "And Tinker."

"Right. And Tinker."

She was looking up at me very solemnly. I reached down, mussed up her hair a little. "Ready?"

She nodded. We got in the car, and pulled back on the road. We drove in silence. Sophie unwrapped some bubble gum.

It was late in the day, and the sun was low and behind us now. We passed through a magical, mysterious landscape of vast vistas, of mesas and buttes and far-away mountains. There were all kinds of colors in the land and the sky, pinks and yellows and blues and browns and grays and violets and greens, and the land seemed to reflect the sky and the sky, the land.

Sophie had been letting Dulwich's cat out of her cage and she had the run of the car. Now she curled up between Sophie and me, and began to doze off.

After a while we saw dark clouds off to the north. Pretty soon they produced gray dragging curtains of rain, and then a spectacular lightning bolt that went all the way down to the ground. But here it was still bright sunshine. It was like the desert was putting on a show just for us.

I thought about Darla, and thought and thought about her, and decided it was okay. After all, it was Gwynnie, whoever she was, that I really loved. And when I got to New York I'd find her and try to win her back from my best friend, whoever he was. Or maybe I wouldn't bother. Maybe I didn't love anybody anymore, except Dulwich, who was dead, and Sophie, who was blowing enormous pink bubbles of gum right beside me.

But suddenly Sophie was covering her face with her hands, and making sobbing, sniffling noises. I was appalled.

"Sophie! Sophie, what's the matter?"

"I miss my mummy!" she wailed. Then her hands dropped, and I saw her dry eyes and sly grin.

"Fooled you."

"Hey," I said. "Don't get wise, BB eyes."

She giggled. The road stretched out before us. And that's about all I've got to say.

ABOUT THE AUTHOR

Tom Epperson is a native of Malvern, Arkansas. He received a B.A. in English from the University of Arkansas at Little Rock and an M.A. in English from the University of Arkansas at Fayetteville, then headed west with his boyhood friend Billy Bob Thornton to pursue a career in show business. Epperson's co-written the scripts for *One False Move, A Family Thing, The Gift,* and *A Gun, a Car, a Blonde.* He's presently living in the Los Angeles area with his wife, Stefani, and three pampered cats.